Cold Stone & Ivy:

Book 2: The Crown Prince

H. Leighton Dickson

ISBN-13: 978-1544111476
ISBN-10: 1544111479

To Hawk,
Battered, Bruised, Bandaged but never Broken

AUTHOR'S NOTE

Like Cold Stone & Ivy Book 1, this story is inspired by real life events, namely the untimely murder/suicide of Crown Prince Rudolf of Austria in 1889. Once again, the timelines are accurate and the characters/locations are for the most part, real. It was a delight doing the research, and even more so in visiting Vienna with my husband Alan. With his camera on silent, he managed to capture the Hofburg, the Stallburg, the Sisi Museum, St. Stephan's Cathedral, Strasbourg and many of the other places that make this story come alive. As you know, life is not 'a given' when it comes to Sebastien de Lacey…

And once again, I owe a huge debt of gratitude to my armchair linguist, Szabolcs Szterszky. While Canadian, Sisi's beloved Magyar blood runs hot in his veins.

Empires of Europe

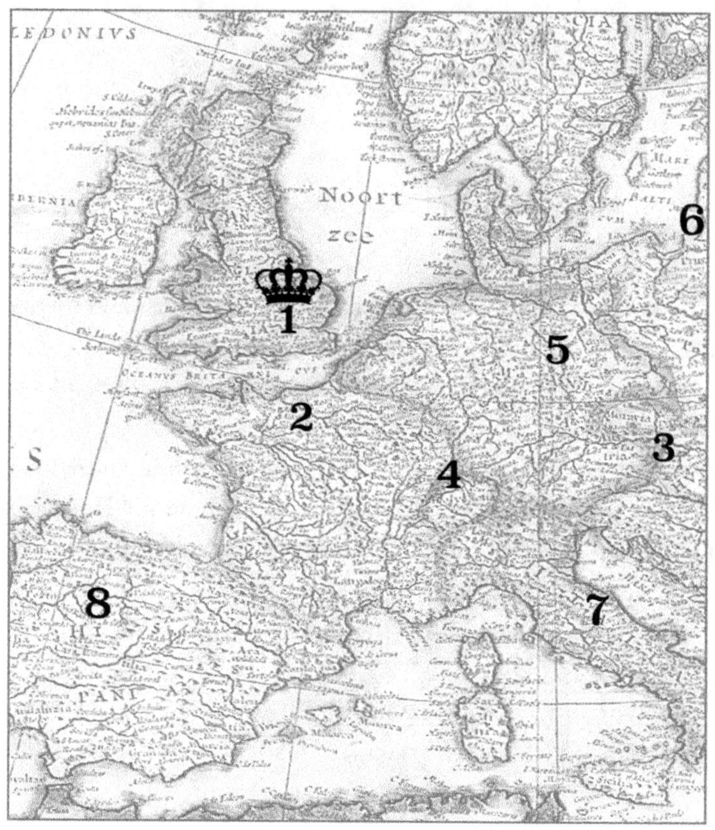

1. London, Empire of Steam
2. Paris, Industrial Republique *de* France
3. Vienna, Guilded Empire
4. Strasbourg, Alsace-Lorraine/Black Forest
5. Berlin, Empire of Iron & Blood
6. Empire of Steel (St. Petersburg)
7. Empire of the Sun
8. Empire of Two Swords

Prologue

Of Bold Boys and Iron Men

January 27, 1889
*The disputed border of Alsace-Lorraine, **Industrial Republic of
France** and Reichsland Province, **Empire of Blood and Iron**, Germany*

The boys slowed as they neared the fence surrounding the distant towers. It was growing dark – the best part of a dare, to be sure – but they could still make out the shapes, tall and angry under an orange sky.

"Drei?" said Bernd, seeing his breath in the cold of evening. "Three towers? When did they make three towers?"

"I know!" said Jens. "I swear, Bernd, they weren't here last month!"

The third boy, Udo, stomped his boots in the snow. "But they look so old."

"This is Reichsland, *dummkopf,"* grinned Jens. "Everything looks old. Jean-Baptiste says the towers are everywhere along the border, in the towns, in the fields, even in the mountains. And Erhard says they are found in threes. Always in threes."

"Are they empty?"

Jens shrugged.

"Do you see anyone?"

Bernd studied the fence in front of them. It was made of wire and rotting wood and looked as if it couldn't keep out a goat, let alone three curious boys. There were signs clipped to the wire at uneven intervals.

Verboten und *Kein Einlass*. Forbidden and No Entry. The border between the *Industrial Republic of France* and the *Empire of Blood and Iron*.

They studied the towers for a few moments, waiting for a flash of lantern or pocket torch, when Jens removed his coat and swung it against the wire. There was no flash, no crackle, no bark of very big dogs. There were rusty barbs however and they had snagged the wool of his coat tight. He abandoned it, dropping into the snow and rolling under the wire with barely a scratch. He bolted the last stretch across the field, his friends following at his heels.

They slowed as they approached, could make out plates of weathered aluminium and narrow windows black from within. They were tall towers, at least three stories and the copper lightning rods on the roofs reached for the setting sun. The ground was well packed despite the snow and littered with pipes, bricks and rusted gears. The smell of metal was sharp on the night air.

Bernd lifted a brick from the ground, tested its weight in his mitten before hurling it through one of the lower windows, sending glass shattering in all directions. The others howled, bolting to the edge of the towers but there was no siren to announce the intruders. Slowly they returned and this time, they needed little encouragement to climb Udo's shoulders for a look inside. In the center of the tower, something very large glinted in the darkness.

"Give me a pebble," barked Jens.

"There's too much snow!"

"Just do it."

Bernd did as asked, digging through the snow to the ground beneath, and all three held their breaths as Jens threw the pebble into the room. The tower echoed with the sound of pinging metal and Jens grinned down at his friends.

"Boost me higher," he said. "I'm going in."

"This is stupid," grunted Udo but Bernd grabbed his friend's boot, pushing so Jens was able to scale the brick. Inside, it was dark and quiet and he straddled the pane, taking a long moment for his eyes to adjust. With a deep breath, he dropped to the stone floor.

Tall, dark and narrow, the tower's interior was like a silo, wooden scaffolding hugging the sides of the walls. Gears moved the air as they hummed slowly overhead and cables hung like jungle vines only to disappear into the blackness of the ceiling. It all smelled of petrol and grease and the sharp tang of metal. But in the center, a dark silhouette stood on twin pillars, gleaming in the moonlight and rising as high as the roof.

"What is it?" cried Udo, standing on Bernd's shoulders this time. "Can you see what it is?"

Jens crept closer, reached out with his hand to rap on the edge of the shape. It echoed like a drum.

"Hit it again!"

He did and repeatedly, growing bolder and louder with each strike. He straightened now, walked around the pillars to study the mechanisms that anchored them to the floor.

"They look like feet," he muttered to himself. "Like big ugly iron feet."

He gasped and staggered backwards, letting his eyes sweep up the pillars to the fulcrum, a girdle of black iron and steel cables. High above his head, a torso as large as a warship hull with clockwork arms hanging from massive shoulders. Almost three stories above him, barely visible in the blackness, a helmet tucked low like a soldier in a bunker.

"Eisenmann," Jens whispered. "An iron man."

It was massive, a giant soldier made entirely of metal standing guard in an abandoned tower in a *Reichsland* field. He climbed on top of the foot for a better look but was dwarfed by the mountain of iron and steel above him. The only sound was his breathing, quick and shallow in the room.

Suddenly, there was a click and under the helm a single red eye opened, piercing the darkness like a beacon.

"Get out!" screamed Udo. "Jens! Get out now!"

With the screech and groan of a hundred grinding gears, the metal giant shuddered and the great helm moved as Jens leapt off the feet and scrambled to the window. There was a flash and the whole world was filled with light.

Chapter 1
Of Lost Girls, Misplaced Men and a Lodge called Mayerling

"Oh Penny, you are a crackerjack shot!" boomed her father, Chief Inspector Charles Dreadful. "Why, I would never have imagined a girl to be so good with a pistol, and a clockwork pistol to boot!"

"Oh father," laughed Penny as she blew the smoke from the triple barrels. "One only needs a good eye and a steady hand."

"Still, my girl, you took out three of the six tires from that steamcar and caused it to career into the ditch! Now, we can finally capture that nefarious rogue, Alexander Dunn! Bully for you!"

Penny smiled and slipped the pistol into the holster at her hip. Breeches, she thought to herself. Marvellous handy for a Girl Criminologist.

With billy clubs at the ready, the boys in blue ran to the ditch where steam and smoke rose from the upended vehicle. They waited for Penny and her father before swinging open the doors. Pearls, diamonds and satchels of gems spilled from within and bags of counterfeit notes flapped out of the windows to be carried away on the breeze.

But of the elusive driver, international jewel thief and rogue

Alexander Dunn, there was no sign.

The End of **Penny Dreadful and a Burglary in Bulgaria**

***

January 28, 1889
Lasingstoke, Lancashire

There was someone coming for her from the shadows.

She knew it, could feel it in every nerve of her body and she crouched low in the gorse bushes on a hill above the Hall. She had never spent a winter in the north, was amazed at the amount of snow that fell and then stayed. In London, a snowfall was a celebrated thing, in part because of the fact that it melted almost as soon as it hit the streets. Here, in the wild north county of Lancashire, the snow had long outlived its welcome. She hated the feeling of wet feet, even if tucked away inside her very fine boots.

There, she heard it again, a soft crunch as another set of boots trod slowly through the drifts. She held her breath. There was a pistol in her hand, a small woman's iron with a pearl handle and compact stock. It was a clockwork pistol, dual chambers holding two balls and she had to admit she was getting pretty good. It helped that she had a crackerjack teacher but still, it would be a long time until she was as proficient as he.

Didn't matter. Ivy Savage was certain she was smarter.

There again, and she grew still. She could feel the little hairs on her neck telling her that he was very near. He was teaching her how to listen to her surroundings, how to feel changes in the air and find signs in the earth. It had been less than two months and she was only beginning to become aware of such clues, let alone read them.

The wind was strong and sharp and she stayed down, hidden by the thicket of gorse branches. The crunching had stopped and she knew he was likely waiting in the dale below, hoping she'd pop up for a look. The first mistake, he had told her. People were curious creatures. A good hiding place could be compromised by a sneak peek. When every inch of her was itching to do that very thing, she flattened even lower, ears straining to hear something of his boots, his flapping coat, his ghosts.

Nothing.

She wondered if they would help him, his ghosts, in something as trivial as this. They did seem to be a capricious sort, looking out for themselves and using him up in their pursuits. She was glad he was setting boundaries. She liked him too much to wish him spent on the dead. Yes, she was beginning to realize she liked him far too much for that.

She cursed her silly, girlish thoughts. He was her partner, nothing more. The Mad Lord of Lasingstoke was easily the most fascinating man in all of England, having spent most of his life in asylums and churches amongst the mad and the dead. Living women hadn't been a part of his world until she pushed had her way into it, breaking that world apart like a child with a new toy. He had given her freedom and she had changed the rules as if it were some sort of great game that she had never been allowed to play. She had brought the house down on both their heads but if she was honest, she was the one who was lost.

The snow was soaking into her knees but still she would not move. It had been at least five minutes now since she'd last heard anything but she could well imagine him, standing with his head cocked like a dog, growing more like the snowy landscape with each heartbeat—

Damn. Ivy closed her eyes and sighed.

Slowly, she lifted her head to see an English Setter not twelve feet away, straight as an arrow, pointing.

Next, the cocking of a pistol very close to her ear.

"Good morning, Miss Savage."

She looked up slowly to see Sebastien Laurent St. John de Lacey, the Mad Lord of Lasingstoke, standing above her, his clockwork pistol pointing three barrels square between her eyes. His greatcoat was flapping in the wind and he was smiling like the sun.

"You finally remembered the dogs, did you?"

"It's not fair," she scowled. "I'm quite certain you would not be bringing your dogs into the field to track a murderer."

"And there you would be mistaken." He slipped his pistol behind his back and reached a hand down for her. "I frequently bring them. Dogs are far more sensitive to other worlds than we."

Reluctantly she took it, allowing him to pull her to her feet.

"Still," she grumbled. "It gives you an unfair advantage."

"Remember, anything that gives you the advantage…"

"Is to be *used* to your advantage," she finished. As she rose, she swung her small pistol up under his coat, finding a home beneath his heart. "Like this?"

"Damnation," he growled. "You see? You posses a great many strategies against which I would be utterly defenseless."

"And what would those be, other than a quick hand with a pistol?"

"Your belligerence, your reason, your pluck." He shrugged. "Also, I'd say your womanly wiles are quite keen."

"My womanly wiles?" she laughed. "Honestly Sebastien, I wouldn't know where to start."

"You're currently holding a pistol to my ribs."

"Good point. But I don't think I would do something like that in the field. It's beneath me."

"I think it's rather effective."

"It shows no cleverness. It's the ploy of a woman of low character."

"You're not a woman of low character, Miss Savage, but you *are* a woman. It may serve as an advantage."

"I *am* a woman," she murmured, her eyes suddenly finding a home on his face. "A grown-up woman. Nineteen in three weeks."

"You now have the upper hand, Miss Savage," he said. "I am entirely at your mercy."

"Indeed."

"What are you going to do?"

"I…I don't understand."

"What do you want to do, Miss Savage?"

She bit her lip. It was *the* question, after all.

There had been no more murders in Whitechapel, no riots on the streets, no mysteries in need of solving. Her mother was awake and picking up the threads of her old life with her father in Stepney. Her brother was happily redesigning the boilers for the great house of

Lasingstoke with Lottie Cook for company. There was no one to care for, no dreams to fight for, no chains to break. Here at Lasingstoke, she had been given freedom to chart her own course and she had no idea where to start.

Three weeks before her nineteenth birthday, Ivy Savage didn't know who she was or what she wanted and for the first time in her life, she was terrified to ask.

The wind was playing with his hair, causing his cheeks to grow ruddy with the sharpness. She noticed the beginnings of a beard on his chin, his ever-changing eyes currently as brown as a colt. She could feel his heart thudding beneath the waistcoat and remembered the time he had held her under the pier at St. Katharine's Dock, the cold of the water and the warmth of his body. She had very much wanted to kiss him then, to throw off the reins of her carefully-ordered life and leap into his chaos with very fine boots. She would have done it, that night under the pier. Nothing save a head in the Thames would have stopped her.

And now that he was here, she couldn't. Perhaps what she wanted terrified her most of all.

Slowly, she slipped the pistol out from under his coat. He stepped back, trying to find a place for a smile on his face.

"Not to worry, Miss Savage," he said. "I think you're ready for the field. What say we go back to the Hall and pull a name? I have a house full at Seventh and would dearly love to reduce that number."

"Without bullets?" she asked. It came out a squeak.

"We shall give it our damnedest."

"Thank you, Sebastien. You're a very patient man."

"And you're an apt pupil, Miss Savage. I'm certain you will outgrow my company in no time. There is still that university in Paris, yes?"

He was giving her a way out. Chivalrous to the core and her heart broke for him. She was a silly, stubborn, confused girl.

"The *Sorbonne.*"

"Splendid. I will have Rupert send a telegram—"

She flinched as the crack of a rifle echoed over the fields.

"Arclight," said Sebastien. He staggered back, eyes changing from brown to green to brightest blue. *"Arcus lux. Ostium ad praeteritum, ad alterum mund."*

"Oh no," Ivy moaned. "Not again."

"Archelicht. Licht des Hauses Habsburg. Bedrohung der Hölle." he said, voice echoing as much as the shot and he dropped to his knees, began drawing in the snow.

"You are a Pandora's Box," she sighed. "If I open you, who knows what will be released. But dashitall if I don't long to do that very thing."

She glanced over at Jo, the English Setter, no longer on point.

"Perhaps he just needs another dog," she said. "I am so much work and dogs are liberal with their kisses."

Jo wagged her tail, smiling as only dogs can smile.

Another shot echoed over the trees. The Mad Lord sat up, blinked and blinked again.

"Who's shooting?" he asked. "Who's shooting?"

"I don't know. Rupert?"

"Rupert doesn't own a rifle."

"Castlewaite?"

"Not with one eye. Terrible shot."

"Well then. Perhaps we should investigate?"

"Well said, Miss Savage." He brightened. "You see? You'll make Girl Criminologist yet!"

He rose to his feet, slipped his fingers between his teeth and whistled, and suddenly five other dogs burst out of the gorse, covered in snow and bounding with happy energy. As he dusted his knees, he paused to study his drawing in the snow.

"Twin eagles?" he asked. "Are those crowns?"

"As long as they aren't angels, Sebastien."

"Life is a wondrous mystery." He turned, greatcoat billowing like a cloak. "Come along dogs, Miss Savage. Come to heel!"

With a sigh she followed, dragging her feet and her very heavy heart through the snow toward Lasingstoke.

***

It took some time to reload the rifle attachment. He was, after all, a left-handed man and now that arm was reduced to a mass of intertwining cables, shafts, pulleys and copper wire. But once loaded, the clockwork rifle was a remarkable device. He was certain he would like it once he learned to shoot.

He was standing behind the little house called Fifth on the southwestern corner of the estate. It was an old stone building surrounded by wild roses and gooseberry bushes, with a low roof and small windows. It was also abandoned, making it perfect for target practice. He had shattered first the windows, then the gooseberries and was moving on to the roses, their winter hips a dark red contrast against the whiteness of the snow.

"Good shot, sir," said VINCE, the Hall's automaton.

He grunted, raised his arm toward the bushes and fired just as two figures appeared in his line of sight. The first yanked the other backwards as roses shattered where a head had been.

"Damn," and Christien Jeremie St. John de Lacey lowered his arm, smoke curling from the end like a serpent.

"Thank you Miss Savage," gasped Sebastien. "That would've taken my head clean off. Christien, you took out the rose hips most admirably!"

"I was aiming for you."

"Is that a pistol attachment like Bertie's? By Jove, it can shoot! What is the caliber?"

He jogged up and Christien shook his head. His brother was worse than a bloody dog. No matter how many times kicked, he kept coming back. He was convinced they would be fast friends one day. Christien was convinced he'd kill himself before he let that happen.

The latch of VINCE's head was open with rifles, golf clubs and copper hands protruding from the top. Christien removed the rifle attachment with a twist and plucked out an aluminium hand, began the delicate process of attaching it to the copper shafts that formed his wrist.

"How are you this morning, Christien?" asked Ivy as she stepped out of the bushes.

He managed to keep his face expressionless. He'd always been able to mask his emotions and it seemed nothing had changed in that regard. He was a master still.

"Fine, as always, Ivy."

"Why are you shooting?"

"Because I do terrible things with a knife, I'm told."

She looked down at the snow. She was pretty and smart and had cut out his heart long before she cut off his arm. Truth be told, he didn't miss the heart.

"Do you still speak to Valerie?" asked Sebastien.

"Valerie?" Christien glanced up. "Marie-Valerie?"

"Of the *Gilded* Habsburgs. Yes, that is the one."

He stared at his brother for a long moment then released a breath, studied the fingers of his metal hand as they flexed and curled.

"In fact, I've only today received a letter in the post. She's invited me to a dinner party in Vienna tomorrow." He looked up, keeping his face neutral. "I would like to borrow the airship."

"Of course, of course," said Sebastien. "I'll tag along, if I may?"

"Why?"

"I just drew twin eagles in the snow. That's the Habsburg Coat of Arms, yes?"

"Oh god," muttered Christien. "I must learn to shoot straight."

"Oh you will!" said Sebastien. "I know you will! You'll be a crackerjack shot in no time with that marvelous contraption!"

"Then I shall shoot you and not the rose hips."

Sebastien laughed and clapped his brother on the arm before turning toward Ivy.

"Have you ever been to Austria, Miss Savage? You will love it, most certainly. We'll collect our bags at the Hall then set off for Vienna at once. It'll take a day, I'd wager. Hmm, given your stomach for air travel, you might need a very large pot."

He whirled and set off in the direction of Lasingstoke Hall, dogs bounding at his heels. Slowly, Christien slipped a black glove over the prosthetic and made a fist, the leather squeaking tight. He slid his eyes in her direction.

"A day contained on an airship with the Mad Lord of Lasingstoke *and* the London Ripper," he purred. "Poor Ivy. Do you think you'll make it to Vienna in one piece?"

She swallowed.

He turned to follow his brother, not sparing a glance at the speechless young writer, nor the rose bush dripping red onto the snow.

***

Mayerling Hunting Lodge,
Vienna Woods, Austria

It was night and quiet in the lodge, save for the crackling of the fire and the sound of sighing, sad and soft, from the bed.

"It wasn't your fault, Rudy," said a young voice. "You tried your best."

"Indeed, my love." A man's voice now and he reached for his cigarette case on the bedside table. "But trying doesn't matter in my world. Only success and power and I have lost both."

"But you haven't lost me." And she pushed up onto his chest, smiling at him with sleepy eyes.

He stroked her hair. Barely seventeen, she was a beauty. A Greco-Austrian Baroness betrothed to a Portuguese prince. He opened the case, lifted a cigarettello to his lips and struck a match, inhaling several times before the stick caught. He blew a long stream of smoke into the dark and smiled.

He was not even remotely Portuguese.

"I will never lose you Mary," he said. "I would lose the Empire before I lose you."

"You still have Hungary." She laid her chin on her hand, caressed his chest. "You could be king in Hungary."

"My father would never forgive me for being his equal not his puppet."

"All the more reason to do it."

He stared off to watch the flames dwindle in the hearth. He would need to build it up soon. There was a bitter wind howling tonight and the windows did little to stop the force.

"I will take the *Archelicht* with me as a gift to the Hungarians. "

"*Archelicht,* " she cooed and her eyes shone with mischief. She was just a girl. "Can it really bring people back from the dead?"

"That is the rumor, my darling. My mother insists it can, but well," he exhaled and the smoke curled above him in the rafters. "You know my mother. She wants to use it to bring glory back to the Magyars, to restore Hungary to its former heights. Wilhelm wants to use it to spin rooms into gold and power his Iron Soldiers. Sophie wants it to bring back her childhood. Everyone wants this little trinket."

"What about you, Rudy?"

He gazed down at her. Anything was possible with this girl. She was iron as she was silk. He loved her more than life. Or death.

"All I know is that, because of *Archelicht,* I now have more gold than any Holy Roman cathedral or unholy Austrian bank."

The girl pushed up on his chest, eyes awake now and dancing. "I want to see it."

"In the morning."

"No. Now. Let me see it," and she pouted. She had beautiful lips, a part of her allure and she knew it. "It must be magical."

His moustache twitched and he leaned in to kiss her, let it linger long and sweet. "Not as magical as you, Mary."

"Still…" The girl, Mary, stoked his face. "I wish to see it, Rudy. Please."

She was the most exquisite creature he had ever known.

"For you, anything. You know I cannot stand against your whims."

The man, Rudolf, rose to his feet and crossed the floor towards the dressing room. He was wearing nothing but a linen shirt that fell past his hips. He was perfectly at ease. With Mary, he never needed to hide. In Mayerling, he was home.

It was for the most part, a hunting lodge, with hides on the floors and antlers on the walls and the bedroom was the same, with only a mirror framed in rough wood and a tapestry that hung from the ceiling. The wardrobe was easily the oldest thing in the lodge, its patina nicked but gleaming with age. He slid open its doors to reveal a pistol case cast in the twin eagles of the House of Habsburg, several vials of clear liquid and an antiquated hex-nut keypad. He punched a code with one hand and stood back, holding the cigarettello in the other. The thin trail of smoke flickered as high above, the raftered ceiling echoed with the sound of grinding gears.

The wardrobe began to move.

Mary sat up on the bed, clutching a sheet to her chest as a strange eerie light shone across her face.

Behind the wardrobe, the wall slid aside to reveal a room that glowed with unnatural light. The walls, floor and ceiling had once been paneled wood but now were gleaming gold. The room was entirely empty, save for a pedestal in the center that had the shape of marble but now shone with the brilliance of liquid amber. On the pedestal sat a glass bell jar and inside the bell, a locket.

It was a clockwork locket, fashioned from brass, copper, silver and gold, each tiny gear a different metal, spinning in connected but opposing directions like a watch. It was housed in a polished glass orb, oblong as opposed to round, like a raindrop or a tear. Encircling the orb were rings of brass, copper, silver and gold and at the bottom apex, a pin.

Rudolf Franz Karl Joseph, Archduke and Crown Prince of Austria, Hungary and Bohemia turned and held out his hand.

"Come and see her, my darling. The greatest treasure in all of Europe."

She rose to her feet and crossed the cold floor, dragging the sheet behind her like a robe. Lights and colour flashed from the glass, creating a kaleidoscope across her face.

"This," he purred, exhaling the smoke yet again. "Is Arclight."

Chapter 2
Of Borrowed Dresses, Bad Ideas and the Airship
Chevalier *of Lasingstoke*

Penny Dreadful and the Villain of Vienna

"The Crown Prince of Austria?" asked Penny and she raised her glass of claret. "But of course Maximilian would ask for me! We're whopping good friends!"

"He's afraid there will be a theft at the ball," guffawed her father, Chief Inspector Charles Dreadful. "What with the globe-trotting antics of that rascal Alexander Dunn! He's a brazen rogue, he is! Completely brazen!"

Penny's fiancé, barrister Julian Terrence Hull, studied her from the shadows, his clockwork arm ticking the night away like a hidden explosive.

"Shall I accompany you, Penny?" he asked. "I would hate for Dunn to think it an opportune time to pounce. He does itch to sweep you off your feet."

"Oh, Julian!" Penny laughed. "All's fair in love and war and international jewel thievery. Dunn has met his match in me, I guarantee you!"

But she did find her breath catch in her throat at the thought, and quickly tossed back the claret in a most unladylike manner.

A fact that was not lost on Julian.

***

It was a remarkable dress - deep red satin with black beading and lace trim, a wide neckline, large bustle and sweeping layers of skirting. Perfect for a royal ball in the capital city of Austria, or so she thought. As a girl from London's East End, Ivy had no idea. She had never worn anything like it in all her life.

"This is a bad idea," she said, balancing on a trunk in her Lasingstoke room. "I've never been to a ball. I don't even know how to dance."

"Ye won't be dancin' child," grumbled Cookie, pins between her teeth as she tugged and pulled. "Ye'll be watchin' it all from the sidelines, ye will, like a regular wallflower."

"Ye do look smashin' though," said Lottie. "The Lady de Lacey 'ad grand taste in dresses."

"But she were a fair sight taller than ye, child," Cookie said. "Ye'll need to cinch it up smart."

"I will," said Ivy. "Most certainly."

Through the window, she could see the rounded back of a canvas rising above the courtyard walls like a breaching whale. She bit her lip. The airship. She was not good on airships and now, she was to be spending an entire day and night on one. Christien had been right. She wasn't certain she'd make it to Vienna in one piece.

"There," said Cookie. "All done. Step out and don't pull nuthin'."

"But don't you see?" Carefully, she stepped out of the dress and into her skirt. "I won't fit in with Dukes and Duchesses. I won't know what to say, even less what to do. I don't even speak German. I'll embarrass myself or worse, I may embarrass Christien or Sebastien."

"Nonsense," said Cookie. "Mr. Christien is a smooth as English cream, and 'is Lordship? Well, you know 'im. Ah doubt anythin' could embarrass 'im."

"But d'ye want to go, Miss Ivy?" Lottie smiled her shy smile. "Is it what ye're a-wantin'?"

There it was again, the question. *What did she want?*

"I don't know. I mean, it's Vienna. Just to think of it – the history, the art, the music, the museums. And this is during Winter Carnival. I would be a fool if I didn't want to go."

"Ye may be many things, child, but ye're no fool." Cookie folded the dress into a brocade carpetbag, pushed it into her hands. "Off ye go, then. Don't keep the boys waitin'. Go. *Go.*"

Ivy grabbed her bowler and dashed out the door toward the stair.

The airship filled the entire courtyard and the draft from many propellers lifted snow from the cobbles. The canvas billowed with a hunt scene of leaping horses and red-coated riders, the elusive fox nowhere to be seen. Cables, wrapped around black iron posts, held the gondola to the ground while the balloon filled with gas. A thick hose ran from the workshop and many hands were needed to hold it steady. She spied her brother Davis among them and waved. He waved back but quickly, needing both hands for the hose and she marveled at the pressure required to inflate such a contraption. It was like a great dragon, hissing and roaring, and her heart pounded inside her chest at the sight.

The Airship *Chevalier* of Lasingstoke.

As she stepped into the courtyard, she spied Sebastien and his uncle, Rupert St. John, in the arch of one of the towers. They were surrounded by swirling snow and dogs. The Mad Lord smiled when he saw her. The Scourge did not.

"Ah, Miss Savage," Sebastien called as he jogged over to her side. "Let me take that bag. Castlewaite will get it onto the ship."

He snatched it out of her hands and made toward the ship, greatcoat whipping like wings in the draft. Much more slowly, Rupert began making his way across the cobbles, dogs wagging around his knees. He was still weak from his surgery, the clockwork heart sapping much of his usual vigor. But his blue eyes were sharp as ever and she stood a little straighter under his gaze.

He came to a halt in front of her.

"Vienna then, is it?"

"Appears so, sir."

"Was this your idea?"

"Not at all, sir," she said, determined to keep her chin from rising. "I'm simply along for the ride."

"Naturally." His smile was a knife, sharp and cutting and she marveled at how she still feared him, just a little. "He's a good catch, isn't he?"

"Sir?"

"You would have gotten very little if you married Remy. Just a fancy house in London and a husband who lived for his work. With Laury, you get all this. It's a considerable trade up for an East End moll like yourself."

"I… I'm sorry, sir I don't know what you're saying."

"Laury is a good man," he growled under his breath. "You may think him a puzzle to be solved or a game to be played, but I can assure you he is much more than that. I didn't think you were such a girl to toy with a man, but then not three months ago, you were betrothed to one of my nephews whilst doggedly pursing the other. And here you are, off to Vienna with them both."

She had no words.

"I still don't know what to think of you, little skirt. What sort of game are you playing?"

Her cheeks burned at the question and this time, she did not stop her chin.

"I'm not playing," she said. "I just don't know anymore. I used to think I knew but now, I realize I don't. I don't know anything – who I am, what I want, nothing. It's sad but true and I won't apologize for that."

The knife slid to one side.

"Well, that's honest, I'll give you that." He glanced over as Sebastien stepped out from the shadow of the *Chevalier*. "He's had much broken in his life, but never his heart. If you're the first, I will toss your bags out the door myself. Am I clear on that subject?"

She swallowed but did not answer.

Sebastien jogged up and the dogs wagged all the more.

"All ready," he said, smiling. "Just waiting on Christien,"

"This is a bad idea, Laury," said Rupert. "You haven't been to Vienna for years."

"Christien and Miss Savage will be with me. I won't get into trouble with them around."

"I can't protect you over there."

"I don't need protection, uncle."

"Vienna is not London," Rupert went on. "Silver Hussars will shoot first, question later, especially in a Habsburg ballroom."

"Don't worry." He reached down to scratch a canine ear. "I simply want to see this year's Winter School horses."

"You're lying."

"Only a little."

Rupert released a long, rattling breath and suddenly, Ivy could see the years on his face.

"I should go with you," he grumbled. "I haven't seen Franzi in a deuce's age."

"Franzi?" she asked.

"Franz Joseph. The bugger still owes me two hundred pounds. Bad day at the Derby."

"You ain't goin' nowhere, Ruby," came a voice from behind. "You can barely puts yer shirt on, let alone spin round a dance 'all."

Mary Jane Kelly, or Marie Jeanette as she was called, swished out into the courtyard. She was a beautiful young woman, made even more so by the fine clothes she had bought during her in two months at Lasingstoke. She had traded her tattered shawl for an elegant high-necked blouse and her strawberry blonde curls were pinned up like a lady. The marvelous dimples, however, were unmistakable and she turned them on full as she slipped an arm around Rupert's waist.

"I won't be going anywhere for quite awhile, *jolie* Marie," he said. "But when I can, I promise I will take you to the finest balls in Europe. Then, you will outshine them all."

"Gads, listen to you," she grinned. "What'd I do to deserve that?"

"You saved my life."

He kissed her forehead and Ivy saw the woman blush. She covered quickly however, pulling a letter from the pocket of her skirt and pressing it into Ivy's hand.

"The post came," she said. "It's fer you."

"It's from Fanny," said Ivy. "I'll read it on board. Thank you, Marie."

"So," she grunted. "You goin' with 'em, are you?"

"Yes," said Ivy. "I am."

"Bad idea, luv." She scowled at Sebastien. "Rotten apples. Both of 'em."

"Enough, *ma chère,*" said Rupert. "You don't understand."

"And she's gravely mistaken," said Sebastien. "Christien is, of all things, a good apple. He's about to renew ties with the young Archduchess of Austria. I am very proud of him."

"'e's the London Ripper," Mary Jane hissed. "'e killed 'em all with 'is own 'and, 'e did. *With 'is own 'and.*"

She bit her tongue as the object of their debate stepped out into the courtyard from another door. He was dressed entirely in black, from trousers and town coat to the top hat held in gloved hands, presenting a dark contrast to the snow. His porcelain face was pale, his cheeks red and his hair, usually so sleek and shiny, was a rumpled mess.

No, thought Ivy, Christien Jeremie St. John de Lacey had not been himself since Whitechapel.

Or perhaps for the first time he was not someone else.

He paused, ran his blue eyes over the company.

"Are we having a family parlay?"

"Come back soon," sneered Mary Jane.

"Perhaps I won't come back at all."

"That'll be too soon fer me."

"Marie, c'est assez!" St. John snapped at her. "I'm sorry, Remy…"

"Nothing personal, uncle," said Christien, gripping the hat tightly. "One can't survive on the streets without developing a good sense for liars, murderers and other such villains. And Mary Jane was very good on the streets."

"Bastard," she hissed.

"Bastien, Ivy, I'll be waiting on the ship."

And he turned and strode towards the gondola hovering ten feet above the ground, and the gangway steps leading up to it.

"That was bad form, Miss Kelly," said Sebastien. He turned to the pack of dogs wagging before him. "Fergis, you're in charge. Clancy, you're second. Birdie and Jo, take care of Dickie. And Tag…"

He bent down to rub the spaniel's long ears.

"Don't worry too much, Tagger, old boy. I'll be back soon."

The dog wagged his back end vigorously.

"Be careful please, Laury," said Rupert and he rapped his chest. "I'm not certain this chunk of tin can take much more."

"Bad idea, luv," whispered Mary Jane, shaking her head. "Very bad idea."

Ivy looked up at the Mad Lord.

"Are you sure of this, Sebastien?"

"Think of it as an adventure, Miss Savage," he said brightly. "What could possibly go wrong?"

And he surprised her by offering his arm. She took it and together they crossed the snowy cobbles toward the *Chevalier*.

***

Dearest and most Darling Ivy,

We cannot tell you that we both have finally finished your story, **Penny Dreadful and a Burglary in Bulgaria**. *This is sure to be a fabulous bestseller! It still begs the question to which of her suitors Penny will choose—scholarly yet troubled solicitor, Julian Terrence Hull, or rogue Alexander Dunn/Alexandre Gavriel St. Jacques Lord Durand. You have left us with baited breath, dearest, and while we Helmsly-Wimpoll women have a good nose for a denouement, we must admit we are utterly at our wits' end regarding this.*

On other fronts, Ninny and I have decided on Lasingstoke Hall as venue for our upcoming nuptials. We have spoken with the Scourge himself—a more miserable man we can never hope to meet, but he is looking surprisingly well in the aftermath of his surgeries. A clockwork heart does suit him so, and we all know Victoria has many to spare. We are also made giddy with disbelief that our mother's sister's husband's sister's cousin's daughter, Mary Jane, is apparently thriving in his company and it is rumored to be carrying his love child at this very hour! But it is mere rumour and scandal—people do love to gossip so.

Franny has also received a most splendid communication from none other than Albert Victor, Duke of Clarence and Avondale. They apparently share a fascination with these Analytical Engines, and while we all know there is no future in computing machines, it is nevertheless an engaging hobby and he has accepted her invitation to join her as her guest at the wedding. As you well know, it is almost impossible to refuse a Helmsly-Wimpoll woman, once she has set her mind on something.

Alas, dear one, we must end this letter. Mr. and Mrs. Helmsly-Wimpoll are calling us down for dinner. It seems we have only just finished lunch! Adieu, dear heart. We await your next communication on proverbial pins and needles.

Much love and affection,
Fanny Helmsly-Wimpoll
Franny Helsmsly-Wimpoll

***

The three-tone call of the bosun's whistle rang through the pipes and Ivy breathed deeply, blinking the sleep from her eyes. She was on a settee in the airship's saloon, holding the letter and an iron pot in her lap. Sebastien had offered her a sleeping compartment but she had declined, preferring to sit alone in the dark with the gaslight, the drone of the propellers and the stars.

It was very early morning now, the first golden haze of dawn outside the round window. Christien was sitting across from her, a cigarette held in the fingers of his clockwork hand. She had never having known him to be a smoker but it was understandable, all things considered. He had disappeared once setting foot on the *Chevalier's* wooden deck but here, in the thin sunlight over Austria, she thought he looked like he finally belonged.

He was staring at her.

"Good morning," she said.

"Ivy." He drew a long drag on the cigarette and slowly let the smoke slip, all the while his eyes fixed on her. "Don't you ever tire of it?"

"Of what?"

"Of being a 'good girl'?"

"I'm not a 'good girl,' Christien," she said.

"Aren't you? Staying here all night in the saloon rather than take a bed of your own?"

"I was fine last night. The saloon is quite comfortable."

"Spoken like a true martyr. If a bed of your own is not up your alley, you could of course, slip into Sebastien's."

Her heart thudded once. She raised her chin.

"Sebastien has not invited me into his bed, Christien."

"You're waiting for an invitation?"

"No. But he is a gentleman."

"He shoots people in the head, Ivy."

"He's stopping that."

"Ah. So you're training him. Well done. He needs that and you've always needed someone to need you." He blew a thin steam through perfect lips. "That's why we didn't work. I never needed you."

"You're so bitter, Christien."

"Call me Remy. Christien de Lacey died a long time ago."

"You're still alive, Christien."

"Remy."

"Remy." She sighed. "Is that why you are pursuing this Archduchess? Does she make you feel alive?"

"Mmm."

"How old is she?"

"Perhaps your age. Perhaps mine."

"Do you love her?"

He blinked slowly, telling her everything.

"Why didn't you marry her then?"

"She wouldn't have been allowed to marry me. Not after my father shot his damned head off. Not even before, if I'm honest. It would have been a morganatic marriage, forbidden for a daughter of the *Gilded*

Empire. Even the youngest and least significant."

"So you chose me."

"Someone younger and even less significant, yes."

He was trying to hurt her, she knew. She probably deserved it.

"What is she like, this Valerie?"

"Beautiful," he answered and raised the cigarette again, the prosthetic whirring softly with the motion. "Beautiful and clever and dangerous and elegant and all to fine for someone like me. But still, she writes and I don't want to be rude."

"So you write back."

"I do."

He exhaled again and she wondered if they could have made a go of it had they married. Had she actually loved him and he her. Had he not been the London Ripper. Had Sebastien not shot his way onto the scene. Had an entire host of unnatural, otherworldly things not happened.

He turned his face to the window and she followed, seeing a silver river snaking through the white below. Dozens of airships gathering in descent. The haze of dawn over a large city.

The cigarette had burned down to his fingers, causing the black leather to smoke and hiss. He looked down but did not move to snuff it out.

"Sometimes I still feel it," he said quietly. "My old hand. This can do many things but it doesn't feel. Not a bloody thing. Not cold, not heat, not softness, not pain. Nothing."

The three-toned call echoed again as Castlewaite spoke through the pipes.

"Enterin' Imperial airspace." His thin voice crackled like paper. *"Dockin' at* Südbahnhof *in twenty, or thereabouts."*

The saloon fell silent, save the drone of the propellers.

"I'm sorry," she said.

"You should have let me go," he said. "That would have been better than this."

"Christien—"

"Remy," he said. "Christien was the name my father chose. I hate it. I hate everything to do with him. Call me Remy or nothing at all."

"I will try," she sighed. "I do wish we could be friends, Remy. You are not the only one who is lost."

He lit another cigarette and they continued to sit in silence watching the sunlight widen over the city, he holding the cigarette, she the iron pot.

With the clanking of boots on metal, Sebastien trotted down the spiral staircase, jumping the last few steps to the saloon's wooden deck.

"Good morning, Christien! Good morning, Miss Savage! Anyone for tea?"

Before they could answer, he turned to a tarnished old trolley stationed against the saloon's far wall. He cranked a handle, the machine gurgled and steam billowed like fog from a coiled hose. A silver teapot sat waiting.

And he turned back to them, smiling like the sun.

"We'll give it four minutes so it'll be nice and strong but not too strong. We don't want cabbage soup."

Ivy sat forward.

"Sebastien?"

"Miss Savage?"

"One of your eyes is green."

"Is it?" He snatched up the teapot, staring at his distorted reflection. "Gads, you're right. I wonder why?"

"Bastien," began Christien. "Why are you here?"

"I'm making tea, Christien."

"Not Christien. Not anymore. Call me Remy or nothing at all. And you know what I mean. Why are you in Vienna?"

"Oh, that. I told you—"

"Yes, you told me. You drew eagles. But you do many strange things yet never go to cities. You hate cities."

"I do hate cities. But Arvin has modified my spectacles. Look!" And he pulled from his waistcoat pocket a pair of spectacles with very large black lenses. He slipped them over his nose. "He thinks they should cut the dead by fifty percent or more. They certainly cut out the living. I can barely see either of you now."

Christien crushed the cigarette between his fingers, dropped the butt to the wooden floor.

"I will take them off when I get to the Stallburg, for I dearly wish to see the horses. The Winter School of Lipizzaners is training in—"

"Did you draw Lipizzaners, Bastien? In the snow?"

"No, Christien, I drew eagles."

"Why would you draw eagles if you wanted to see Lipizzaners?"

"I—"

"And it's Remy, Bastien. Or nothing at all."

"I'll try," Sebastien sighed. "You know that will be difficult. Father forbade nicknames."

"Father is dead."

"I don't understand."

"You are *not* going to the party."

"I know that. Of course, I know."

"I doubt you'll see any Habsburgs at all on this trip. In fact, I'll make sure you don't."

Sebastien cocked his head, looking odd in the large dark lenses and his brother eased back onto the settee. The airship shuddered as they began their descent into Vienna.

"That's fine, Christien, although I don't see what any of this has to do with the colour of my eyes." Sebastien pulled the lenses from his nose, tucked them back into his pocket. "Do we have rooms at the *Sacher?*"

"*I* do. I didn't call about you."

"Not to worry," he said, brightening. "We'll make due, won't we, Miss Savage?"

Ivy studied him, his childlike manner, his eager smile. Sebastien was brilliant and gifted and unpredictable and raw. Christien had been right. She often found herself wondering what it would be like to slip into his bed. If it would grow them both up and draw them together or shatter everything that was good and strong and pure between them. It was a grown up thing, part of a world just outside her grasp, a door she was unwilling to step through quite yet.

Nineteen in three weeks, yet she felt like a spinster.

"Well, I believe the tea is ready." Sebastien turned back to the trolley, began assembling three china cups, a sugar bowl, a creamer. She leaned forward.

"Sebastien?"

"Miss Savage?"

"In the gorse bushes, you said a word…"

"You take milk and sugar, Miss Savage, yes?"

"When Christien started shooting—"

"Remy," said Remy.

"When Remy started shooting, just before you began speaking in Latin, you said a word."

"A word?"

"You said 'Arclight'."

"Arclight?" said Christien.

"Arclight?" said Sebastien and he turned, spoon in hand.

"Oh god," said Christien.

"Yes, Sebastien. You did."

"Oh god," repeated Christien. "That's why you're here."

"Arclight?" repeated Sebastien.

"Oh god." Christien placed his human hand over his eyes, rubbed his forehead.

"Do you know what an Arclight is, Remy?"

"A locket." Christien rose to his feet. "You came here for a locket, didn't you?"

For his part, the Mad Lord had frozen in place, the spoon dripping tea onto the wooden planks of the floor.

"Answer me, Bastien," growled his brother. "You're here for a bloody locket."

"Arclight," Sebastien repeated slowly, the word rolling off his tongue like honey.

"I won't," said Christien "I won't do this again with you, Bastien. I can't."

Sebastien cocked his head and Christien leaned in, raised a clockwork finger.

"Ghostlight…"

And another one.

"Arclight…"

And another.

"Lostlight."

But instead of a finger, this time a dagger sprang up, its blade gleaming like a razor in the morning light. He stared at it, his face draining of colour while his brother's eyes began changing to brightest blue.

"Three?" Sebastien breathed. "There are *three?"*

"God, I hate you."

Christien whirled and left the saloon and the airship shuddered again.

"Batten down the 'atches," called Castlewaite through the pipes. *"We've a bumpy ride this mornin'."*

And Ivy sat, arms wrapped around the iron pot and counted off the bad ideas as the airship began its descent into Vienna.

***

Vienna News
29 January 1889

The Imperial family will be holding a dinner and dance at the Hofburg Palace on the evening of 29 Januayr, to celebrate the birthday of Kaiser Wilhelm II of the **Empire of Blood and Iron***, Germany and Prussia. Dignitaries from all of Europe will be in attendance, with both political and fashion correspondents camping out at the Hofburg gates.*

Unfortunately, Kaiser Wilhelm II is not expected to attend.

Chapter 3

Of Marble Halls, Renaissance Stalls and a Booking at the Hotel Sacher

Winter in Vienna was a study in monochrome. White snow, grey sky, black carriages. Over the skyline, smokestacks puffing coal and steam into the morning sky. All buildings looked as if made from marble or limestone, although given the city's reputation, Ivy suspected it was concrete. The *Gilded Empire* was renown for its industry, leading the civilized world in automated factories, shops and agriculture and while it was very proud of its six hundred year history, they were even prouder of their future. Paving the way for the next six hundred was the steel-and-clockwork vision of the young, liberal-thinking Crown Prince.

The *Südbahnhof* was packed with travellers, the airship docks towering high over the rail yards and Ivy was grateful for the automatons carrying her bags down the many steps. After the conversation in the saloon this morning, she was convinced her heart was heavier than any luggage.

The brothers had not spoken a word to each other since the airship's mooring and she had lost sight of Christien in the mob outside the station. People were hailing cabs, mechanical porters were hoisting bags, street boys were hawking tickets for a hundred Viennese balls. They were carried along by the crowds toward a row of steamcabs parked along the street, when Ivy spied the flash of a top hat. Christien stepped up into a cab.

Sebastien bolted across the walk in pursuit but the steamcab jerked once, twice, before peeling off onto the road. The flash of a pale face in the window was the last they saw before the cab disappeared into the crush of black on the street. Sebastien had turned back then, his breath falling like snow to the ground. The look he gave her broke her heart.

Now, they sat in a steamcab of their own, bumping along the crowded *Ringstrasse* of Vienna. Sebastien stared out the window, his dark lenses blocking most of the dead and much of the living. As they drove into the heart of the city, Ivy was surprised to see no horse-drawn carriages, only steamcars. Their cabbie was a squat tin-plated automaton with handlebar moustache and copper top hat named MAX and he rode the stick as if part of it. All of the drivers were automatons, their human passengers little more than blank faces in icy windows. It was unnerving, but she had to admit she hadn't seen any accidents either, four-wheeled or otherwise. It was a very different world than she had expected and the words of Mary Jane Kelly ran through her head.

She didn't even notice the vehicle lurch to a halt until the Mad Lord reached a hand to help her out of the cab.

"Where are we?"

"Hofburg Palace," he said, pushing the lenses up onto his forehead. "It has almost twenty wings."

She stepped out, marveling at the labyrinth of the tall white buildings that rose up on either side. Pillars and arches, cornices and buttresses, statues and domes and peaks in a maelstrom of architectural styles. It was impressive, it was claustrophobic and it went on as far as she could see.

"Twenty wings! I believe it."

"It's a bloody rabbit warren. Built up since the twelve hundreds or thereabouts."

"Almost as old as Rupert," she grinned.

"Marginally." And he smiled. "Driver, keep our place. We'll be heading to the *Hotel Sacher* next."

"*Ja, mein Herr,*" squawked MAX, his language program translating the English words as quickly as Sebastien could speak them. "Ve vill vait here."

She took the Mad Lord's arm and together they headed through the narrow laneway into the square.

Gentlemen in black towncoats, women in furs. Soldiers everywhere standing guard in the snow and a single statue towering in the center much the way Charles I towered over Trafalgar. A man on horseback – an emperor most likely, with a name etched in copper. She craned her neck but Sebastien kept on, dragging her toward an angled building with grey capstones. For the first time since arriving in Vienna, she could smell horses and wondered if this was the 'Stallburg' of which he spoke. If it were, then these would be the first horses she had seen since leaving Lasingstoke Hall.

Uniformed automatons in white-plumed helmets stopped them at the door. They were Vienna's Silver Hussars, with no faces and heads shining like mirrors under their Shako helms. Their arms were sabres and pistols but they were wearing cloth uniforms instead of metal. Ivy wondered who had dressed them, or if they came that way.

"*Darf ich Ihre Papiere?*" asked one, its voice layered and inhuman.

Sebastien pulled an envelope out of his great coat and handed it over to the guard.

Almost immediately, the automata clicked heels. They were wearing wheels like Arvin Frankow and while one spun off with the envelope, the other led them under the arched ceiling and down a white corridor. She raised a brow by way of asking.

"Silver Hussars," said Sebastien. "Quite terrifying but not very clever."

"Not them," she grinned. "Your secret papers."

"Ah," he said. "From Sisi,"

"Sisi? Not…"

"The *Gilded* Empress, Elizabeth, yes. She and my mother shared a love of horses, dogs and all things mystical. It's an open invitation to tour the Imperial Stables. It seemed like an opportune time to fetch it out of the drawer."

"All because you share a love of horses."

"The love of animals cuts across all classes, Miss Savage. It is a very common denominator."

"Like mystery."

"Or murder."

"Or love."

"I wouldn't know."

The smell of horses, pine and leather grew stronger and soon, the guard stepped aside, ushering them into the largest arena she had ever seen. It was easily over three stories in height with marble pillars, crystal chandeliers and grey trim on the walls. It looked like a museum, she thought, a museum with sand floors, leaded windows and opera seating. But in this museum, the artwork was alive.

Horses as white as the snow were dancing, rearing, leaping, prancing in place. There were perhaps eight men working five horses, some mounted, some on the ground, each of them intent on their exercises to the exclusion of all else.

"The Spanish Riding School," said Sebastien and he led her over to a row of chairs under a balcony. It was the only seating on ground level – all else were in the galleries high above. "These are the morning lessons. It's been years since I've seen the Lipizzaners of Vienna."

"Why is it called the Spanish Riding School when it's in Vienna?" she asked as they took chairs in the second row. There was no one else in the arena. It echoed with the sound of working horses and men.

"The horses are of Spanish stock, descended from Andalusians of Lipica."

"And there you go," she said.

It was quiet save for the jingling of tack, the squeak of leather and soft voices in German. The movements of the horses were fluid and hypnotic. The lightness of hoof, the ripple of mane and soon, she felt the strain of the morning begin to lift. This was truly a magical place.

Next to her, Sebastien leaned forward, folded his arms across the chair in front.

"There are at least thirty in here," he said. "Thirty that have noticed me. I would slip on the lenses but that would cut my view of the horses."

It took her a moment to understand. She leaned forward, copying his pose.

"Surely, the thirty are long dead?"

"Yes, long. Which is why they're only looking. I'm grateful for that fact." He dropped his chin on his arms. "Why does he hate me so, Miss Savage? Am I truly such a terrible brother?"

She sighed.

"It's not you, Sebastien," she said. "I'm sure of it. We've all had a rough go. He needs time to heal, and not just his arm. We all need time to heal."

Sebastien grunted and they sat for a while longer, allowing their spirits to dance with the horses.

"Ghostlight," he began softly. "Changed me."

Her heart thudded in her chest. He never spoke of Ghostlight, the locket that had caused such devastation in London's East End.

"She opened doors for me, doors to worlds I can't begin to explain. The ice is not ice. The frost is not frost. I don't know what they are and I want to know. I want to know more and I want her back. As corrupting as she was, I want her back."

"She's gone."

"I can still hear her. She moves the blood in my veins."

"She sank in the Thames along with the rest of the Docks."

"She didn't. She's with the Ghost Club in London, although how she got there is beyond me." He blinked slowly. "I could call her anytime. She would come like a bullet from a pistol."

Ivy swallowed, trying to still the dread rising inside her. And, truth be told, more than just a little anger. She looked back.

"That would be a very bad idea, Sebastien. Ghostlight is a diabolical device. At least five women murdered that we know of, likely more, and then what she did to poor Christien."

"That was my father, Miss Savage. Ghostlight was merely a tool."

"Ghostlight almost killed you."

"Would that have been such a terrible thing?"

"Yes, Sebastien, it would have. Death is not an option, not when life is yours for the taking."

"Life." He sighed now. "I do try, Miss Savage. I try to be good, I try to be strong, but when all I see is death and dying, sometimes 'life' is very hard to see."

She studied him, felt the rush of conflicting emotion that always accompanied his darker moods and cursed Christien for being so damned perceptive. She took a deep breath.

"Look at me," she said.

He did.

"Tell me what you see."

He blinked slowly.

"Dark hair, green eyes, a sprinkle of freckles on your nose. A very pleasant smile when you do choose to smile. Which is not as often nowadays—"

"No," she said and she turned in her chair to face him. "When I look at you, I see freedom. I see freedom and courage and wonderment and hope. When you look at me, what…do you see?"

And she captured him in her eyes, forbade him to look away, pulled him deeper than she had ever dared before, deeper even than that night under St. Katharine's Pier. Now, like then, he swallowed.

"I…"

She arched a brow. "What do you *see?*"

"I see…"

She grinned her lop-sided grin.

"I see…" He swallowed again. "A horse…"

"A horse…"

"A horse." He turned back to the arena, released a breath that traveled up like snowflakes. "There. A white horse."

"There are five white horses, Sebastien," she grumbled and sank back, folding her arms across her chest. "Which one of them is me?"

"He has red eyes. The shake of his mane looses arrows."

She looked over at the horses. Of the five Lipizzaners, not one of them matched his description.

He rose to his feet.

"Ekeí prin apó ména ítan éna áspro álogo!"

All activity in the arena ceased, the horsemen stopped to stare. Someone began barking in German but Ivy was convinced German was not the language on the Mad Lord's tongue at the moment.

"Sebastien?"

"Anavátis tis pragmatopoiíthike éna tóxo, kai tou dóthike éna stefáni, kai o ídios odígise os kataktitís lygisména gia tin katáktisi."

He yanked her to her feet.

"He's coming this way, Miss Savage. Best to duck or get out of the way!"

And without warning, he pushed her into the walls as a blast of cold air struck like a fist. It blew the bowler from her head and lifted the Mad Lord off his feet and into the chairs with the sound of shattering ice. The Lipizzans bolted in different directions, men chasing after them and soon, the arena filled with silver soldiers, sabre-arms pointed and rifles at the ready.

She pushed herself off the wall, knelt down at Sebastien's side.

He was covered in frost, from his hair to his boots, and tentatively, she touched his arm, remembering the vivid description of a dog shattered into a thousand pieces.

"Laury?" she asked. "Laury, are you alright?"

"Yes, Miss Savage," he panted. "I think so."

He released a deep breath before pushing himself to hands and knees. He looked up at her, ice sliding in thin plates from his face to the sandy floor. It was then that she saw his eyes.

Like the Lipizzan horses of the Spanish Riding School, his eyes were as white as the snow.

***

Le Petit Journal – Strasbourg,
29, Janvier 1889
The search has begun for three young boys who have gone missing in the territory west of Kolmar last evening. The boys are thought to have gone exploring the Roman ruins around the city. If the public has any knowledge of their whereabouts, they are asked to come forward to

police at once.

***

The *Hotel Sacher* was very different from Lasingstoke Hall – veined marble instead of aged wood, statues instead of bookcases, the heavy odor of fresh flowers instead of horse or wet dog. It was elegant, located across from the State Opera and served a fine cup of coffee. Coffee was all the rage in Austria. Rupert loved his coffee. Christien doubted that he could say the same, no matter how long he spent in Vienna.

At the moment, it was a Scotch he was nursing and he stared out the window at the snowy Opera roof. Another thing he would have to learn to love if Valerie asked him to stay. He lifted the Scotch, hearing the gears and pulleys work to move the glass, and he wondered what she would think, if she would allow him to touch her with a clockwork hand, if it would be considered a crime against the Empire. He grinned darkly to himself. If she only knew what else that hand had been guilty of, she would surely not let him touch her at all.

He was alone in the room save for an automaton busy steaming the wrinkles out of the suit and tails. It was a white tie affair and he had come prepared, although he had no hopes of impressing her with a suit. He was not a fine dancer, he was not given to polite conversation, and while he did have a keen mind for politics, he doubted that subject would be on the table given the nature of the party. Kaiser Wilhelm was not a popular figure on the international stage. It was a good thing he wasn't expected tonight.

No, there was nothing he could use to impress the daughter of an Emperor save for his fine, fine face. At least the Ripper had left him that.

He looked down at the photochrome she had sent him last month. Valerie was a beauty with dark blonde hair, long elegant neck and lips that begged a lingering kiss. But it was her eyes that captivated him. Clever, deep and quick and he could read the stories that they told, stories of a harsh father, a free-spirited mother and a life of duty, obligation and privilege. It was a story he understood well. He knew those eyes hid almost as much as they told, if not more.

There was a knock at the door and he downed the Scotch before crossing the carpet. The door opened onto the sight of an Imperial Hussar, dressed in red coat and tall *shako* helmet. He was accompanied by a brigade of silver-faced automatons and in the center of them all, a woman.

His heart thudded in his chest.

The woman spoke to the soldiers and they wheeled aside, allowing her to move to the door. She was very young and slim, dressed in a town coat with sable at the collar and her hands were hidden in a roll of black fox. Her hair was tucked under a fur bonnet, her lips full and painted the colour of peaches, her eyes hazel, deeply set and sharp as steel.

Marie Valerie Mathilde Amalie von Habsburg, Archduchess of Austria.

She lowered her lids, all the while a smile playing with her mouth.

"Lord de Lacey," she said, her English accented in high German. "Is the room to your satisfaction?"

"The room is exquisite. Thank you, Your Royal Highness."

And he inclined his head. He had no idea if he should bow, kiss her hand, fall to the floor in genuflection. He was the second son of a deceased minor Baron and not a Lord at all. These were games played by those of higher society, ones she had been playing all her life.

"I would like to see for myself. To be certain."

There was a murmur from the Hussar captain but she silenced him with a flash of those eyes.

"By all means, Your Royal Highness," said Christien and stepped aside, holding the doors as she swept through. "Would your guard care to inspect the room as well?"

"No need," she said. *"I* booked the room. *I* will inspect it. My captain is no expert in hotel décor. That is something he will leave to me. Is it not, Captain?"

The Hussar clicked his heels and Christien closed the door behind her.

The Archduchess stood with her back to him, head held proudly with the carriage of a swan. There was only the ticking of an ornate mantel clock, the hiss of the automaton working the steampress, the thud of his heart in his chest.

"We are alone?" she asked, sweeping the room with her eyes.

"Yes, Your Royal Highness. Completely."

She turned those steely eyes on him now, swept up and down his lean body clad only in trousers, shirt and braces, paused for only a heartbeat at the tangle of cables that was his arm, finally coming to rest on his face.

"Yes," she said. "The décor is acceptable. Does it meet with your approval?"

"I have never seen anything as beautiful in my life," he said.

Slowly, she reached down to the key, locking the door with a click.

He was certain his heart stopped at that moment.

She rushed at him, catching his face in her hands and crushing his mouth with hers. He gasped and together they staggered backwards, stopped only by the wall and she quickly covered his surprise with kisses until there was nothing left but the want of her. His fingers fumbled with her buttons but her hands were the experts, moving across his body, pulling at the braces, sliding under his shirt, into his hair. She tasted like peaches, like peaches soaked in brandy and he couldn't get enough of her, her cheek, her throat, her velvet hair when he began to feel the Hussars pounding the door on the other side.

"Ihre königliche Hoheit! Öffnen Sie die Tür!"

"Einen Moment, Kapitän," she snapped. *"Die Möbel umstellen…"*

She tore herself away, her breath coming in shallow gasps, but quickly composed herself, smoothed her hair under the bonnet, fastened the buttons he had managed to undo. She glanced up at him, her eyes steely once more.

"Fix your hair," she ordered and he did as best he could, trying to pull himself together before she turned the key in the lock. The Hussars wheeled in, sabre-arms at the ready and she turned to them.

"We were rearranging the furniture," she said. "Silly hotel. You never place a side table at the wrong end of a room."

"Of course," said the Captain. "Sacher décor is held to the highest standard."

The Captain glanced down at the fox roll on the floor. She bent to retrieve it, hiding her hands inside it once more and smiled.

"We shall see you again tonight, Lord de Lacey?"

"I am looking forward to it, Your Royal Highness."

"I shall have a coach sent for you at eight."

And with that, she swept out of the room, the Hussars in tow and he closed the door behind them all, sagged against it for a long moment, waiting for his heartbeat to return to normal.

Yes, he thought wryly, *he was likely to be committing many crimes during his stay in Vienna.*

He turned back to the window and the Scotch.

***

The *Hotel Sacher* was very different from Lasingstoke Hall – veined marble instead of aged wood, statues instead of bookcases, the heavy odor of fresh flowers instead of horse or wet dog. It was elegant and posh and far too sophisticated for his tastes, but it was well located and served a fine cup of tea. Coffee was all the rage in Austria. He couldn't fathom it but there was nothing new in that.

He felt like a statue and he was grateful for the black spectacles that hid his eyes from curious staff and guests alike. However, Ivy had to lead him all the way from the arena to the steamcab, from the concierge desk up the stairs. He felt much like the night back in Milnethorpe when he'd shot Frederick Easterton Crumb and been shot himself in return.

The Concierge manager, a trim little man with a bald head and thin moustache, was escorting them to the very best room in the entire hotel. Sisi had been notified of their arrival and, after the incident in the Stallburg, her staff had arranged accommodations within the hour. A minor diplomat had been displaced to a smaller room several floors above and he wondered if the diplomat was going to the party. It would be an interesting turn of events if that were the case.

The manager pushed open the doors into an elaborate suite that smelled like clean cotton and hot-water heat. Ivy led him to the sofa where she removed the dark lenses and pushed him to sit. He could see her clearly now, a little furrow between her brows. He cursed his frailty although he welcomed her hands.

"I shall have a light lunch brought up for you in twenty minutes, *mein Herr,*" said the manager. "And an Imperial coach will be waiting just before eight, at the doors."

"For what exactly?" asked Ivy.

"For the dinner party," he said. "The Empress insisted that we take care of these things for you, as our guests. One of our other guests is going as well. Imagine that, two English Lords on the same floor, both with the last name de Lacey. That's is French, is it not?"

"Christien de Lacey?"

"Ya, Fraulein. In the room across the hall. Perhaps you would like to share the coach?"

"I don't think we'll be going, sir, but thank you."

"One does not say no to the *Gilded* Empress. You will be going." He smiled wanly. "Is there anything else you need, *mein Herr?*"

He felt her squeeze his hands. Everything was sluggish. Slow.

"Sebastien, did you bring a dinner jacket?"

The manager cleared his throat. It sounded like the boom of a cannon.

"White tie, *Fraulein.* It is an Imperial dinner party."

"Sebastien?"

"No," he moaned. "I wasn't expecting to go."

"I shall see to it," said the manager. "The Sacher is renown for taking excellent care of our guests. We are Vienna's preferred hotelier."

He gave a little bow and slipped from the room.

Ivy bent down in front of him now, cupping his cheeks and lifting his face to examine him. Her hands were warm and the green of her eyes reminded him of forests.

"Can you see?"

"Same as ever," he said.

"Hm. How do you feel?"

"Cold."

"What happened?"

"A horse ran me clean through."

"A dead horse?"

41

"Must have been. A living one would have left bruises."

She grinned and he thought he could die a happy man.

"What am I to do with you, Laury-boy?"

"A cup of tea and a blanket?" *Although a kiss would not be turned away.*

"Done." She pushed him down on the sofa and he did not fight as she dragged a blanket over his legs. "Sleep now. I'll have tea waiting when you wake up."

He rolled over, hugged a pillow to his chest. Could see snow when he closed his eyes.

"I wonder," he heard her say, "What Christien will think when he sees us at the party?"

But he hadn't time to answer as sleep claimed him almost immediately. With it came dreams of dead horses and clockwork lockets and the Seventh House of Lasingstoke at the center of a dying world.

Chapter 4

Of White Ties, Black Swans and Red Dresses at the Hofburg

Penny smiled and spun from the mirror.

"What do you think, Julian darling?"

The barrister nodded as he slipped out of the shadows, a black cigarette holder in his clockwork fingers.

"I think you look splendid, Penny," he said, between puffs. "But then again, you always do."

"Oh Julian! You are too kind!" She slid an opera glove over her hand. "But I have a small pistol tucked away in case that ruffian Alexander Dunn tries to steal the second locket. You remember surely how valuable the first one was."

"Surely."

"And dangerous." Her eyes flashed at him. "Are you ready for a little danger, Julian?"

"Always."

Penny clapped her hands and snatched her sable wrap from the chair, sashayed out of the hotel room towards the hall. Behind her, Julian slid his cigarette free of the holder to reveal the gleam of a thin

dagger. He smiled as the blade shone in the gaslight.
   "We'll both be ready for Dunn tonight."
   He slipped the cigarette back and followed her out the doors.

***

Christien would not look at them.

Even sitting across an Imperial coach, he found places for his eyes other than his brother and one-time fiancée. In fact, the entire coach ride from the Sacher to the Hofburg was spent in silence and Ivy thought it the most uncomfortable ride in all her life. Both brothers looked very fine in their white ties and tails, but Sebastien insisted on wearing his black spectacles and a blanket draped across his shoulders for warmth. His eyes were still the colour of the snow and Ivy wondered if they would ever go back to brown. Brown was for him, she realized, the colour of humanity. Everything else was a roll of the dice.

The coach slowed at yet another wing of the labyrinthine palace known as the Hofburg and the Imperial coachman sprang from the dickey to the cab door. Christien stepped out first and did not wait, crossing the snowy walk with swift strides. Sebastien next, but he turned and held out a hand and she was grateful for his help. The dress she was wearing was long, very full and a little too big. She prayed it would stay pinned the rest of the night.

"Möchten Sie mir, das zu nehmen, mein Herr?" asked the coachman, looking at the blanket on the Mad Lord's shoulders.

"Nein danke," said Sebastien. "It will serve a dual purpose tonight."

The night was black and gaslight was pouring from lampposts, lighting their way to the palace entrance. Hussars, both human and silver, were everywhere and Ivy leaned on Sebastien's arm as they approached.

"Do we have an invitation?" she whispered. "We only have the word of the concierge manager that the Empress invited us. What if he's mistaken?"

He smiled at her, looking odd with dark spectacles on such a black night.

"Oh, he might very well be. Still, the evening has been worth it, hasn't it? If only to see you looking so beautiful."

She felt the heat rush to her cheeks.

"Besides, it is Carnival in Vienna. Surely, we will find another ball somewhere."

An automaton looked up at them at the door. He was fashioned as a Hussar as well, complete with gold-plated uniform and *shako* helmet. But this one was different from the others she had seen. He had a face, and she had to admit that the metalwork was amazingly detailed, right down to the tooling on his large copper moustache.

"Namen, bitte?" he asked, voice sounding like the growl of a steam engine.

"Sebastien Laurent St. John Lord de Lacey of Lasingstoke and Miss Ivy Savage of London, *Empire of Steam,* Great Britain."

Lights flashed across the faceplate.

"Honoured guests of Empress Elizabeth," it announced in perfect English. "Welcome to the party. Long live Kaiser Wilhelm."

As they entered the palace, Ivy wondered if she would ever grow accustomed to splendid places. The ceilings were as ornate as the walls, the portraits were huge and of important figures, the floral arrangements lush and larger than life. In fact, everything seemed that way, larger, bolder, monumental, giving the impression of power and authority. She wondered if she would find Buckingham the same had she ever the chance to call.

They followed the stream of well-clad guests to a ballroom, where they were halted before entering. The music of Strauss was lively and from the door she could see couples sweeping around the room in dance. She remembered waltzing around her sitting room when she was very young, pretending to be a princess in a ballroom just like this. Her father had been her make-believe prince but now, as she looked up at the man on her arm, great black lenses on his face, blanket still across his shoulders, she realized she could never have made up anyone as fantastical as the Mad Lord of Lasingstoke.

The couple before them was announced and entered the ballroom. Ivy and Sebastien stepped forward.

Against a far wall, she could see Christien with an exquisite young woman. She was wearing a ball gown the colour of pearl that shimmered like champagne in the light and suddenly, Ivy realized that in this room, all of the dresses were light. Ivory, blush, white and cream, undoubtedly the height of fashion here in Vienna. She swallowed, stepping forward now in her borrowed dress of deepest red.

"Sebastien Laurent St. John Lord de Lacey of Lasingstoke!" announced the man at the door. "And Miss Ivy Savage of London, *Empire of Steam,* Great Britain."

It was unnoticeable at first, a mere glance from a few nearest the door, but quickly all eyes in the room turned to look as a hush fell across the crowd. Even the musicians stopped playing and for a long terrible moment, there was silence in the ballroom of the Hofburg.

Ivy swallowed, glanced down at her dress. Yes it was red, but it was still in place. She could see Christien slap a hand over his eyes and turn his back. Bewildered, she glanced up at Sebastien.

"Blast," she said.

The Mad Lord of Lasingstoke had just been announced to Viennese high society with a blanket over his head.

"Sebastien," she hissed. "Could you take that off, please?"

"There are more dead in here than living," he answered in a muffled voice. "I think I'll leave it on for now."

"But the lenses—"

"Cut out most, yes, but there are simply so many dead. That has been the problem since Ghostlight. I wish I knew what it meant."

She swallowed again and cast her eyes about the crowd before slipping an arm through his.

"Oh, what am I to do with you, Laury-boy," she muttered under her breath and she raised her chin. "Hello, Vienna…"

"Sebastien?" called a musical voice from the crowd. "Dear Sebastien de Lacey, is that you?"

The crowd parted, bowing low to the floor as a very beautiful woman swept toward them. She had bright eyes, ivory skin and dark hair that fell in a massive double braid down her back. She was wearing a diamond coronet in her hair and was, Ivy noted with some measure of relief, also wearing red.

She paused in the center of the room, turned to look back at the musicians.

"Is there a break, gentlemen?" Her accent was continental and sophisticated. "I thought this was a party?"

The music resumed and the crowds began to dance once more. The woman continued over, raising her gloved hands to catch his.

"Sebastien de Lacey. How long has it been?"

"Sixteen years or thereabouts, Sisi."

"You were just a little boy."

And he pulled her to the blanket, giving her a kiss from underneath its woolen drape. She smiled at Ivy, her eyes mischievous, and she lifted the edges of the blanket to peer under.

"Ah yes. Just like your mother. I remember Jane never liked to follow rules." She turned to Ivy. "My name is Elizabeth. You may call me Sisi."

Ivy didn't know what to say. She curtsied low to the ground, heart louder than the waltz.

"This is Miss Ivy Savage," said Sebastien. "Writer and Girl Criminologist."

"Girl Criminologist. How exciting."

Ivy straightened. "Your Most Royal Highness."

"Sisi."

"Sisi."

"What a lovely dress," Sisi went on. "Jane used to wear one like that on occasion. She had wonderful taste."

She slipped her arm through Sebastien's and together the three of them strolled through the crowd.

"So, Sebastien," purred the Empress. "Are there too many spirits in this room for you or simply too many Germans?"

And she smiled slyly, eyes flicking to a loud corner where a party of mustachioed men were drinking and laughing in highly un-Austrian fashion.

"Representatives of *Blood and Iron?*" asked Sebastien.

"Willie's drinking partners," she went on. "I'm not overly fond of Wilhelm but diplomacy is fragile thing. We must all do our part to keep

Europe whole, yes? Even open up our countryside to German hunting parties. Franzi knows I shall now press for parity for my Hungarians."

"Many a national issue could be resolved behind a brandy, a pheasant and a fine hunting dog," said the Mad Lord.

"Although there might be too many bullets on the field for peace." And she smiled wickedly. "So, Sebastien? Germans or spirits?"

"Spirits," he said. "Aristocrats invariably bring the dead."

"That is to be expected, I suppose. The human soul is a capricious thing. I heard about what happened this afternoon in the Winter School. Was it a spirit that attacked you?"

"I don't know what it was, Sisi. But it *was* a horse."

"How wonderful," she smiled again and Ivy thought it was the most radiant smile she'd ever seen. "I knew horses had spirits, but such a powerful one? Of course it would be a Lipizzaner. I do prefer the Spanish breeds. Mystical creatures. Very hot blood, you know. Do you ride, Miss Savage?"

"A little, Your Most Royal Highness—"

"Sisi."

"Sisi."

Trumpets blasted over the sounds of Straus and Sisi looked up.

"My son's coach is arriving. Sebastien, you must say hello to Rudolf once you are able. I will introduce you to his wife Stephanie and to Mary, his special friend. If you will excuse me…"

Ivy curtsied again and Sebastien bowed, careful not to dislodge the blanket and Sisi left them, disappearing into the parting crowd like a drop of red ink in a well of champagne.

A waiter passed by and Ivy snatched a glass, downing it in one go before setting it back on the tray.

"Is it beautiful, Miss Savage?" Sebastien asked. "Is it everything you had imagined?"

"Everything and more, Sebastien. Thank you for bringing me."

"I'm not certain I would have come without you. I would never have found the courage."

She grinned. The Mad Lord was many things, but not a coward. She doubted very much there was anything he feared – living, dead or in-between.

As her eyes swept across the ballroom, she couldn't help but sigh. Such beauty, such pageantry as couples swirled and dipped to the music. It was a fairy story, she realized. She, the scullery maid in a borrowed dress on the arm of a prince. It didn't matter that the dress didn't fit or that it was red or even that the prince was currently sporting a blanket on his head. It was a magical story, a fantastical mystery, one she could never have written herself.

Or perhaps, with the choices she was making along the way, she had.

There was a ripple through the ballroom at the flash of a ghostly white face, the crowds parting like Moses through the Red Sea.

"Sebastien," she whispered, breath catching in her throat. "I think its Sophie von Habsburg…"

"She's still alive, then?" asked the Mad Lord. "Gads, that's a miracle. Is Gisela with her?"

"A terrifying blonde military person?"

"That would be Gisela, yes."

Ivy swallowed as two women moved toward them like arrows to a target. Sophie and Gisela, the eldest children of Franz Joseph and Elizabeth. Gisela was imposing in a military uniform of black and gold, breeches instead of skirts and two sabres at her hip. Her blonde hair was pulled back severely from her face and her sharp gaze did not waiver.

But Sophie.

It was Sophie who drew the stares, Sophie who turned the heads. There were as many rumours about Sophie as there were about Sebastien – even still the tabloids thrived on her story. She had succumbed as an infant to Typhus and was revived days later with a miracle of modern science – a set of clockwork lungs. Her torso seemed a separate part of her body, covered by an intricate corset of hammered steel and it could be heard drumming as bellows controlled her breathing. Her throat, tiny midsection and shoulders were a mass of cables, much like Christien's arm. Her baby blonde curls were piled in ringlets on top of her head.

It was her face however, that was as enigmatic as it was disturbing. It was completely covered by a mask of white porcelain, with slits for eyes, nose and mouth; her brows, cheeks and lips painted like a china doll. No one had ever seen what lay behind and it was rumoured that she was either the most beautiful woman in the *Gilded Empire*, or a machine.

Ivy curtsied low and long.

"Guten Tag," said Gisela. *"Willkommen in der vergoldeten Reich."*

"Gisela," said Sebastien through the blanket. "I'd like to introduce you to my companion, Miss Ivy Savage."

"English yes?"

"Miss Savage does not speak German so English would be preferred."

"My sister insisted we come pay our respects. She heard you were dead."

"Tabloids," said Sebastien. "They would be out of business if not for our misfortunes."

Sophie stepped closer, her porcelain face expressionless, inhuman.

"You remember me?"

Her voice was like a baby bird.

"No," he said.

"But I remember you."

"I broke my skull in several places. Very little stayed put."

"Your doctor was skilled, then."

"Apparently."

Ivy swallowed again. Of all the surreal and unnatural things she had experienced in the last six months, now a clockwork princess with porcelain face carrying on like old friends with the Mad Lord under a blanket. Oh yes, in the middle of a *Gilded* ballroom no less. Her circles had widened considerably. She wondered when they would be considered orbits and she would attract some little moons of her own.

Sophie stepped closer and Ivy could see eyes behind the slits, bloodshot and blue.

"You see them, don't you?" she cooed to Sebastien. "A room filled with the dead?"

"Enough of this," said Gisela and she took her sister's arm. "Pappa wants us to join his tribute to Wilhelm."

"I do not pay tribute to a false prince," Sophie said, her mask not leaving Sebastien for a moment. "The real crown is much nearer. Have you seen the red horse?"

"The *red* horse?" asked Sebastien and he lifted a corner of the blanket to peer out. "What do you mean, a *red* horse?"

"I thought it was white," said Ivy.

"The red horse is next," trilled Sophie. "He will come with fire and a sword, taking peace from the world. You are prepared to take your sword, *Bruder?*"

"Bruder?"

"Sophie!" snapped Gisela, and she clicked her heels. "Forgive my sister. She speaks of nonsense, intrigues and mysteries, when this is a night to celebrate the Kaiser. *Heil Wilhelm!"*

And dragged her sister away toward an alcove painted with trees.

"That was odd," said Ivy. "You honestly don't remember meeting her before?"

"I must have," he said, the blanket dropping back down over his face. "But I don't remember much of anything before that night."

That night. The night everything changed. The night his father murdered his mother, threw young Sebastien out a third story window and shot himself in the head while an even younger Christien watched it all. There was no other way to speak of it. *That night* spoke volumes.

Ivy sighed, took a deep breath.

"Sebastien," she said. "Look at me."

"Again, Miss Savage?"

"Just lift that damned blanket and look at me."

He did, but only so that his eyes peered out.

"What do you see?"

"Well, there's a decapitated fellow standing behind you—"

"No, dammit." She surprised herself with her vehemence, but then again, she had downed an entire glass of champagne and just survived an encounter with two of the three terrifying Habsburg sisters. "I know the room is filled with the dead, but you need only look at me."

He swallowed.

"Look. At. Me."

He did.

"No horses, no dead, just me. What do you see when you look at me?"

This time, he allowed himself to fall into her eyes and all time seemed to stop.

"What do you *see?*"

"Life," he said finally. "I see life."

And he smiled like the sun.

"Shall we dance, Miss Savage?"

"Oh God, let's."

He reached for hand and together they stepped onto the floor, the blanket falling to the ground behind him.

***

"God, I hate him," grumbled Christien as he tossed back another champagne. "Why can't he just stay home? He's manageable back home but no, he has to go to London. He has to go to Vienna. I swear, Valerie, I will kill him myself someday."

The Archduchess lifted a flute to her lips.

"Brothers," she said. "I do love Rudolf but he will never be Emperor. Not if Father or Wilhelm or Taaffe have anything to do with it."

"All I ask is to take the airship. It belongs to the estate. I shouldn't even have to ask."

"Your brother is Lord of Lasingstoke, not you. We are all slaves to something." She smiled cryptically. "That is the woman you were to marry? The one in red?"

"Ivy," he said and he shrugged. "I was aiming for a sensible life."

"She seems very sensible, wearing a red dress to a *Gilded* Ball."

He grinned, despite his dark mood.

"Forgive me, Valerie. I don't usually talk like this. I don't—"

She placed a finger on his lips.

"I am the same when talking about my father. It proves to me that you are not always so cool, so in control..."

And she leaned forward, kissing him lightly on the cheek, lingering just a moment as if to steal the breath from his mouth.

"*…and* that you don't have swans for sisters."

She grinned wickedly, eyes flicking toward an alcove where her sisters had retreated, watching everything with cold Habsburg eyes.

"Swans?" he asked. "Black Swans?"

She merely smiled and he raised a brow. The Black Swans, or *Schwarze Schwäne,* were rumours, urban myths, curious whispers in Ghost Club meetings. Generations of European noblewomen, trained in the arts of politics, espionage, seduction and murder. Intelligencers circulating at the highest levels. Many an assassination carried out by a woman of cunning and beauty.

Or so the rumours went.

"So," she purred. "We are equal, yes?"

"You are superior to me in every way," he said, raising her hand to his lips. The clockwork gears whirred softly. *Is that why Sophie spoke to him? God, I hope she's not planning to seduce him. He wouldn't know what to do with that.*

"They have a mutual past and according to Sophie, a mutual future. She has been obsessed with your brother for as long as I can remember. She calls him the Crown Prince."

"Why?"

"Infatuation perhaps, or shared experience? Both children of a mystical mother and an iron father. Died as children, restored to life by a Czech doctor. I don't know. Women are enigmatic creatures."

He kissed her palm.

"And Gisela? She is married, yes?"

"To Prince Leopold of Bavaria," she said. "But she has no time for marriage. They are estranged."

"I thought you told me she was in love with Wilhelm."

Kissed her wrist, up her thumb. Didn't care that they were in a crowded Habsburg ballroom. No one would stop them, short of the *Gilded* Emperor.

"She would do anything for Wilhelm and my father would do anything for *her.*" She followed his progress with her eyes. "That is why we are having this Ball. Not for Wilhelm. For Gisela."

"She doesn't seem the romantic type."

"As I said, women are enigmatic creatures. Why do you think there are German hunting parties in the Vienna Woods? Wilhelm asked her to entertain his friends and she could not refuse."

"As you said," he looked up at her though his lashes, unleashing his blue eyes on her like a weapon. "Enigmatic creatures."

She arched a brow, undaunted. She was a warrior. She had defenses.

"Valerie! Dear cousin!"

He released her as a woman wheeled toward them from the crowd. She was slim and bejeweled with dark hair, flashing eyes and a smile as sharp as a knife. She grabbed his arm as if he were an old friend or a new possession.

"Is this your secret friend, the English baron?"

"Christien de Lacey," said the Archduchess. "Of Lasingstoke, *Empire of Steam*. Remy, this is my cousin, Countess Marie Louise Larisch von Wallersee."

The woman named Marie grinned wickedly and leaned in to study his face.

"Well he's as pretty as you've described, cousin," she said. "No wonder you are nearly making love on the ballroom floor. How scandalous. How delicious. And he's managed to avoid the clutches of the London Ripper! All the world is aghast, eagerly awaiting his next strike."

"The Ripper has closed up shop," he said flatly. "You'll hear no more from him."

"Oh, one can never be so sure. Blood and fame are wicked companions." She glanced at Valerie, lights dancing like fireworks in her eyes. "Forgive me, *Liebling*. You know how I love to play."

"I do know," said Valerie.

Marie turned those fireworks back on him.

"And your brother," she said. "Is he always so entertaining at parties? First blankets, now dancing with little girls in red dresses?"

He looked to see Sebastien sweeping Ivy around the floor, dark lenses pushed up on his forehead, eyes locked on her face. They were both beaming.

"Good lord," Christien said and he reached for another glass. "She may be the making of him yet."

"Men are hapless," purred Marie. "But I'm afraid I must leave you now. I would hate for my husband to find me. He might make me dance with him and that would be very bad for my reputation."

She reached up to snatch his flute, tossing it back and laughing before wheeling into the crowd.

Valerie slipped her arm through his.

"Dance with me."

He took her hand and led her onto the floor.

Under the gaze of two Black Swans.

***

Penny swirled around the ballroom on the arm of first one duke then another. But while she twirled and flirted and drank champagne, she could not help but keep one eye open for the sight of a tow-headed rogue in white tie and tails.

The Emperor of the Known World sat on a Gilt Throne next to his wife, the Empress of Avalon. She was the most beautiful woman in all the empires, and around her neck, the Star of Morocco. A clockwork locket of unspeakable beauty and unimaginable power.

Next to them, their son, Crown Prince Maximilian of Pomerania, his special friend, Baroness Annaliese Goethe, and the three Princesses, Rosamunde, Sieglinde and Isolde.

The music ceased and the Emperor rose to his feet, extending a hand to his wife. She took it and rose as well, accompanying him to the center of the ballroom. He was shorter than she and bald, save for an enormous white moustache that ran up to his ears, and all the crowd watched as he placed one white glove on her hip. The Star of Morocco twinkled and gleamed.

The orchestra breathed in, raised their bows, and immediately, the room was plunged into darkness.

Chapter 5

Of Arclight, Ghostlight, Moonlight and a Bullet at Dawn

The music was loud and the waltz a lively quick three-four rhythm. Even though she was not a dancer, Ivy found it easy to follow Sebastien's lead. In fact, he was completely at ease on the floor and she wondered how and when he would have had the chance to learn. *Arvin Frankow,* she realized, his surgeon, psychiatrist and surrogate father. The man would have done everything in his power to give Sebastien the hope of a normal life. She smiled as she imagined Agnes Tidy twirling the young lord around the dining hall, while Carl Feigenbaum played viola and a mad orchestra kept time.

Around and around they whirled, her red dress swishing across the floor and she could feel tendrils of her hair breaking free of the twist at her neck. But she was happier than she had been in a very long while and chalked it up to a glass of champagne and a marvelous dancer. She began to wonder what it would be like to stay in his arms all night when suddenly, in the midst of a spin, Sebastien froze.

It was as awkward as it was sudden, sending her stumbling into the pair beside and causing angry rumblings from across the floor. She glanced up at him and her heart began to thud. No longer white, his eyes were cycling through all the colours of the rainbow and she knew immediately that Arclight, the enigmatic second locket, was in the building.

Through a far door, a uniformed man of about thirty pushed into the room, dragging a young girl behind him. A shorter man with silver chops was on their heels and Ivy recognized him in a heartbeat. Franz Joseph, the *Gilded* Emperor, Apostolic King of Austria and Hungary; King of Bohemia; King of Croatia; King of Galicia and Lodomeria; Grand Duke of Cracow and therefore arguing with him, his son.

The crowd parted as Rudolf spun around and shouted again. The girl clutched his hand but around her neck swung the locket.

"Arcus lux," said Sebastien. *"Ostium ad praeteritum, ad alterum mund."*

"Damn," said Ivy. She tried to pull him to the door but his feet were stuck to the ground, unmovable as the marble pillars along the walls.

The argument escalated on the ballroom floor as the crowd formed a circle around Emperor and Heir. Sisi had joined them, taking her husband's arm but it was obvious that her heart was with her son. Politicians watched, soldiers tensed, even the loud German hunting party had ceased their laughter and were now watching the spectacle with a keen interest.

All music and dancing had died and Ivy could not help but count the number of sabres, bayonets and rifles in the room. A now-familiar wind – deadwind, Sebastien had called it – picked up, causing the many candles in the ballroom to flicker. With dread, she watched as Sebastien's eyes cycled from snowy white to silver and across the room, the locket began to flash in response.

"Rudolf?" The young girl grasped the pendant in both hands. *"Was ist das?"*

"Sebastien," Ivy pleaded. "Please, let's go now."

"Fumus et specula," said the Mad Lord.

"Sebastien, please…"

Suddenly, along the walls the gaslight roared then just as suddenly died, plunging the ballroom into darkness. People screamed and so did the girl when the locket flared with brilliant light. Beams of colour shot out from it, flashing across the ceiling and scattering throughout the room, slowing as if called back by her gravity. The beams disappeared leaving the ends to hover, breathless and still, like spotlights without a source.

"*Re obscura,*" said Sebastien in a voice that echoed as if through a drum. "*Re obscura, veniat ad me.*"

The deadwind died away and the room hummed with the sound of a great engine, although there was none in sight. It was the heartbeat of the locket, she knew it full well, and the entire ballroom held its breath as the strange round lights floated over their heads, splitting like large soap bubbles, slick with oil. They hovered above faces open-mouthed in wonder, spinning like tops, twinkling like stars. Orbs like mirrored coins, they were beautiful, magical, more phenomenal than all the sparkling lights of Carnival.

A collective murmur rippled through the crowd.

"*Was ist los?*" said the girl.

The locket had begun to spin, now rising from her chest as if pulled by invisible strings. Just like Ghostlight in the sitting room of Easterton Frederick Crumb.

"Rudolf? *Helfen Sie mir!*"

"*Wer ist das?* Sebastien de Lacey?"

Rudolf drew the girl into his arms, even as his eyes fell upon the figure at the far end of the ballroom. Sebastien's hand rose in the air, the locket mirroring his movement.

Ivy grabbed his arm, tried to pull it down but it was unyielding as iron.

"Sebastien, please…"

Gisela pushed through the crowd, hands on the hilts of both sabres.

"Stop this now!" she snapped.

"*Arcus lux,*" said Sebastien, his voice hollow and echoing but now, everyone could hear. "*Veni ad me.*"

In the crowd, a woman reached for an orb, catching with both hands. Light flashed across her face and she stared into it, smiling. Others moved toward her, entranced by the otherworldly beauty of the thing. It was like a mirror made of light, a fragile bubble that teased and whispered at the edges of the soul. Her hands, glowing with light, seemed to dissolve within it and her eyes grew larger, her mouth wider. Suddenly, the orb shattered like glass into a thousand pieces, revealing the woman's hands as mere bones without flesh.

There was a heartbeat of silence before the ballroom of the Hofburg erupted in chaos.

Orbs burst and guests screamed and the deadwind roared now as people fled for the doors, pushing and shoving in a mad dash for escape. Blood ran down the young girl's throat, staining the fine ivory gown as the locket dug into her flesh, began to drag her across the floor.

"Es ist er!" shouted Franz Joseph and mechanical Hussars wheeled across the floor, weapons pointed at the man with the silver eyes. *"Haltet ihn!* Stop him!"

"Arcus lux," repeated Sebastien. *"Mortem tuam et timebunt."*

"Kill him!" shouted Gisela.

The girl screamed and a Hussar raised his rifle when Christien de Lacey snatched it out of his hand.

He rushed his brother, swinging the rifle in a savage arc across the blond head. Sebastien staggered and immediately the orbs disappeared in a shower of ice. Christien swung again, this time sending his brother to his knees. Immediately, the winds died, the gaslight sprang to life and the young girl sagged into the Crown Prince's arms, Arclight swinging sweetly about her neck.

"Bekommen ihn hier!" barked Gisela, using her sabres as punctuation. "Get him out, now!"

"Leave this country, the three of you!" echoed Emperor Franz Joseph. "Leave and never return!"

A unit of Hussars surrounded them.

As they hauled Sebastien to his feet, Ivy could see the odd masked face of Sophie von Habsburg, head cocked like a china doll, watching everything from the far alcove. Together, Ivy and Christien dragged the Mad Lord out of the ballroom and down the grand staircase of the Hofburg, leaving the blanket in a corner of the floor.

The Crown Prince, Mary Vetsera and Arclight left through another door, into a carriage bound for Mayerling.

***

New Vienna Daily: Special Edition
Scandal in the Hofburg

*According to sources close to the Imperial family, a riot broke out tonight at the Hofburg Palace. Causes are not yet known but it is said that explosives were set throughout the palace in an attempt to disrupt birthday celebrations for Kaiser Wilhelm II of the **Empire of Blood and Iron**. A trio of French anarchists is suspected, as tensions between the **Industrial Republic of France** and the **Empire of Blood and Iron** are at an all-time high, and the Anarchist movement is wreaking terror across the continent. State police are currently investigating a variety of suspects, however, including a German hunting party taking up temporary residence at a lodge in the Vienna Woods.*

On a separate note, Vienna's own Turf Angel, Baroness Mary von Vetsera was introduced to society last night at said party, wearing the most exquisite jeweled necklace. Had there not been such excitement caused by the anarchy, she would have surely won the day with her poise and charm.

Her fiancé, Prince Braganza of Portugal, has declined to comment.

Regarding the debacle at the Hofburg, police are continuing to investigate

***

The annex was dark, the vault dripping with condensing steam. Even so far from the hydraulic lift, the place hummed like an engine.

"Jackie," came a voice. "I didn't expect to see you here."

Dr. John Williams grimaced. He hadn't even heard the footfall on the grated floor. He had been assured the annex was vacant, guarded only by CHARLES, the Club's automaton. He forced a smile and turned.

"Just popped down to admire the collection, Bookie," he said. "That locket has made it damnably fine."

"Indeed, Jackie," said William Crookes, chemist and physicist and chairman of the Ghost Club. "She has indeed, although she hasn't made a peep since you brought her here last month. Not one bloody peep. Are you certain you've given us the right device?"

Williams studied the trim man in white beard and labcoat. Hidden beneath his bushy white brows, his eyes looked like pebbles in the snow.

"It is identical to the one young Remy had these last months and according to the letter, it was pulled out of the Thames after the incident at St. Katharine's Docks. I have no reason to believe it to be a fraud. Do you?"

Crookes smiled a little before turning his gaze to the object in the glass and lead vault. The inside was gleaming with a faint gold sheen.

"None whatsoever. I must get that thing into my lab post haste."

"Old Vic has strict orders—"

"I know, I know, old boy. But what Old Vic doesn't know won't hurt her. Besides," he raised a bushy brow. "Don't you want to know what makes her tick?"

"Did you see what she left of the docks?"

"Oh come now, where's your scientific spirit, Jackie? Don't tell me that bloody heart shook you like a sapling? You used to be made of sterner stuff."

"Past tense, Bookie," said Williams. "I have retired from practice."

"One never retires from the Ghost Club, Jackie."

"Too true. Perhaps one day I'll take you up on it."

Crookes narrowed his pebbly eyes.

"You're afraid."

"Petrified, old boy. We've awakened forces beyond our control."

"Spirits?"

"Worse, Bookie. Much worse." Williams grunted and clasped his hands behind his back. *"Royals."*

The men turned and left the dark annex. From the subterranean vault of the Ghost Club, the locket called Ghostlight sprang to life, flashing light and colour like the birth of a star.

***

Accompanied by two squads of Silver Hussars, they rode back to the Sacher in silence.

There was nothing to say. Ivy could think of nothing at all. Christien was sitting across from them once again, arms folded across his chest, his face a porcelain mask. For his part, the Mad Lord just sat, arms limp, head low. But his eyes were brown once again and for that, Ivy was grateful.

Finally, the carriage rattled to a halt outside the hotel, as did the Imperial coaches before and behind. Hussars streamed out, flanking the carriage and Christien sprang from the cab. Ivy thought he would disappear but he swung back and leaned in on the door.

"I don't care what you do, Bastien," he said quietly. "I don't care where you go. You have no place in my life, now or ever. You are dead to me. Once we get to England, I will take ownership of Holbrook and you can go to Hell or Lasingstoke. Wherever you belong."

And he disappeared into the hotel foyer, leaving the carriage door open. She could see the soldiers lining the way and her heart tightened in her chest, remembering Rupert's words. Remembering Marie Jeanette's. Remembering her own. Bad ideas all around.

Ivy looked at Sebastien. She wondered if he knew what was going on, if he'd heard anything his brother had said or if he was locked in a world of dead and dying and otherworldly lockets. There was no frost, there was no ice. That, she reckoned, was a good thing.

"I'm sorry, Miss Savage," he said finally and he dropped his face into his hands. "I don't know why I do these things. I just don't know."

She sighed. There were no words for a night like tonight, no apology, no excuse. Truth be told, she was as responsible as he.

She slipped her arm through his, leaned her face on his shoulder. But still, she had no words for him. Her throat was too tight and the Hussars too terrifying.

"I'm a greedy, greedy man," he continued. "I want so many things but can't have any of them. I wish I could die. I have tried. God knows I've tried. It doesn't take and I don't know what that means."

"It means you're meant to live."

"Why? So the dead can have an avenger? Is that all there is for me? Death for the dead?"

"No," she said. "There is more for you than that. I know there is."

"I belong in Hell with the damned."

"No," was all she could say but it sounded feeble, even to her.

"I'll leave first thing in the airship. You can stay longer in Vienna with Christien, I mean with Remy. I mean…" He sighed. "I don't know anymore. But you can stay if you wish. The Sacher will take good care of you and you can come home when you wish."

"I go when you go. Do you understand? I go with you."

He released a deep breath, then another, wiped his cheeks with his palms. He looked up and smiled.

"Thank you, Miss Savage. You are a good friend."

For some reason, that cut to her heart.

"The doorman will see you to your room. I think I need to walk."

"Not bloody likely, Sebastien. Do you see those soldiers? They're not about to let you go walking the streets of Vienna tonight. Not on your own."

"They won't give me any trouble. I just need to be moving."

"Sebastien—"

"Locked up actually, but for now moving will suffice."

"They won't let you."

"Good night, Miss Savage. I'll see you in the morning."

And he leaned in to give her a kiss on the cheek, silencing her long enough to slip out of the cab. There were words in German, footfall but no shouting, no gunshots and soon, nothing but the sounds of blackness and the snow.

She sat in the carriage a while longer, realizing that for the first time, the world was colder without him.

***

New Vienna Daily: Second Special Edition
Graveyard Horror
According to an eyewitness, vandalism of a most horrific nature has

occurred in the graveyard of St. Marx Cemetery. It involved the removal of long-dead corpses from their resting places and the scattering of the body parts throughout the grounds. The method of removal of these bodies is not known, as the graves themselves were opened with neither spade nor shovel. Rather it appears as though they were dug by hand from beneath the ground. It is rumoured to be a gruesome farce on the part of medical students from the Vienna General Hospital. Many of the bodies are reported half-in, half-out of the frozen earth and the bones are impossible to move without shattering them entirely.

Police are continuing to investigate.

***

He sat on the edge of the bed, moonlight streaming in through the frosted window. The white tie, shirt, vest and black tails were discarded on the floor and while he hadn't bothered lighting a fire, he wasn't cold. He wasn't warm. He was nothing at all, just a shell. A pretty porcelain shell, and even that wasn't pretty anymore.

He stared down at his hand, moved the fingers one by one, felt the tug of the cables on the tendons of his upper arm. His flesh had finally stopped chafing under the metal brace as if growing weary of the fight, and scar tissue was building up along the stump. He had been instructed not to remove it for at least six months to allow the flesh to incorporate the brace as part of its healing, but he often found himself wondering what would happen if he simply disconnected the device and chose to live one-handed. It was a macabre thing, this clockwork arm. Life without it couldn't be much more so.

He willed it and the dagger sprang up, the same as on the airship earlier. He had killed with a dagger such as this. Couldn't remember but it didn't much matter. He was guilty, a murderer, the London Ripper no less. He'd been a fool to think he could leave it all behind and find redemption in Vienna. Neither life nor Sebastien worked that way.

He twisted the blade, catching the moonlight and watching it reflect in circles across the dark walls. A swift stab up and into his heart would be painless and clean, but he didn't deserve either. A severing of the carotid artery would be a better fate. That's how he had killed in the back streets of London. He himself had attended the necroscopies, remembered them vividly. It would be poetic justice. A part of him yearned for such a symmetrical, symbolic end.

"That is a remarkable device," said a voice and he looked up to see a woman silhouetted in the bedroom doorway. "You could be an assassin with an arm like that."

"Valerie," he breathed. "How did you get in? I bolted the door."

"I have many skills, Remy. All the Habsburg women have them."

"Are you a Black Swan too?"

"If I tell you, I will have to kill you." But she slipped over to sit on his bed, brushed his cheek with her fingers. "And that would be bad, yes?"

She was joking but he had lost his sense of humour long ago.

Slowly, he folded the dagger back into the shafts of his wrist.

"What else do you have in there?" she purred.

He stared at her a long moment before looking back down.

"A screwdriver, a flint, a wrench, a fountain pen."

"So dangerous." She nuzzled his neck. "What else?"

"I have an attachment for a pistol."

"That," she kissed his throat. "Is very dangerous. When do you leave?"

"Tomorrow morning. Your father made that perfectly clear." He gazed at her. "Come with me."

"I might. It depends." She bit her lip. "Have you ever made love to a Swan?"

"Your father would have me killed."

"Then maybe I would have to kill him too."

And she pushed him down onto the bed, covering him with her feathers.

***

She sat in the most beautiful room in the hotel, alone.

The Silver Hussars had accompanied her and somehow her legs had managed to hold her up until she closed the door behind her. Then they failed and she slid down the wall to sit in a pile of red lace, arms around her knees, eyes fixed on the window and the moonlight through the glass.

She was numb.

One day, one night and everything was gone, changed, shattered like those damned orbs of light in the ballroom. Rupert had been right. She should have listened, she should have stayed and she derided herself for being so weak. A part of her had wanted the madness, she knew it in her bones, had welcomed the chaos that was Sebastien de Lacey and she wondered what part of her it was. Certainly not 'the good girl.' No, Trevis Savage's good girl was long gone. It was someone else entirely, someone who was living with two unmarried men in the wild north country of Lancashire and loving it.

The moon was bright tonight. It looked cold. It looked like those damned orbs, if she was honest, or like his eyes made white after the ghost horse of the Stallburg. As if seeing the dead weren't bad enough, now he was dealing with flaming hooves and manes of arrows. And Sophie, eerie, otherworldly Sophie, the clockwork princess in her porcelain mask. The world was ghost horses, clockwork corsets and shattered mirrors now. Just another Penny Dreadful in the making.

She blinked slowly, wondering where he was, her Mad Lord of Lasingstoke and if he was as incomplete as she at the moment. Funny, that and she cursed Christien once again for his perception. She had always been needed. By her father, by her mother, by her brother and now, it seemed, by Sebastien. Maybe she needed him just as much. She would never, could never admit it. She would rather die than become just another simpering girl, smitten by a dashing smile or a tortured soul. She was made of tougher stuff. She would be a Criminologist if it killed her.

But if she was honest, she did need him. She couldn't afford the Sorbonne so if she went, it would only be because of Sebastien's deep pockets. He was good that way. So very good.

She raised her chin, dreading the tightening of her chest, fighting the war of want inside her.

The Sorbonne or Lasingstoke. Her fate would be sealed when the airship touched down and she needed to decide where that would be, how that would look. One path would be alone, pursuing a career independent of Sebastien, sharpening her mind and her skills and her writing in the process. The other, well, the other path would *be* Sebastien, as his right hand, his moral compass, and if Christien were to be believed, his bedfellow.

All of nineteen in three weeks and if tonight was any indication, she had lost all hope for even a kiss.

She wiped the tears from her eyes, cursed herself for being so weak.

The moon had moved across the window, tracing icy fingers along the glass and illuminating the door to the suite's only bedroom. Only one bed. She hadn't thought it out, hadn't thought it through. Not surprising for Sebastien, but for her, it was uncharacteristic. And in Victoria's world of steam and stigma, it was scandalous. But then again, she was living in the north with two men. Perhaps she was making choices after all.

So here she was in a room with one bed, finally wondering about that kiss, that chaos that was Sebastien, and she was sitting on the floor, alone.

And so she curled up on that floor, wrapping herself in borrowed lace and waiting for the morning or for Sebastien, and unsure of which she wanted more.

＊＊＊

The sun is beginning to rise over the hunting lodge known as Mayerling. The snowdrifts glisten with slick crusts, the branches are heavy with ice, the windows are frosted like sugar cake. Ravens and crows perch in the trees, feathers ruffed to keep in the warmth. Black smoke drifts quietly into the pink sky, and servants are only starting to rise for morning duties. It is a picture of rural Austria – cold, severe, austere. Lived entirely on the inside.

A shot inside the lodge shatters the quiet and sends the crows flying up with the smoke, as Death comes to Mayerling.

Chapter 6
Of Imperial Escorts, Russian Roulette and Iron Maidens in the Sky

"But how did he do it, Penny?" asked her father, Chief Inspector Charles Dreadful. "We were in the ballroom the entire night!"

"Alexander Dunn is a wily fellow," said Penny and she stroked her chin with a manicured finger. "I'm still not sure if he took it right out from under our very noses, or if he waited until later that night…"

"Are we sure it was Dunn?" asked Julian. "We were keeping an eye out for him but what if he had an accomplice?"

Penny spun around, eyes wide.

"Oh Julian, that is brilliant! You will make Criminologist someday!"

"I'm content with my barrister's calling, Penny," purred Julian. "But I appreciate the sentiment."

"However, I believe you to be completely wrong." Penny swung back to the floor, where she was examining a footprint with her magnifying lens. "It was Dunn alright. Only he would have the audacity to pull off a caper this outrageous. No, this has his signature all over it."

"Of course, you're right, Penny," said Julian.

He smiled to himself and reached for his cigarette.

***

Ivy glanced around as she stepped out of the steamcab at the *Südbahnhof* Station. It was the morning of the thirtieth and she wondered if she had just set a record for shortest trip to Vienna. She shouldn't have been surprised. The Mad Lord of Lasingstoke hadn't returned to the hotel that night and with this many Silver Hussars hovering, she was lucky not to be in chains.

"Remy, wait!" she called as Christien began to disappear in the crowds. "Can we please wait?"

"Why Ivy?" He swung around, arms wide. "He's not here, is he?"

"But he said he'd come. We can't leave!"

"Oh we can and we will. By all means, stay behind and look for him if you wish. But I'm taking the airship back this morning, with or without you. Your choice."

And slipping the top hat onto his head, he turned and strode off, quickly disappearing into the crush of travellers. A row of mechanical porters clanked after him, bags rolling along on track-wheeled carts. She had one bag only, the carpet bag with the red dress, and she clutched it to her chest as she scanned the crowds for a flash of golden hair. Nothing. Only the mirrored-faced stares of six Silver Hussars assuring her departure. She sighed, hiked the bag and followed the top hat toward Airship Tower C.

She lost him on the catwalk and had to ask an automated steward who was assisting passengers to the docks. He confirmed the mooring and she was relieved to find Castlewaite running through departure protocols with three small automatons at the *Chevalier's* gate.

"Ahoy there, Miss Ivy," he said, grinning his gap-toothed grin and reaching for her bag. "Tha' were a short trip, weren't it?"

"Oh Jerry, you have no idea. But we have to wait for Sebastien. Please, we can't leave without him!"

"'is Lordship *is* onboard, miss."

"But…" She gaped at him. "But, but when? And how?"

"Walked, far as Ah know," and the copper eyepiece clicked once. "Came on sometime this mornin', 'e did."

"Escorted?"

"Alone, far as Ah could see."

"But why didn't he tell me?"

"Ah can't say, miss. But 'e's 'ere on board and we're ready to leave when ye are."

The thin man turned and shuffled into the gondola. She remained standing for a moment longer, struggling to keep her chin from rising. *Here.* Sebastien was here, on the airship. She didn't know what to think, even less what to feel but she suddenly understood Christien much better. Living with the Mad Lord was like walking along a tight rope – stepping off to either side would result in fury or madness. The skill was in keeping the balance.

Christien, she realized, had simply given up the walk.

"Bad form, Laury," she growled to herself. "Very bad form."

And she followed Castlewaite into the gondola as the automatons sealed the door behind her.

***

Sebastien sat on the floor under a porthole of the airship, waiting for the call of the bosun's pipe. He needed to leave the city, needed to get home as soon as possible. Bad things had happened last night, bad things were continuing to happen. The white horse was an omen and somehow he knew life was going to get worse before it ever got better.

He looked down at his hands, the stars circling between his palms. *Ghostlight.* Just the thought of her caused the stars to become snowflakes and he watched them dance and spin. She had been his teacher, his mistress, his opiate. He had learned so much from her, could feel her singing still in a glass and iron case in London. The last he'd seen, she'd been sucked into the rushing waters of the Thames along with the rest of St. Katharine's Docks but he knew that somehow the Ghost Club had found her. Didn't matter. He could call her anytime. She would come in a shot, despite the iron or the glass.

He had called her sister last night. He had called her name and she had leapt at the touch of his mind. She had opened doors last night, invited him in and he had followed into wonder and terror and death. Always death. Damn the Habsburgs and their petty soldiers and swords. Arclight was his by right. She belonged with him, with the stars and the snow and the dead.

He wondered what they might do if reunited, Ghostlight and Arclight. If together, they might destroy the world, or remake it.

Suddenly, the stars caught fire and a ring of flames leapt to life within his palms. He snatched his hands away and the flames disappeared, leaving the faint scent of gun smoke and sulphur in the air.

"The red horse is next," Sophie had said. *"He will come with fire and a sword, taking peace from the world."*

Fire and brimstone, smoke and mirror. It would all end in fire and madness. A single bullet had changed everything.

There was a pounding and his cabin door rolled aside.

"Miss Savage," he asked from the floor. "I thought you were staying?"

"How dare you," she snapped. "How dare you leave me in a carriage after what happened last night? How dare you just walk away without a thought of what I might need or what I might want or how I might feel?"

"I don't understand."

"No, you don't. I'm quite convinced of that. I was terrified for you last night, Sebastien. For all of us. What were you thinking? Or were you thinking at all?"

"I *was* thinking, Miss Savage." He struggled to his feet. "A great deal, in fact, and about you. About how you don't know what you want—"

"Oh, I know now, Sebastien. What I want is to be returned to English soil so I might figure it out for myself."

Castlewaite's whistle called down through the pipes.

"Tower's given us the all-clear. We'll be pullin' out in five, God willin'."

The *Chevalier* shuddered as the mooring hooks fell away and they could hear the thunder of the gas in the drums.

"Miss Savage?"

"English soil and that'll be the end of it. Perhaps you don't need me at all in your investigations. Perhaps, all you need is another dog."

And she rolled the door shut behind her.

He stood for a moment, wishing he could have told her any of what had happened last night but he knew it was impossible. She would never kiss him if she knew how utterly unnatural he was.

He reached into a trouser pocket for a slip of folded paper. *1 Rue Victor Cousin, Paris*, written in Castlewaite's scrawled hand. Rupert had telegraphed it last night.

He slipped it back into his pocket as the airship groaned and heaved, leaving the *Südbahnhof's* docking tower and the monochrome of Vienna behind.

***

January 30, 1889

Dear Fanny and Franny,

I'm afraid my first foray outside the Empire has been rushed on account of a locket. Yes, another of the accursed things has shewn up in Vienna, at the Emperor's very party! I won't go into detail about the scene that was made, just rest assured that it's be unlikely any of us will be allowed back into the Gilded Empire *ever again.*

Dear friends, I must ask you both a very serious question. Is it wrong for me to want both a career and a man? I struggle with wanting the one over the other and I never rest on either side. I would be perfectly happy to devote my life to writing and crime solving and I can think of no better way to do this than working with Sebastien de Lacey and his house-full at Seventh. But then, when I am near to him, I find my heart racing, my tongue stammering and I long to steal more than a kiss. It makes me furious to lose so much of what I have fought for, all because of a man!

Is it a betrayal of suffrage or is it simply biology? Must it always be war – heart against head, mind versus emotion? Is it at all possible to have both, or am I simply a greedy girl, as Miss Lizzie Borden has insisted. I wish I knew, for I fear that poor Sebastien will bear the brunt of this battle. And yet, I will be nineteen all of in three weeks, and still never been truly kissed! I wish I could put it out of my mind, but every time I see him, that is my very first thought! Even my own thinking betrays me.

I'm sure I'll see you both to deliver this in person, as we're on the airship bound for home at this very moment.

Love to you both, with much confusion,

Ivy

***

She stood on the bridge with Castlewaite, waiting for the ink to dry and watching the Black Forest of *Blood and Iron* drift below them. The flight had been smooth, the iron pot discarded in a corner, and she was fascinated by the technology required to keep the ship afloat. A large captain's wheel with three massive brass gears — one controlling the rudder of the main canvas and the others the secondary sails; a series of pedals to angle the propellers; a wall of levers to direct the fins. Compasses, clocks and steam gauges could be monitored from this very room and the large window offered a panoramic view of the forecastle, masts and main deck. He had assured her that an automaton could just as easily pilot the ship and that a helmsman was required purely for the comfort of the passengers. People, it seemed, still needed a human face from time to time.

She was dressed and ready for Lasingstoke. Breeches, red corset over a loose white blouse and of course, very fine boots. Her brother's peacoat and Rupert's bowler warmed her as the bridge was rather cold. Even a cup of hot tea couldn't stop the chills from shaking her to her toes.

"So the wheel controls the rudder, just like in a sailing ship, correct?"

"Much the same, Miss Ivy," he said. "But in an airship, we 'ave a rudder, fins, props, sails, jigs, furnaces, trip-masts and o'course, the balloon."

"Trip-masts?"

"Aw, ye'll never need 'em."

"But what are they?"

"A set o' masts that crank out of the sides o' the gondola. They're canvased and work a bit like wings on a bird, only fer glidin'. Great fer catchin' an updraft if ye're a mite too low." He grinned at her. "It's summat complicated."

"*Everything* is summat complicated, Jerry."

"Aw, Miss Ivy. 'is Lordship's givin' you a turn, ain't he?"

"He is, indeed." She sighed and leaned against a tarnished banister, cupping the tea in her hands. "Is it wrong for me to be angry, then? I'm not certain he can help himself. Those lockets are so bloody powerful."

"We can all 'elp ourselves, miss," he said. "But 'is Lordship's 'is own man. 'e ain't yers t'fix."

He pulled down a reticulating hose, attaching it to his eyepiece.

"M'wife Flora tried t'fix me fer years. Drove her nigh mad, Ah did. But Ah knew she loved me, despite it all. And she knew Ah loved 'er. Ye can forgive much when ye know ye're loved."

Both eyepiece and hose clicked once, twice and she grinned.

"So you believe in love, then, Jerry?"

"Ah do, Miss Ivy. Don't ye?"

"I suppose I do. It's just well…"

She lifted the cup to her lips, but stopped before it reached.

"Well, things change, don't they? People change. The world is full of possibilities and you're going to take them all on together and then, he gives you a ring…and everything changes."

She shrugged.

"A woman may have a career but if she's bound for the altar, well, I suppose she is well and truly bound."

"Yer young t'be so cynical, Miss Ivy."

"I know. Sad, isn't it?"

Through the helm window, she could see the entire main deck and forecastle, the furnaces that heated the steam and the cables that held the balloon. She could also see Christien, leaning out over the railing, hair whipping in the fierce winds. She wondered what he was thinking, if he regretted leaving so soon. It was good that she had not married him. The

Archduchess was a beautiful, complex woman. There would have been no way of escaping her shadow.

"Are we in France, yet, Jerry?"

"Almost, miss. We're over Reichsland. A prized bit o' land, Ah suppose. French and Germans always fightin' over it, though Ah can't see why."

She grinned.

Castlewaite disconnected the hose and slid it her way.

"Now then, take a look 'ere…"

She peered through as lens upon lens moved across each other like a kaleidoscope. Something began to take shape in the clouds.

"What is it?"

"An airship, miss. Been followin' us since the *Südbahnhof.* Ah reckoned it were a sort of escort and also Ah reckoned it would stop once we passed out of *Gilded* airspace, which we 'ave indeed done…"

She could make out the balloon, large and easily identified by the twin eagles on the canvas. She swallowed, remembering the Hussars and their sabres and swords.

"Now, move the scope up ten degrees," he said.

She did, and this time she could have sworn her heart stopped dead in her chest.

"Guess Ah reckoned wrongly, didn't Ah…"

Above the shape and behind it, there was an entire fleet of airships bearing down on them.

***

Christien flicked his cigarette over the side and leaned over, watching as it whipped away into the clouds. It was damnably cold out here on the main deck even as he stood near one of the three furnaces, the fans blowing heat up into the double canvas. The inner balloon was filled with hydrogen and he'd often wondered at the combination of open flame and combustible gas. But then again, he was a physician, not an engineer and he trusted that some measure of sound design had gone into the engineering. Surely, more of them would have gone up in flames had the combination been even remotely dangerous.

Dangerous. Even the word made him think of her. She had tasted like peaches in brandy. He couldn't help but smile.

Marie Valerie von Habsburg. She was a loaded pistol, a game of Russian Roulette. She was intoxicating and he was addicted, altogether a new experience for him. Women had never made much of an impression. For the most part, they fawned or they preened, desperate to attract his attention. He had never really cared until Ivy. She had ignored him into curiosity, then captured his imagination with the macabre. He still didn't understand how. Didn't matter. She'd moved on to stranger pastures. He'd moved on to wilder ones.

He pulled the glove from his clockwork hand, popped another cigarette when the door from the sterncastle swung open and Sebastien rushed out onto the main. Looking like a mad man, he grabbed the railing and bolted up the steps to the aft deck.

It was impossible to see him from the main, so he lit the cigarette and slowly followed up the narrow stair. Last night, he had hated his brother more than he had ever thought possible. Now, he merely studied him as he leaned over the railing, greatcoat open and whipping in the winds. They were very high up and snow was swirling in the drafts of the propellers but Christien doubted whether his brother could even feel the cold, given his companions were ice, frost and the dead.

He shook his head. Their lives could not have been stranger.

Sebastien was staring over the railing and Christien lowered the cigarette, narrowing his eyes. There were a great many airships on their tail.

"Are those Habsburg ships?"

"They're flying the twin eagles so yes, I'd wager," said Sebastien. "I was afraid of this."

"Of what?"

His brother turned a sideways glance at him. "Can Castlewaite go any faster?"

"Answer my question."

"There's been an incident."

"An incident?"

"Yes. Crown Prince Rudolf is dead."

Christien slowly exhaled the smoke, stared flatly.

"What did you say?"

"Rudolf is dead."

Cold swept from his ears to his toes, threatening to sink into his bones, pushing all thoughts of Valerie aside.

"Bastien…?"

"Damnation. They're gaining."

"How do you know this, Bastien? He was very much alive when we saw him last night."

"Arclight shewed me."

"Arclight." He crushed the cigarette with his mechanical fingers. "How did Arclight show *you* when Arclight was with the girl?"

Sebastien looked at him, eyes cycling from brown to blue. Christien felt sick.

"Where did you go last night?"

"We need to go faster…"

And the Mad Lord pushed off from the railing and leapt down the stairs to the deck. Christien looked back at the fleet, shocked to see cannon-fire flash from the largest ship. He could hear the boom over the roar of the propellers, the shrieking whistle as a black object hurtled past, narrowly missing the *Chevalier's* port fin before disappearing through the clouds below.

A warning shot, he realized. They'd fired a warning shot.

He tossed his cigarette and bolted after his brother.

***

"Crew of the Chevalier, *heave to and prepare to be boarded."*

Ivy skidded onto the main deck as the huge gondola of the Imperial Warship *SMAS Stahl Mädchen* lowered from the skies. The double canvas and many sails were white, black and gold, the twin-eagled flag of the *Gilded Empire* whipping from the mizzenmast. She could see gun ports and cannons open like angry mouths. But the thing that made her breath catch in her throat was the fact that the gondola was a charcoal grey and studded with bolts.

"Oh my stars," she whispered as she fell in between the brothers. "Is that an Ironclad?"

"A dreadnought," said Christien. "Nothing will pierce that hull."

"An Ironclad airship? Does Victoria have anything like that?"

"No idea," Christien grunted. "We have two cannons and Sebastien's pistol. We're dead in the air."

Barely visible on the *Stahl Mädchen's* deck, three women dressed in funeral black stood in the company of airshipsmen. Gisela in military coat and boots, her blonde hair pulled back severely, twin sabres at her hips. Next to her, Marie Valerie, in leather corset, boots, leggings and split skirt, goggles perched on her elegant forehead. Behind them both, the ghost in steel, furs and porcelain mask.

"Surrender the criminal and the ship will be spared," boomed Gisela, through a loud-hailer. *"If not, prepare to be blown from the skies. You have one minute."*

"The criminal?" asked Ivy. "What is she talking about?"

"Crown Prince Rudolf is dead," said Christien, clutching the railing with both hands. "Ask Bastien."

"Sebastien? What is he talking about?"

"The dead and I are on intimate terms, Miss Savage," said the Mad Lord. "And there were many dead last night."

"But surely they can't suspect you. You were…you were…"

"Thirty seconds!" boomed Gisela over the roar of the *Stahl Mädchen's* engines.

"Sebastien?"

"Not to worry, Miss Savage. I can stop the cannons."

"How the hell can you stop the cannons, Bastien?" growled Christien.

"Arclight is on the dreadnought."

"So? What does that mean?"

"Sebastien?" Ivy looked up at him. "Where *did* you go?"

"To Hell, Miss Savage," he said, eyes beginning to cycle from blue to silver. "I went to Hell."

And as he held out his hands, mirrors began to form, folding in the space between his palms. Just like in the ballroom of the Hofburg, orbs of silver sprang into life, circling through the expanse of sky between the airships and bearing down on the *Stahl Mädchen.* Airshipsmen surrounded the Habsburg princesses, swords drawn, but with every slice of a sabre, the orbs multiplied like soap bubbles.

A cannon was wheeled onto the dreadnought's iron deck. In it's mouth was a hook the size of a calf.

"Damnation," said Christien. "It's a grappling hook. They intend to draw us close enough for their corvus."

"A corvus?" repeated Ivy. "Is that a boarding ramp?"

She could see it, a metal bridge pulled taut on an hydraulic spring, with spikes like the fangs of an iron adder.

"Chevalier! *Prepare to be boarded!"*

"I can stop the cannons," said Sebastien.

"Then, you'd bloody well better do it now!"

"Have they fired yet?" He turned to her. "Miss Savage, could you tell Castlewaite to prepare for a vertical drop? And I need a date."

"A date? What do you mean, a date?"

"Past, future, it doesn't matter. Just give me a year even. Now!"

"Um, ah…"

"Now please."

"1895?"

"Thank you."

And the deck cannon boomed, hurtling the massive hook toward the *Chevalier's* gondola. The Mad Lord swung back and raised a palm. Suddenly, an orb appeared between the two ships and the hook sailed into it, disappearing entirely save for a length of cable trailing in its wake. Immediately, ice shot up the cable and back, growing white slicks along the deck and railing of the dreadnought.

Airshipmen began scrambling for cover.

"Arclight and I will stop the cannons, Remy," Sebastien said and he looked at Ivy once again. "Now please, Miss Savage. Vertical Drop. Go."

She bolted for the quarterdeck while the *Stahl Mädchen's* cannons boomed at her heels.

***

January 30, 1895
North Sea
The S.S. Elbe *rises and falls with the waves. The storm is the worst this year and they've discharged warning rockets into the black skies to alert all ships to their presence. There is a small steamship, the* Crathie, *close by on an intercept course. She is not heeding the rockets. They fear there may be an incident until suddenly, out of the skies, something large and hook-like appears, hurtling through the clouds and smashing a hole in the Elbe's prow. Cannonballs are next and within twenty minutes, the* Elbe *is under the sea losing all but twenty, one lifeboat surviving for hours until the* Wildflower, *a fishing ship, pulls them from the water. The steamship* Crathie *sails on to Amsterdam with no mention of the* Elbe, *the* Wildflower, *nor the hook and cannonfire that appeared from the sky.*

Later, shipsmen are interviewed and without exception, all attest to the cannonfire being the cause of the incident but no warships were reported in the area. A U-boat, Sous-boat or submersible is being blamed but the action was unprovoked and would be considered an act of war. Three hundred and thirty people lost their lives on January 30, 1895 and the cause is still listed as unknown.

***

"'ang on, Miss Ivy," shouted Castlewaite as he leaned into the wheel, sending the *Chevalier* in a steep downward arc away from the *Stahl Mädchen*. "And close those dampers, if ye'd be so kind…"

She swung around to twelve bronze levers on a panel. They looked very old and she wondered if they'd been used anytime in the last century.

"All of them?"

"All please, aye."

With a deep breath, she grabbed the first of the twelve, swinging it downward and the airship shuddered with the closing of hydrogen

80

dampers. A second and then a third, the groans almost as loud as the boom of cannon fire outside. The ship was losing altitude as the balloon vented far too quickly, dropping several fathoms in as many seconds. Ivy was forced to hang on as bowler, teacup and iron pot flew to the ceiling.

"Last one!" she cried and she threw a glance to the coachman at the helm. "Here we go!"

Suddenly the wall behind them both burst inward, sending timber, gears and shrapnel flying and they were thrown across the floor.

Chapter 7

Of Cannon Balls, Metal Skulls and the Snowy Fields of Reichsland

"You missed one!" shouted Christien as he damped the mizzen burner. "It's taken out our rudder!"

The air was shattered by another boom and the *Chevalier* shuddered as a second ball tore through her stern, sending planks of oak raining on the snowy German landscape far below.

"Bastien! Did you hear me?"

"What does she want? I don't understand…"

"Bastien, dammit! Pay attention! If they hit the balloon—"

He was thrown off his feet as a cannonball smashed the burner beside him, tearing up timber and sending live coals flying across the deck. He lay a long moment, time stopped, movement slowed, all sound muddied as if underwater. His breath was aching in his chest, arms and legs heavy as iron. It seemed to take forever to push himself to his knees and as he did, he noticed a twisted slice of steel embedded in his clockwork arm. The burner had been shattered and coals had caught canvas as flames raced up the rigging to the sails. The sky was dark with airships above them and bright with orbs flashing between and in the middle of it all, Sebastien.

He stood like a statue, arms held out, hair and greatcoat whipping in the winds. High above him, on the deck of the *Stahl Mädchen,* ghostly Sophie was his counterpart, arms extended, ringlets flying behind the eerie mask. They were mirror images of each other and the orbs had frozen between them like panes of silver glass. He could still see the sisters, Black Swans both, watching from the railing but it was Sophie, only Sophie, with her blank stare and golden curls. The long guns on the dreadnought had fallen silent, overextended as they tracked the *Chevalier's* rapid descent. In fact, it was as if the very air was holding its breath.

As if in a dream, he could see Sophie's clockwork arm move, the slow deadly glint of metal and he realized that she was aiming a pistol across the steep flashing expanse of sky.

"Bastien!" he cried, scrambling to his feet but the shot rang out, sending his brother sailing backward. His body hit the deck hard, sliding across the smooth wood before coming to rest against the rail.

And in that instant, the glass between the ships shattered and the cannons boomed again one after another. The *Chevalier* pitched starboard as balls of iron tore into her sails and her balloon erupted in flames.

***

"Jerry!"

"Grab the wheel, Miss Ivy!" shouted the coachman and he pushed up onto his knees. "Grab and hold fast! We're going down and if we capsize, we're done fer!"

Ivy sprang to the wheel. It was spinning wildly as it followed the shattered rudder and she was yanked off her feet with the force of it. She hauled back with all of her strength but the bridge deck was angled so steeply that it was impossible to get her boots beneath her. Winds whipped from the breached stern and smoke billowed in from the blazing sails. The *Chevalier* lurched starboard, arcing from the sky like a pheasant shot in the wing

"Shot in the wing," she breathed. "Like a bird!"

With a snarl, she braced her boot and yanked the wheel, arms burning with the effort and feeling the gears strain as they turned backwards against gravity.

"Jerry!" she cried over the groan of the airship. "The trip-masts!"

The coachman had dragged himself to the prop-pedals and was working them like a fireman on a steam engine. He grimaced over his shoulder.

"What about'em?" he shouted back.

"They're like the wings of a bird! If they catch an updraft, can they help stabilize us as we descend?"

His single eye grew round.

"Tha' might just do it! Keep your hand on the wheel! Ah'll crank 'em loose!"

The bridge was inclined so steeply that he was forced to crawl on hands and knees to the port wall. The cannonball had made a hole in the stern bridge the size of a carriage and the wind made it impossible to move without grips. Finally however, the coachman reached the wall, pried a brass handle from the panels and began to crank.

Ivy felt her stomach lurch as she battled to keep the wheel level. The *Chevalier's* nose was dipping as it plummeted earthward and through the window, she could see white fields and black trees growing larger, more distinct by the second. It suddenly occurred to her that she hadn't seen Christien or Sebastien for some time. Throat tightening, she gripped the spokes and leaned in, desperate not imagine either one being lost over the rail.

"No!" she snarled. "Not today! Jerry?!"

"Almost there, Miss Ivy! 'ang on!"

The *Chevalier* shuddered as the trip-masts began to detach from her ribs but the snow and the trees were growing closer, faster still. The roar was deafening and she fought the stinging of her eyes and the ice in the back of her throat, willed her hands to grip the freezing spokes and hold fast until the ship hit or soared on the wind.

"Jerry!!!"

Trees and snow filling the entire pane. The roaring of the winds.

"Almost…there…" he cried.

The screeching of the masts, the howling of the hull, trees and snow and three towers in a field. She turned her face away, closing her eyes and prayed it would be quick.

Suddenly, there came a deafening boom as canvas unfurled like great leathery wings, catching the winds and jerking the nose up with such force that Ivy almost lost her hold. The entire ship leapt upwards and for a brief moment, she was suspended in midair, her grip on the spokes the only thing keeping her from disappearing out the breach and into the clouds. For a very brief moment, the *Chevalier* hovered, sounding like a ship on the seas - the flapping of the sails and the creak of the trip-masts, the soft whistle of the wind. For a very brief moment, she opened her eyes to see sky and clouds and the horizon level through the large window. For a very brief moment, the loudest, strongest, most frightening thing in the world was the pounding of a young girl's heart. But it was a very brief moment.

There was a boom and crack as both trip-masts snapped under the pressure and the *Chevalier* dropped the final hundred feet to the snowy fields of Reichsland.

***

*Penny leaned over the rail of her airship, the **HMS Scarlet Pimpernel**, her white scarf whipping in the winds.*

"I see him, father!" she shouted over the flapping canvas. "He's in his sporty little steamster on the motorway!"

"By George, Penny, you're right!" boomed her father, Chief Inspector Charles Dreadful. "Boys! Bring us closer! Penny will shoot out a tire or two! She's a crackerjack with a pistol!"

The boys in blue scurried to hoist sail, heave to and all things airshipsmen did to increase speed in a vessel. Penny could see Julian, lounging in a deck chair and looking particularly content with his cigarette and broadsheet. Good thing, she reckoned. Alexander Dunn was quickly becoming an all-consuming pursuit.

"On the lamb with the Star of Morocco, are you?" she muttered to herself. "I wonder...?"

She lifted a pair of pince-nez to her eyes to study the racing *steamster. There were **two** blond heads in the dickey, one undoubtedly female and she scowled at the thought that not only might Dunn have an accomplice, but that the accomplice might in fact be a woman.*

"Very well, Mr. Dunn," she growled. "You are weaving a most curious web of intrigue but do not doubt, I know a thing or two about spiders."

*And she grabbed an airship cable, tucked her hair up under her touring hat, and leapt from the deck of the **Pimpernel** in a perfect swan dive to the hood of the speedster on the motorway below.*

***

There were snowflakes everywhere.

She lay for a long while, blinking them from her lashes, feeling the fairy pinprick as they settled on her nose and lips. She was warm under a soft blanket and the sky stretched white above her. She wondered if she was dreaming. If so, it was a very peaceful dream. She could happily dream this dream forever.

"Ivy?"

A very beautiful face hovered into her dream.

It was Christien. She could recognize the clear, perfect blue of his eyes, the measured timbre of his voice. There was blood on his cheek, soot on his forehead. She frowned. This was not how the dream was supposed to go. This was not how it was supposed to be.

"Ivy, lay still. I want you to wiggle your fingers and toes."

She reached up to touch his cheek when she smelled smoke and suddenly, she remembered that this wasn't a dream and that the airship had crashed and her breath rushed out of her body as she flung her arms around Christien's neck and began to sob.

"Oh Remy!" she gasped. "The trip-masts…And then Jerry… but there were cannonballs! And all the ships…"

She wept into his shoulder and he held her until finally, the accompanying shudders ebbed and it was all she could do just to breathe. She lifted her head, sniffed and sniffed again, tried to smile.

"Well done with the fingers," he said. "Now the toes."

She stared at him for a moment before beginning to laugh. Release of tension, she knew. Her father had talked about it with accident victims but the strength of it surprised her. She wiped her cheeks with her palms and looked up at him.

"Jerry?"

"He's a tough old bird. It would take more than a crashing airship to dent that fellow."

"And…" Once again her throat tightened and she fought back the tears that welled up. "And Sebastien? Is he…?"

Her words deserted her.

"Come on," he said and he helped her to stand. "This way."

They were in the middle of a snowy field, the gondola of the *Chevalier* in smoldering pieces and she tried to make out the various parts of the ship. Sails flapping with smoking edges, rigging tangled around splintered masts, the balloon caught in the treetops and heaving like a dying whale. Cabin debris was scattered across the field and she saw a fold of red lace, sizzling in the snow. In the distance, three towers stood like giant tombstones.

"Where's the *Stahl Mädchen?*" she asked, squinting at the sky. "And, and the rest of the fleet?"

"I don't know. We're very far from the Austrian border. They shouldn't have been here at all."

He led her to the edge of the trees where a small fire was crackling, throwing sparks into the grey morning sky. She could see two figures and her heart leapt to her throat. She rushed to the fire, dropping to her knees in front of the Mad Lord and this time, she didn't stop the tears.

Head in his hands, he looked up at her, eyes baleful but thankfully, brown.

"Miss Savage," he moaned. "I'm so glad you're alive. I was rather hoping you would be."

She nodded quickly, swallowed back the lump in her throat.

"I didn't kill him," he said. "The Crown Prince. I didn't really."

She reached forward to smooth his hair from his forehead and he grimaced.

"Is that a bullet wound?"

"Sophie shot him in the head," said Christien, tossing fractured deck planks onto the fire. "The bullet's embedded under the scalp. If it weren't for that damned metal skull, he'd be dead."

She frowned. "It looks bad."

"She didn't want to kill me."

"She shot you in the head," said Christien.

"Still."

"And she shot down our airship, Bastien, with four people on board. Would have been quite happy to kill all of us just to get at you."

"She didn't want to kill me." He rubbed his head with both hands. "Valerie was with her, yes? Maybe they wanted to kill you?"

Christien glowered at him, hands on hips. "I'm going to those towers. We need to get back to England and there might be a telegraph or a steamcar or something."

"Or soldiers," said Ivy. "With sabres and swords."

Christien twisted his wrist and the dagger sprang out. "I can manage."

"So are we in France?" She looked over at Castlewaite and her heart swelled at the sight of him, bruised and bloody but very much alive. "Jerry, you are the best airship pilot ever in the history of airship pilots! Ever!"

"Aw Miss Ivy," he grinned and she could have sworn he had one less tooth than before. "It were yer idea to spring the trip-masts."

"Only after you told me about them."

"Only because ye're a clever girl and a-wantin' t'know."

"Then I'd say we owe our lives to the pair of you," said Sebastien, and he tried to smile. It didn't work and he groaned again.

"*Are* we in France, Castlewaite?" asked Christien.

"Alsace-Lorraine, sir."

"Or Reichsland," Ivy added. "Disputed territory."

"Aye."

"Well," Christien shoved his hands into his topcoat pockets and looked toward the towers. "If they're French towers, *nous serons bien.* But if German…"

"*Wir tot sein,*" finished Sebastien. "I'll come with you."

"No, Bastien, you're not fit—"

"I'm fine. Miss Savage will stay here with Castlewaite—" He rose to his feet but staggered as he did so. Ivy slipped an arm around his waist to steady him.

"*Ivy* will come with me," said Christien. "*You* will stay with Castlewaite."

"I don't need—"

"That's a good idea, Remy," said Ivy and she turned her green eyes on the coachman. "Castlewaite, you need Sebastien to stay with you, don't you?"

"Ah do," the coachman said slowly, his mechanical eye clicking between Ivy and Sebastien. "T' discuss replacin' the *Chevalier*. If yer Lordship don't mind, tha' is."

"No, I don't mind," said the Mad Lord with a sigh. "The ground is upside down right now. I feel like I'm wrong way in a hole."

"That settles it, then," said Ivy as she helped lower him to the ground, bent to button his greatcoat, which all too often flapped open to the elements. She cupped his chin, lifted his face. "You will stay here and discuss airships with Castlewaite, yes?"

He blinked slowly and she fell into his eyes once again, now as brown as a cup of sipping chocolate. She cursed the beat of her own heart.

"We'll be right back."

Snow was falling, dusting his cheeks and hair and she leaned in to kiss him on the forehead, beside the bullet wound. He closed his eyes at her lips, breathed deeply as she pulled away.

"I don't want to talk about airships," he said. "I want to sleep."

"No sleeping," said Remy. "Castlewaite, whatever you do, do not let him sleep."

"Aye, Mister Christien, sir. No sleepin'."

Sebastien growled but did not protest. Christien stared at him a long moment, face once again like fine porcelain, perhaps more of a mask than Sophie. He shook his head and turned his back, pushing through the snow and debris across the field.

He was more of a puzzle than ever.

She followed the path he was making toward the towers, looking like upended torpedoes in the gray skies. It was hard going through the field, with ice forming crusts on the drifts and the smoldering debris causing snow to melt into puddles. It was also cold and she rubbed her arms. She was wearing nothing more than her torn blouse, corset and breeches, having somehow lost both bowler and peacoat in the crash. She kept telling herself that she might still find them in the debris. Hope, she'd learned from St. Katharine's Docks, was a difficult thing to kill.

"By god you're stubborn," said Christien, turning his head. "It's cold as hell out here and you have yet to ask me for my coat."

"Perhaps you have yet to offer it," she said.

"Is that why you haven't kissed him then? You're waiting for an offer?"

"What? No!"

"I thought you were tougher than that."

"Well, you're wrong and I'm not."

"You are. That's what I first saw in you. You were a tough, smart, bricky little thing. You knew what you wanted and you went for it, no matter what people thought."

They slowed as they approached a fence of twisted wire. She could see his breath in the grey light.

"I liked that in you, but you changed."

"*I* changed? I never changed! You changed, Christien! We used to talk about forensics and murder and writing and crime, but once you put that ring on my finger, I was bound for babies and whist and elegant parties!"

"You're a silly girl, like all the rest. Just wap him and get on with it."

"You're rude."

"You're welcome." He studied the fence, the twisted wire and rusty barbs. There was a dark shape on a post fifty yards east. "Is that a coat?"

"Looks like one." She raised her chin. "A gentleman would fetch it for me."

"I'm no gentleman."

"But there's no path," she said. "And the snow is very deep. What if that fence is ionized? I could be shocked and killed in a most gruesome way. Remember when I helped you with the necroscopy of that old bludger in Cobb's yard? His eyes bulging out of his head, his hair fried like kippers on Sunday. It was a horrible way to go."

"You want the coat?"

"I do."

"Go get it."

"Why are you doing this?"

"It's time to grow up, Ivy."

She scowled at him before turning and stomping through the snow. But she did fetch it and wasn't fried in the process. It was a boy's coat, small and snug but warmer than nothing. She cinched the belt and trudged back.

"Right," she snorted. "Shall I get us through the fence as well?"

"No entry," said Christien. "That's what the signs say. *Kein Einlass* and *Verboten.*"

"Of course you speak German."

"Part of an expensive and now completely wasted education."

"*Verboten,*" said Ivy and she narrowed her eyes. "Forbidden?"

"Likely. I gather we're ignoring it?"

"Definitely."

And he reached out with his clockwork hand, twisted the wrist and a pair of tiny snips popped out. She grinned wickedly.

"What else have you got in there?"

"God knows," he grumbled. "I find new gadgets every day."

He cut the wires and they sprang back into large barbed coils at the base of the post, leaving a new and open way to the towers.

"After you," he said.

She rolled her eyes.

They stepped through the fence and into the snow.

***

Mirrors, mirrors, smoke and mirrors. White horses filled with arrows, red horses with manes aflame. The dead were coming for him, calling him, setting a crown upon his head—

"Aw now sir," said Castlewaite as the man nudged his arm. "No sleepin'. Tha's what Mister Christien said."

"I'm not sleeping," he lied, opening his eyes. "There are simply so many dead on this field. Thousands, in fact. I've never seen so many. And these poor little boys."

"Boys, sir?"

Three boys had appeared before him, crackling into existence like frost on a window. Three boys not more than twelve. It should have broken his heart but he was as cold as stone.

"I'm just, it just…" He looked away. "Gads, what has she done to me?"

"Sir?"

"Arclight." Her name on his tongue, filling his head with glimpses of power, time, life and death. "*Arcus lux, quid vis tibi? Quid tibi opus est?* I don't know…"

The little fire roared and he scrambled to his feet.

"Castlewaite?"

"Sir?"

The flames, dancing, rearing, rushing, burning.

"Do you see any horses in the fire, Castlewaite?"

"Naw, sir. Just a few bits of wood. Why? Do you see an 'orse, sir?"

"Not yet."

"Why don't ye sit down wi' me?" Castlewaite patted the snow. "Right 'ere."

He looked across the field, past the towers, past the world. He could see all of the *Industrial Republic of France* from here, all of *Blood and Iron* too. Austria, Poland, Russia and Slovakia, an entire continent on fire because of one man. One man and a set of lockets.

"He's dead," he said, his voice echoing and hollow. "The Crown Prince is dead, shot in the head. War is coming on iron feet."

"Sir, ye're scarin' me and yer bleedin' sommat fierce. Please sit down wi' me, sit 'ere…"

Sebastien dabbed his forehead, looked at the fingers shiny with blood. With a grunt, he reached behind to pull his pistol, the remarkable clockwork pistol, from his belt. It was a fine musket-bore walnut and steel officer's piece, with carved ivory laid in the grip. He spun the chambers once, twice, three times.

"Three balls," he said. "Three balls of lead. Still three."

He looked at the coachman and smiled like the sun.

"You see, Castlewaite? I didn't kill the Crown Prince."

And he bolted through the snow toward the towers.

Chapter 8

Of Mechanical Monsters, a Shooting Mishap and a Maritime Disaster of Titanic Proportions

Reuters, Int., January 30, 1889

Excitement in Vienna

Sudden Death of Gilded Crown Prince

Intelligence has just been received from Mayerling, a small village in the vicinity of the Gilded *capital, announcing the death of Crown Prince Rudolf. There are conflicting reports on the manner of death, one indicating a stroke of apoplexy while another mentioning the notion of a single gunshot wound to the head.*

State Police have begun an official investigation.

***

"These are strange, don't you think?" Ivy asked as they approached the towers. "Are they grain silos? Windmills without vanes? Very ugly huts? And why has no one come out to meet us? Someone has been here recently – look at all the footprints in the snow. But surely, if someone were here, they'd have seen something as monumental as an airship crashing in the fields outside their homes."

"Surely."

"And it's almost noon, so we certainly don't have the element of surprise."

"Certainly."

"Do you think it's an army base? It looks rather like an army base. But if so, where's the army?"

"God, I'd forgotten how much you talk."

"You used to like talking. Now you're a grumpy old buffer."

He smiled to himself. Not that he would let her see.

She spied a mound under the trampled snow, nudged it with the toe of her boot.

"Oh look, Remy," she said. "It's a cap!"

He shook his head. She was such a contrast, a 'good' girl who dreamed of more. Change couldn't come fast enough for Ivy Savage, not in Victoria's *Empire of Steam* but still, he couldn't fault her for the dreaming. He had dreamed once. It had all come to ruin at the edge of a very sharp blade.

She pulled the cap out of the snow, slapped it a few times before slipping it on her head.

"You look like your brother," he said.

"Don't I though?" She dug a little more with her toe. "Now what's this?"

He turned to study the towers, all gunmetal gray and industrial like the airship hangers at the Heath Row Fields. One of the windows was shattered and the metal was blackened as if by a torch.

"It's a boot," said Ivy.

He studied the panel doors of aluminium. They looked to slide on inside tracks but the towers were tall as opposed to wide, with lightning rods atop like the peak of a helmet. This was a wine region. He wondered if they could be filled to the ceiling with barrels and oak.

"Remy," said Ivy.

Now if they were houses, they'd be the most unusual houses he'd ever seen. He'd heard of houses made of grass in deepest Africa, houses of snow in colonial Canada. Perhaps, in the border regions of *Blood and*

Iron, houses of aluminium were all the rage.

"Remy, please," said Ivy. "I need you to see this…"

He sighed and turned, eyes flicking down to the shape at her feet.

"Yes, Ivy. It's a boot."

"Not just a boot."

Frowning, he crossed over to where she was standing, peered into the leather.

"Oh god," he breathed.

The sound of propellers echoed down on the breeze and they looked up.

Led by the *Stahl Mädchen*, the Imperial Fleet of airships had begun their descent on the snowy field of Reichsland.

***

Suddenly, an orb folded into life on the path before him and he skidded to a halt, twisting into the snow as he did to avoid sliding into it. He had no idea when or where he would come out if he did, or if in fact, he would come out at all.

He pushed himself to stand, looking up at the skies as the underbellies of airships appeared through the grey clouds. They looked like whales, he thought. Like great black and white whales, lowering as if to land. The *Stahl Mädchen* was nearest and on her decks somewhere, Arclight. He could hear her singing to him, calling him to her the way a siren called seamen to their deaths. He would go and willingly if only he knew Ivy Savage would be safe. As long as she was with Christien, she should be. Surely, he would protect her. His hatred could not go that far.

The orb hovered above the snow and he studied its surface, at once silver and mirrored as well as black and shiny. It was like a pearl, he thought, a large black pearl and he could see something as it spun before him. He stepped closer. It looked like a face.

No, three faces, three mouths open in a scream, three heads separating, three bodies with arms and legs, young arms and legs running toward him in the snow. Three children, boys, the same ones from the fire and suddenly, they appeared before him again, dead and pleading and so very young.

A red flash crossed the orb and from the towers, the sky lit up with lightning.

***

The sky was dark with the underbellies of ships as the fleet hovered over the field, preparing to land.

"Airship docks?" asked Ivy as she staggered back to look at the towers. It was something she had not considered. "But they're not tall enough."

They could hear the rumble of the gunports, saw the black iron glint in the grey sky and suddenly, a flash of red and the boom of cannon fire.

"Run!" Christien shouted as the earth in front of them exploded with the impact, sending clods of frozen mud raining down like shrapnel. A second boom hit the ground near the fence and they slid in the snow as they tried to stop.

A siren rose from the towers and the lightning rods began to crackle between them. Suddenly, the skies thundered as beams of light arced from the roofs to the *Stahl Mädchen,* racking its iron hull. The dreadnaught heaved forward, sails engaging and propellers straining to gain altitude.

"*Anti-*airship docks," Ivy gasped as Christien pulled her to her feet. His face was streaked with mud. "So do we try to get in?"

"No," he said. "To the trees."

But they ducked as the lightning struck again, this time catching only the rudder as the ironclad rose upward into the snowy skies. The fleet dispersed, taking position low in the clouds as if awaiting orders from the *Stahl Mädchen.*

"Listen," said Christien. "Do you hear that?"

Between the towers, there were voices. Thin and tinny, a man was shouting orders like Castlewaite through the bosun's pipe. It sounded a world away.

"That's German," she said. "Is it a photophone?"

"*Aktivieren die Eisenmänner,*" and he frowned. "Activate the

97

iron…*men?"*

"Iron men?"

Suddenly, with the screech of metal on metal, a tower door shuddered, revealing a crack of red.

"Iron men," she breathed, stepping back.

And with the groan of a train on a track, the tower doors rumbled open on massive shapes within. Almost three stories high and illuminated by red a glow, they looked like ironclad warships. Beams of light swept from their helms.

"Sentinels," she whispered. "Remy, they're Sentinels…"

"Ivy," said Christien, shielding her with his body. "To the trees. Run!"

And he grabbed her hand and bolted for the trees.

***

His heart sank as the *Stahl Mädchen* lurched upward, her hull racked by lightning from the towers. He could see her gunports darkening however, flinched at the boom, watched as the cannonballs tore up the ground. More lightning and the fleet broke to hover, deadly and silent over the snowy field. The air was holding its breath.

Something was happening with the towers.

He pushed through the boys and ducked around the orb to study them. The towers were splitting open like over-ripe oranges, rumbling with the sound of thunder and shaking the ground beneath his boots. Three shapes could be seen through the wide panel doors, three silhouettes in red and he thought they might be giants until they moved into the light.

"Good Lord," he breathed.

The boys appeared before him once again. He turned, watched the orb for a moment as it spun and flashed with red. Suddenly he understood.

He turned back to the boys.

"Those things? Did they kill you?"

One of the boys nodded. Another began to cry, his tears forming an icy slick along his cheek.

"I'm sorry," he said. "But there's nothing I can do. I can't kill them for you. They're machines."

Sentinels, he corrected himself. Huge mechanical soldiers moving on iron legs out of the towers, iron legs churning up the ground like the strides of very large horses. One raised its massive arm, pointing it toward the dreadnought as one would aim a pistol. Its fingers were artillery shells, five on each metal hand and fire leapt from its wrist as four rockets flared up to the sky.

Arclight sang and he raised his own hand, trying to understand her song.

"Wilhelm, Children, Red, Peace!" he shouted, naming each rocket as she flew.

The orb disappeared only to reappear beneath the *Stahl Mädchen,* swallowing all four rockets in succession in a kaleidoscopic burst of ice. Another Sentinel fired, sending a fifth rocket hurtling towards the Maiden but she swung hard to port, taking her well out of range of the hovering orb. The rocket pierced a hole through a starboard sail and the *Stahl Mädchen* soared up, up, up into the cloudy skies, taking the rest of the fleet, and the orb, with it.

The Sentinels turned their attention away from the ships and it was only then that Sebastien noticed two figures racing across the snowy fields.

Beams of red swept along the ground – targeting mechanisms built into the Sentinels' helms. Another rocket flared from the arm and the earth erupted as if struck by a cannonball. Christien and Ivy dodged the snow, dirt and sparks that rained down on their heads. Another rocket and Ivy was thrown into the air. Only Christien's clockwork grip kept her from being crushed by the massive feet.

The boys stared at him with vacant eyes.

Sebastien studied the pistol.

Three bullets. Three Sentinels.

"Crackerjack," he said.

He spun the chambers, raised his arm, and fired.

***

January 30, 1945
Baltic Sea

The MV Wilhelm Gustloff is evacuating civilians and navy personnel from the threat of the Red Army. It is not flying the Red Cross to mark it as a hospital ship and its navigation lights are on to avoid collisions with the many minesweepers in the area. There are upwards of ten thousand people on board, most children and the fact that they are fleeing signals a turn in the war.

Suddenly, the night sky is lit up by rocket fire as four torpedoes strike the Wilhelm Gustloff, the first in the port bow, second amid ships, third below the funnel while the fourth sputters harmlessly into the water.

It is rumoured that the ship has been attacked by a Steel Kosatka, or Killer Whale U-Boat, although the only submersible in the vicinity returns to port with a full bay of faulty torpedoes. Alexander Marinesko, Captain S-13, will take credit for the sinking and be awarded the Order of the Red Banner, but will later be dishonourably discharged from the Navy of Steel.

While the minesweepers are able to save some, it is reported that over nine thousand people, including the five thousand children, lose their lives in this most tragic of maritime disasters.

***

She was grateful for Christien's hold as they flew across the field, wave after concussive wave threatening to send them into the air like kites. She could hear nothing but the wail of sirens and boom of exploding earth, could see nothing but his black-clad shoulders and the line of trees in the distance. Another blast and this time, the impact sent them both skidding sideways, the snow immediately melting under the heat. Her hand slipped out of his grip as another rocket blast stuck like a wall, and she was flung high and far only to hit the ground hard, forcing the breath from her lungs. She spat out the dirt and lifted her head, freezing at the sight of barbed wire not inches from her face. She scrambled backwards only to slam into a huge iron foot that went up and up and up.

The Sentinel had stopped, groaning as it angled its helm to look down at her. The red eye began to glow and she felt her heart grow numb. She thought of the little boy's boot, felt a rush of sadness to know she was likely wearing his coat. She wondered if he had been afraid before he died, if his parents missed him, if there had been pain. She looked over at Christien pushing himself out of the snow, saw the dread on his porcelain face, felt the world shrink to the sound of her own heart. After everything that she had lived through these last six months – the human heart in the post, the Milnethorpe murder, the Whitechapel Ripper and finally the horror of St. Katharine's Docks, it was all reduced to the simple beating of her heart.

The crack of a remarkable pistol changed everything.

The Sentinel's helm jerked back and sparks flew from the eye to the snow around her. She scrambled to her feet and threw herself to Christien's side, grabbing his hand and pulling him to his feet as the Sentinel staggered back, each footfall booming like a cannon and forcing deep ruts in the ground. It was all they could do to avoid the massive legs as they dashed between and she could feel heat building up from the second Sentinel when another pistol shot echoed across the field. It lurched like a marionette with strings snapped and sparks rained down on their heads, sizzling into the snow around them.

A roar and flare as a rocket sliced through the sky above her head. Across the field, the ground erupted as earth, snow and fire rose up where the Mad Lord of Lasingstoke had been.

"No!" she cried, swinging her own pistol and firing but the bullets pinged harmlessly off the metal. With slow, ground-shaking steps, it roared past her through the fence, catching it with its iron legs and dragging the barbed wire and the posts as it went.

To her utter surprise, Christien rushed after it and with catlike grace, he leapt up onto a moving foot and held fast. His shoulders barely came up to the gears that worked its knees but as it carried him further, she could see him changing attachments on the clockwork hand. Further still as he connected his arm to the knee bolts with a click. Even further, she could hear the whine as both attachment and knee bolts began to spin. She reloaded her pistol and gave chase.

Like an ironclad on the open seas, the Sentinel plowed across the field until a loud clang echoed caused it to stop in its tracks. Christien sprang from his perch, rolling and coming up, hand dipped in snow for balance. The helm swiveled and from across the field, Ivy could see the red eye stare down at him, unblinking and inhuman. Slowly, carefully, Christien straightened and for a brief moment there was only the rush of the wind on the field.

The Sentinel struck, swinging a savage backhand and sending him sailing like a ragdoll into the snow.

She raced toward him and dropped to her knees, gathering him in her arms. He was not moving, the side of his face covered with mud, grease and blood. She scanned the field for sight of his brother. Not fifty feet away, Sebastien was pushing himself up out of the snow, face blackened, coat smoking from the blast. She doubted he could find his pistol now, let alone take out the Sentinel's eye. As it stood above and between them, the helm swiveled first her way, then his. She could see the artillery fingers reload, hydraulics squealing and clicking with each motion. It was as if it was deciding which one of them to kill first and she cursed the analytical programming that was allowing such machines to think.

With a deep breath, she pushed out of the snow, drew her pistol and aimed, waiting for the head to turn her way.

It did not. It turned toward Sebastien and her heart leapt into her throat as she saw him scramble to escape. It took a step but only one, earth booming as the foot struck the ground. With the screech and groan of straining gears, the mechanical knee buckled, plates of the thigh sliding over pistons of the lower leg. Slowly, ever so slowly, the towering machine began to fall.

"Sebastien!" she screamed, losing sight of him as the Sentinel crashed to the field, arsenal-arms flailing, iron legs shattering, wires springing from the joints and sparks leaping into the air, melting the snow as they landed. Bits of metal rained down like arrows and she threw herself over Christien, shielding him from the deadly hail. The

Sentinel twitched and shuddered but finally, hissed into the sky and did not move to get up.

After a moment, she raised her head, searching but seeing nothing but smoke, steam and snow.

"Miss Savage?"

She blinked back tears as the Mad Lord of Lasingstoke sank down beside her in the snowy field of Reichsland. They sat that way for a while, the only sound being the soft rush of the wind until finally, Castlewaite's voice calling their names.

***

Death of Crown Prince Ruled a Shooting Mishap
Illustrated London News
We are informed that, according to a telegram from official sources in Vienna, the death of Crown Prince Rudolf has been deemed a fatal accident whilst shooting. According to Gilded *Ambassador Count Kinsky, his Royal Highness was present at the state reception in honour of Kaiser Wilhelm II's birthday and was reported in the best of health and spirits, full of his forthcoming visit to the shooting box at Mayerling, where his death has taken place.*

*The funeral is to be held on February 5. The Prince of Wales will be the representative of Queen Victoria and the **Empire of Steam**. Prayers are being offered in the Austrian Chapel at Berkeley Square for the repose of the deceased Prince.*

It was originally reported the Prince's death due to a state of apoplexy but examinations have proven death by a single gunshot wound to the head. State police are continuing to investigate.

Chapter 9

Of a Traveling Locket, a Dented Brace and the Matter with Dark Matter

London News

Theft in Pall Mall

The preeminent Ghost Club of London and Cambridge is reporting a most unusual burglary at their Pall Mall address. There is no evidence of a break-in and there is only one item missing from their archives. According to Chair Dr. William Crookes, the stolen item is a several-hundred year old locket from the Normandy region of France. It's said to have little monetary value, but is valuable in terms of its physical, anatomical and parapsychical properties.

Police are continuing to investigate.

***

"Kaffee, Fräulein?"

"Oh thank you," said Ivy and she took the mug, welcoming the heat in her hands. It was a bitter brew but it reminded her of Rupert's fireside smokes at Lasingstoke. She smiled at the memory and wearily, looked around the room.

The farmhouse was very old with walls of black stone and a low timbered ceiling but a fire was roaring in the hearth, filling the room with warmth and light. They had been rescued by a search party who had seen the smoke, and brought to this farmhouse near the town of Kolmar. Debris from the airship was strewn across a table and at least twenty people were going through it, speaking to each other in French, German or both. Sebastien had been invaluable earlier on, speaking both languages as he did, and somehow Ivy felt safe in this room filled with strangers. Life, she had realized, was infinitely stranger.

For one thing, the party had not been searching for them.

"Miss Ivy?"

She looked up. Castlewaite was in a doorway, separated from the rest of the house by a woolen blanket. She leapt to her feet and met him, laying her hands on his sleeve.

"Jerry?"

"'e's awake, miss," he said. "And askin' fer ye."

She slipped past him into a tiny room with a single chair and a cot. A man straightened as she entered. Dr. Schoenguar was Kolmar's sole physician and on the cot, Christien. His face, throat and chest were in the ripe stages of bruising and one eye was almost swollen shut. Still he was the most beautiful man she had ever seen.

She looked up at the physician.

"He'll live, yes?"

"Ich werde leben?" Christien translated, grimacing with the effort.

"Yah. You'll liff," the doctor scowled. "I vill find somevone vor zis."

And he held up the brace for the clockwork arm.

The arm itself was usually hidden by brace and sleeve and she couldn't stop her eyes from going to the stump she had made so many months ago. It was affixed to the prosthetic by a long bloody screw, with wires and cables disappearing into the flesh of his upper arm. It looked like a mass of copper snakes entwined around a hydraulic crane and to see it exposed like this made her stomach turn.

Christien sighed, mask falling into place like always.

"It was dented," he said flatly. "Dr. Schoengaur will find a blacksmith or something."

"Sie müssen ruhen," said the doctor. "He must rest."

And he slipped out under the wool blanket over the door.

She sat on the edge of the cot.

"You did it," she said. "Unscrewed that knee like a machinist."

"Medical man, machinist, murderer. Impressive list of accomplishments."

"It was very brave," she said.

"I knew you couldn't save us with that pistol of yours." He tried to move, hissed, settled back down again. "I don't think it could dispatch a spaniel, let alone a Sentinel."

"I'm not the marksman Sebastien is."

"Is he dead yet?"

He was trying so hard to be indifferent.

"No," she said. "He carried you until the villagers found us."

"Of course he would."

"They're going to take us to Strasbourg tomorrow. There's a telegraph office and steamtrain station. We can get to Paris from there. Maybe Rupert can arrange transport to London."

"You've got it all worked out, haven't you?" He closed his eyes, turned his face away. "You haven't reckoned on the long arm of the *Gilded Empire.*"

She frowned. "What do you mean?"

"It's a very, very long arm…"

He was asleep before she knew it. Or a perfect likeness. All a part of the mask, she knew. Very fine, very fragile porcelain. She had seen it crack more than once but still didn't know the man who lived behind it.

With a sigh, she leaned forward to kiss his forehead on the one spot that wasn't blue and rose to her feet, returning to the crowded kitchen.

They stole curious glances at her while they talked, knowing she couldn't understand. She sighed again, looking for but not finding Sebastien in the mob. They had found his pistol but not his black spectacles. She did see her bowler however, crushed and sitting on the wooden table along with her tattered peacoat and vestiges of the red lace dress. Canvas, gears, pipes and rope had all been salvaged and she suspected the towers had been looted as well. People were combing the wreckage for items of use, of value or curiosity and it felt strange. They were going through bits of her life like it was market day, her possessions little more than cabbages or carrots or beets. Still, she was in a kitchen, warm and sheltered. She could still be out in the snow.

The door blew open as an older couple entered and suddenly, all conversation in the farmhouse ceased. The woman moved into the kitchen but the man hung back and Ivy heard a name whispered between villagers. Face grey and cheeks gaunt, the woman eyed her coat. Ivy swallowed, slid the cap off her head.

"I'm so sorry," she said. "I didn't know. I just found it in the snow by the towers."

She held out the cap.

The woman took it, turned it over and over in her hands and Ivy could see tears welling in the deep-set eyes, felt her own throat grow tight. She looked down at the coat she was wearing, remembered how it had hung, lost and lonely, on the post.

"This is his too, I think. Mine was lost in the wreckage, but it wasn't really mine. It was my brother's. I borrowed it from him and never gave it back. Rather like my hat. And you see this corset? I borrowed that too from a lunatic asylum. Now that is crazy, isn't it? I seem to be borrowing everything. Clothing, adventures, storylines, companions. All borrowed from someone else, never given back. I am a greedy girl who wants everything at once. But I did buy the boots myself. Honestly, I did."

Her words ran out as she fumbled with the buttons and she couldn't stop her chin from quivering.

"*Nein, Liebling,*" said the woman. "You keep."

"No, no. Your son…"

"Jens gone. You live."

She couldn't stop the tears spilling from her lashes and the woman wiped them, smiling and sad. The old hands lifted the cap, took a long fond look and carefully set it onto Ivy's head, tugging it down snug. She kissed her cheek and stepped back.

"You live."

With a deep breath, Ivy nodded and rushed from the farmhouse and into the snow.

***

The little girl struggles with breath, her normally pink cheeks pale, blonde curls slicked onto her forehead. Her mother is there, as is her father, but it is her mother who is the strong one. The physicians shake their heads. The sickness will kill her, they know this now. For all the Habsburg might and power, this sickness will kill her. There is nothing they can do.

Unless the one from Slovakia can make a miracle. He has been experimenting on orphans in Prague with great success. So much success that all the royal houses of Europe want him. He is a clockwork genius, this little man, and he's on his way from Prague to Budapest as fast as horses can fly. But little Sophie is so very sick...

Sophie.

Sebastien opened his eyes, not surprised to see orbs like silver coins floating between his hands. Arclight was near, he knew, most likely on the *Stahl Mädchen* somewhere overhead, heading for Strasbourg or Paris. He wondered if it were allowed, a *Gilded* warship flying the *Republic's* skies. But then again, it was a Habsburg ship. No one would protest. Protesting would mean an international incident and those were to be avoided at all costs.

Something he'd never managed to learn.

He was sitting in the open mouth of a very old stone barn. It was more of a dugout built into the hillside, with thatched roof and straw covering the earthen floor. There were goats, cows, chickens and one horse, all housed in various timber stalls. The farm dog was sitting beside him and he was comforted by its presence. Dogs were good that way. He missed his dogs, hoped Rupert would treat them well. He doubted he would see them again.

His head was throbbing and he reached to touch the bullet wound. Fresh blood oozed onto his fingers and he grimaced as he pressed it forward between his scalp and the plates in his skull. The dog whimpered but he steeled himself, pressing all the more. Finally, it slipped out from the wound and into his palm, bloody and white and clearly not lead. He turned it over, not entirely surprised to find it a bullet made of bone.

Sophie.

He slipped it into a pocket and sighed, looking out over the fields. Behind him, the farmhouse was well-lit and warm but he didn't belong inside. Too many living, too many dead. Orbs circled like snowflakes, like mirrors, like coins. It was impossible to keep them away now and people, it seemed, did not do well with the orbs.

He heard the farmhouse door and knew it was Ivy. He could smell the life on her. Life and leather and rose petals, her very peculiar scent and he breathed her in, wishing for so much more but knowing it was for the best. Death followed him, and so did she. It was only a matter of time before they met.

He could hear the crunch of her boots in the snow, felt her warmth as she lowered down beside him. The dog wagged again. It was a good dog.

"Christien's sleeping now," she said. "I think he'll be fine."

"Good."

"Those Sentinels killed three boys."

"Yes."

"You knew?" She turned to study him and he could tell she had been weeping. "Are they gone now, the boys?"

He nodded. "Released."

"I thought only murdered people sought you out, not those killed by machines."

"Apparently not anymore."

"Not since Ghostlight?"

"Ghostlight changed everything."

"How many do you see?"

"Thousands. Thousands upon thousands."

She sighed and he watched her from the corner of his eye. An orb circled before her like a firefly, throwing light across her face. She reached for it.

"Don't touch it please," he said.

"Why? What are they?"

"*Re obscura.* Dark…matter. I call them orbs."

"Orbs." She frowned as if trying to find a home for the word on her tongue. "But the guests at the Hofburg were screaming."

"The lockets open doors or windows into other worlds, yes?"

She nodded.

"I think these are Arclight's doors. Dark doors. Very dark."

"What do they lead to?"

"Moments of death, Miss Savage." And he shrugged. "No one needs to see that."

"Oh…"

He felt his chest grow tight. His world was far too macabre for such a soul. As fascinated as she was, she could never share it and he hated himself for even entertaining the thought.

She shifted in the snow. "Have you…"

"Looked into one?"

She nodded again.

"One."

"That's where you were last night." She looked at him. "So you didn't kill Prince Rudolf. You saw it."

He sighed.

"You didn't kill him. Right, Sebastien?"

"I didn't kill him. Not directly."

She stared at him.

"I called Arclight and she tried to come. The girl tried to bring her but Rudolf stopped them."

"Oh dear…"

"So," he cleared his throat. "So, in a way—"

"No," she said. "You're not responsible, Sebastien. You're not."

"That must be why I can't see him. I've never had the dead point a finger at me. Would I see it? How would I help? If I shot myself in the head, it wouldn't take."

She sighed, wrapped her arms around her knees and he felt his heart almost break in two. He wanted her to hold him, tell him it would be alright, kiss his forehead as she had done in the field. But she wasn't a romantic sort of girl and he was a fool anyway.

"You said the girl tried to bring her."

"Yes," he said.

"So how did she try?"

He blinked slowly, not following.

"I mean," and she made a face as she stared over the fields. "Was she stealing it?

"I don't know."

"Ghostlight was damnably clever," she continued. "She would use people to get what she wanted. That's what made her unnatural and frankly, terrifying. Ghostlight didn't 'do' anything, except make people do everything."

"She wanted to come to me."

"Exactly. What I'm trying to say is this: If Arclight is like Ghostlight, and Arclight wanted to get to you, then how do it? What did you see?"

He looked at the snow as he remembered. It was not something he wanted to remember.

"The girl was wearing it," he said. "She was leaving him but he grabbed it and they struggled at the top of the stairs. The chain broke and she fell."

He reached up to touch his forehead. The blood was still fresh.

"And she died from the fall, then, yes?"

"He carried her back up the stair, laid her in bed with a rose…"

"Hmm. And what about Rudolf? How did he die?"

"I don't know," he lied. "I didn't want to see anymore."

She frowned, looked away and his heart ached at the sight. He should leave now but every minute with her was a gift and he was a greedy man. It was only a matter of time. A dark matter of time.

He made a fist and the orb disappeared.

"But the locket," she murmured, obviously thinking out loud. "It was on the *Stahl Mädchen* this morning. That's how you were able to stop the cannons, right? By calling the orbs."

"Yes," he said. "She's still trying to come to me."

She turned to him now, eyes large and shining.

"But Sebastien, if the girl had the locket last night, how did it end up on a dreadnought over Kolmar this morning?"

His heart skipped a beat.

"Who brought her onto the *Stahl Mädchen,* Sebastien? How did they get her, and why?"

"How did they get her?" he breathed. His mind was racing now with possibilities.

"And why?"

"And why?"

"There is murder afoot, Sebastien, and if not murder, then most definitely some manner of wickedness and treachery. We need to get to the bottom of it to clear your name. To clear all of our names."

He released a deep breath, and then another as he stared into her eyes, so quick, so bright, so full of life. She had done it again, gleaned hope out of ashes, turned everything upside down with the strength of her will. He was a fool for her. Had been since he'd first met her, less than six months ago. A lifetime.

He so wanted to kiss her.

"You have saved me once again, Miss Savage."

"Ivy," she said. "I'd be pleased if you called me Ivy, Sebastien."

"Ivy," he said, feeling at the same time both light-headed and heavy. "Ivy."

He looked out over the snowy fields. The white horse stood, eyes red as sunset. It shook its mane and arrows were sent flashing into the sky.

"Whoever has Arclight has the answer," he said after a moment. "I need to go back."

"That's what I was thinking."

"We'll go to Strasbourg where you will accompany Christien and Castlewaite to Paris. Perhaps check in on that university you were thinking of before crossing the channel to London. I'll stay on the continent, see what I can suss out."

"Sebastien, can you honestly remember a time when I ever did what you said?"

He looked back at her. She was hugging her knees and grinning a little grin that tugged into one cheek. He wondered what her lips would taste like.

"Never," he said.

"Right. We *will* go to Strasbourg but Castlewaite will take Christien to Paris. You and I will catch the train to Vienna."

He shook his head but the dog wagged happily beside him.

***

Dr. John Williams could see the rooflines of Sandringham in the sights of his rifle as he followed the flight of the pheasant across the sky. The setter had flushed it and now it flew, her wings beating a steep arc over the grounds. He squeezed the trigger ever so gently and immediately relaxed as the recoil butted into his shoulder. The bird's arc changed dramatically and the setter bounded off into the snow.

"Capital shot, Jack! She was a fast one, that bird."

Williams turned. Big and bearlike, his companion sported a thick beard and upturned moustache. His arm was held straight down at his side, right sleeve buttoned at the shoulder. It was a prosthetic, all metal shafts, copper gears and a cable pulley system that mimicked the movements of both muscle and tendon. At the moment, there was no hand attached to the arm, but rather the barrel of a well-oiled hunting rifle. With an arm like that, it was amazing how well he shot.

Albert Edward, Prince of Wales. The King with the Clockwork Arm.

"Indeed, sir," smiled Williams. "A lucky shot."

"Tosh, man. You're a natural behind the stock."

"Thank you, sir."

He lowered his rifle and the two men stood, awaiting the dog that would retrieve the prize. It was not the only prize however. A porter stood nearby, a flush of grouse and two more pheasants hanging from a cob. All in all, it had been a good afternoon.

A second porter approached holding a tray filled with shot glasses. Both men appropriated one, Williams with his right hand, Edward with his left.

"And so, have you had any luck with those *Peniarth* texts, Jack? Last I heard, you were angling to get 'em."

"Alas, that Wynne is a bastard, Bertie. He won't part with 'em for any sum."

"Tell him it's for the library on behalf of the Prince of Wales, wot!"

"The Prince of Wales Library! Capital idea, sir!"

As the men tossed back the whiskies, the setter returned, dropping the pheasant at their feet. The porter snatched it up, slid it onto the cob.

"Let's call it a day, shall we? I like to end on a good note."

Wales held out his arm and an automaton approached, groaning on track wheels over the snow. Several rifles protruded from the top, along with several mechanical hands. The porter twisted the rifle extension, popping it off with a click and dropping it into the canister. He carefully selected a forearm with its wondrously designed network of pulleys and began to twist it onto the elbow joint.

It was a rather ghastly image but over the last few months, Williams had seen much worse.

He cleared his throat.

"Ahem, Bertie…"

"Jackie?"

"That matter you had asked me to look into…"

"Ah yes."

"I've taken care of it, sir."

And he reached into his waistcoat pocket, producing a small black pouch.

Pleasant but sharp, the Prince of Wales narrowed his eyes.

"That's it?"

"It is, sir."

"Balderdash! You would have me believe something so powerful could fit in such a tiny bag?"

"Without the key," said Williams, "It's just a locket."

Wales dumped the contents of the pouch into his hand, held it up to swing at the end of its chain.

"What do you boys call it? Gaslight? Spooklight?"

"Ghostlight, sir. Or the French equivalent."

The locket spun sweetly, no flashing colours, no spinning rings.

"Hmph. Can't see what all the fuss is about then. Pearls, lockets, trinkets for the bunters. My nephew Willie is swaggering bully, you know that! Insisted I bring this bloody thing to the damned funeral! Franzi doesn't want us to go but dashitall, Rudy was a friend. Be damned if I'm not going to pay m'respects and all that rot."

He glanced up.

"I say, you weren't seen, were you?"

"Not at all, sir. I slipped in, nicked it from the case and slipped out again. The only one who might suspect is Bookie and he's as loyal to the Club as you or I." Williams smiled grimly. "After all, it's only on loan to the Club, isn't it? It belongs to the de Lacey family. I was merely the unfortunate recipient after the debacle at the Docks."

"Indeed. Indeed. You know that boy is still alive, don't you?"

"Sebastien de Lacey? Yes sir, I do know. I keep in touch with Remy from time to time."

"How he manages is beyond me. That boy has been dead more times than a cat! One day, he'll meet himself a bulldog and be done with it all! Ah ha! Ah ha!"

The Prince of Wales swung around to the porters.

"Webster, take these birds and roast us up a spread."

"Yes sir," said the porter.

"Jackie, let's call us a day," said Wales. "I'm off for Vienna tomorrow and can't abide the thought of their sweet wines and bitter coffees. Stay and nosh it up with me. God knows I'll have no fun once I set foot on *Gilded* soil."

"I would be happy to, Bertie."

He raised the locket to his eyes.

"I can't wait to see Willie's face once I pull little Spooklight out of m'pocket. Why, he might just declare war there and then! Imagine that! A European war all on account of a bloody locket! Ah ha! Ah ha!"

As the pair began the short walk back to Sandringham, Williams could not help but wonder if that wasn't precisely what the bloody locket had in mind.

Chapter 10

Of Archduchesses, Pillars of Angels and the Empire of Blood and Iron

"Where are we going, you rogue?" asked Penny as she struggled against her bonds.

"Why, Strasbourg of course," answered international jewel thief, Alexander Dunn. *"It's wine country. Where else would I take two beautiful women?"*

Penny growled but did not respond. She was trussed like a Christmas ham in the rear seat of his speedster, flying down a country road in Alsace-Lorraine. A woman was seated in front of her, wearing a tiny top hat with an enormous feather, a striped corset and goggles that were as dark as coal. She also had a white powder wig and a rather large mole on her cheek, and had been introduced as Antoine Marionette.

The woman turned and smiled at her.

"Penny Dreadful, Girl Criminologist, oui?"

"I refuse to answer," said Penny.

"But of course," said Antoine, her accent undeniably French. "You are the most celebrated criminologist of all time, oui?"

"Mais oui," said Penny, knowing it to be quite true.

"You think I stole the Star of Morocco, don't you Penny?" said Alexander from the stick. "But I didn't."

"I say again, you are a rogue, sir. Why should I believe you?"

"Because it's true and Penny Dreadful does not rest until she uncovers the truth."

She harrumphed but held her chin high, eyes fixed on the road before her.

*"I **would** have stolen it," he said. "But the Star of Morocco wasn't in Vienna."*

"Of course it was," she snapped. "I saw it myself."

"You saw a copy, a replica."

"A forgery," cooed Antoine.

"A forgery, exactly."

"A forgery?" gasped Penny and she looked up, eyes flashing. "But where is the original?"

Dunn threw a glance over his shoulder at her, grinning like the rogue he was.

"And that, dear Penny, is why we're going to Strasbourg. We have a train to catch."

*She sank back in the seat, bonds tight but mind racing. So if the Villain of Vienna was NOT international jewel thief Alexander Dunn, she thought to herself, who WAS he and why would he frame Dunn? Suddenly, she was very glad she had leapt from the **Scarlet Pimpernel** and into the speedster, for she was currently on to the road to answers in Strasbourg and the **Empire of Blood and Iron**.*

***

Strasbourg had been a part of the *Empire of Blood and Iron* since the Franco-Prussian War of the Wire and its historic buildings were being restored with a distinctly Germanic feel. As they floated along the icy River Ill, Ivy could see half-timbered houses beside grey gothic spires, shops selling French wines and German beers. Black banners with golden eagles waved from every post, the clockwork fleur-de-lis from every pillar. Easily a town conflicted, Ivy thought, as if serving two masters.

She was tired.

It was twilight when they pulled up near a bridge and a set of stone steps that led to the city's waterfront. The town center was an island surrounded by the Ill, much like the Seine surrounded the heart of Paris. They had taken Dr. Schoengaur's buggy into Kolmar and from there, a wine barge along the river until the very tall spire of Strasbourg cathedral came into view. The bargeman had charged a hefty sum and Ivy began to worry about the depth of Sebastien's pockets. She wondered what he had lost in the crash and if they could even afford a train to Paris.

Cold, damp and bone-tired, she was glad to set foot on solid ground once again, even if it was to trudge up the stone steps from the canal to the quay. It was dark but the snow had stopped and the gaslight burned on streetlamps all along the bridge. Below her, the bargeman was speaking in German as Castlewaite and the de Lacey brothers followed her up the stair.

"Damn," muttered Christien. "Apparently, we've missed the nine o'clock train."

His face was purple now and his breathing laboured from the bruised ribs. But the doctor had worked a miracle, finding an iron-monger able to fix the metal brace and a tonic to shrink the swelling. The prosthetic would make an odd clicking sound from time to time. He looked miserable and Ivy was certain he felt even worse, but he was alive and moving and she was grateful for that.

"The fellow says there's one at half-past midnight," said Sebastien. "We'll take a meal in town and head out tonight."

The bargeman pressed a sheet of paper into the Mad Lord's hands.

"Fahrplan," he said.

"It's a train schedule," said Sebastien, handing it to Castlewaite.

"Und Bahnhof Straßburg," the bargeman said. "Station. Train station."

And he pointed down the street to a distant building, bright with gaslight.

"Good lord," said Christien. "Are those airships?"

Above the station, shapes floated like bloated dragons against a darkening sky. There was a fleet of them in close mooring but one easily dwarfed them all.

"The *Stahl Mädchen*," breathed Ivy. "Why is she here?"

"*Stahl Mädchen, yah*," said the bargeman, heading back down the steps to the river. "*Kaiser Wilhelm ist auch hier. Es ist sein Geburtstag Besichtigung.*"

The brothers glanced at each other.

"What?" said Ivy. "What is it?"

"We're all dead," said Christien. He turned and trudged off across the bridge toward the center of town. He was a silhouette in moments.

Castlewaite looked between them, copper eyepiece clicking in the gaslight.

"Sebastien?" Ivy prodded.

The Mad Lord shoved his hands into the pockets of his great coat.

"Apparently, Kaiser Wilhelm is doing a tour of the *Empire of Blood and Iron* for birthday. He's here, in Strasbourg."

She narrowed her eyes, straining to catch a glimpse of the canvases hovering over the station. A single black eagle crowned in gold.

"*Two* Imperial airships here at the same time. That's hardly a co-incidence, is it?"

Sebastien made a face. She swallowed, fighting the knot in her chest.

"Did he know Rudolf? I mean, they were having a celebration for his birthday, weren't they? That's why we went to Vienna. I would imagine all European royalty would all know each other somehow or another, right?"

"I would imagine."

"Do you think he's here because of the sisters?"

"Not at all. Well, unlikely. Quite probably, actually. Christien is right. We might all be dead before the night is through."

From the far end of the bridge came a rumble like distant thunder and Ivy's breath caught in her throat. She turned to see a shape flashing between the gas lamps, a familiar red beam sweeping the ground as it rolled toward them onto the bridge. Ivy felt a wave of cold wash down her body.

It was a Sentinel but instead of legs, it was moving on a carriage of track wheels that shrieked and groaned like grinding gears. In a strange disconnect of thought, she remembered reading that the *Empire of Steam* was using track wheels to enable iron-clads travel over land. *Track-Armoured-Naval-Carriers* they were being called, or TANCs, but never in her wildest dreams could she have imagined those track-wheels carrying a Sentinel. Her knees began to tremble and she wondered how long they would hold.

She barely felt it as Sebastien pulled her out of the way and the three of them stood with backs against the stone as the Sentinel rolled across the bridge. It was huge, the tracks as high as a man and Ivy could feel the cobblestones rumble under her boots. It squealed to a halt when it reached them, it's tiny helm swiveling and the red eye flashed across their faces.

She wanted to run. She wanted to scream. She wanted to wake up from this nightmare with its inhuman gaze and terrible power, but she was trapped on a bridge and her legs wouldn't move. She had never been so terrified in her life.

"Heil Kaiser Wilhelm," said Sebastien. *"Geburtstagsgrüße von Kolmar."*

And he smiled like the sun.

For several long agonizing moments, Ivy simply forgot to breathe.

Finally, the helm returned forward and the Sentinel rumbled its way across the bridge.

"Well," said Sebastien. "That was unexpected."

Ivy sagged back against the stone, her breath coming in ragged gasps.

"Let's go find lodging, shall we? I'm famished and perhaps we could catch forty winks."

And he turned to follow his brother, leaving her on the bridge with Castlewaite. He looked at her, eyepiece clicking twice.

"Ye're right, Miss Ivy," he grinned. "'e might need a bit o' fixin' then, sure enowt."

And he held out his elbow.

Still shaking, she took it and followed the Mad Lord into Strasbourg.

***

London Times

Complex Case surrounding Crown Prince

Funeral services for Rudolf Franz Karl Joseph von Habsburg-Lorraine, Archduke and Gilded Crown Prince of Austria, Hungary and Bohemia, will take place on February 5, 1889. According to sources, interment will take place in the imperial crypt of the Church of the Capuchin Friars in Vienna.

*While the shooting was initially reported to be a tragic accident, police are beginning to suspect the involvement of foreign nationals in the shooting death of the Crown Prince and sole heir to the **Gilded Empire** of Austro-Hungary. The man, reported to be a French anarchist, is said to have caused a scene at the Hofburg celebration for Kaiser Wilhelm II on the evening of January 29 and was believed to have left the country via airship on the morning of the 30th in the company of an English lord and lady. Anyone with any information regarding this man or this crime is asked to come forward to the police.*

***

They had found Christien drinking in a tavern but he refused to join them, so they ate without him a meal of black bread, old cheese and cold sausage. The tavern owner had let them a room over the pub for three *sous* and forty winks. Ivy had flopped into the mattress that served as the room's only bed. She was asleep in seconds.

Sebastien sighed as he watched her, how her hair spilled across the pillow, how her lashes brushed the curve of her cheeks. He was a greedy man, he knew. Greedy and selfish and cold. Her death would be on his shoulders. He wasn't certain how he would ever stand under the weight.

"Castlewaite," he said, turning to the man sitting under the window. "I'm going to the church down the street for a bit. You will watch Miss Savage for me, yes?"

"Aye, sir," said the coachman. "Ah will indeed."

He nodded distractedly. "And Christien? You'll watch over Christien too? If it's not too much trouble."

"Ah'll try, sir. But Mr. Christien is 'is own man, sir."

"I know it. I do know."

He stood for a moment longer, heart heavy and conflicted, before turning and trotting down the stair.

The tavern was dark with only a fire in the hearth for light. A woman was wiping tables and a man was putting up chairs. Christien sat at the bar, with what Sebastien assumed was his sixth beer of the night. Sebastien cleared his throat.

"I, ah, I'm going to the cathedral."

His brother said nothing, merely lifted the stein to his lips. The prosthetic wheezed and clicked as if broken.

"I need to clear my head. To think. To pray."

Still nothing.

"Well, there's a room upstairs. It's not very big but if you push Miss Savage against the wall, I think you both should fit."

Christien stared into his beer.

"Right," he said. "Well, I'm off. I do hope the cathedral is open. I don't feel right about picking the lock of a church."

He hiked the collar of his greatcoat and stepped out into the night.

After a moment, Christien looked up at the tavern owner.

"Did you deliver my message?" he asked in French.

"To one of the Palace guards," said the man and he grunted. "No one is allowed in. They've kicked out all the students."

"Students?"

"The *Palais Rohan* has served as a university since the War of the Wire. The first Bonaparte lived there, did you know that? With Josephine. Before that, Louis XV and Marie Antoinette. And now, it's a damn German university. But oh, when the Kaiser and his *Gilded* princesses show up, it's a palace once again. *Merde."*

Christien raised a brow, followed soon after by the stein.

***

He did, in fact, have to pick the lock for one of the cathedral doors and he cursed the loud creak that echoed through the nave. The lighting was dim and he closed his eyes, breathing deep the smell of candles and incense, old wood and marble. He loved churches. The arches and the spires, the stained glass and the quiet. Most of all he loved the quiet. The dead left him alone when he was in a church. It was one of the few places he could ever find peace.

And so he walked slowly up the nave toward the presbytery, taking his time and admiring sandstone walls that gleamed like wine in the candlelight. It was a very tall cathedral, its vaulted ceiling pulling his eyes heavenward and his soul with it. A perfect place for prayer, he thought. To ask forgiveness for his latest, most dire sin. He wondered if he would indeed go to Hell as his brother had suggested or if Hell was reserved for those who died. He slid into a pew and sank to his knees.

Time always slipped through his fingers when his thoughts were turned heavenward so he couldn't tell how long it had been but at some point, a strange chime drew his attention back to earth.

At the far end of the transept was the largest clock he had ever seen. He loved clocks, was fascinated by the mechanisms that made them work, the very fact that a device could track time, yet was so immune to its reach. Much like the orbs and he wondered if the maker of the lockets was a clocksmith.

He rose to his feet to study it.

Easily sixty feet tall, it reminded him of a pipe organ, with inlaid copper, brass, iron and polished wood. At the same time, it was more than a clock, with etched glass, carved panels and moving gears. Near the top, puppet-like mechanisms moved in perpetual motion, chiming the bells of midnight. Early automatons, he realized, like windup toys for children but infinitely more complex. Angels spun hourglasses, mechanical saints circled the savior, a copper cock crowed and carved figures circled a terrifying rendition of Death. *Of course.* Death as the skeleton, scythe held high judging all ages and stages of human life that passed before him. Infants, children, lovers and old ones, all dancing under the sickle of Death. Death himself rang the chimes, eye sockets empty, cheeks sunken, draped in tattered robes of grey. Sebastien touched his own cheeks, relieved to find them still covered in flesh.

In the candlelight, he could see that this clock not only told the time, but the day, week, month, and year. There was a case enclosing a *Computus Ecclesiastique,* a set of gears that calculated the position of the moon, the planets and the zodiac. A celestial globe spun in the center of the device and it hummed with energy. A complex machine, he realized, not unlike an Analytical Engine. A computing device of higher function, of astronomy and chronology and metallurgy, of earth and spirit and beauty and he had to remind himself to breathe as he tried to take it all in.

His gaze wandered to the left where a pillar of angels rose up to the vaulted ceiling. Tall and slim and meticulously detailed, he wondered how such a thing could possibly serve to support the roof. It was carved with saints and symbols but the most impressive were the angels. From the Book of Revelation, he knew, angels of death blowing trumpets of judgment, calling the dead from their graves at the end of all days. It was heartbreaking and profound and so very sad. He held his breath, waiting for the white horse to leap out from the marble but nothing came.

The clock ceased its chiming and the church fell silent once again. There was a sound however, muffled and rhythmic, like a heart beating inside a drum. His eyes rose once again onto the figure of Death high above him, its motion ceased, its sickle frozen over a clockwork child with golden curls and rosebud lips.

"Bruder, " came a childlike voice behind him.

And the eerie figure of Sophie Friederike Dorothea Maria Josepha von Habsburg, Archduchess of Austria, appeared from behind the Pillar of Angels.

***

Dearest Wilhelm,

Your warm words of sincere participation in our grief have deeply moved the Empress and myself and done our sorrowing hearts good. Accept our warmest thanks for your loyal friendship and also for your intention to come here for the funeral. If I ask you not to do so, you may judge you deeply crushed my family is if we have to address this even to you.

Franz Joseph

***

Willie,
Do NOT come to the funeral.
Gisela

***

He was almost asleep in his stein, alone with the dwindling hearth and the remnants of his stale beer. The tavern door swung open, bringing a blast of cold wind and with a final gulp of ale, he turned in his chair. There was a woman at the door.

"Valerie," he said.

She stood like a statue, her face unreadable under a sable hood. Her eyes were gathering storms.

"Do you still like the décor?" he asked. "It's been banged up a bit since yesterday."

She moved forward, lowering the hood as she came. She was wearing a dress of rich burgundy with a deep neckline and full skirts parted on one side. Underneath, he could see breeches, high boots and what looked like a pistol holster strapped to her thigh. Ready for a ball, he thought, or a barney. Either one would suit her.

"Why are you here?" she asked.

"Because I didn't die. Good idea to get on with life then, generally."

"Why did you send a message?"

"I was cold and alone and I missed you." He shrugged. "And I needed someone to pay for the beer."

She stopped in front of him, raised a hand to stroke his face.

"Does it hurt?"

"Yes," he answered and without hesitation, she hit him.

He went with it, catching himself before it took him off the chair. Slowly, he raised his eyes to meet hers, steel against steel.

With a snarl, she swung again but he caught her wrist in his clockwork hand and pushed to his feet, pulling her roughly to him.

"Don't," he warned, catching her other wrist. "Don't or your hand will drop like a stone to the floor."

And he increased the pressure on the mechanical grip, hearing cables ping with tension. Her eyes watered but her lips drew back in a snarl.

"Where is your brother?" she spat.

"Why did you shoot us down?"

"Where is your brother?!"

"He didn't—"

"He shot him!" she cried. "Shot him in the head!"

It stung more sharply than the slap.

"Oh yes, we know," she hissed, her face only inches from his. "We all know what your brother does, Remy. Bertie knows so my father knows. He shoots people in the head for your clockwork Empress."

"No," he lied. It was a feeble attempt and it was she who pulled him now. She was trained. Could probably kill him with a flick of her wrist.

"He wanted that locket. We all saw it, yes? At the Hofburg. Your brother killed Rudolf to get that damned locket."

His words had fled. Shot in the head.

"You know it's true, Remy. You know it."

"No."

"Where is he?" And suddenly, she melted into him, bones soft, body supple, leaned in close enough to kiss him.

"We only want him, Remy," she purred. "Not you. You are innocent …"

Her lips brushed his cheek and she pressed her forehead against his.

Peaches. She smelled of brandied peaches.

"Just tell me where he is, and you can be with me tonight. And many nights after tonight."

His breath left his chest and he felt lightheaded. He looked at her. She was so very beautiful.

"Dead," he said. "He's dead."

"Dead? Are you sure?"

"Your sister shot him on the airship." He turned her, began to move her slowly backwards to the wall. Like a dance. "You know that. You were there, Valerie. When you shot us out of the skies."

"Yes. I was there."

He pressed her into the wall, raising her arms over her head. But she was not his prisoner.

"Your brother is dead," he said. "And now my brother is dead. The *Gilded Empire* has had justice after all."

She closed her eyes, turned her face away, exposing her long, elegant throat. He kissed it.

"And your girl?" she murmured. "Your little girl who dances with madmen and wears red to a ball?"

"Dead, as well."

"Mm. That's sad."

"Isn't it?"

His lips moved along her throat, up her jaw, could have kept going when he heard a footfall on the stair.

"Remy, is it time to go? *Oh...* "

He froze mid-kiss, sighed and lowered his eyes, but couldn't help the grin that slid to one side.

Valerie pulled away.

"The girl?"

Ivy Savage was standing on the stair.

Chapter 11

Of Airships, Steamtrains and All the Strange,
Surreal Places One May Go with a Plan

A porcelain-faced ghost slipped out of the shadows
"Bruder," she said.
"How did you find me?"
"You carry a piece of me with you. I will always find you, *Bruder."*
Sebastien reached into his pocket, studied the ivory bullet in his
palm.

She moved toward him with unnatural grace, cloak of sable
sweeping the ground behind her. It rather reminded him of Victoria's
wheeled crinoline and he wondered if her legs were as inhuman as her
face. He could see her eyes through the slit in the mask however,
bloodshot and blue and rather small. She wheezed as she held up her
hand, enclosed in a glove of thickest leather.

"It is from my little finger."

Her voice was thin and he wondered if it were because of the effort
required to work the iron lungs.

"Why did you shoot me?"

"To find you. If you do not wish to be found, toss it into the gutter.

Or better yet, into the bowl of holy water near the nave. That would be macabre. Magical."

He thought a moment, before slipping it back into his pocket.

"You didn't want to kill me."

"You did not die."

"I never do."

"Neither do I."

"I don't understand."

"Flesh of my flesh, bone of my bone," she said. "You are my *Bruder.*"

"I'm not your brother."

"You are," Sophie said and she inclined her head, mask like a China doll. "My father is your father."

"My father is dead, while your father is the Emperor of half the world."

"Our father lives."

"Our father?" He glanced around at the angels, at the altar, at the statues. "God? God is our father?"

"*Dummer Junge,*" she said and she laughed. It was like a child, delighted with the gift of a toy. "God does not live in the *Empire of Steam.* God is a Habsburg."

Her white face tilted upwards to the astronomical clock, where Death held his sickle high above the ages of man.

"Profound," she said and he swallowed, remembering he had thought the very same only minutes ago. "Death rules all things, yes? He is the last, best master."

"I didn't kill your brother."

"But we both know who did."

"Who?"

She cocked her head and the drumming of her heart and lungs echoed softly though the church. He could see the iron sheen of her corset, the copper and steel cables that were her throat. Her golden curls were the only human things about her.

"*Archelicht* killed Rudolf," she said after a moment. "Archelicht, and love."

"Love? Love dies."

"Love kills." And she moved forward. "Do you remember what it is like to die, *Bruder?*"

He moved back. "I'm not your brother."

"I remember what it is like to be dead. It is beautiful, calm and quiet. I remember it well, like dawn at *Gödöllő*. That is where I died."

He frowned, trying to follow her train of thought but finding himself lost. She was a labyrinth of wax and cobwebs.

"I was raised from the dead by my father, just like you. Like the Savior was raised by the Father. You and I are Children of Death."

"Children of Death," he repeated. "I understand."

"Nein," she said. "You do not. But you will."

And she reached up to unhook the clasp, letting the cloak drop to the stone floor. He could see the iron corset clearly now, more function than fashion with its bolts and rivets merely outlining the shape of a woman. There was a key protruding from her breastbone, and she twisted it once, twice, three times. The corset clicked and swung open on a hinge, revealing a cavity as complex as any airship or steamcar or Difference Engine. Cables quivered like blood vessels, copper wires tangled over and through a central device that looked like a heart. Sparks leapt between the lungs, expanding and contracting as metal slid across metal and he wondered if there was anything even remotely human about her.

"You," she said. "Are much better."

She held out her gloved hand, and in it, an orb was spinning.

***

"Lie," Valerie hissed. *"You lie!"*

Her ankle hooked his knee and she swung him around against the wall but he rolled, taking her with him and keeping her off-balance. She was skilled and it was a vain attempt to gain control.

"Ivy!" he shouted. "Grab your coat!"

Ivy whirled and bolted back up the stair.

Valerie sent the heel of her palm up but he caught it and pushed her again into the wall. She thrashed like a wild woman until he drew his clockwork arm up, his hand still locked around her wrist, and he pressed both across her throat. He twisted and she gasped in pain.

Suddenly, the door swung open and a squad of silver guards wheeled in. Behind them with twin sabres came Gisela.

"Kill him," she barked in German, but through the leather of Christien's glove, a dagger sprang out. He hugged Valerie tight and pressed it into her throat.

"Don't," he said. "Once I get started, there's no telling when it will stop. Or so I've been told."

A line of red sprang up beneath the blade and Valerie grew still, struggled to control her breathing. He could feel the strain in her muscles, knew if he released any pressure, she would snap like a coil and send him to his knees.

"You will not leave," said Gisela. "These Hussars have pistols built into their arms. It is nothing for them to shoot you."

For emphasis, a mirrored captain raised his arm, aimed it between Christien's eyes with a click. It was an odd sensation, having an automaton threaten him like this, but after the *Eisenmanner* of Reichsland, nothing much surprised him anymore.

"I wouldn't. I have a very sharp blade at her throat. If you shoot me, the autonomic spasm will sever her carotid artery, causing death within seconds. But in the extremely odd case that it doesn't and she does survive the prolific blood loss, I must warn you that this prosthetic has been malfunctioning of late, courtesy your cannonball and Wilhelm's iron man. If you shoot me and do manage to remove the attachment from my arm, you will not be able to remove it from her wrist. It will continue to tighten, until it cuts off her circulation and her hand grows blue. Depending on how long it takes to either amputate the hand or find a metallurgist to remove the clockwork, gangrene will set in and she will die within days. Either way, if I die, she dies. Trust me, Gisela. I'm a physician."

The woman glanced at her sister.

"Ihn erschießen, " growled Valerie. "Shoot hi—"

Her words were choked as he pressed the blade deeper against her throat.

The Hussars did not move. Indeed, he wondered if they felt anything either way. Life and death placed in the clockwork and steel hands of machines. It was inevitable - the rush of science for the sake of science. Nothing more noble than that. The world was a strange, surreal place.

Finally, Gisela straightened, slid her sabres home.

"What do you want?" she asked.

"Safe passage to the train station," called Ivy from the stair. "And use of one of the airships."

As one, the Hussars swung their arms and Christien cursed her belligerence. She could have escaped through a window. She could have crawled across a roof. But not Ivy Savage, daughter of calamity, bringer of chaos. He shook his head but said nothing. They couldn't be seen to doubt. They were in control. It was the only way.

"You will not leave Strasbourg," said Gisela.

"We *will* leave Strasbourg," said Ivy as she reached his side. "We will leave with Archduchess Valerie and once we are safe, she will be freed."

"You have no clockwork attachment," said Gisela and she wrested a pistol attachment from the captain of the silver guards, causing sparks to rain to the floor. It wheeled into a corner, flailing its arm while Gisela aimed the pistol at the young writer's head. "I will shoot you now."

"Pistols are loud," said Ivy. "And Christien is highborn, delicate and prone to hysteria. Besides, I have a pistol of my own."

And she raised the tiny woman's iron to Valerie's head. She glanced at him as she did so, coaching him with her eyes. He tugged Valerie closer, producing a gasp and another drop of blood.

"Wait," said Gisela.

She stepped toward Ivy and Christien couldn't help but notice the difference. Gisela with her black military uniform and severe blonde hair, Ivy looking like a newsboy with her cap and tweed coat. It would have been absurd had there not been so many pistols.

"We didn't kill your brother," said Ivy.

"I don't care," said Gisela.

Ivy lowered her pistol and for a long moment, there was silence in the tavern. Finally, Valerie grew still in his arms.

"I will go with them," she breathed through clenched teeth.

"No—"

"I will go."

"She will be safe as long as we are," said Ivy.

"You will all be executed," said Gisela but she stepped back. "Go. There is a coach waiting outside. I will arrange for an escort to the station and access to one of the lesser ships. As far as it depends on me, you will be allowed passage through German airspace. I cannot speak for the French."

"Thank you," said Ivy.

"Don't," said Gisela. "I will see you dead before the week is up."

And with Valerie still locked in Christien's arms, the three of them shuffled slowly through the guards toward the door. Cold air blew in and Christien turned his head.

"I've had seven pints of local and there was also a meal and a room let. Kindly take care of that for us, will you?"

And he closed the door behind him.

***

"Because I could not stop for Death, he kindly stopped for me. The Carriage held but just Ourselves and Immortality."

"I know that," he muttered, but could not tear his eyes from the orb. "What is that?"

"Emily Dickinson. A spiritualist from the Americas."

Slowly, Sophie closed the latch on her clockwork corset. The orb was spinning just above her gloved hand. He could feel it like his own heartbeat.

"You wish to take it," she said. "Take it. Look into it. You will understand."

The orb began to flash, reminding him of Ghostlight and the colours of her world.

"Where is Arclight?"

"Arclight is not your master. You are hers."

Spinning, flashing, warping all light around it. He could fall into it like a river, like a lake. She stepped closer.

"Death is the last, best master, brother."

Sisi sitting by a bed, hands folded limply in her lap

"Let it crown you."

On the bed, a bundle wrapped like a loaf of bread, covered in white linen

He stepped forward now, his palms aching to hold it, knowing it would destroy him, longing to feel the burn as it seared the flesh off his bones…

A small, bearded man rushes into the room

"There y'ar, Yer Lordship, sir!"

He stepped back, blinking, as Castlewaite's thin frame hobbled down the nave toward him. He held up a slip of paper. It was the schedule for the Strasbourg rail.

"We've a bit of a wicket, sir!" he puffed. "Ye've got a train t'catch!"

Sebastien glanced around the church. There was no sign of either Sophie or the orb. A fact that did not surprise him.

***

Peering out the window, Ivy could see the gaslight of Strasbourg station growing brighter as the Imperial coach raced along the street. Mounted Silver Hussars led the way, more followed behind and she prayed this would not simply get them shot somewhere more convenient than a tavern in the centre of town. She sat back and sighed.

Valerie was sitting next to Christien, his hand still firmly locked around her wrist. The Archduchess was scowling but Christien was staring across the cab at Ivy.

"What?" she asked.

"Delicate and prone to hysteria?"

"I'm a writer," she grinned. "Exaggeration comes with the territory."

He grunted. "Where's Castlewaite?"

"He went to fetch Sebastien," she said. "We made a plan."

"You and Castlewaite?"

"Made a plan, yes."

"Good lord. Don't you ever stop thinking?"

"I got us a coach to the station while you were busy discussing gangrene with a mad woman. I think I'm doing rather well."

For the first time in a very long time, he smiled. Beside him, Valerie snarled and Ivy raised her chin, trying to marshal her best, most stubborn resources.

"My name's Ivy," she said.

"An English weed."

"A very tenacious English weed," said Ivy. "Almost impossible to stop, once it's got a foothold. Can crack a stone wall in a matter of years."

"But not the heart of a de Lacey."

"We won't hurt you. I promise."

"I'm sorry I can't say the same."

"Enough," said Christien.

"Let me go," she pouted and she glanced at his prosthetic. He had managed to fold the dagger back into the shafts of the wrist but the fingers were locked like a vise. "That thing. It's hurting me."

"I can't," he said. "I wasn't lying. The damned thing is well and truly stuck."

"The moment your back is turned, I will break your neck like a dog."

"Then I shall not turn my back."

"The moment you close your eyes, I will gouge them out and crush them under my boot."

"You look like your father."

She growled and sat back, would have crossed her arms if she could.

And Ivy swallowed, wondering if they had not just made the biggest mistake of the journey.

After what seemed like hours, the coach finally rattled to a halt at the entrance to the Strasbourg station. Just like at the Sacher and the *Südbahnhof,* Silver Hussars flanked them as they exited the coach and strode through the door, Valerie only mildly protesting. Ivy turned to face the guards.

"Go," she said. "Go now. We don't want you here. Go."

No one moved a whisker.

"Gehen!" snapped Valerie. *"Ich sagen, gehen!"*

Immediately, the guards peeled off, mounting their horses and trotting back down the snowy road like a parade. *Odd*, thought Ivy. Automatons riding horses. The world was such a strange, surreal place.

Valerie released a long breath, held her head a little higher.

"You are both dead," she said.

"That's the plan," said Ivy, looking around for the stair to the airship docks. "This way."

***

For such a late hour, there were many travellers in the station and gaslight blazed up into the night. Sebastien could see the bellies of the fleet high above. German, French and Austrian but none could match the iron giant that was the *Stahl Mädchen*. He wondered how canvas and heated gas could keep such a weight in the sky. Surely devastation would result if any of the systems were to fail.

He could see Castlewaite's breath making clouds as they crept around the station to the yard. Dozens of cars were on the tracks, several of them hissing steam as they made ready to move out. Black gleamed blue in the moonlight and the labyrinth of tracks looked like the inner workings of a clock. He could smell the coal, the wood, the oil and he shook his head. The world was a strange, surreal place, what with the modern need for transportation. Give him a horse any day and not for the first time, he thought of Gus.

A whistle echoed across the yard and one of the trains heaved forward. He glanced at Castlewaite but the coachman shook his head and pressed on across the tracks, stepping over couplings and slipping between the cars. Another whistle, another train. Castlewaite peered at his paper but again, shook his head. Strasbourg was a terminus for both French and German rails and quickly the yard became a moving maze as train after train headed out into the night. Across the tracks, over the couplings, between the cars, his world shrunk to the smell of coal and iron and steel. His coat caught and his shins scraped and he cursed this turn of events. It wasn't like this with horses.

A different whistle now, this time accompanied by a series of bells and he looked up as mooring hooks fell away, releasing one of the airships into the night sky. There was an eagle painted across its belly and he could see flashes of moonlight reflected from the propellers. Snow swirled in the downdraft and slowly, the dirigible glided away from the dock like a ship leaving the shore.

"Yer Lordship?" called Castlewaite.

He cocked his head as high above, the airship clanged and trip-masts began to detach from the ribs of the hull.

"It shouldn't do that," he muttered. "It's too close to the other ships."

"Quickly now, sir!"

The Mad Lord sighed and tore his gaze away. The coachman pointed at an engine chugging east, dragging at least ten cars behind. The first seven were passenger cars, bright inside the many large windows but the following three were black. Baggage cars, he knew. Baggage and mail and sugar and tobacco and suddenly, he saw a face hanging out a cargo door, waving at him in the darkness.

"Ivy."

"Ah said quickly, sir."

He turned to the coachman.

"And you?"

"Ah have me own plan, sir. Now off with ye, or ye'll miss 'er."

And without another thought, Sebastien sprinted across the yard, leaping iron bars and wooden ties and ducking the yard signs that threatened to take off his head. Ivy was leaning out the baggage car, one hand on the door, the other reaching out for him. The car was picking up speed but just the sight of her caused his heart to work harder, his legs to move faster and soon he was reaching for her hand, his coat whipping in the cold.

"Come on, Laury!" she shouted. "Hurry!"

He leaped for her but missed, swore as his wrist banged against the side of the car. Leapt again and felt the brush of her fingers when suddenly a flash lit up the entire night sky. It was an explosion among the airships, the force of the blast lifting him from his feet and throwing him violently into the side of the moving car. It was too fast and he couldn't even think to grab hold, felt himself thud then roll as his body hit the snowy tracks and fiery debris rained down from above.

He pushed to his feet and bolted after it once again but he had lost so much ground. He could see her face like a beacon in the dark but she was so far ahead on a train gaining speed when there was another boom from above. He turned his head and immediately wished he hadn't, for a fireball was hurtling toward him across the track. Dashitall if it didn't look like a galloping horse.

And it was red.

He ran faster.

"Laury!"

Even faster as flaming wreckage rained from the skies. The cargo door was just a heartbeat away but the horse was behind him and closing in. He could feel the fire of its breath on his neck, teeth sharp and biting his skin like a sword. He could hear the thunder of hoofbeats on the ground and with a shout he leapt toward the speeding car, knowing he would fall short. But the flaming horse leapt too, carrying him up and into the dark like a fireball. He hit the floor, sliding into steam trunks and carpetbags and sacks of mail heading east. Suddenly Ivy was there, batting out the flames that raced across up his arms onto his back. He pushed to his knees and scrambled to the open doorway, searching for the horse but the sky was ablaze with colliding airships and Christien slid the door shut.

***

Petit Journal, Strasbourg
DISASTER IN THE SKIES
The sky lit up last night as several airships collided over Strasbourg Station. According to witnesses, an Austrian dirigible engaged its trip-

masts in close proximity to other ships, puncturing their balloons and igniting the hydrogen gas. A chain reaction is said to have occurred, as one after another, the moored ships exploded, causing a fireball that could be seen across the Vosges Mountains to the Black Forest. Only three casualties are reported, despite the widespread carnage.

This is the second airship accident to have occurred in as many days, the most recent being the crash of an English airship near the town of Kolmar.

According to reports in the London Times, it is believed that French anarchists are at the root of these incidents, and all wreckage is being examined for traces of incendiary devices. The Anarchist movement is known for political assassinations and bombing campaigns across Europe, possibly including the murder Crown Prince Rudolf of Austro-Hungary. Already Kaiser Wilhelm II and Chancellor von Bismark are calling for the unilateral cessation of liberal policies throughout the **Empire of Blood and Iron.** *It is confirmed now that the heads of the* Three Empires League *will be meeting in Vienna early next week to discuss the current situation in Europe and form a solid alliance to meet the campaign of liberal terrorism with unity and strength.*

Regarding the deployment of the airship's trip-masts, police are continuing to investigate.

Chapter 12

Of Fairy Kisses, Colonial Cigarettes and an Abrupt Exit from the Orient Express

When the train pulled into Paris *Gare de l'Est* early that morning, no one was allowed to leave. It was a thing unheard of and caused a commotion as a unit of *gendarmes* swarmed aboard, pistols and batons at the ready. After much protest, the Wagon Lit conductor was forced to lead them to Sleeping Compartment Number Two. In the hall outside the room, he protested once again, saying the guests in Comp. Two were English gentry and had paid over-and-above the standard rate for privacy. They were strictly 'Do Not Disturb' and the English were well known for their private natures. It would not look well on 'the Company' to have English patrons angry at the appalling manner of French *gendarmes.*

Naturally, the *gendarmes* did not care about the private natures of English patrons and insisted the compartment be opened at once or the very expensive door would be broken down.

Once opened, the room revealed a lone man of about seventy years with a remarkable copper eyepiece attached to his thinning scalp. He sat up and smiled at them, showing an equally remarkable lack of teeth.

The entire train was searched with no English gentry, Viennese Archduchesses or French anarchists to be found.

***

Christien opened his eyes to find Valerie staring at him.

He sat up slowly, wishing to stretch the ache from his limbs but the baggage compartment was close and cold and her body was closer and warm. His clockwork hand was still locked around her wrist and he had to admit it was uncomfortable, although he reckoned it was worse for her. Light beamed in through seams in the train's outer jacket but there were no windows and very little could be seen except steam trunks and carpet bags, boxes and huge sacks bound in canvas.

The train rocked to the rhythm of his heartbeat, and as his eyes adjusted, he could see his brother asleep on the floor. Behind him Ivy slept as well, head against his shoulder, arm across his ribs. They fit, he thought abstractedly. They always had and he wondered how he could ever have wanted her for a wife. But that was a lifetime ago and he had been a different man, set on a different path. He had no idea who he was now, or where he was going. Didn't matter. Life could never get worse than it had been these past few months. Even death by a *Gilded* firing squad would be preferable to that.

He looked back down at the Archduchess wrapped in her coat of luxurious sable. Her hair was spilling from the coif at the nape of her neck and her expression was colder than the air in the compartment. He resisted the urge to kiss her. She'd probably hit him and every muscle in his body ached.

"Thank you," he said softly. "For not gouging my eyes out while I slept."

"I am your prisoner," she said and he could see her breath frosting at her lips. "It would not be helpful."

"You're not my prisoner."

"And there is still tomorrow."

He reached into a pocket, slipped out a handkerchief and lifted it to her throat. She hissed as he dabbed the wounds he had made with his dagger. There was no fresh blood, but still.

Her eyes had not left his face.

"My mother raised me," she said as he tended her. "My grandmother raised Sophie and Gisela and Rudolf, but my mother raised me."

"Your mother is a remarkable woman."

"She is a very good mother. When I would fall from my horse or prick my finger with a needle or stumble on the path at *Schonbrunn*, she would kiss the *petit* injury with a fairy kiss and it would heal like a miracle."

She lowered her eyes, her lashes the colour of honey.

"No matter what the *petit* injury was, a fairy kiss would make it better."

He stared at her for a moment.

"You might break my neck like a dog," he said.

"Not today," she said.

"And there is still tomorrow."

And he leaned in to kiss her throat with fairy kisses and she pulled the sable coat over them both.

***

white horses with manes of arrows, red horses with hoofs of flame, pillars of angels calling the dead from their graves, hands pushing from beneath the earth, decayed corpses walking the streets, Death towering over the people, sickle raised, setting the world on fire while a small, bearded man rushes into the room

Sebastien awoke, heart thudding to the rhythm of the train. It was dark and he lay very still as his eyes adjusted to the darkness. Across the floor, someone was moving under a fur and he remembered that he was in fact in the baggage compartment of a train bound for Vienna and that Christien was hopelessly in love with a very dangerous woman and that there was someone breathing at the back of his neck.

Sophie.

No, he realized with relief, not the terrifying child-woman with the mask of porcelain and the clockwork heart. He breathed in deeply, thankful for the scent of rosehips and leather and his heart thudded once again as he saw the hand draped across his chest.

Ivy. She had asked him to call her by name. Ivy.

He lay terribly still, desperate not to disturb her. His side was cold but his back was warm because of her and he never wanted this moment to end.

"I remember what it is like to be dead," Sophie had said. *"Beautiful, calm and quiet."*

Did he remember what it was like to be dead? He had been dead so many times. Even now, there were dead watching him from the walls of this compartment and he wondered how that could be. It was a train. People weren't murdered on trains, surely. He sighed and concentrated on the feeling of her breath on his neck.

Breathing, he thought, was a precious gift. He was glad he was still doing it.

He wondered what it might be like if he rolled over toward her. He would be able to see her sweet face and the freckles on her nose but other parts of her as well. He felt the heat in his cheeks and cursed himself for being such a greedy man, so he didn't.

And so he lay very still, unwilling to move as the train rocked onward to Vienna with Ivy at his back.

***

The train was as beautiful as she had expected, and she gazed out the etched windows as the trees and mountains of the Black Forest rattled past. In fact, she had been gazing out at the scenery since setting foot onboard. It was infinitely safer, she reckoned, than gazing at her companion.

"Have you enjoyed your dinner, Penny?" asked international jewel thief and rogue Alexander Dunn. "Only the finest on the Orient Express."

She raised a flute of champagne to her lips but still did not look.

"The oysters were cold, the turbot meely, the coq a-la-chasseur weak and the chateau potatoes over-mashed. The Chocolate pudding was tolerable."

"Penny," he grinned. "Do you honestly hate me so?"

"I am your prisoner, sir," she countered. "It was only for appearances that you cut my bonds. I'm surprised you didn't have me tossed in the baggage compartment like a carpet."

"I had thought of it," he said. "But carpets are much more useful when they're underfoot."

"Useful," she said and now, she did look at him. "Is that all I am to you?"

Here, on this luxury train speeding to cities such as Vienna, Belgrade and Istanbul, he was at home as his other self, Alexandre Gavriel St. Jacques Lord Durand, Baron of Greystoke, Yorkshire. His hair was tamed, his suit dapper with a white carnation in the lapel. No one had ever suspected his altar ego as international jewel thief Alexander Dunn. No one, until her.

"No Penny," he said and he reached a hand across the table to brush her gloved fingers. "I find you intoxicating, enchanting, fascinating, infuriating, beguiling, bewitching…"

He sat back, raised his flute.

"AND useful."

She sniffed and turned back to the window.

"I suppose that is what you say to your French paramour, Antoine Marionette, oui?"

"Antoine is not my paramour."

"Of course she isn't."

He rose to his feet and reached for her.

"Come. I'll show you."

Reluctantly, she took his hand, bade farewell to the rushing forests and mountains of Germany and followed him to their compartment. The aisle was polished cherry wood and very narrow, and when they stopped at the door, he was forced to lean across her to open the latch. She held her breath, bound to master her racing heart. No rogue would ever get the better of Penny Dreadful, Girl Criminologist. Certainly not one as blatantly seductive as Dunn. But as he pushed open the door, revealing the narrow bunks, she couldn't help but wonder if she might need to teach him that lesson before the case was well and truly solved.

She was frankly surprised when a voice came from behind the door.

"Alexandre? Est-ce vous?"

"Oui," he said. "Et Penny."

"Ooh Penny!"

Antoine stepped into the center of the room and Penny's breath caught in her throat.

With only a wire crinoline for clothing, Antoine was an automaton with clockwork arms, cable-length torso and pistons for legs. The back of her skull was open and Penny could see the tiny gears ticking as they ran her Analytical and Difference programs. Her heart hissed steam into mechanical lungs and her eyes were astrolabs housed in wrought iron. The rest of her face however was almost completely human, with fleshly cheeks, painted lips and flawless skin.

Alexander smiled at her.

"Antoine is not my paramour," he said. "She is my sister."

***

Ivy realized that it had all started with Christien wanting a cigarette.

He had been without one since the last morning on the *Chevalier*, and had lost his case in the crash. Without warning, Sebastien rose to his feet and knelt beside one of the steam trunks, placing his hands over the drawbolts and closing his eyes. His lips moved and the deadwind had picked up and soon ribbons of white frost ran the length of the metal clasps. The Archduchess watched with disbelief when he kicked with the heel of his boot and the steam trunk shattered into a hundred pieces across the floor.

Methodically, he distributed the contents of the trunk – blankets, jumpers, scarves and coats, including a silver case of colonial cigarettes for his brother and a box of Turkish Delights wrapped in parchment for Ivy. He slipped one particularly sharp metal piece into his boot before gathering the shattered trunk into a mound in the center of the car and pulling a paper from his greatcoat pocket. Ivy recognized it as the train schedule from Strasbourg Station.

"That was clever," he said to her. "Strasbourg to Vienna. An express train."

"The Orient Express," said Valerie, eyes still fixed on the Mad Lord. "I usually ride in a first-class double compartment, not like this."

"Welcome to Lasingstoke," Christien grumbled.

He leaned forward and raised his clockwork arm, bringing hers along with it and lighting the schedule with a flint attachment buried in the cables. Sebastien stuffed it under the mound and soon, a small fire was crackling in the baggage compartment of the Orient Express.

"Where did Castlewaite go, then?" he asked and Ivy hugged her knees. The Turkish delights were making her teeth stick together.

"He booked passage on the night train to Paris. Under Christien's name."

"A red herring. Well done. And the airships? That *was* an airship explosion, wasn't it? It looked to me rather like a horse."

Ivy laughed.

"No Sebastien, not a horse. Castlewaite had told me that an automaton could easily fly an airship, so when we reached the station, we commandeered the use of one of the ships, told the personnel that all drinks in town were on the Kaiser and programed the docking steward to take it out."

"Valerie had the Imperial codes," said Christien. He lit a cigarette, inhaled deeply to make it catch. "No one would question her orders and no one did."

Sebastien looked at Ivy. "Did you program the 'bot to release the trip-masts too?"

"I did. I only thought it might cause some extra chaos and allow us to catch this train. I didn't expect everything to explode the way it did. I am a calamity."

"Well," said Christien and he released a long stream of smoke through his lips. "I expect they'll think we're dead now or in Paris. Either one."

"Death," said Sebastien, "Is the last, best master."

"Sebastien?" asked Ivy.

"Because I could not stop for Death, he kindly stopped for me. The Carriage held but just Ourselves – and Immortality."

They all stared at him. He shrugged.

"Well I'm glad it was an exploding airship, then and not a fiery horse. I couldn't abide the site of a horse on fire."

"You are mad," said Valerie in a quiet voice. "Just like Sophie."

"Death does that to a person."

They sat in silence for a moment longer, each staring into the flames and occupied with their own thoughts. The Turkish Delights had suddenly grown bitter and Sebastien slipped the candies into his pocket.

"This is the Orient Express," muttered Ivy and she looked up. "Would there be a telegraph on board?"

"Of course," said Valerie. "The Express has all the modern conveniences. But we won't need it. We should be in Vienna by dinner."

"Well, I think we should get off before Vienna," said Ivy. "We're still fugitives."

"So why are you going, then?" Valerie's eyes glittered like steel as she reached for one of Christien's cigarettes. He lit it for her and she inhaled deeply. "If you insist you're innocent, you must realize that are going to your deaths."

"We *are* innocent," said Ivy. "Sebastien didn't kill Rudolf. We have to prove it."

"By kidnapping an Archduchess?"

Ivy grinned. "In for a penny…"

"Arclight killed Rudolf," said the Mad Lord. "Arclight and love. That's what Sophie said."

"Sophie?" asked Ivy.

"When did you speak with Sophie?" asked Valerie.

"In the cathedral. She shewed me an orb, a memory of when she was dead."

"Never speak of my sister," growled Valerie.

"Then kindly tell her never to speak to me," he said. "Who was her doctor? The man who gave her life."

"I don't know," said the Archduchess. "It was years before I was born."

Ivy leaned forward. "And what about Arclight, Sebastien?"

"What is this Arclight?" asked Valerie and she blew out a stream of smoke. *So very like Christien,* Ivy thought. "Is it the locket?"

Suddenly the swingdoor into the compartment flew open on a steward in brown cap and uniform. He froze, very much surprised.

"Was ist?"

"Blast," said Ivy.

The steward turned back to the corridor.

"Sicherheit! Eindringlinge! Zigeuner!"

The four of them bolted to their feet.

"Christien," said Sebastien as the temperature in the baggage compartment began to drop. "Open the cargo door, if you will."

The steward raised a baton but Sebastien caught it in his hand, shattering it into a hundred tiny pieces. Those were instantly sucked out of the train as Christien hauled the cargo door to the side revealing a snowy landscape. Trees, bluffs, snow and riverbank, all rushing by at breakneck speed.

"Jump!" Ivy cried over the roaring of the winds.

"Don't be ridiculous!" snapped the Archduchess. "I will tell them who I aaaa—"

Christien leapt out of hurtling car, taking her with him.

"Sebastien!" called Ivy, looking over her shoulder. "Come now!"

"Verdammt Zigeuner!" barked the steward and he grabbed the Mad Lord's coat. Sebastien swung around to catch him by the throat, forcing him back against the wall. Immediately, the steward's face drained of colour and he opened his mouth in a silent scream.

"Let him go!" Ivy shouted. "We have to jump!"

She could see frost running up the wall beneath the steward, even as the edges of his clothes glowed like cinders. Flames leapt up the Mad Lord's sleeves, across his shoulders and down his arms, but they did not burn. The steward's uniform caught however, and the compartment filled with the smell of burning cloth.

"Sebastien, no! We have to jump!"

Steam hissed as frost met flame and the steward began to convulse violently under Sebastien's hand.

"Laury, no!" she screamed. "Let him go! Now!"

With a growl, Sebastien shoved the steward out the door and closed it, running a palm along the frame and sealing it shut with a slick of ice. He strode across the compartment and took her hand and she caught one look at his face before they leapt from the train.

His eyes were as red as the flames.

***

Over and over and over and over and over she went, head over heels over head over heels down the steep snowy side and it was impossible to stop, impossible to grab hold, impossible to get her feet underneath as her feet went over her head over her heels through the snow. Ribs, legs and back and shoulders thudding for a heartbeat, replaced by shoulders and back and legs and ribs and then suddenly for a moment, a brief terrible eternal moment, there was nothing but air around and above when below she saw a river, realized it was the Danube and that it was indeed beautiful and blue and coming at her very quickly and then she hit.

It slowed her fall but barely. She couldn't breathe, couldn't find the way to up, to the surface and air and life and she thrashed wildly but she began to sink, her coat and boots too heavy, her legs leaden, her arms numb. It was so cold, freezing and dark and she tried to hold her breath but her chest ached, swelled with pressure until finally it burst out with the rush of bubbles then a tide rolling in, panic and burn and terror giving way to thick and distorted and quiet and finally still. In a vague distance she could feel the ripple of another splash, the tug of her arm and then floating, ever-so-slowly, like a balloon over Piccadilly, like a feather on a westerly breeze, up to a dappling grey light and silence.

It was remarkably like the crash of an airship.

Suddenly, pain in her chest again and pain in her throat and she began to cough and gag as water bolted from her mouth and air flooded back in its wake. She was kneeling in the snow, coughing and retching and trying desperately to breathe as much as she could, as quickly as she

149

could. The cold was biting every inch, stabbing with many sharp daggers. She tried to become very small but there were arms moving across her back, trying to rub the feeling back into her body and the hands were very warm. Her breathing grew steady, her shaking less pronounced. After a while, she raised her head to see Sebastien, clearly worried, hands running over her limbs as if looking for breaks. He lifted her chin, hands cupping her face.

"Are you alive, Miss Savage? Please tell me you're still alive!"

"I th-th-think so. D-do I l-l-look d-dead?"

"Everyone looks dead now. I can't be sure."

In snowy gorse once again, her feet cold, her cheeks frozen. Somehow she managed to smile at the thought.

"Y-y-you were r-right."

"Right? About what?"

"My w-w-womanly wiles?"

"Miss Savage?"

"I w-would have you comp-ple-pletely at a disad-v-vantage," she chattered. "I-if only I could f-find my p-pistol."

He froze, hands still cupping her face and he blinked at her, eyes thankfully brown, before he did a most unusual thing.

He kissed her.

It was sweet and completely unexpected and her breath caught in her throat from the surprise. He pulled back.

"I'm sorry, Miss Savage," he gasped. "Please forgive me. I'm so relieved that you're alive and that was out of turn. I'm so very sorry."

The Danube was dripping from his hair, off his forehead and down his cheeks and she couldn't imagine a world without such a fantastical man. She could go to the Sorbonne in Paris, she could go to balls in Vienna and chase down criminals in London and sell all her books to grand publishing houses in New York but without the Mad Lord of Lasingstoke, it would be for nothing. There could be no adventure without his adventure, no mystery, no plot, no storyline. He had ruined her. There was no way back to normal from him.

She fell headlong into his arms, pushing him down into the snow and pinning him with her body. Her mouth found his, delighting in the river taste of him, the feel of his lips as they moved to discover hers, his breath filling her lungs.

"Bastien!"

It was a voice from far, far away and she was happy to ignore it. She was an explorer and Sebastien an undiscovered country. Her hands were eager as they slipped under his coat, his fingers clumsy as they tangled into her hair.

"Bastien! Ivy? What the deuce?"

She looked up. Tattered, torn and still attached by the clockwork grip, Christien and Valerie stood in the drifts above them. The young physician raised a brow.

"Did someone go into the drink?"

"I haven't had a drink in days," said Sebastien, pushing up onto his elbows. "I would love a Scotch."

"The Danube," growled Ivy. "I nearly drowned."

"Ah," said Christien. "So is this resuscitation, then?"

She scowled at him.

Valerie raised her free hand to point to the hillside towering above.

"Melk," she said. "We go to Melk."

They followed her point to a treed bluff where spires of gold and towers of ivory rose up to the skies. A fortress, a castle and a cathedral, the Abbey of Melk perched like a war crown high on the banks of the Danube.

Chapter 13

Of Hot Baths, Cold Banter and the Man of Jewels and Bone

London Times
EMPIRES ON ALERT
*International leaders from the **Empires of Steam**, **Blood and Iron**
and **Steel** will be joining the **Gilded Empire** of Austro-Hungary on Feb 6
for a summit of the Three Empires League, in Vienna, Austria. On the
agenda will be the rise of the French Anarchist movement in certain
sectors of high society, including and most prominently their suspected
the death of Crown Prince Rudolf of Austro-Hungary, whose funeral is to
be held Feb. 5. Heads of state expected to attend include Kaiser Wilhelm
II, Chancellor Otto von Bismark, Tsar Alexander III of Russia and
Edward Prince of Wales. The **Empire of Steam** is not officially a
member of the League but has been known to consult from time to time
on matters of international importance.*

*French President Bonaparte IV has refused to comment on the
summit, saying the **Industrial Republic of France** has no ties in anarchy*

*and is an independent government, having strong diplomatic relations with both the **Empire of Steam** and the **Empire of Steel**. To show his confidence, President Bonaparte will be visiting his godmother, Queen Victoria, for a tour of London whilst Edward Prince of Wales attends the summit as the representative of the **Empire of Steam**.*

*It is not known whether Umberto I, King of the **Empire of the Sun,** Italy, is expected to attend or if, according to accounts, he has even been invited. The Italian Prime Minister has assured this reporter that the Triple Alliance is still in effect and that Chancellor von Bismark often consults King Umberto on the matters of international politics, anarchy and Tuscan wine.*

For the French Anarchist suspected in the death of Crown Prince Rudolf, the hunt is still on and police are continuing to investigate.

***

A hot bath was a beautiful thing. A hot bath with water deeper than six inches was heaven. Hot water had been a rare treat growing up in London's East End. Even at Lasingstoke where she was spoiled with the luxuries of a northern barony, Rupert St. John had kept such a hold on finances that a hot bath was a hard fight. She wondered how long that would last when Mary Jane Kelly became the woman of the house.

She sighed and sank deeper into the water, barely even noticing the splendor of the water closet. Although it *was* splendid. Incredible. Magnificent. Golden, just like the abbey itself. The Abbey of Melk was huge, a Benedictine monastery clearly not known for austerity or poverty. She could soak in this claw-foot tub of pure gold forever, she reckoned, just staring at the curved ceiling with cherubim and seraphim painted in Raphaelite detail above her. She could have soaked forever, had not her heart been racing.

Sebastien had kissed her.

He had kissed her.

He had saved her life and he had kissed her. Two weeks before her nineteenth birthday, Ivy Savage had been well and truly kissed. And what was more, she had kissed him back.

She lifted a foot out of the water and curled her toes, not even seeing the bruises along her shins. She ran the bar of glycerin along her arms, equally black and blue, not remembering how she'd even come by them. She couldn't imagine her back or hips or ribs. She didn't care. It had been worth it. The taste of him had made her toes curl in entirely different ways. On the snowy banks of the Danube, she had flung open a forbidden door and ran headlong through it.

Sebastien, it seemed, had been quite happy to follow.

She sank deeper 'til only her eyes and nose were above the steam, remembering Christien's words on the fields of Reichsland. She was not a romantic girl, never had been, but she had been hard pressed to stop with just kisses. The memory of his hands in her hair made her wonder what they would feel like along the rest of her.

The cherubs were watching from the ceiling and she wondered what God might think of a girl who had such thoughts. She had never been religious but she had always considered herself a good girl. Did good girls kiss Mad Lords? Could good girls do more? What of Valerie and Christien? Of Mary Jane and Christien, of Mary Jane and Rupert? She knew so little the ways of women, but even less the ways of men. She'd always believed her dad had loved only her mother but she had been young, preoccupied and willingly blind. Seven years was a long time. He'd had to have been lonely and even good women were cheap in Whitechapel.

She blew little bubbles in the water as she sighed.

And what of Sebastien himself? Christien had once called him a child, a wild child who needed to be protected from the world and the world protected from him. Surely he'd had as much experience with women as she'd had with men, or less so if his brother were to be believed. Was she more than simply the first girl to take the time, or was that a delusion of her heart?

"He's had many things broken," said Rupert in the courtyard at Lasingstoke. *"But never his heart."*

And his eyes, first white then mirrored then, this morning, red as flames. He was being pursued by ghost horses and it made no sense. But then again, he rarely made sense. He was the Mad Lord for a reason. She was only beginning to see with the eyes of a cat.

Suddenly, the deep hot bath was suffocating, drowning her thoughts and damping her energy. She rose up from under its steamy depths, stepped onto cold marble and reached for the robe.

***

It was the most beautiful church he had ever visited, more beautiful than St. Paul's, more beautiful than Notre Dame. In fact, it's beauty was overwhelming and he sank to his knees in a pew near the High Altar to take it all in.

Carved marble pillars held up a ceiling frescoed with baroque cherubs, fiery seraphim and lions pulling celestial chariots, all drawing his eyes to heaven once again. A massive pipe organ towered over the pews and he wondered if he might be allowed to play. The pulpit was hammered gold and the cupola above the central altar rose easily three stories with a tiny window at the top, where the skies opened to the realms of heaven.

There was a smattering of worshippers in the pews, praying through the stations of the cross, twisting strings of beads through their fingers. He watched with fascination as they went through rituals that were foreign to him but obviously meaningful. Physical reminders, he thought, of a spirit world unseen by most.

His own faith was entirely different.

Non coronabitur nisi certaverit. The motto of the abbey inscribed above the High Altar. 'There is no victory without a battle.' Life was a battle, he reckoned. Everyone knew that. But so was death. Most people never fully understood the battle of death. He couldn't remember a moment without it.

Unlike most churches, there were dead here. Some sitting in pews, some moving through the alcoves high above. They had noticed him but, since Ghostlight, they simply noticed. They weren't asking, weren't seeking him out. These, like all the others of late, just stared at him as if waiting. In a small way, he was grateful. It was easier to tell the dead from the living, for in his general experience, the living ignored him altogether.

There were two altars in alcoves on either end of the transept but he realized they weren't ordinary altars. They were actually sarcophagi of ebony, marble and chiseled gold. He watched with curiosity as a woman bowed before one, touching the stones and bringing her fingers to her forehead, lips and heart. There was a whisper of wind and he knew it. The deadwind, he had taken to calling it. Being a writer with entirely too much imagination, Ivy Savage had approved of the name. He rose to his feet to follow.

Each sarcophagus was holding a 'relic' – a holy skeleton of a saint or martyr. Common in older churches, he knew, but he had never seen the likes of these before. These two, on either side of the transept, were encrusted in more jewels than Victoria on a holiday. Ribs ornamented with gold filigree and rubies, arm bones laden with sapphires and emeralds. Skulls crowned with diadems of diamonds and pearls. Cuffs of lace circling the wrists, brocade covering the loins. The faces were covered in sheer linen but the empty hollows of eyes, nose and teeth were visible as through a window fogged with steam.

Just like in Strasbourg, Death had found him in a church and breath frosted from his mouth at the memory. He reached up to touch his cheeks, his eyebrows, his lips. Flesh still, but it was only a matter of time.

He remembered the white horse – bringer of arrows. He remembered the red – flame and fiery swords. The woman on her knees gasped and he looked down at her.

"Was ist das?" she moaned and struggled to her feet, pointing at his hands. *"Was bist du?"*

In the palm of one hand, snowflakes were circling and in the other, tongues of fire.

Another worshiper moved toward him and then another but Sebastien didn't care. The deadwind was blowing now and he looked to the first skeleton in its jewels and fine brocade. It wasn't a martyr. It wasn't a saint. It was just a man and he closed his eyes to see better. A man with dark hair and a large nose. Tall and thin with the hands of an artisan. Antonio Figliomeni, a cabinet maker from Milan. And with eyes still closed, he turned to see the other. Short, stout with thinning hair and a kind face. A family man from Italy who had died of the plague years ago, years upon years, centuries ago and he did not wonder how he knew anymore. The lockets had changed everything.

He opened his eyes.

The dead in the church were crowding in on him but this time, the living had surrounded him too. Six months ago, he would have been terrified. Six months ago, he would have been mad. Now, standing in the place between the living and the dead, he was home.

Behind him, there was a sound. A ruby dropped to the floor and rolled past his boot.

The woman screamed as the man of jewels and bone began to move.

***

"Another, if you please," said Christien and a third magnifying lens was added to the goggles strapped to his head.

"You look like a *verrückte Wissenschaftler*," said Valerie.

"A mad scientist?" he grunted. "You have no idea."

They were sitting at a small table in the abbey's kitchen, working on the prosthetic to release her wrist. He had rolled up his shirtsleeves to expose the brace and was currently holding a tiny brass chisel in one of the cogs like a surgical instrument. It was delicate work and not for the first time, he found himself cursing the loss of his left hand. Even penmanship was a bugger with his right.

"Another?" asked Matthias Johannes Phillip, Abbot of Melk. He was not at all what Christien had expected, being a plucky man with an intelligent face, a simple set of black robes and comfortable shoes. It was clear he recognized the Archduchess but was saying nothing about her current situation. Rather, he was eagerly helping with coffee, carpentry tools and magnifying lenses and had given them license to use the abbey as they needed.

"Sie sind ein Mechaniker?" he asked as he hovered over the operation.

"A machinist? *Nein,"* said Valerie. *"Ein Chirurg."*

"A surgeon once," said Christien. "No longer."

He changed the angle of the chisel. She hissed but did not pull her arm.

"Sorry."

"Work," she said. "Don't worry."

"You haven't got that done yet?" came another voice and he threw a glance over his shoulder as Ivy strolled into the room. She was wearing a plain dark skirt that swept the floor, a white blouse and woolen shawl.

"Good lord," he muttered. "You're a girl."

She grinned at him.

"My clothes are drying," she said. "Apparently, the monks don't approve of a woman wearing breeches."

"They are men of the cloth," growled the Archduchess. "You should respect that."

"Oh, I do," she said. "But the respect isn't mutual, is it?"

"You are clean, warm and dry. Be thankful."

"Spoken like a member of an Imperial family."

"Warum hast du sie heiraten wollen?"

"Hush, Valerie," he said. "Almost...*there.*"

Inside his arm, a gear clicked, the fingers sprang open and Valerie sank back with a sigh. He pulled the goggles from his forehead and flexed his clockwork fingers as bowls of warm water, cloths and astringent were brought to the table. Valerie's wrist was raw from the metallic grip and he reached for it, began to dab with the astringent and cloths. Ivy stepped forward, watching the procedure with interest.

"Have you seen Sebastien?"

"This is an abbey, Ivy," he said, wrapping the wrist now with strips of linen. "He could be lost for days."

"We need to talk about our plan once we get to Vienna. I have some ideas."

"Of course you do. Let us freshen up a bit first, then we can plan Vienna."

He sat back, looked up at the abbot. *"Können Sie für ein heißes Bad zu arrangieren?"*

"Yah," said Matthias, and he spoke to the monks. They moved to

the door but the Archduchess did not. She looked at him.

"Thank you," she purred. "You have bound the wing of the swan."

And she leaned across the table, placed a slow, lingering kiss on his lips that he was hard pressed to break. Ivy had never kissed him like that, not even when she was his fiancée.

Finally, Valerie rose to her feet and followed the monks but at the door, she turned back.

"You. Writer girl. You like books?"

"Very much," said Ivy.

"Gerhardt will take you to the Library. There are twelve rooms and over eighty thousand books." She arched a brow. "Perhaps *you* could be lost for days."

And she left the room, taking most of the air with it.

"She's charming," said Ivy after a moment. "You two are well suited,"

He smiled to himself, knowing it to be true.

"You should see this place," she said. "I never knew there was this much gold in all the world. There's an entire room made of marble!"

"I don't spend much time in churches."

"I never have, either. This is grander than St. Paul's. It is…it is… Oh what's the word? It is sheer resplendence."

"Sheer resplendence," he said, flexing his fingers one last time. "Puts you in the kissing mood, does it? I should have thought it would be a morgue."

"Hush," she grumbled and threw a glance at the abbot, looking like an ordinary monk as he wiped the table, the counters, the floors.

"I doubt he speaks English, Ivy," said Christien. "He can't hear your confession."

"Remy, please don't be cruel." She bit her lip. "I don't know what to do."

"Looked to me like you were doing quite fine on the riverbank."

"But it's not the same."

He said nothing, began to roll down his sleeves.

"I mean, a man shouldn't… but he can. But a woman shouldn't and she can't."

"She can, Ivy."

"But don't you think—"

"All the time. Is that what this is about? I thought you were tired of being a good girl?"

"I am! I mean—"

"Well then, what is it, Ivy? What are you afraid of?"

She swallowed.

He rose to his feet, snatched his jacket from the back of the chair.

"Do you love him? You can say it. I don't care. Probably didn't back when I was supposed to."

"I think I do. In fact I'm quite certain I do. It's just…"

"Yes?"

She leaned against the table, hands wringing like damp dishcloths.

"I'm not certain it's what I want."

"What you want?"

"Yes. Is it what I want?"

He harumphed.

"Well, you're not going to find someone better suited to you, in my opinion. Nor will he ever find anyone who can put up with him the way you do. Like Valerie and I, you two are quite well suited in that regard."

"No, I know that. But…" She looked up at him now. "I'm not certain I want a husband at all. Not now. I mean, I've never lived on my own. Ever. I've always looked after someone, taken care of everyone's wants and needs. My mum, my tad, Davis. I've never thought about myself. Never ever."

"Has Bastien proposed, Ivy?" He slipped the jacket on, rolled his shoulders, smoothed the creases. "Has he offered to take you as a wife?"

"Well, no. But—"

"You don't want a husband. Bastien will never take a wife. I think you both can be as selfish as you please."

She stared at him for several seconds, her eyes large, round and wondering and he prided himself on such a small victory. Corrupting the incorruptible. Perhaps he had a purpose in life after all.

Suddenly, a monk burst back into the kitchen and from the hall there was the sound of panic. In fact, he was certain he could hear screams as the abbot hurried from the room.

"Good lord," Christien groaned. "Five minutes? He couldn't even give me five bloody minutes?"

"What's that?" asked Ivy. "What's going on?"

"*Who,* Ivy. *Who* do you think is going on?"

"Blast," she said and together they bolted from the kitchen.

***

Many corridors and sets of stairs from the abbey kitchen to the sanctuary and they pushed against the current of terrified worshipers on their way out. The abbot and monks stopped dead in their tracks. Altogether a fitting image, she thought, as she herself skidded to a halt at the sight before her.

In front of the High Altar, Sebastien stood like a figure from a holy painting, one eye white as the moon, the other burning with flame, hair and greatcoat whipping in unnatural wind. Fire burned in one hand, a storm of snow and ice in the other. It was as strange as the night in Easterton Frederick Crumb's sitting room. But here, now, there was something even stranger that stopped her heart and made her question her sanity.

From opposite sides of this elaborate golden church, two skeletons were trudging toward the Mad Lord, clad in brocade and dripping jewels like blood.

"Ivy," said Christien in a very small voice. "Have you ever seen this before?"

"Never," she said, equally small.

There were no words for such a sight. In fact, she wasn't sure there was breath left in her body. It was like a nightmare. Ghastly, horrific creatures stumbling, jerking across the floor towards the Mad Lord of Lasingstoke. It was all they could do to keep their bones in places as they dragged skeletal legs, losing jewels with each footfall. Linen around their heads flowed with the wind, revealing skulls yellowed and brittle with age.

From the corner of her eye, she could see the abbot, mouth moving

161

as if in prayer but silent, not a word coming forth. His attention was, like theirs, riveted on the creatures shuffling to the centre of the crossing.

First one, then the other, they reached skeletal arms toward Sebastien and he reached back, one hand fire, the other snow.

"Antonio Figliomeni," he said, his words hollow and echoing. *"Quia pulvis es, et in terram ibis. Dimissa es."*

Fiery finger met dry bone and suddenly, the man called Antonio Figliomeni burst into flames and the jewels scattered across the floor like rice at a wedding. Ash rose up on the wind, spinning through the cupola of the High Altar until it disappeared through the tiny plate of glass at the very peak. The swaths of brocade dropped to the tile, unscathed.

Ivy watched, astounded and speechless, as the man she'd kissed this morning turned his attention to the second creature.

"Nein," said the abbot. *"Nein, nicht die Reliquien!"*

And without regard to skeletons and Mad Lords or other unnatural things, the man rushed forward, his own black robes whipping in the wind. Sebastien looked at him, cocking his head like a dog. He did not touch the second skeleton.

"Sie ein Kind des Teufels!" the abbot shouted. "A child of the Devil!"

"Quoniam filius mortis," said Sebastien in his hollow voice.

"These relics are sacred! They are martyrs for the faith! You are committing sacrilege!"

"Et mortui sunt atque percussi."

"Stop speaking Latin! It is the language of God!"

"Mein Gott," said another voice, and Ivy saw Valerie beside them now, eyes fixed in unbelief. "Is this real?"

"You're dreaming," said Christien. "This is my nightmare. All mine."

For her part, Ivy was overwhelmed by the spectacle on the floor. The abbot moved forward.

"You have destroyed the holy relic of St. Frederich! Leave St. Clemens in peace, creature, and we shall pray for your forgiveness."

"His name is Alberto Tassone from Milan. How can you see him?" He turned, shocked to find others in the church. "Miss Savage?

Christien? Can you see him too?"

She nodded and slowly, the storms in his hands died away. He turned to the relic of St. Clemons (or the skeleton of Alberto Tassone of Milan) and shook his head.

"I'm sorry," he said. "I can't help you."

Abruptly, the deadwind died and the creature crumpled to the marble floor, a mass of bones, brocade and rattling jewels. For a long moment, there was silence in the Abbey of Melk.

Sebastien sighed and sighed again, becoming somehow smaller and more human with each breath.

Finally, he looked up and she was grateful that at least one eye was brown.

"I know you do like your coffee in Austria," he said quietly. "But I would very much like a cup of tea, if that's not too much trouble."

Ivy ran to catch him as he sank to his knees.

***

Mystery In Melk

Melk Daily News

Several graves in the Melk cemetery were looted sometime today, said manager, Ernst Grundl. Caskets were pushed open in the familial crypts and human remains have been scattered all across the grounds. The groundskeeper, Ivor Kuhlmann, has been fired for dereliction of duty. Police are continuing to investigate.

Chapter 14

Of Controversies, Conspiracies and a Hot Conversation in a Cold Carriage

It seemed they had worn out their welcome in the Abbey of Melk.

The entire church had been closed down and they had been ushered out of the sanctuary to the Prelate's Courtyard. Even a woman of Valerie's status couldn't change the abbot's mind and he had commissioned a carriage from the village to transport them to Vienna. It was snowing again so he had also arranged for extras coats, a flask of black coffee and a blanket for the cab. Now as the coach bumped along the icy roads, Ivy realized they could have used a second blanket. The first was currently over Sebastien's head, blocking the dead lining the way to Vienna.

She sighed and looked at her companions across the cab. They had spoken little in the last four-hours. Small talk didn't suit any of them and it just seemed best to leave it rather than engage in conversation either pointless or destructive. The Archduchess stared out the window, her profile elegant and unreadable. Even under better circumstances, Ivy knew that they would never have been friends.

Christien stared out the opposite window, a colonial cigarette in his clockwork grip but she hadn't seen him smoke. He was trying to make sense out of what he had witnessed, she was certain but the perfect porcelain mask was tight. She wondered who he would be if and when he ever let it slip.

For his part, Sebastien merely sat with the blanket over his head. The last she'd seen of him, one eye had still been white and she wondered if it had gone back to brown in the last few hours. Nothing was guaranteed unless that happened.

And not even then. Not anymore.

She sighed and sank back, her mind rolling back to his behavior after the abbot had chased them from the sanctuary. They had been forced to wait for the carriage in the Prelate's Courtyard and when it rolled under the great stone gate, she was surprised to see it pulled by horses.

"Look," she had said to the Mad Lord. "Horses."

He had done a very strange thing, then – he rose to his feet and walked away to hide behind the cloisters.

She sighed and followed, finding him behind an arch, wringing his hands.

"Are you alright?" she asked.

"Yes, yes," he said. "Fine."

"The horses are here. Did you want to see them? You said you did."

"No. No I'm fine."

"They look quite nice. Are they Lipizzaners too?"

"Friesians. Lipizzans are grey, although you do find the occasional bay. You need a bay. They bring good luck."

She really had no idea what he was talking about. All the horses in her world were black, brown or white, Thoroughbreds, Clydesdales or now, French Warmbloods.

"Don't you want to see them?"

He shook his head.

"Why not?"

"They're black."

She had looked back then. Both horses were indeed black, with long manes, tails that dragged on the ground and feet with plumes like feather dusters.

"I don't want them to see me," he had continued. "Just in case, you know. I've already had white and red. The black will come for me next and everything will change."

"What is it, Laury?" she sighed, took his hand. It was shaking and she gave it a squeeze. "Do you not want to go?"

"No, no. That's fine. Good, in fact. I don't like it here, Miss Savage. Far too many dead for a church. But I don't want to go to Vienna. I want to go somewhere else."

"We need to go back. We have a two days to figure things out before the funeral—"

And quite suddenly, he caught both of her hands, pulled her behind another arch.

"We *can* leave," he'd said. "Right now and they'll never find us. There are places we could go where there are no empires, no airships, no soldiers or guards or Hussars or policemen, only green grass and fields and water and horses and dogs and tea. I'm certain we could find books. Or if there aren't, you could write them. Naturally we'd need fountain pens and ink and paper, so we'd need a place that had a few shops –"

She'd placed a finger on his lips then. His eyes were wide but at least one was brown.

"You know we can't do that, Sebastien."

"We can. We could go to India or Corfu or Morocco or Istanbul. They won't find us there. They're coming, Miss Savage. They're all coming and I can't escape. Not here. Not when there are black horses in the courtyard."

"Ivy? Bastien?"

It was Christien, leaning around the arch. The wind was lifting his dark hair, making his cheeks red in contrast to his pale skin.

"Sorry. The coach is read – Oh god."

She glanced back at the Mad Lord. He'd slipped the blanket back over his head.

"So the horses don't see me," he said.

And her heart broke all over again.

He had allowed her to lead him to the carriage and it reminded her of the night in the flat of Easterton Frederick Crumb, when he'd avenged three murdered women and shot a man in the head. She would never forget that night. It was seared into her bones like a brand.

The coach bumped now as it skidded through wet snow, rousing her from her thoughts. Valerie too breathed deeply as if awakened.

"We will be in Vienna soon," she said quietly.

"Bully," said Christien.

"We will go to the Hofburg. I can't wait to tell my mother."

"Your mother?"

"She will be overjoyed at this turn of events."

Christien blew out a thin stream of smoke. He blinked slowly and Ivy thought at this moment, he'd never looked more like Rupert.

"What are you talking about?" he said flatly.

"What happened this afternoon," she said. "With the relics. My mother will be very pleased."

"Valerie, you don't think—"

"How could I *not*?" she snapped, eyes glittering. "I saw, Remy. I saw a miracle!"

"That *miracle* will get us all killed."

"If we don't go to the Hofburg," she growled. "*I* will have you all killed."

"Not the most persuasive argument, darling," said Christien.

"My mother will understand. She knows the spirit world. We will explain everything and then we will take your brother to Rudolf."

"What's that?" Ivy sat up. "What did you say?"

"Him." Valerie pointed at the blanket. "He can speak the words and bring back my brother from the dead."

There was only the sound of wheels digging through the snow. Christien dropped the cigarette to crush it under his shoe

"That," he said. "Is impossible."

"For you, yes. For me, yes. But for him?"

"Valerie—"

She swung toward the Mad Lord.

"You can do this, yes?"

"He can't," said Ivy. "No one can."

"Those relics were hundreds of years old, perhaps a thousand! He made them live!"

"He can't do it."

"Ask him!"

Ivy bit her lip. It was a fantastical question.

"Sebastien?" she asked. "Sebastien, what do you think?"

"Is there tea?"

"Can you, Laury? Can you bring someone back from the dead?"

He sighed, breaking her heart with that one small thing.

She reached up to slide the blanket from his head, surprised that he didn't resist. Ran a hand through his hair, took a moment to examine the wound that only yesterday had been oozing with blood. It was almost healed over, but she could see the aluminium sheen beneath the skin. One eye was still white, both bloodshot, and she thought his cheeks had sunken, just a little.

"Can you see Rudolf, Sebastien?" she asked quietly.

He shook his head.

"Why not?"

"I don't know. The world is upside down, Miss Savage."

"Ivy."

"Yes, that too."

"Can you bring Rudolf back from the dead?"

"Maybe." He blinked slowly, as if trying to focus. "I've never done anything like that before."

"You moved those skeletons," said Christien.

"I didn't. They moved themselves."

"How?"

"I don't know. You'd best ask them."

She resisted the impulse to kiss him. Odd, that.

"Right," she sighed and sat back. "We've been rather preoccupied with running these last days. Now that we're closing in on Vienna, I think we need to talk this through."

Christien grunted and snapped open the stolen case, began to light another cigarette. "You did say you had a plan."

"Well, it may have to change some, given the current circumstances but we can do quite a lot of sleuthing from this very cab."

"From here?" asked the Archduchess.

"We have all the tools we need." And she tapped her head. "We just need to clarify the chain of events. Valerie—"

"Marie Valerie Mathilde Amalie, Archduchess von Habsburg," said Valerie.

Ivy blinked slowly.

"And I may call you…?"

"Your Most Royal Highness."

Ivy tried a smile. It was thin, but still.

"I shall do that very thing," she said. "So we don't know much, only that Rudolf—"

"Rudolf Franz Karl Joseph—"

"*Valerie,*" growled Christien.

The Archduchess smiled wickedly. How like the wind she changed. Ivy went on.

"The Crown Prince was shot the night of the party, yes?"

"Sometime during the night, yes."

"And where? He wasn't at the Hofburg, was he? Tell me, where did he die?"

"Mayerling," she said. "His private hunting lodge in the Vienna Woods."

"Are there stairs in Mayerling?"

"Of course. Why?"

Ivy thought for a moment, remembering the conversation in the Kolmar barn. If Sebastien was right about Arclight, things could get sticky very quickly. She would have to be careful.

"Who was the girl he brought to the party, the one with the locket?"

"That was Baroness Marie von Vetsera," Valerie said. "But she preferred to be called Mary. I don't know if she had other, more appropriate names. I never cared to ask."

"Was she his mistress?"

"His 'special' friend."

"Special Friend?" Christien arched his brow. "I had thought the

Viennese more creative than that."

Valerie growled but Ivy ignored him.

"Is it customary to bring your 'special friend' to a court function like that?"

"No. It was a breech of etiquette."

"That's why your father was angry then."

"My father does not approve of Mary," said Valerie. "No one does."

"Hmm." Ivy chewed her bottom lip. "She was with Rudolf the night he died, yes?"

"It was first thought she poisoned him."

"But she didn't, did she?"

"Someone murdered him. It is the only explanation."

"Not the only explanation," muttered Ivy. "Not by half."

"With someone of his status, a political motive is the most obvious," said Christien. "Rudolf was a liberal prince in a conservative country."

The Archduchess nodded swiftly.

"Liberal, yes."

"Surely that would bring him into conflict with the government."

"Taaffe hated him," she said quietly. "Our prime minister. He felt Rudolf was courting anarchy with his socialist views."

"And was he?"

"Rudolf loved Austria. He would never do anything to bring it shame."

"He was tipping the velvet with a seventeen year old girl, love."

She struck him on the cheek and he held his breath before slowly exhaling a thin line of smoke. Slowly he smiled, but naturally, without his eyes.

"So this Taaffe," said Ivy. "Would he have anything to gain from Rudolf's death?"

"Nothing. He would have nothing. Rudolf may have been Liberal, but he was the heir to the Empire. Even a liberal heir is better than none."

"Is Taaffe like Bismark? Controlling the government with a puppet king?"

"Taaffe would love to be von Bismark," Valerie grunted. "But my father is no puppet."

"Other factions in the government?"

"There are no other factions in the government."

"A different government, then?"

"A different government?" Valerie narrowed her eyes. "What do you mean?"

"The *Gilded Empire* must have enemies."

"Or allies," suggested Christien. "Sometimes allies are worse."

"Our allies are loyal."

"Are they?" he said, took a long drag from the cigarette. "Is the Three Emperors League allied with the Triple Alliance or the Triple Entente or both?"

"Or neither?" added Ivy.

"And how would a very conservative Wilhelm react to a very liberal Rudolf on the *Gilded* throne? Easier to remove him, put someone less threatening in his place. Someone like, oh say, Gisela? Now *that* would be an alliance."

Valerie swore at them in German. Christien grinned again through the smoke.

"What about Rudolf's wife, then?" Ivy asked. "Could she have shot him? That must have been a terrible embarrassment for her at the party."

"Stephanie is an oaf," said Valerie. "She would not have the courage to shoot him. Besides, she has her own *Liebhaber.*"

"Liebhaber?"

"Lover," said Christien.

"Right. So do we know for a fact that he was shot?" Ivy frowned. "Because I'd very much like to know how. I mean, was it a distance shot like from a rifle? It is a hunting lodge, after all. Or if it was close, how close? Were there powder burns? What was the angle of the bullet?"

"Mein Gott!" snapped the Archduchess. "This is my brother and the Crown Prince of Austria!"

"These are important questions, Valerie," said Christien. "It used to be my entire world."

"Your world is gone, without a hand."

"So is yours, without an heir."

Ivy thought a moment longer.

"So we really need a necroscopy report, yes? Remy, how could we get that?"

"Hm. Let's think that through. A necroscopy report for a Crown Prince suspected to have been killed by foreign anarchists, to be given to those same foreign anarchists? Not bloody likely, Ivy."

"Drat." She made a face. "Well, if we are denied forensic evidence, we must move on to circumstantial."

"God, I'd forgotten how your brain worked."

She grinned, threw a glance at the Mad Lord. During the entire conversation, he had stared blankly out at the road and she wondered if he was thinking about his dogs back at Lasignstoke. She took a deep breath.

"Because, on the night of the party, Sebastien looked into an orb."

"*I* looked into a bottle of Scotch," said Christien.

"An orb?" asked Valerie. "Like those in the ballroom?"

"Exactly," said Ivy. "He saw the girl die. She was trying to steal the locket and they struggled at the top of a set of stairs and she fell. That's why I asked about the stairs in the lodge."

There was silence in the cab.

"This is true?" asked Valerie. "This is what you saw?"

"If I say yes," grumbled Sebastien, "May I have the blanket back?"

Ivy sighed but passed it over. It was over his head in a heartbeat.

Christien blinked slowly, blew out a long thin stream of smoke.

"So who killed Rudolf then, Bastien?"

"Arclight," said Sebastien from under the blanket. "Arclight and love."

"You said that before, " said Christien. "What does it mean?"

"He is a madman," Valerie snorted.

"A moment ago, he was a miracle," said Christien.

The Archduchess looked away.

"We don't know much about Mary but we know even less about Arclight, so we still have a mystery," said Ivy. "You seemed to know about the lockets, Remy. What do you know?"

"Just what the Ghost Club told me," he said and he flicked the cigarette while he thought. "That there were three made centuries ago by a French metallurgist in Holland. Or perhaps it was a Dutch metallurgist in Normandy. I remember the name Tycho Brahe and someone named Ashmole. It was months ago."

"I wonder who the third one is," mumbled Sebastien. "I can't wait to meet her."

"*Archelicht,*" murmered Valerie, "Is the Habsburg locket. Gisela told me—"

"It's not a Habsburg locket," said Christien.

She ignored him.

"Gisela told me it was appropriated from an estate in Normandy, France—"

"The de Lacey estate in Normandy," said Christien.

"—by Louis XVI and given to his wife Maria Antonia Josepha Johanna von Habsburg as a wedding present."

"Marie Antoinette?" asked Ivy.

"And you bloody Habsburgs have had it ever since," said Christien,

"Habsburgs preserve history. The French Empire fell during their reign. It was one of the few pieces that wasn't chopped up and sold for cake."

"Spoken like an Imperialist," said Ivy. "Blaming the people for not wanting to starve to death."

"As I said, Habsburgs preserve history. It is not our duty to preserve people. My grandmother gave it to my father, and my father gave it to Rudolf when he was born. Maman told me the locket spun rooms of gold, and was therefore the perfect christening gift for a *Gilded* prince."

Ivy swallowed, remembering the night in the Engineworks house at St. Katharine's Docks. In a matter of moments, Ghostlight had turned every gear, every piston, every copper wire, into gold.

Valerie sighed.

"The locket was always kept locked up. I had never seen it until that night."

Ivy sighed now, stared out the window at the snowy road, the black skeleton trees, the mountains. The Alps, if she remembered correctly. They had looked so different from an airship.

"So who had the locket on the *Stahl Mädchen?*"

"What do you say?" asked Valerie. "No one had the locket."

"*Someone* had the locket," said Christien. "Where do you think those damned orbs came from?"

"I – I don't know."

"One of your sisters?"

"How would they get it? It belonged to Rudolf and neither of us saw him before his death."

"That's not true," he said. "We all saw him the night in the Hofburg. He had a crackerjack barney with your father."

Her eyes flashed at him. "Are you suggesting—"

"Nothing," he said. "And everything. No one is above suspicion, Valerie."

"Rudolf is the heir to the *Gilded Empire!* The *only* heir! My father would never even consider what you are suggesting!"

"Political assassinations happen all the time, love. And never bank on family loyalty. It can turn fatal over a crock of mummie's china."

"Not in my family."

"A family of Black Swans?"

She snarled at him.

"I want to go home," moaned Sebastien from the blanket. "And I will never leave Lasingstoke ever again. I promise."

Ivy wrapped her arm in his, leaned her head on his shoulder. But that did not, could not stop the racing of her mind.

"So," she continued, "If what Sebastien said is true and Mary died because they were arguing over the locket, then we need to find out what happened to the locket. We'll know what happened to Rudolf once we find the locket."

"The German hunting party," said Christien. "They were staying at a nearby lodge, weren't they? Could they have been sent to steal it?"

"Wilhelm is a personal friend," Valerie hissed. "He would not have the nerve."

"He's a *very* personal friend to Gisela," said Christien. "So how about this? Mary tries to steal the locket but Rudy stops her and she dies. Then Gisela shows up, they quarrel, she shoots him and takes it to the Germans. It would have been suspicious but Bastien's outburst gives her a perfect cover and we get shot down over Reichsland with French Anarchists to blame. Gisela divorces her husband, marries Wilhelm, and Germany and Austria are reunited at last. Well done all 'round, I say. Well done."

Valerie swung again but he blocked it with the clockwork hand. They both stared, transfixed, before he slowly released his fingers, one by one. She folded her arms across her chest, sank back in the cushion.

"I want to go home," moaned the blanket.

Ivy sighed.

"Well, I'm afraid Her Most Royal Highness may be right. We may have to go to the Hofburg after all."

Christien stared at her flatly, blew the smoke out again. It was rather like punctuation, she thought. He could write entire paragraphs with that thing.

"Bastien is *not* going to the Hofburg," he said finally.

"I don't want to go to the Hofburg," Sebastien said. "I want to go home."

"We need Sebastien to see what happened," said Ivy. "And he can do that if he has something of Rudolf's. You and Valerie could go."

"Yes," said Christien. "Fine. We'll go."

"No. Not you," said Valerie and she narrowed her eyes at Ivy. "Her."

"Her? Why?"

"Me? Why?"

Slowly, the Archduchess reached out a hand to caress his cheek. He watched her as one would watch a cobra, waiting for the strike.

"This face," she purred. "No one could forget this face. If a Habsburg sees you after such an unceremonious kidnapping in Strasbourg, you will be shot on sight. And that would be sad."

She smiled, though it was not a pleasant sight.

"No, you and the madman will go to my cousin's. The girl, however, will come with me. She is unremarkable. No one will recognize her."

"Jolly good," said Ivy.

"Besides, she is the clever one. And her arm does not lock."

Christien blew smoke into her face. She grabbed him and kissed him so fiercely that his cigarette dropped to the floor.

Ivy rolled her eyes, looked back at the blanket that was Sebastien.

"Will you be alright at Valerie's cousin's place? I'm certain there will be no saints for you to break."

"I didn't break him, Miss Savage."

"Ivy."

"Yes, Ivy. I didn't break him, I released him. And they weren't saints, simply men who died a very long time ago. Although he seemed like a very kind fellow. He may have been a saint after all."

She smiled.

"Is it Arclight?" she asked. "Is it because of her?"

"The horses, I suspect." He shrugged. "I don't know. I only went into the church to pray but the dead had other ideas. They always do."

She didn't know what to say to that, leaned her head back onto his arm.

"I don't understand how you saw them," he muttered from the blanket. "No one ever sees what I see. Ever."

"Everyone saw them because their bodies were actually there. You literally called dead men out of their crypts."

"Like Ezekiel and the Valley of Dry Bones," he said.

"How biblical."

She threw a glance at Remy and Valerie. They were clearly engrossed, bussing it up and not caring who watched. This was not the man who had been her fiancé so many months ago and it made her wonder if this was the real Christien de Lacey or if now, like then, he was playing a part. Perhaps she would never know. Perhaps he didn't know himself.

And they sat for a long moment, Ivy's mind spinning in so many different directions and she wondered why she should be thinking of crimes when she was wrapped around the Mad Lord's arm. She wished that once, just once, she was a normal girl and that it wasn't always such a war between her head and her heart. Still, she had never been anyone other than herself with Sebastien and he seemed quite fine with it. Perhaps Christien was right once again. Perhaps she didn't have to make a choice. Perhaps, she could reach a little higher, take what she wanted, with or without those very fine boots.

She slipped under the blanket, let it fall over her own head.

Sebastien looked down and her heart soared to see both eyes brown as chocolate.

He smiled.

"You see? It's very peaceful in here, isn't it? No dead. No spirits. No mountains rushing by. And now you. Marvelous things, blankets."

She grinned and leaned her head on his shoulder, letting her body enjoy his while her brain continued to spin and for the first time in months, there was no war inside.

***

Illustrated Grazer Special Edition
Graz, Austria

Funeral preparations for our beloved Crown Prince continue with public viewing of His Imperial body, now moved from St. Stephen's Cathedral to the Court Chapel at the Hofburg. Reports from Vienna say the crowds that came to pay respects were so numerous that the chapel could not be closed at the regular time and prelates were forced to maintain public viewing throughout the night. In a solemn ceremony, the Crown Prince will be interred in the Church of the Capuchin Friars on February 5.

In an unrelated story, young Viennese socialite Baroness CENSORED has reportedly died this week in CENSORED, and has been laid to rest in CENSORED.

Chapter 15

Of Tuscan Princes, Turkish Delights and Bergl Elephants in a Viennese Palais

It was twilight when the coach plowed into the snowy streets of Vienna. Twilight and grey and very sad. Black flags flew half-mast from every post, window shades were drawn like closed eyes. There was no music. There was no Carnival. There were no cakes or coffee or flowers for sale. Vienna was mourning her beloved Crown Prince in a monochrome of smoke and steamcabs and funeral black.

They had driven in using back roads but soon, the monumental buildings of the Ringstrasse slipped past the cab windows. Narrow laneways alternated with stained glass, gothic spires with Greco-limestone, all of it thick with industrial soot. It seemed as if fate was closing in and Ivy began to fear none of them would escape the Silver Hussars or their sabres. Finally the coach rattled to a halt in the courtyard of a city *palais* that reminded Ivy of the aristocratic white homes of Pall Mall and Piccadilly.

"Wait here," said Valerie. She pushed open the cab door and disappeared into the shadows thrown by the gaslight.

They sat for a moment before Christien leaned forward.

"Bastien," he said. "Are you thinking what I'm thinking?"

Sebastien pushed the blanket up on his head, leaned forward as well.

"Kill the driver and make off with the coach?"

"No killing!" Ivy snapped. "That won't improve our chances!"

"Valerie telegraphed someone before we left," said Christien. "I'd say our chances couldn't get much worse."

"You promised, Sebastien," she growled. "No shooting."

"I wasn't going to *shoot* him," said Sebastien. "I have no bullets left."

"No killing."

She sighed and sank back, folding her arms across her chest but to be honest, Christien was right. Their chances couldn't get much worse than they were now, sitting in a coach mere blocks from the Hofburg. Suddenly, her plan to uncover this murderous plot didn't seem nearly as clever as it had only hours ago.

Despair, it seemed, was a contagious thing.

"This could all go very wrong very quickly," said Christien. "Whatever you do Ivy, don't trust her. Not one bit. She is a Black Swan, as dangerous as she is clever and she may just sell you out for a page in her father's good book."

"A Black Swan?"

"I've told her that I personally know the London Ripper and if any harm comes to you, he will slit her throat and take out her heart. I think that gave her pause. She's terrified of Sebastien and she thinks it's all part of the de Lacey curse."

"Which, of course, it is," said Sebastien.

"If you do get the sense that you're being duped, leave her. Find a safe place and lay very low. Do whatever you need to do to get back home. They'll want someone to hang for the Prince's death and they won't care whom. Do you understand?"

"Do you want my blanket?" asked Sebastien.

Suddenly, the cab door swung open on a tall man in a military uniform. He had sleek dark hair, a sporty moustache and bright eyes.

"You are *von Steam,* yes? I will speak English. Come out, come out."

Reluctantly, they obeyed as Valerie appeared beside him in the gaslight, hair newly piled, the sable wrapped around her shoulders. Ivy sighed. Easy to be unremarkable around such a woman.

"This is my cousin Archduke Franz Salvator Maria Joseph Ferdinand Karl Leopold Anton von Padua Johann Baptist Januarius Aloys Gonzaga Rainer Benedikt Bernhard of Austria, Hungary, Croatia and Bohemia."

Ivy blinked.

"Call me Franz," said the man, offering his hand. "You must be Remy.

"Christien de Lacey," said Remy.

Interesting, thought Ivy, how he suddenly preferred his Christian name.

"And you the miracle man," he said, turning to Sebastien and offering his hand. "I am fascinated to meet you sir."

Sebastien took it.

"Is there a church nearby? I would dearly love to pray. Last time I tried, it went very badly."

"Ah yes, the relics! Valerie has told me. Are you a practicing Catholic, sir?"

"Practicing?" asked Sebastien. "Yes, practicing. Haven't quite got it right yet."

And he began turning Franz's hand over and over in his, running his fingers up to the wrist and holding it there for a moment. For his part, the man called Franz just stared until the Mad Lord released the unusual grip and smiled.

"Italian, yes? Do you prefer Austria or Tuscany?"

"I—" He looked at Valerie. She arched a brow. "Austria, sir, but I must admit Tuscany is considerably warmer!"

"Do you have tea?"

The Archduchess stepped forward.

"Remy, you and your brother will stay as guests of my cousin. He understands you were not responsible for Rudolf's death and will afford you as much protection as any minor prince can give. Do not leave his company. We cannot guarantee your safety otherwise."

"You cannot guarantee our safety at all," said Christien.

"Do not leave his company," she growled.

And she climbed back into the coach and threw a glance at Ivy, ordering her with that simple gesture.

Ivy turned to the men.

"Remember what I said," said Christien. "Be careful."

"I will." She swallowed, looked up at the Mad Lord. The blanket was draped across his shoulders like a cloak. "Sebastien?"

He stepped toward her and she marveled at the rush of her heart. His cheek brushed hers and she held her breath, waiting for the feel of his lips on her skin.

"Beware of horses, Miss Savage," he breathed into her ear. "They are duplicitous creatures and will turn the world upside down with their hoofs."

And with that, he turned to the 'minor prince' called Franz.

"Did you say there was tea?"

"Writer girl!" came the voice from coach. "Come now!"

And for the first time she could remember, Christien laughed. It was a bitter, cynical bark of a laugh and the three men turned to head into the *palais,* leaving her to climb into the carriage alone.

***

Vienna Daily News

Vienna

We are shocked to report that the offices of our sister newspaper, **Illustrated Grazer Special Edition,** *have been raided and looted overnight, their presses damaged and across the city, newsstands burned. It is rumoured that the Grazer broadsheet was publishing falsehoods and slander regarding the unfortunate death of beloved Crown Prince Rudolf but state police have denied any involvement in these acts of vandalism. They have also assured other presses that as long as they continue to print the truth, they should fear no public backlash or private retribution on behalf of outraged citizens or vandals.*

State police are continuing to investigate.

***

Obviously Archduke Franz's circle of friends didn't include many lunatics or madmen, judging from the look on his face. The 'minor prince' had been pleasant as he led them through the grand city *palais,* with both footman and valet at their heels, but all had changed the moment they entered the guest suite over the courtyard. The footman turned up the gaslight and suddenly, the guestroom was transformed into an exotic place with leafy jungles and fantastical creatures painted over walls and ceiling. Smiling in wonderment, Sebastien stretched out on the floor, fingers laced across his middle to study it.

Christien didn't smile. He didn't even try.

"Thank you," he did say to the prince. "This is very generous."

"You are friends of Marie-Valérie," said Franz. "That is enough for me."

"You might find yourself in a world of trouble on our account."

"Well then, we will face it like Austrians. With a stiff drink and a large cigar."

He gestured to the footman, who moved around the Mad Lord to the fireplace. It was painted to look like a jungle volcano. He began to prod it with a poker and embers gleamed, erupting as the fire finally roared to life.

"These are quite remarkable," said Sebastien from the floor. "Much better than most frescoes I've seen."

"The Bohemian, Bergl," said Franz. "He painted rooms in the Hofburg and Schoenbrunn, as well as the Abbey of Melk. Have you ever been to Melk?"

"No," Christien lied.

"I don't like Melk," said Sebastien. "No tea. Only saints."

Franz looked at Christien.

"Your room is the door opposite. But before I show you," he held up three cigars. "Would you care to join me in the smoking room? You and your brother are fascinating company and these Havanese are too rich for an idle smoke."

Christien studied the man, his military posture, his bright eyes, the eager way he carried himself. There was something about him, however and for Christien, trust was not a thing easily lent.

"Delighted," he said after a moment.

"And the Miracle Man? Will he join us, yes? Marie-Valérie told me of the relics, how he made them come to life."

"Is there a tea trolley?" asked Sebastien from the floor.

"Surely not when we have Grüner Veltliner and Muskateller in the cellar?"

"Bastien will stay here, won't you Bastien?"

"I'll stay here," said Sebastien.

Christien turned.

"Might you give us a moment? I do need to speak with him."

"Of course. The valet will wait outside and will show you to the smoking room when you're ready."

And with that, the minor prince, his valet and footman left the room to the de Lacey brothers – one on his feet, one on the floor.

There was silence, only the hiss of gaslamps and the crackle of the hearth. The painted walls gleamed with firelight.

"You will stay in this room, Bastien. Promise me you won't get into any trouble."

"Why? Are there skeletons here too?"

"There are skeletons *everywhere,* Bastien, most of them well and truly buried. Would that stop you?"

"It's not me."

"Well, it's not anyone else, is it? How the bloody hell did you do that? And don't tell me they did it themselves. I don't believe it."

Sebastien slid a hand into his greatcoat pocket, pulled out the bag of Turkish Delights he had stolen from the train. He popped one in his mouth and held up the bag.

"They're sweeter than cigars," he said.

Christien grunted and snatched the bag, reached in with a pick attachment rather than a finger. The candy was delicious and stuck to his teeth.

"You're looking for horses, aren't you?"

"I am."

"Do you see any?"

"None on the ceiling," said Sebastien. "But two on the walls. At least they're only white. I was curious about those brown things in that corner but I realized that they have humps so I think they're camels. Did you see the elephants?"

"I see *painted* elephants, Bastien. What type did you see?"

"Why, painted elephants of course. What other kinds are there in a Viennese *palais?* "

"I would love to ride an elephant."

Christien plucked another Delight before tossing the bag back to his brother. Even from the floor, Sebastien caught it easily and slipped it back into his coat.

"I'm going for a smoke. You are staying here."

"Yes, of course."

"No chasing horses through the *palais*. Do you understand?"

"Yes, completely."

"I'm serious, Bastien. I don't care if all the horses in the world come calling, you will not go after them. Is that clear?"

"Why do you hate me so, Christien?"

Because you're laying on the floor looking for horses. Because you see the dead and call skeletons from their graves. Because I was chased out of Vienna's halls and Valerie's bed on account of you. Because I lost everything to your damned lockets and your damned ghosts and grew up in your mad shadow and because you were a terrible brother and because of you, our father killed himself and I've hated you since I was born. Is that enough for you to chew on, or do you need more damned Turkish Delights?

"Because you don't keep your word," he said flatly. "And then, you don't think about the consequences."

"Hm. You may have something there. Might you bring tea after your cigar?"

Christien sighed.

"Only if you promise to be here when I get back."

"I promise."

"Do you hear yourself? You are promising to stay here, even if there are horses."

"Yes, I hear myself."

With that, he turned and headed out through the painted doors toward the steps when he heard his brother's voice call after him.

"But what if the horse is black?"

He closed the door behind him.

***

Ivy could see flashes of limestone between the narrow streets, covered in fresh snow and illuminated by streetlamps. It was very dark now, but not late. Winter did that to a place. In winter, the sun was a welcome commodity, like sugar or plums.

She was warm now, her red corset under blouse and shawl, her breeches and boots hidden under the long dark skirt of Melk. It served not only to keep her warm, but disguised her rather unorthodox wardrobe. On this trip, she was to be unremarkable, unmemorable, forgotten.

Easily done, she reckoned, when travelling with an Archduchess.

"I'm sorry about your brother," she said as the coach rattled down the cobbled streets.

Valerie didn't look at her. It was impossible to guess the thoughts that ran through her head.

"Were you close then?" Ivy asked. "You and Rudolf?"

"No," was all she said.

"Still," said Ivy. "I am sorry for your loss. After all of this, I am truly sorry."

"Rudolf is ten years older than me. I rarely see him. *Saw* him. I rarely saw him."

The Archduchess turned her face now. It was as much a mask as Christien's.

"Do you have a brother?"

"Yes, Davis. He's almost sixteen."

"What is he like, your brother?"

Ivy smiled. "Wild, clever, stubborn. Resourceful. Currently besotted with a maid-girl at Lasingstoke. I miss him."

"Rudolf was clever," Valerie said. "And resourceful. Perhaps he was stubborn but he hid it well. We all do. It is how one survives as a Habsburg."

"How so?"

The woman's eyes were like cold steel and Ivy tried her best not to feel small.

"When you are born Habsburg, you have one role and that is to perpetuate the *Gilded Empire*. For men, you learn the art of war. You learn strategy, diplomacy, tactics and politics. You travel and make allegiances, break alliances, placate the barons and please the church. You marry whom they tell you to marry, produce an heir and chart the best course for the Empire."

"And for women?"

"You marry whom they tell you to marry and produce an heir."

They were birds, Ivy thought, beautiful birds in gilded cages. She had once thought that about Christien but now anyone would be hard pressed to cage him.

"You are very fortunate," Valerie continued. "You have none of this weighing on you. You write your little books and live a life of freedom. You may marry whomever you wish to marry and have children, or stay a spinster and have none. You may go to school or bake bread all your days. You have your will and your life goes as your choices, for good or ill. Not so, a Habsburg."

Through the window, distant sights of the Ringstrasse rolled by. The Opera House, the Parliament Building, the Museum of Natural History. No longer regal or imposing, she thought, just sad.

"So why aren't you married?" she asked. "I would have thought that a princess of your status would have dozens of suitors by now."

"I was betrothed at Christmas," said Valerie. "To my cousin."

"Your cousin?"

"Franz."

"Franz? The minor prince Franz?"

"Archduke Franz Salvator Maria Joseph Ferdinand Karl Leopold

Anton von Padua Johann Baptist Januarius Aloys Gonzaga Rainer Benedikt Bernhard of Austria, Hungary, Croatia and Bohemia." She sighed. "My cousin."

Ivy gaped, at a loss for words.

"He is a physician in the *Gilded* cavalry."

"Does, does Christien know?"

"Why should he know?"

"He loves you!"

"I'm sure he does," she said. "But I am a Habsburg and a Habsburg does not marry for love."

"Oh my," sighed Ivy and she sagged against the carriage seat. "Oh my."

"First you, then me. Our Remy does not choose his women well, I think."

If you do get the sense that you're being duped, leave her. Find a safe place and lay very low.

She'd never run from anything in her life. Not likely to start now.

She narrowed her eyes.

"What is a Black Swan?"

The Archduchess looked away.

"Remy said you were a Black Swan," Ivy pressed. "What is that?"

"Remy talks too much."

"Why am I going with you in the Hofburg?"

The woman smiled and Ivy felt a rush of cold sweep down from her ears.

"You are here to help me find who murdered my brother," she said. "And if not, you will die in front of an Imperial firing squad for treason and murder."

The carriage rattled to a halt.

"Well then," said Ivy. "We'd best get started."

And the coach door swung open on the marble arches and Silver Hussars of the Hofburg.

***

Sebastien rose from the floor as the fire sputtered in the hearth. Even though the room was painted like a jungle, the many windows conducted the winter air like an icebox. He was relieved to have found the hearth loaded with wood. There was a set of clockwork bellows and an ornate pot that must have been used to boil water. For tea, he thought glumly. Not that he would get some anytime soon but Christien had promised and Christien was a man of his word.

He sighed and looked at the frescoed walls. Camels, elephants, baboons and tigers, cockatoos, parrots and peacocks with tails that dragged on the ground. People too, from far-away lands with turbans on their heads and sarongs across their hips. Palm trees and ferns and oranges, mountains and rivers and deep jungle vines. The hearth itself was painted like a volcano, seams of red gleaming along the marble. It was a world of coloured fantasy, utterly unnatural yet serene as a dream.

He popped another Turkish Delight in his mouth, chewed slowly as he studied the baboons, thinking them a refreshing change from the cherubs and saints of Strasbourg or Melk. He'd never seen a baboon or an elephant, but then again, he'd never seen a cherub either. Saints, he reckoned, were a littler trickier to spot.

There was a flash outside one of the many windows and he moved to peer out at the courtyard one level down. Nothing. Not a brother bearing teapots or a Girl Criminologist who had somehow become his whole world. Only snowy cobblestone, gaslamps and steamcars. In the distance, the gothic spire of St. Stephan's as it towered over the city. And the dead.

There were so many and he missed his dark lenses. Even inside this room, there were easily a hundred, rising up the walls, hovering across the ceiling, pressed on each other like a tapestry, becoming a part of the Bergl frescoes themselves. They were staring at him as if waiting and he would have turned away if there weren't more outside.

There again – a flash of arrows and this time he saw it, tossing its mane as it pranced below, a horse as white as the snow with eyes like burning embers. It was a beautiful horse, he realized. A Lipizzaner but he remembered his promise and ran his hand across the glass of the window, causing frost to crawl across the pane and turning it opaque within seconds. Arrows shattered into another window, then another, and he followed, frosting each and every one until his breath hung in the air like crystal. But he had promised Christien and now he couldn't see the horse.

Suddenly from the hearth, there was a boom like the cannons of the *Stahl Mädchen* and smoke billowed out from the box. Slowly, he stepped toward it, heart racing like the horse outside when an unearthly squeal shattered the silence and the fire roared in its wake. The red horse, he knew, trying to reach him from the fireplace. He had been a fool to let them light it. Live coals rained down from the chimney and embers spewed across the floor. Smoke boomed again and he knelt down next to the hearth, took a deep breath before reaching a hand up into the firebox to close off the flue. His shoulder pushed against the hot marble and he called the frost to combat the sizzle of his sleeve and the puckering of his flesh. His fingers brushed against the damper. It was wedged, so he threw his weight behind it, pulling so violently that he fell backwards and soot spilled out like a river.

In his hand was a sword.

He stared at it, not fully believing. It was a beautiful sword, the hilt old gold, the blade a folded Damascus red. A sword in the chimney was an odd thing and he wondered what it meant, when suddenly the horse squealed again. The sword burst into flame, burning blue and yellow and he threw it to the floor. It shattered instantly, leaving an outline of ash on the tile.

He rolled to his knees and reached up again, this time closing his eyes and calling the dead. He could feel them moving to him, into him, freezing the life from him and the fire sizzled and sputtered and finally died, plunging the painted room into semi-darkness. He sagged back and studied the box, the Bergl volcano now sealed within a massive block of ice.

Even for him, it was unnatural.

He sat for a long moment, concentrated on the breath entering and leaving his body, marveled at the mechanics of breathing, when as if from a great distance, he heard a sound.

"Christien?" he called. "Christien, is that you?"

It was like the boom of cannon fire and it echoed through the rooms of the *palais,* bouncing off walls and ceiling and floor. There was a second boom and a third, shaking the very foundation with each pulse.

Slowly, he rose to his feet to stand in front of the doors that led to the hall.

"Is that the footman, sir? Are you bringing tea?"

The Bergl room boomed again and the doors shook and he peered through the keyhole, praying he might catch a glimpse of someone with a trolley on the other side of the door.

What he saw was the chest and shoulder and flaming eye of a black horse.

***

Neueste Nachrichten
Munich, Empire of Blood and Iron
Headline: MARY VETSERA!!

■■

■■

■■

CENSORED by order of His Imperial Majesty, Wilhelm II

Chapter 16

Of Black Wax, Red Ice and a Fatal Pronouncement

Valerie lived in a residential apartment in the Amalienburg wing of the Hofburg, attached to her mother's suites by antechambers that could have housed entire families. They had entered through the Guard's Gate, up several sets of stairs and Ivy's chest had tightened with each step. Surely she would be recognized if either Sisi or Gisela set eyes on her and that, she reckoned, would not bode well for sleuthing.

Valerie opened her suite by punching a code into a keypad on the door. Steam hissed and the door groaned open, gaslight glowing along the walls to reveal a very beautiful apartment papered in blue crewel. It was surprisingly feminine and Ivy wondered if Valerie had been allowed to choose her own furnishings or if they had been handed down over six hundred years of *Gilded* rule. While they could kill with a look, it seemed that for the most part, Habsburg women did what they were told.

Closing the door, Valerie pushed past her and tossed the sable onto the bed.

"My mother will have been notified," she said. "She will be here within minutes. You will help me with my buttons, then I will find something for you."

"Your mother can't see me," called Ivy as the woman disappeared into another room. "She knows I was with Sebastien."

"I will handle my mother. Wait here."

Ivy sighed and looked around the suite. It was larger than her entire house in Stepney, with chairs of gold, paintings of rural landscapes and draperies that could have made a dozen fancy dresses. There was a writing desk under the window and she crossed the room to study it. The papers and envelopes showed a woman clearly involved in many correspondences. She thought of the Helmsly-Wimpolls and smiled sadly. She hoped she would see them again one day.

On the corner of the desk, a stamp-press and black wax. Black was an unusual colour for letter-wax and she lifted the stamp to study the imprint in the gaslight. It was a swan, she realized, the arched neck and elegant wings unmistakable.

She is a Black Swan, Remy had said, *as dangerous as she is clever.*
What on earth was a Black Swan?

She returned the press as Valerie swept back into the room, clad now in funeral black. Ivy was certain there was a dagger strapped to her thigh, wondered if the locket around her neck contained poison and if the pins in her coif were secretly needles that could puncture arteries or veins. Her face, it seemed, took care of the hearts.

The woman tossed Ivy a grey frock coat and turned her back, revealing an open bodice in need of buttoning.

"Do this, now. Quickly."

Ivy shook her head but didn't argue. Already half-way Habsburg.

"Quickly!"

Ivy growled under her breath. The buttons were tiny black pearls, there were at least thirty and the Archduchess was considerably taller, but finally she finished with a twist of the clasp at the nape. Valerie slapped her hands away and spun, smoothing her clothing and arching her neck, poised like a swan. Like a beautiful black swan.

And with a click and hiss of steam, the door swung open and Empress Elizabeth of Austria strode into the room.

***

The smoking room was moderately less elaborate than the Bergl room, with the paintings restricted to the insides of gold frames. Servants waited discreetly, topping up the wine, refreshing the cigars and in another part of the *palais,* Christien could imagine a footman standing outside the Bergl door, waiting for Sebastien to be done with the ceiling.

He inhaled the cigar smoke deeply, let it bite inside his lungs like bitter teeth. Franz had been right. It was a good blend, earthy and sharp but he had to admit, his experience was limited to French cigarettes. Cigars waged a peculiar war on his tongue.

"Your clockwork arm is a marvel, yes? Like your own Wales," said the prince, and he blew out a ring of Havanese smoke. "I've heard France's Bonaparte owes half his body to piston and gear. Since Africa, you see. Too many spears."

Franz lounged on a green settee, cigar and wine glass poised in the same hand. The bright eyes rested for the most part on the dancing fire, but darted his way from time to time. Christien didn't care. Life had become entirely too surreal for him.

"You have known Marie-Valérie since you were children, yes?" asked Franz.

"So I'm told," said Christien, volunteering nothing.

"She is a remarkable woman, so tender, so modest."

Christien stared into the flames, remembering her modesty.

"She has fallen under the spell of the orphans," Franz continued. "She has always loved children. Such a tender heart."

The memory of her mouth on his, brandied peaches, Turkish Delight

"She wishes to found a hospital for children," he said. "In honour of Sophie and her courageous battle for life over death. She loves her family so very much."

Her hands under his shirt, pushing him onto the bed

"They protested at first but I knew they would come around. I am, after all, family."

"Come around?" asked Christien, only vaguely interested. The flames and his memories were much more seductive.

"To our marriage," said Franz. "We needed their approval but Rudolf would not give it. Not until this Christmas."

"Marriage?"

"Yes, we were betrothed this December. Of course, she will renounce all claims to the throne to marry me but we will be happy. I am certain of this."

Christien stared at him. The minor prince from Tuscany raised his glass in a toast.

"You would be fortunate to find a woman like Marie-Valérie, my friend. Perhaps you will be invited to the wedding?"

And he sipped the wine, his moustache wicking the amber like a straw.

For his part, Christien raised his glass and tossed the entire contents back in one go.

In the fire, he could have sworn the flames leapt a little higher.

***

Sebastien rushed to the door, twisted the skeleton key with both hands to lock it. The horse was as big as any he had ever seen, as black as night with mane and tail fairly dragging on the ground. Through the keyhole again, he could see it back up, toss its wild head, paw the air. Could see the flame burning in its eyes and he wondered how no one could hear such a creature in the elegant halls of the *palais*.

He glanced over his shoulder. Over a hundred dead, hundreds upon hundreds now, crowded and hungry, staring at him with empty eyes, watching, waiting for him to fail. Why did they want him to fail?

"Adiuva me," he said.

They stared at him. Did not blink, for most had neither eyes nor lids.

"Adiuva me," he repeated. "I need your help!"

Slowly as if immersed in tar, they opened their mouths. Wide and then wider, until they collectively became one large caverning mouth, breathing out the frost like a strong and biting wind. He closed his eyes and spread wide his arms, let them take him to the dark, to the empty, to the frozen, lost himself in their bitter landscape. It was where he belonged, he knew.

He turned and laid his palms on the white-washed wood of the door and soon, it was sealed shut with a thick layer of ice.

The horse struck again and ice splintered across the floor. Sebastien staggered back, knowing it would not hold for long. He needed something else and wondered if the *ligaturae spiritus* would protect him from such a creature. He had no pen. He had no ink. There was a blade in his boot however, the sliver of metal from the steam trunk he had shattered. He pulled it out and dropped to his knees, whispering prayers as the horse struck the door again.

The dead in the pavilion shrieked and writhed along the walls as he pressed the makeshift blade into his thumb. A pinprick of red popped up. He drew it down now, down his thumb, across his palm and stopped at his wrist, marveling at the immediate welling of red along the line. There wouldn't be enough blood, he knew. There was never enough blood.

He dipped his finger and began to write.

***

She was dressed in a gown of funeral black, her train at least ten feet long and fashioned from calendared silk. She said nothing, her deep blue eyes flashing between them and Ivy could see the losing battle against the tears. She watched the expressive hands curl into fists, wondered if the tight boning in her corset was to restrict her breathing and thus keep her calm. It was clear she was near her breaking point.

"Maman," said Valerie and without another word, she rushed into her mother's arms.

Ivy looked away as the women wept, for Rudolf, for each other, for the fractured state of the *Gilded Empire*. She couldn't help but remember her own mother at Lonsdale, taking her first steps after years of catatonia. She remembered the first smile, the first light of recognition in her eyes, that very first hug that could have broken all bones. All because of Sebastien, she remembered. The Mad Lord of Lasingstoke.

Sisi began to speak very quickly to her daughter and Ivy shuddered, hoping it wasn't a death sentence. Once again, she cursed her lack of linguistics. It was a handicap. If she survived, she promised herself, she would learn both French and German and maybe Latin. And then fisticuffs.

Valerie took her mother's hand. Together, Empress and Archduchess faced her, Elizabeth clutching her daughter to her side.

Ivy curtsied. It seemed the thing to do.

"My daughter tells me that she has *not* been kidnapped," said Sisi in her elegant accent. "But rather, she chose to accompany you and the de Lacey brothers from Strasbourg to Vienna. Is this true?"

"Yes, Your Most Royal Highness," she said. "Sebastien is being falsely accused. He has nothing to hide."

"He was under a blanket the last I saw."

"Hiding from spirits, Your Most Royal Highness. Not people. He has no interest in people."

"My son is dead," said Elizabeth. "I saw his body. He was shot in the head and I know what dear Sebastien does for his Empress."

"Not anymore," said Ivy. "He's exploring other methods for bringing villains to justice, but even still, I'm quite certain your son was no villain."

The blue eyes were heavier than anything she had ever borne, those of a mother grieving the loss of her child. That grief had destroyed her own mother. It was something Ivy understood all too well.

"I wish Sebastien to tell me this himself," said Sisi after a long moment. "Here, in the Hofburg. Have him come to me and tell me. I will know if he is telling the truth."

"And if he is shot on the way?"

"Then he will join my son in death."

"Why would Sebastien shoot Rudolf? What would he have to gain?"

"The locket," said Sisi. "It was very clear he wanted the locket."

"But he doesn't have it."

The Empress looked at Valerie.

"That would be a very foolish plan, don't you think?" Ivy added. "Murder a prince to take something, and then not take it? Sebastien is many things, but he is no fool."

"She is telling the truth," said Valerie. "Someone on the *Stahl Mädchen* had *der Archelicht*. I don't know whom or why."

Elizabeth glanced between the two of them.

"You are sure of this?"

Valerie nodded.

"Gisela?"

"We don't know," said Ivy. "But whoever has that locket is involved somehow in Rudolf's death."

There was silence in the suite and Ivy swallowed, summoning all her courage.

"And we need to know, Your Most Royal Highness…" Valerie shook her head. Ivy ignored her. "We need to know if he was alone."

Sisi's eyes flashed. "What are you saying?"

"Was he alone or was the girl Mary with him?"

She watched the battle play out on the Empress' flawless face. Watched the tears press, watched the nostrils flare but most of all, she watched the chin rise, telling her all she needed to know.

"Right," Ivy said. "And was she shot in the head as well?"

"How dare you—" snapped Valerie.

"No," said Sisi and she released her daughter's hand, stepped forward like the monarch she was. A most remarkable woman, Ivy thought. She wished she could have known her under other circumstances. "Not shot. But a blow, yes. A blow to the back of the head."

"A murder weapon?"

"None found."

"So she may have died from a fall down the stair?"

"An accident?"

"Perhaps."

And Ivy released a deep breath. Death by a firing squad was still a possibility but perhaps with a few less rifles.

"And who had access to the room after their bodies were discovered?"

"Loschek…"

"Loschek?"

"His valet," said Valerie.

"Loschek and Bratfisch, Count Hoyos, Dr. Widerhofer and Gisela."

"Gisela?"

"She was seeing to the German hunting party in a neighbouring lodge. Naturally, she was notified immediately."

Ivy glanced at Valerie. The woman was unreadable.

"Did you *see* the locket?" asked Ivy.

"Half of my son's head was missing," said the Empress. "I was not looking for jewelry."

Blast.

"Forgive me, Your Most Royal Highness," said Ivy and she curtsied again. "I have the mind of a detective. I often forget about the feelings. Please accept my apologies."

"I accept them," said Sisi. She drew herself up, regal and tall. "The state funeral is in two days. You have until then to tell me why my son died. After that, I am leaving for Corfu. I will not help you if you fail."

Valerie kissed her mother on the cheek.

"I will not fail you, *maman.*"

"My only child," said Sisi and stroked her face, tears welling once again. *"Kedvenc."*

"Szeretlek," said Valerie. She turned to Ivy. "We will go now. Quickly."

She released her mother and strode from the room, Ivy trotting at her heels. But before they left, Ivy swung back.

"Why he died?" she asked. "We have until the funeral to tell you *why* your son died?"

"Yes."

"Not *how?"*

The most beautiful woman drew a deep breath, gathering all the air in the room.

"I told you. He was shot."

"From afar?"

Silence for a long moment. Ivy squinted.

"From up close?"

Still nothing.

"From *very* close?"

And suddenly, all the scandal in the world couldn't compare to the despair in those most beautiful eyes.

"Blast," said Ivy.

"Mein Gott," whispered Valerie. *"Maman, nein…"*

"But how could you think Sebastien—"

"It was not Rudolf's pistol!" snapped Sisi. "His pistol is missing. He used a weapon belonging to someone else."

Her face was a stone, eyes like glittering sapphires, and Ivy felt a wave of dread sweep down from her temples. She swallowed, took a deep breath.

"Have you determined the owner of this pistol?"

"If we had, you and I would not be having this conversation." She raised her chin. "I have already given the word to the Silver Hussars and the order is being written into law. As of this moment, you – Miss Ivy Savage *von* Steam, are a marked woman, with the sentence of death upon your head. Sebastien de Lacey, Christien de Lacey and you will find no peace in Europe until I have justice for my son. There is nowhere you can run that the *Gilded* arm of the Habsburgs cannot reach."

This would be the time to run, Ivy thought, *if only her legs would move.*

"There is one chance for you and only one."

"What is that?" Ivy whispered.

"You say you have the mind of a detective. You have two days to prove it. Find out who made my son put a pistol to his head, or my Silver Hussars will do the same for you."

Her knees were shaking. She couldn't move.

"And if I can't?"

"You will use your influence over Sebastien de Lacey."

"I don't…" Her voice, it seemed, had fled. "I don't understand?"

The tears that had been so threatening, began to spill.

"I've lost my son," the Empress said. "And I want him back."

Her own mother watching Tobias sink below the Thames, sinking herself in the black waters of despair.

"No," said Ivy.

Valerie squeezed her mother's hand, straightened like the swan she was.

"Your Miracle Man can do this. I know he can. I saw it."

"Please, no," Ivy said again. "You can't ask that."

"Go now," said Sisi. "And do not fail."

Without a word, Valerie whirled and swept from the room, Ivy a pale vapor behind her.

***

Austrian wine, Christien mused. Heavy on the sugar, easy on the tongue, the alcohol hitting his blood like poison. Had nothing to do with Valerie or the wedding or his miserable, wretched life. Nothing at all.

"Now we'll have to delay the wedding yet again," said Franz. "Most unfortunate time for the prince to die, if I may be honest. I wonder what really happened at that hunting lodge? And where on earth is Mary Vetsera? I can't believe she killed him. She was barely eighteen. Charming girl, if a little vulgar. She had dancing eyes, you know. There was definitely something special in those eyes."

Franz had been speaking nonstop about the details, but for Christien, it had become a blur of Imperial ritual and church custom. A holy Habsburg blur.

Footsteps across the tile and the valet hurried into the smoking room, moving quickly without appearing rushed. He stopped beside Franz, gave a little bow, leaned in to whisper in his ear.

The prince sat up abruptly, glanced his way.

"Oh god," Christien rubbed his forehead with his human hand. His left was currently a flint, in the process of lighting another cigar. "What has he done this time?"

"I don't know, *mein Herr,* " said the valet. "The Bergl room is on fire but the door is frozen shut."

"Another miracle?" asked Franz.

Christien sighed and rose to his feet. "By any chance, do you have laudanum?"

"I am a physician," said the prince. "Laudanum is a god-send."

Together, the two men accompanied the valet up the short flight of marble stairs and down a series of corridors. Christien could smell the smoke long before they reached the room however, and he was surprised to find the door covered in sheets of silver ice. Servants were hauling at it with axes, shards scattering with each blow while ash floated down from the ceiling like snowflakes. Snowflakes and ash. It was a contrast. Only Sebastien could manage something so unnatural.

"Is he still inside?"

"We do not know," said the footman. "We cannot open the door."

Christien strode past him, reached to push on the handles and realized, with an odd detached thought, that one of his fingers was still a flint. It was utterly surreal and not for the first time, he wished Frankow had just let his brother die.

He ignored it, pushed on the door, felt it as solid as brick. Damn Sebastien and his ghosts.

"He's sealed it from the inside," he said. "Is there by chance another door?"

"Down the hall," said Franz. "But it is for the guests' servants. The door is always locked and the key is inside."

"I can unlock it."

Franz nodded, leaving the frozen door and moving east down the corridor to a second very small door. Franz rattled the handle but shook his head.

"No one has used this in months," he said. "It was for the servants, for refilling the firewood."

Christien held up the clockwork hand, pressing down the flint and punching a key on his wrist. An iron digit popped up.

"Skeleton key," Christien said and leaned in to the door, inserting the key into the lock. His wrist spun once, twice, three times and the door clicked open. He took a deep breath and pushed his way in.

It was like nothing he had ever seen before and immediately his breath frosted from his lips. The Bergl jungle had been transformed into a cavern of polar glass. Walls of ice curved into the frescoed ceilings, swept across the tiled floors like a frozen lake. Every inch of wall was coated so thickly he could barely see the paintings beneath. In fact, the fantastical animals were distorted, transformed into creatures of horror and myth with eyes too large and teeth too fierce. The ceilings were the same, as exotic jungle birds took on predatory airs, beaks and talons like blades under the refraction of the ice.

He was in an antechamber, he realized, unlit but flickering from the fire in the room beyond. Smoke was hovering like a blanket and Franz followed him carefully as he made his way across the floor. Even under his shirt, the cold ran down the metal brace to bite the flesh of his upper arm. He wondered how the fire could have no effect on the ice, or if ghost ice could even melt, but the questions left his mind when he spied the first of the blood.

Red in frozen stalactites from the ceiling, red in horrific scratches along the walls, red in icy rivers across the floor. The Bergl room of Archduke Franz Salvatore was a cavern entirely of red and in the middle, his brother knelt, flames dancing across his shoulders, arms in tattered ribbons at his sides.

"Mein Gott," breathed Franz.

"Bastien?" he asked, his voice echoing through the foyer and he moved carefully across the icy tile. He spied the blanket, discarded on the floor and he scooped it up, laid it across his brother's shoulders causing the flames to hiss and die beneath its weight. He knelt down, careful not to shatter anything into a thousand pieces. With Sebastien, one never knew.

"Bastien?" he asked again and he raised an eyelid. Pupils wide and unfocused, tiny blood vessels had ruptured in the sclera. Not surprising given the blood loss and the violent manner in which he had likely lost it. His carotid pulse next, weak and thready, his breaths shallow and quick. The cheeks were sunken, his colour grey but he was alive. Christien realized that he was supposed to be grateful, but he wasn't. Sad state, all things considered.

"Hypovolemic shock," said Franz. "I will call for more blankets."

"No," said Christien. "They won't help."

He reached down now, took one of his brother's hands, turned it over to study the wounds. Likely an attempt to write those damned Latin prayers but he had not stopped at his palms, and the slices traveled up his wrists and across his forearms. Both forearms, and he remembered that his brother was proficient with both right and left hand. Perfect for killing oneself, if only one would die.

His brother was insane, it was evident now. Not merely troubled, not odd or eccentric or even mad. Violent and paranoid schizophrenia was the first of many on the tip of his tongue, and that would be a fitting diagnosis if this were any other man. It didn't explain the ice and frost, didn't explain the winds and the ghosts and the walking dead, couldn't explain the supernatural landscapes through which his brother moved. Insanity came the closest, but even insanity couldn't explain all this.

Truth be told, he wasn't sure anything could.

Slowly, Sebastien raised his head.

"I didn't leave," he said in a very small voice. "I tried to write the *ligaturae spiritus* but it was too slippery and I made a mess. But the horse didn't get in and I didn't leave. I am trying, Christien. I am, honestly."

Yes, insanity was far too easy a diagnosis.

Christien sighed, slipped an arm under his brother's. Franz joined him and together they helped him to his feet.

Chapter 17

Of Bohemian Skulls, Biblical Woes and the Surprising Skillset of a Swan

It didn't matter that it was late and dark – she would have been lost anyway. Narrow passages, steep marble steps, doors behind doors. The Hofburg was a labyrinth with every wing telling a different story as six hundred years of history played out in frame, furnishing and fabric.

Under normal circumstances, she would have been delighted. Now she was terrified. Now she was numb. Now there was nothing else but Rudolf.

Finally, the Archduchess stopped at a door, turned her elegant face toward Ivy.

"Rudolf's private apartments," she said. "No one but Loschek was allowed."

"He didn't live here?"

"In another wing, with his wife and daughter. But he spent much time here."

She pressed a code into the panel. No steam this time but the sound of grinding gears as the door slowly swung open. As she turned up the gaslight, Ivy was surprised to see a suite very different than anything she would have expected in the Hofburg. It was a strange room, a sad room and it was distinctly Bohemian.

Fabric of burgundy velvet draped the walls, Persian rugs atop Oriental rugs atop Berber, two black fireplaces at opposite ends of the room. Candles and Geisler tubes and stargazing telescopes and all manner of animal skeletons. Encyclopedias crammed in every shelf, cork frames with butterflies pinned, crystal decanters and cigar trays and clockwork spinning gadgets and Hungarian-embroidered cushions and strange bulbs with copper filaments. Atop an elaborate writing desk, a human skull watched everything with empty eyes.

It was the room of a thinker, an inventor, a reader, a man of reason and philosophy and science, a sharp mind filled with modern ideas and the natural world. A liberal, as Valerie had put it, though not by any stretch of the imagination, a Habsburg.

Of all the times she needed to be sharp, Ivy Savage felt like stone.

"This was *his* room?" she asked as she moved to the windows, darkened with black sashes.

"His bachelor's apartments," said Valerie. "He lived here before his wedding."

"But that was years ago." She paused at the desk. The skull grinned up at her, cynical, taunting. "He was a writer."

"Histories and treaties, studies of environments and the ways of men upon the land."

She lifted a stack of letters. Envelopes with names such as Tesla, Edison, Clemenceau and Szeps. One from Edward, Prince of Wales and she knew they had been friends, although it was a vague remembrance from a headline or broadsheet long ago. No letters from Mary Vetsera, no mystical stamps of swans in black wax, no 'smoking pistol' as the term went. Nothing to assist her and she had to admit, with a man of this status and his sheer breadth of domestic and foreign affairs, she was completely out of her depth.

One thing was clear to her, however. The Prince of the *Gilded Empire* was very much a bird in a gilded cage. And if his mother was to be believed, this same man – heir to the Habsburg dynasty and half the known world, had blown his head off in a rural hunting lodge.

No wonder the room felt heavy.

"He loved these rooms," Valerie sighed. "He spent more time here than in his home these last months."

"Unhappy marriage?"

"Habsburg marriage."

Ivy replaced the letters, ran her fingers across the dome of the skull.

"What about the lodge? What was it called again?"

"Mayerling. For a town in the Vienna Woods."

"Is that far from here?"

"Twelve miles or so. Why?"

"Did he spend much time there?"

"It was his escape. Away from the mire that is the Hofburg."

"Vienna Woods." She looked up. "Is that where the German hunting party was staying? Your mother said Gisela was attending them."

"What would that matter?"

"Well, is it customary for foreigners to stay so close to a royal residence?"

"With an Imperial guest, yes. Very. But if not, then no. It is odd."

"Hm. The hunting party was at the Hofburg that night and saw everything that happened. We need to talk to them. We need to find out why they were there."

"I will ask Taaffe about this. He will have names." Valerie crossed the floor to stand near the dark window, pulled the sash with the tip of a finger. "I want him back."

The sentence of death upon your head.

She took a deep breath.

"Does it make sense to you, what your mother said?"

"About?"

She bit her lip, not wanting to say the word. Valerie looked away, tears welling behind the steely eyes.

"My brother was not a happy man. He was being stifled politically and domestically. He and Father would always argue over the course of the Empire and our choice of allies. Rudolf wanted stronger ties with France but Father wanted none of it. We all hate Wilhelm but he is

Kaiser of *Blood and Iron* and we are Germany's first and dearest friend."

"Empires have come and gone since the beginning of time," said Ivy. "Princes generally wait for their turn to take the throne, not kill themselves as a means to avoid it."

"Rudolf was not a normal prince." She smiled sadly. "He was the people's prince. They loved him so very much, but they were unhappy, so he was unhappy."

Ivy looked around at the wild décor, more befitting a poet than a prince.

"He was a romantic," she said.

"An Austrian romantic," Valerie shrugged. "If such a thing can exist. We are a proud people, a pragmatic people. We are known for our quiet passions. But new Vienna has embraced this Bohemian fascination with truth, beauty, freedom and death. It started with the revolutions in France but the philosophies have swept across all of Europe. Here in the city, at least a dozen young men and women kill themselves each week."

"That's terrible."

"Terrible and romantic. A terrible, romantic illusion. My father refuses to think about it. He says it is the foolish and destructive pursuit of a foolish and destructive age. He rejects the notion, but along with it, the age."

She sighed, peered out the window again.

"It was the first thing I thought when *Maman* told me he was dead. But then I heard Mary was with him. That made no sense."

"To die with your lover?" asked Ivy. "But it's the ultimate romance isn't it? A love that lasts beyond death? It's Romeo and Juliet."

"There is no love beyond death. There is only death. And Mary Vetsera was no Juliet."

Outside, the snow had turned to sleet, wet slicks sticking to the glass and sliding down like icy tears. The moon flickered in and out as clouds, turned silver and black, moved across its face.

"Pick something," said Valerie.

"Sorry?"

"You said Remy's brother needed something of his. Pick something."

She looked down at the desk. There was a gleam from inside the skull's empty eyes and she lifted it to reveal a simple band of gold.

"A wedding ring?" She held it up in the dim light. "He leaves his wedding ring under a skull?"

"As I said, Habsburg marriage."

"This should do then." She slipped it over her thumb. "And may I take these letters?"

"They might be important state documents. You could be shot for that alone."

"If you want me to figure out why he died, there may be clues, motives, suspects hidden in these pages."

"You don't read German."

"But you do." Ivy picked up the letters, flipped them through her hands. "Tesla and Edison – they are inventors, but these?"

"Politicians and liars," said Valerie.

"The Prince of Wales?"

"A friend."

"Why has no one gone through these?"

"They are personal."

"They are evidence."

Valerie took the letters, slipped them inside her bodice.

"They will tear this room apart after the funeral but they will not find the pistol."

"Is there actually an investigation being conducted or am I it?"

"It will be dealt with the way any Habsburg scandal is dealt with. By ritual cleansing. He will be erased from our history."

"Erased? How?"

"After the funeral, his name will never be uttered again. Stability, Strength, Holiness, Order. It is the *Gilded* way."

There is nowhere you can run that the Gilded arm of the Habsburgs cannot reach.

Valerie crossed the room to a bookshelf. She pressed a beam of wood and it creaked aside, revealing a hidden door and long dark flight of stairs. Ivy peered down. It smelled of dust and grease and six hundred years of secrets.

The Archduchess paused, swept one last look around the room of her brother, Crown Prince and heir to half the known world. He would be erased, she had said, from the political arena of nations, erased from the history of a dynasty extending back over centuries. Erased from the landscape of *Gilded* politics and policies and dreams. But as Ivy looked at Valerie - younger by ten years - she wondered if he could ever be erased from heart of his little sister.

No wonder she wanted him back.

With one last glance, Ivy left the strange sad room of a Crown Prince and the all-knowing gaze of the Bohemian skull.

***

He measured the opium in careful drops, stirred the teaspoon into the wine and watched it change from red to inky brown. He was amazed that Franz had given Sebastien another room, let alone wine. Apparently, the man was fascinated by the arcane and believed Sebastien a miracle sent by God. Now, when they had nowhere else to go, Christien was not about to dissuade him.

They were in room far removed from the Bergl jungle, with arched ceilings, crystal chandeliers and shelves filled with very old books. There were two beds draped in green brocade, club chairs and a porcelain chiminea for warmth. After the jungle of fire and ice, it felt like heaven.

Christien passed the glass to his brother.

"Here, drink this."

"Is there cinnamon?"

"No Bastien. No cinnamon."

"Nutmeg?"

"We're lucky to get the wine, otherwise your laudanum would consist of one hundred percent opium. Believe me, that would be worse."

Sebastien sighed and reached for the glass. Both hands and forearms were bandaged and the blood had finally stopped seeping afresh into the linen. He looked terrible, with dark circles under his eyes and hollows in his cheeks. His shirt had been stained beyond repair and the prince had arranged for another from his own personal wardrobe. It was military grey linen but better than counting all of his ribs.

"Drink."

Sebatstien obeyed, slowly, unhappily and made a face before tossing it back.

"Swallow."

He did, stuck out his tongue in displeasure. Handed back the glass.

"Right," said Christien. "Look at me again."

Christien examined his eyes, brown for now, pupils dilated, schlera ribboned with red.

"So," he said. "The black horse."

Sebastien looked away. "I don't want to talk about him."

"Why are these horses coming for you, Bastien? Do you know? Is it something you've read in a story somewhere?"

"Crown Prince Rudolf is dead," he said. "And so is the girl. It's my fault."

"There's no mention of the girl in the papers."

"She's dead."

"Did you see her die?"

"I don't want to talk about it."

"Did you see her *die?*"

"There were Germans in the forest."

"Germans?"

"Germans and ravens and Arclight and her…"

"Her? The girl?"

Slowly, he reached into his pocket, pulled out a small white shape, clutched it tightly in his wrapped hand.

"Blood of my blood," he said. "Bone of my bone."

"God, Bastien…"

"I need to think," he said. "I need to remember. Because I can't fight. There are too many arrows and a sword. Why a sword? I don't use swords. Bullets weren't invented but surely God must have known about bullets."

"Bastien, you're making no sense."

"The crowns, Remy. The Crown Prince gets the crown. They want to give me the crown and I don't want it. I don't want any of them."

Christien sighed, watched his brother sink back into the pillows, eyes growing glassy and dull. Laudanum was one of the few things that kept Bastien controlled. Arvin Frankow had introduced it years ago when Bastien was barely fourteen. It was remarkable how his brother wasn't an addict. He'd seen the effects of overuse in hundreds of patients, of the euphoria that gave way to depression, the relief that quickly became a horror all its own. He wouldn't wish that on anyone, not even his brother.

He rose from the bed, taking the bottle of wine with him as he strolled over to the door. Sebastien was not to leave the room, nor was he to be left alone – those were Franz's two conditions. Not until the Archduchess came back and knowing Valerie, it could be a very long time.

He wondered if a locked door would stop a ghost horse?

And he shook his head. Delusions, clearly. While there were many, many things about his brother he couldn't explain, that was an easy one.

Still, he dragged a walnut chair and propped it under the knob, just in case.

He sank into one of the club chairs and stared out the window at the night sky. The world outside was black, cold rain now freezing against the pane like icicles. He wondered what Valerie and Ivy were doing, if they were in the Hofburg, if they had been discovered and if so, how it would have played out.

And here he was, sitting in a library, waiting for horses.

On the table between the chairs, there was an old bible with gold-edged pages and parchment as thin as an eyelash. He reached for it, flipped it open to browse through the illustrations. They were very colourful and he was certain that they would have had some meaning if only he knew the stories. He had never read the Bible. It was not a thing his French family had ever encouraged, even with a church on the property. Religion was Sebastien's obsession, not his father's, not Rupert's and certainly not his. Rules and regulations, clean and unclean. So foreign to the world of science. Although he had to admit that in a forensics lab, rules and regulations had to be followed and 'clean or unclean' might mean a world of difference in the integrity of evidence chain.

He didn't believe any of it, however. Life was life, death was simply the end of it. There was no God to pronounce judgment, only a jury of twelve and a hanging at the Ol' Bailey. But then again, what the deuce did Sebastien see? What were ghosts anyway but spirits of the dead? And if there were spirits, did that mean there was a heaven? Was there a hell? Who determined entry, one way or the other and why?

He flipped through the pages, trying to find cherubs like the ones in the paintings at Melk. He couldn't imagine a heaven where flying babies were a part and wondered if God had a sense of humour. Not likely but then again, God had created Sebastien.

He paused in his flipping to study his clockwork hand, a hand given him by Ivy and the London Ripper. If there was a God, what he might think of a man who had killed so many, so viciously, now sitting here reading his book? Would it matter that he had no recollection, or that it was the spirit of his father or a cataclysmic, world-ending locket? Would he still be held responsible for the sins committed by his missing hand?

He flipped to the very end. The illustrations were bizarre – dragons and lambs, lampstands and plagues. There had to be something in the pages of this dusty old book but the truth was, he didn't know what he was searching for. There was a mystery but no evidence. Or perhaps, so much that it boggled the mind. *If we are denied forensic evidence,* Ivy had said, *we must move on to circumstantial.* He raised his clockwork arm and pressed a hex-nut key on his wrist. A fountain pen popped out, replacing a finger.

At the end of the book, there was a page with an illustration on one side and blank on the other. He glanced around before quietly tearing it from the spine. There was no hellfire, there was no brimstone. Not even a valet to reprimand him. He was entirely alone with only his mind for a tool. *Given the current circumstances,* she had said, *we can do quite a lot of sleuthing from this very place.*

"By God, Ivy," he muttered. "Perhaps you were right. Old buffer, indeed."

And he poured himself a glass of Sebastien's wine, settled back into the chair and began to write.

***

A private steam carriage awaited them as they snuck out a side door onto an empty lane. The air was cold, her clothes damp and Ivy shivered, seeing her breath in the dark cab. She was grateful to be leaving the Hofburg and she stared out the icy window, trying to rein in her racing thoughts. Outside, the sky was black save for a moon that ducked in and out of clouds like the Mad Lord with a blanket.

She missed him.

There was simply no way he could do what they were asking. It was impossible but knowing him, in order to save their lives he would do the impossible. She had been set on a path of madness and destruction, with Sebastien as the target. Perhaps better to lead them away from him, give him a chance to escape the tightening noose that was currently around all of their necks.

She should have gone with him to Istanbul. She should have gone with him to Corfu. Anywhere would have been better than this.

There is nowhere you can run that the Gilded arm cannot reach.

"Remy spoke very highly of you."

She looked up, blinking.

"He did?" She frowned. "When?"

"During your engagement," said Valerie. "He would write letters telling me all about your adventures in the morgues and mortuaries of London. He was quite fascinated."

"Didn't last," she said. "Fascination turned to expectation, once there was a ring."

"It always does."

The Archduchess looked away and Ivy watched the streetlamps flash across her elegant face. Wondered who she might be had life been different, had she not been born Habsburg.

"So why did you write him?" she asked. "You had princes. You had a purpose. Why bother with someone like him? What could he possibly mean to you?"

The steely eyes lingered a moment on the streets.

"As you said, expectation comes with the ring. With Remy, there could never be a ring. Fascination lived." She blinked slowly. "It still does."

You marry whom you are told to marry and you produce an heir.

The Habsburgs of Vienna wore despair like a crown.

Time dragged as the wheels slid and bumped through slush on the streets. The cityscape was changing from monumental to residential, with rows of fine white houses and wide boulevards reminiscent of Pall Mall. Ivy wondered if they were heading back to Franz's city *palais* when finally the carriage pulled up in front of a palatial home with many doors and even more windows, all drawn and dark.

"The Vetsera mansion," said Valerie after a moment. "The house will be empty. It is a good time. Helene is not in Vienna. She would have been removed from the city along with her other children and most of their personal staff."

Through the carriage window, they stared at the building, its wrought-iron fence and skeletal cherry trees, bare branches covered in icicles. There were no lights from inside and Ivy swallowed, remembering once again the night at Easterton Frederick Crumb's. She prayed there would be no singing lockets, no ghostly frost nor shooting. Most of all, no shooting. Death, she was beginning to realize, was a very persistent suitor.

Valerie stepped from the carriage and Ivy fell in like a hound at the heels of a hunter as they pushed through the gate and up to the front door. The Archduchess rapped the knocker once, twice and drew herself to stand tall and regal. Ivy watched how easily she slipped into the role, how easily the mantle fell across her shoulders. She was every bit a monarch as her mother, thought Ivy. And just as deadly.

There was no answer, no movement from within the house, and swiftly, the Archduchess slipped a set of pins from her hair. Ivy watched with wide eyes as Valerie bent to the lock. *Aristocrats,* she thought. Crackerjacks and screwsmen, the lot of 'em.

Together, they slipped into the empty house, a crime witnessed only by the sleepy, hide-and-seek gaze of the moon.

***

The *HMAS Royal Carolina* rolled like thunder over the Hofburg, her fleet covering all points to protect her flanks. She was a grand airship with a canvas of black and gold, scalloped brass fins and copper rudders, rings of aluminium and girders of polished steel. Beneath it, the cabin was as ornate as a royal frigate, her hull painted a gleaming white with alternating ebony and gold fittings. The bowsprit was a woman of solid gold and on her stern, silver mer-people frolicked in ivory waves.

She was flying the colours of the House Saxe-Cobourg and Gotha.

"Prepare for docking," called a tinny voice through the pipe and the airship shuddered as cables were dropped.

Inside the saloon, Albert Edward Prince of Wales lifted the scotch to his mustachioed lips and stared out the window at the moon rising over the dome of the Hofburg. He hated the Hofburg. Bloody labyrinth, all rococo and red. He hated the Habsburgs too, the lot of 'em. Pompous Franz Joseph, sylphlike Sisi, spooky Sophie and terrifying Gisela. Hated the Germans too, if he was honest. Wilhelm was a boor, as undeserving of a kingdom as a pauper or scullery maid. Bonaparte and the Frenchies were sworn enemies but marginally more tolerable than the entire eastern block. The Russians were another story, and another allegiance, entirely.

The only Habsburg he'd even remotely fancied was Rudolf and dashitall if the bugger hadn't just shot his damned head off with a pistol.

A shudder as docking ports were engaged and he reached into his waistcoat pocket, held the locket up to the moonlight.

"Do you do anything?" he asked her. "Anything at all? If I was to believe Bookie or Jackie or any of the Clubbers, you've a regular host of angels inside but dashitall if you don't do a bloody tip for me."

The locket gleamed innocently.

"Well, don't tell 'em that I had you nicked," he said. "Or there'll be hell t'pay! And I'm not giving you to Willie, that's damned straight! All he wants is another British trophy and wouldn't you be just the trinket? We may just start a war over you yet! Ah hah! Ah hah!"

As he guffawed at his own joke, he slipped the locket back into his pocket and prepared to descend the gangplank for the symposium at the Grand, the funeral and then the meeting of the French Anarchist Summit.

He never thought of it as destiny. Just another carefully-scripted step in an illustrious career of carefully-scripted steps, all over the globe, all over the map. Step, step, step. Such was the life of a monarch-in-waiting.

Impossible to believe that something like an innocuous little locket could ever orchestrate such steps.

Chapter 18
Of Romeo and Juliet, a Holy Roman Bible and
Stories Steeped in Blood

With all the automatons in the city of Vienna, Ivy was shocked at the lack of them in such fine, fancy homes. Once again, it proved to be a blessing.

As her eyes adjusted to the darkness, she gazed over the grand foyer of the Vetsera mansion. Wallpaper and lace, portraits and potted palms. A winding staircase led to the bedroom suites the next floor up. The house had a distinctly bourgeois décor. New money, Ivy reckoned, trying to make its mark in an old city. It did fit, however, with the concept of a bold young girl stealing the heart of a disillusioned prince.

The house was dark and quiet as the women moved up the stairs. There was a corridor with many doors and without hesitation, Valerie entered the very first one. Ivy followed and the Archduchess closed the door, turning the key in the lock behind her.

"The room of Mary Vetsera," she said, not bothering to whisper.

"Have you been here before?"

"Never."

"Then how do you know this is the one?"

"Austrian protocol," she said. "Youngest to oldest to the parents down the hall. Mary was the youngest."

"You're serious?"

"Stability, Strength, Holiness, Order. Welcome to Vienna."

And she reached up for the gaslamp, twisted the brass screw but there was no customary hiss or catch.

"The gas has been turned off," she growled. "I expected this."

And she slipped a hand to her thigh, pulled a device that Ivy recognized immediately.

"A pocket torch," she said. "Do all Swans carry them?"

"Only the clever ones."

Beams of light swept across the room and Ivy spied her third desk of the night.

She crossed the floor towards it, relieved to see matches and a candle on a brass stand. She lit it and immediately the room was bathed in warm light.

"Oh my," she said and her heart sank inside her chest.

It was the room of a young girl, no more than a child. Rose-painted walls, large iron bed with pink coverlet. A locket on a wardrobe, ribbons on a mirror, dried flowers in the large window. Dolls propped against pillows, their eyes empty and black.

And just like the room of the Crown Prince, it was sad.

"I'm surprised Taaffe hasn't had it cleaned out," said Valerie. "He will have her erased from public record as well. He is already censoring the papers and the broadsheets."

"How old was she?"

"Seventeen perhaps."

"Seventeen," said Ivy. "And already seducing a prince."

"As I said, welcome to Vienna."

Ivy gazed around, taking it all in and wondering where to start.

"Sebastien said she was stealing the locket, but why? For whom? This place is a palace. Certainly they couldn't have had a lack of money."

"You know nothing of the ways of the second society."

"Second society?"

"Bourgeois, Neu Monde. New money." The Archduchess began moving around the room slowly, methodically, the beam from her pocket torch flashing from bed to wardrobe to the embroidery on the walls. "First society is that of well-born, aristocratic families. Long histories, noble ties, well-established at court. Those in the Second Society live their lives trying to become First."

"And how would they do that?"

"The *Gilded* way." Valerie turned back, arched a brow. "By marrying into it."

Ivy grinned.

"It was impossible of course, for Mary to marry Rudolf. We are Catholics. The pope would never permit a divorce and my father would never allow it. She knew this."

"You can know something," said Ivy. "And still not *know* something. The heart is always at war with the head."

"The head should win." Valerie snorted. "She wanted his money."

"You don't think she loved him?"

"Mary Vetsera loved Mary Vetsera. No one else."

"And Rudolf?"

The Archduchess returned to the desk, slid open a narrow drawer.

"I think my brother loved the idea of her. He was trapped in a Habsburg marriage, remember? Stifled by my father and the *Gilded* court. He loved her freedom, her frivolity. She was wicked and young and daring and free and she was his last, best attempt at independence."

"So," said Ivy. "No Romeo and Juliet, then?"

"There is no such thing. Love always dies."

On the desk, there was a document framed in gold. Ivy picked up and held it to the candlelight.

"*Institute for Daughters of the Nobility,* Highest Standing. What is this?"

"A Finishing School for the Second Society, " said Valerie, reaching instead for a stack of letters.

"What did they learn?"

"I wouldn't know. Habsburgs are born finished." She flipped them in her hands, studying the addresses, the names. "My cousin Marie…

Maureen Allen from America… the *Freudenau Racing Club…*"

"Racing?" asked Ivy. "She enjoyed racing?"

"Her uncles breed race horses. Successfully, I might add. The papers called her the 'Turf Angel', for she was always at the tracks. In fact, I believe it was at a racetrack where she met your Crown Prince Edward. Epsom Downs, I believe, in Surrey."

Ivy gaped at her.

"She knew the Prince of Wales?"

"I said she *met* him," she said as she continued to rifle the envelopes. "I did not say she knew him. They did not move in the same circles."

Ivy bit her lip. Edward, Prince of Wales, had been a player in the affair of the London Ripper. To have him shew up again, connected to both Rudolf and Mary, was suspicious. She remembered the intelligence in his eyes, the subtle threat of his hand over hers in the eight-wheeled steamcar. She still had his cane at Lasingstoke.

She looked back at the desk. There was a wooden letterbox near the candle and she took it in her hands. It was heavy but locked with a tiny latch and gear set. She held it up to Valerie.

The Archduchess snorted. "You learn nothing in your English schools."

"Reading, Writing and 'Rithmetic. For lock-smithery, you must go to Oxford."

Valerie took the letterbox and placed it back on the desk, slipping the pins from her coif. Ivy watched as she worked her picks, cursed the fact that she had not mastered the art. Sebastien had promised to teach her but she'd put it off in favour of shooting.

Her heart tightened in her chest at the thought of him. She missed him. Desperately.

Three twists and a press. The lock clicked, the gear whirred and slowly, the wooden lid began to rise.

Inside were letters, some in envelopes, others tied with ribbons, but the one thing Ivy noticed above all else was the fact that without exception, each one bore the imprint of a Swan stamped in black wax.

***

Christien's eyes were growing heavy, due in part to the Austrian red on top of the Austrian white. He was sure it had to be morning but through the window, the sky was still black as pitch. He glanced over at Sebastien, unmoving on the bed, lost to the effects of the laudanum. He wondered if his brother dreamed and if so, of what? The dead or the living? Of the two, he didn't know which was more frightening.

The bible lay open on the table. It was a strange book, all poetry and prophecy, promises and blood. Adam and Eve, Abraham, Isaac and Moses. Cain and Abel, brothers with different sacrifices, set against each other from the beginning of time. Before he'd gotten fully into the wine, he'd reached a peculiar chapter called Ezekiel. There had been a very odd part with a valley of bones that had miraculously come to life. It had reminded him of Sebastien and the skeletons of Melk and he couldn't shake the sight of them from his mind. It was something he had never expected, could not explain using any vein of scientific or rational thought. But then again, he was a de Lacey. 'Rational' was not in the family vocabulary.

He sighed, feeling the melancholy begin to weigh on him once again. He raised his clockwork hand and with only a fleeting thought, the dagger sprang up instead of a finger. The edge of the blade was fascinating, beautiful and clean and gleaming in the gaslight. He wondered if he should indeed kill himself, as he had contemplated that night after the debacle in the Hofburg. There would be nothing to return to in England. Rupert was moving on with Mary Jane, a shrewd and beautiful woman who had promised she'd be his forever. Even an East End whore had found a better prospect than Christien de Lacey.

His brother moaned and Christien turned his eyes toward the bed. Perhaps he should do the world a favour and kill Bastien before he turned the blade upon himself. He wondered how to do it, if he would sever the carotid artery or slide the shiv into his heart. The shiv, most certainly. It would minimize the cleanup afterward. Franz would have enough on his plate with providing harbour for two 'French Anarchists', without the bother of so many bloody sheets.

He looked down at the bottle, its contents dark as syrup. He had saved just enough to afford Bastien a second dose of laudanum. Perhaps he would wait, give his brother another shot before sliding the blade home. It would be a quiet way to go, all things considered. According to one of those first stories, Cain offered the wrong sacrifice to a holy God, earning nothing but wrath and condemnation. But with the brothers de Lacey, both sacrifices were steeped in blood and still the wrath came down like brimstone.

He raised the glass, watched the dark contents swirl and slip. Cain had killed Abel, then wandered in exile for the rest of his life. Perhaps he wouldn't kill himself. Perhaps he would just live a life of exile and debauchery in the streets. Cigars, drink, the occasional prostitute. Perhaps become one. Forget medicine, forget science, even forget England. There was nothing left to keep him elevated and proper and he wondered what Paris would be like in the winter.

He picked up the page he had written, held it up to the light. ***Questions that need answering.***

- *What the deuce is on with Sebastien and these horses? White, Red and Black?*
- *How can the dead walk? Is there a scientific explanation to explain this? Is there a spiritual premise?*
- *Who is Mary Vetsera and how was she involved?*
- *What is Arclight and what does it do? Did it kill Rudolf and if so, how?*
- *Do I love Valerie von Habsburg?*

He stared at the last question on the list. He hadn't intended to write that, didn't in fact know where it came from. He was not an emotional man, not one inclined to the notions of love and romance. A love story was simply a quirk of the endocrine system, a mutual attraction to ensure offspring as the end result. He loved Valerie as much as he had loved Ivy, which was to say not at all. Although Valerie was a wicked roll, she was as damaged, if not more so, than himself.

Besides, she was engaged to her cousin, the minor prince from Tuscany. A much better prospect, obviously.

Meticulously, he crossed the last question off the list, turned the paper and his attention was caught by the illustration he had so unceremoniously torn from the book.

Vivid sky, thunderclouds, four horses trampling the world under their hoofs.

He was certain his heart skipped a beat.

Four horses. A white, a red, a black and one that was pale, ashen, barely a colour at all.

He swallowed.

His brother was waiting for horses.

He tossed back the remains of the wine and grabbed the Bible, flipping it open to the very end.

***

"A Black Swan?"

"Impossible," growled the Archduchess. "Mary was not a Swan."

Ivy reached into the letterbox, flipped through the jumbled stack. There were at least twenty letters, perhaps more, all stamped with a swan in black wax.

She looked up, locked eyes with the Archduchess.

"I think you should tell me what it means to be a Black Swan."

"It is forbidden to speak of it."

"If you don't, I shall throw all these out into the street. You can tell *me* or you can tell the people of Vienna."

"I will kill you before you do that."

"I don't think you will. You want to know the truth as much as I."

The Archduchess looked away, tiny muscles in her jaw twitching and Ivy felt a rush of pride. Not six months ago, she would have cursed her impetuous tongue, derided herself for being so bold. Now she was learning to use her words like swords, to parry and slice, to challenge and measure and test. It felt like iron in her bones.

"The Swans?" she prodded.

"*Schwarze Schwäne,*" said Valerie. "A loose affiliation of women with training in specific skills."

"Those being?"

She turned her steely eyes on Ivy.

"Seduction, espionage, sabotage, extortion, procurement of state secrets and the like."

"Murder?"

"Not usually. Men are easily led once you have been in their bed."

I wouldn't know, thought Ivy. The rate she was going, she wasn't sure it was something she would ever know.

Valerie picked up the framed document from the desk.

"If she *were* a Swan, she would have been recruited from this place. This *Institute for Daughters of the Nobility.* A place where these young *bourgeoise* are trained for lives as aristocratic wives. As such, it is a breeding ground for avarice and greed."

"It says Mary took Highest Standing."

"So it says."

Ivy looked down at the letter in her hand.

"So if Mary Vetsera were a Swan—"

"She wasn't."

"But if she was, what did she want from Rudolf?"

"The locket, obviously."

"But why? It wouldn't be a matter of stealing the locket for her own gain, surely. She probably didn't even know what it was. If she were a swan—"

"Which she wasn't."

"Then someone would have paid her to steal it." She glanced back down at the letters. "Edward? But why?"

"He would have known about *die Archelicht,* surely," said Valerie. "He was a frequent guest at the Mayerling hunts."

"Was Wilhelm?"

The Archduchess thought a moment.

"Not as frequent but yes, he was."

"What if…" Ivy ran her fingers over the wax, traced the raised edges of the swans. "What if Wales tapped Mary to stop Wilhelm from stealing it? No one likes Wilhelm, not even his uncle. What if he wanted to get it before Wilhelm got the chance?"

"So he hired Mary to do it for him. That is possible. Mary had been circling Rudolf for years and thanks to your Prince of Wales, she finally met him at Freudenau. My cousin Marie arranged a separate, more personal introduction later."

"That is a very long con."

"It was a very long seduction. We Viennese are careful and circumspect lovers."

The pocket torch gleamed from the desk and Valerie held a piece of jewelry up to the light. It was an iron ring, engraved with initials on the inside.

"Is that a wedding ring?" asked Ivy and she lifted the candle to peer closer. "What's this? ILVBIDT."

Valerie hissed.

"What does it mean?"

"In Liebe vereint bis in den Tod," she said. "United in love beyond Death."

"You see?" said Ivy, slipping the ring over her other thumb. "Classic Romeo and Juliet."

"This Juliet traded a symbol of undying love for a locket that spins rooms into gold." She took the letter from Ivy's hand. "I will go through these and see if it is Wales or Wilhelm or someone else who is guilty of this orchestration."

"You?" said Ivy. "I don't think that's a good idea."

"Well, certainly not you. You can't read German."

"These may not all be in German. Besides, you are a Black Swan *and* a Habsburg. If you take them, they will be erased from *your* history and we will all be shot for something we didn't do."

Slowly, ever-so-slowly, Valerie closed the lid of the letterbox and the gears clicked the lock back into place. Ivy grabbed it and the box hung between them.

"Don't do this," she said. "Sebastien is innocent. You know that now. Let us prove it, please."

"Let it go," said Valerie.

"Unless there is something to gain from seeing him dead." Ivy tugged the box her way. "Is there? You're a Swan too."

"Let it go, little writer. There are things in this world that are too big for you."

"Why have you been writing Christien de Lacey? What do you want from him?"

"Let it go and I will speak to my mother. She will relieve the sentence."

"I don't believe you."

"You don't have the choice."

And before Ivy could stop herself, her small woman's pistol was in her hand, swinging up and under the black corset of the Archduchess, pressing into her heart.

"Apparently I do."

Valerie smiled. It was as sharp and cold as her eyes

"So naive."

And her hand sliced down on Ivy's wrist, knocking the pistol to one side.

Ivy sprang back but an elegant heel lashed out, catching her behind the knee and spinning her around to face the desk. She thrashed but within a heartbeat, Valerie had her pinned, the small pistol firmly pressed into her temple.

First linguistics, Ivy reminded herself, then fisticuffs. If she lived.

"I *said,*" hissed the Archduchess. "I will speak to my mother."

"You are a liar and a treacherous creature. What do you want with Christien?"

"It is too big for you."

"You don't love him, but you want something. Why? You are a Habsburg. You have everything. What could you possibly need from him?"

Suddenly, there was a click and both women froze. At the door, the skeleton key was turning. Someone was picking the lock.

***

227

It was not good laudanum.

He knew enough to be able to tell, even from the deep, twisting blackness of the opium. Frankow's was the best. It was beautiful and quiet and he welcomed its cold dark depths. *This,* this was a carnival of madness, as terrifying as a house of mirrors with no way out but time.

Thoughts and memories blurred together, watercolour with far too much water and the bed was a rack, pressing his body deeper into the tile even as it spun in dizzying circles across the floor. He could hear his brother turning eyelash-thin pages, the sound magnified to the crack of lightning. His own heartbeat was the boom of cannons, his breathing the roar of thunder. Above him, spiders scuttled along their silk, waiting for the promise of flies after the long winter. He could hear mice in the rafters, rats in the cellar, servants in the halls as they began cleaning the Bergl rooms in a far wing of the *palais.* The mattress was stuffed with daggers and each blade stuck into his flesh. Skin, he remembered, was supposed to be a beautiful thing. Now he couldn't wait for it to be gone, for the bones to be free of their prison of flesh.

He wanted to scream but no sound would come. He wanted to run but his legs were gone, lost to the cruelty of the laudanum.

Sophie.

The little white finger in his palm echoed like voices, like her baby bird voice, sweet yet oh-so unnatural.

Sophie sophie sophie.

He knew he could call and the orb would open and he would see the little man with the beard but he was afraid. Afraid of the man and afraid of the horse and afraid of the crowns they would put upon his head. The bed twisted and rushed to the ceiling, stopping just short of the rafters and the spiders. Dropped now, stopping just short of the tile floor and the dust. He had lost his stomach some time ago, wondered if he would ever eat again. Pity, he thought. All he ever wanted was a cup of tea.

A cup of tea but a kiss would not be turned away.

Sisi sitting by a bed, hands folded limply in her lap

His eyes were pressing out of his skull and he wondered how he would see without them. Would his other senses become sharper or would he linger in twilight, waiting for death. Death. His entire world was spent waiting on Death. He would happily trade it for the spiders but the horse had other plans.

Sophie.

On the bed, a bundle wrapped like a loaf of bread, covered in white linen

He had killed a girl, an innocent. He had called the locket and she had come and taken the girl with her. It was on his head, in his soul and yet she hadn't come for him, hadn't shewn up to point a pale finger. It was only a matter of time. It was always a dark matter of time.

Because I could not stop for Death, he kindly stopped for me.

He couldn't fight it, he had told his brother. He didn't know how, had lost the will long ago so he surrendered and fell into it, the tiny slip of white that was her finger, letting the *re obscurum* come. It spun into life, a flashing circle of light and mirror, and he wondered if it were really there or if it were a product of the drug. Still, he reached with hands as he tumbled headlong into it and to the sad quiet room in Hungary where she died.

The Carriage held but just Ourselves — and Immortality.

He is waiting for the small bearded man.

He is terrified of the small bearded man, for somehow he knows that seeing him will change everything.

The door opens.

He closes his eyes. He doesn't want to see the man who has been practicing on orphans in Prague, replacing their limbs with metal, their organs with machines. He doesn't want to know because he knows, deep in his bones, he knows. Nothing will ever be the same once he knows.

"Your Most Royal Highnesses," says the little bearded man, and he pulls large reticulating spectacles from his eyes. "My name is Arvin Frankow. I will save your daughter."

Chapter 19
Of Swans, Crowds, Eyes, Horses and Tears – All Black

The bedroom of Mary Vetsera was plunged into darkness as Ivy blew out the candle and ducked into the shadows of the wall. Silently, the Archduchess stepped away from the desk, slowly raising the pistol to the level of her eyes. Silhouetted darker than the foyer, the figure closed the door and slipped into the room.

It was a woman, lithe and shadowy and she moved like a cat toward the desk. She was dressed entirely in black— long hunt coat, breeches, fine-heeled boots. Her hair was wrapped in black silk, nose and mouth with black lace and Ivy knew she was looking at yet another of the European intelligencers known as Black Swans.

Black gloves reached for the letterbox but the woman paused at the whiff of candle smoke.

"Nicht bewegen," growled the Archduchess with the cock of the hammer.

The woman lunged, knocking the pistol aside and the two Swans became indistinguishable in a flurry of dark limbs and flashing steel.

"Schwarze Schwäne," hissed Valerie. "Stop this!"

"Valerie?" The intruder pulled down her scarf. *"Was machst du denn hier?"*

Immediately, the struggle ceased and the pocket torch flashed on. "Marie?"

As they began to argue, Ivy slowly reached across the desk, gathered the letterbox into her arms.

This was a very dangerous place, she reckoned and began to inch toward the door when the women turned to face her, little more than silhouettes in the dark room.

"This is my cousin," said Valerie. "Countess Marie Larisch. Marie, this is—"

"I know who this is," snapped Marie. "The French anarchist's woman!"

"I'm not French!"

"You were at the Hofburg that night," the woman hissed. "You were with the man who shot Rudolf. Valerie, what are you doing with this fugitive?"

"Sebastien didn't shoot Rudolf!" said Ivy. "Rudolf shot himself!"

"Genug!" barked Valerie.

"What? Is this truc?" The Countess released a breath. "I heard rumours. *Mein Gott…"*

Her remorse lasted but a moment as her gaze flicked to the letterbox. Ivy could see the machinations going on behind those flashing eyes and was entirely prepared for the lunge, ducking out of the way and clutching the box to her chest. Valerie stepped between.

"I *need* that, Valerie," the Countess growled causing Ivy to hug the letterbox all the more. "Give it to me."

"What is it to you?"

"It is worth my life."

"Why?"

"My patron…" She bit her tongue, stopping her words.

"You?" the Archduchess gasped. *"You* were her sponsor? *Mein Gott,* it was you!"

"Yes I was her sponsor! Mary was a brilliant candidate. She could work a room of men like a showgirl. She wasn't even fifteen when she took down an English colonel in Cairo! Imagine that, Valerie! Fifteen and already an expert!"

"She was common and vulgar."

"She was effective, Valerie. That is all that matters."

"So," began Ivy, inching toward the door. "Am I to understand that Mary Vetsera was indeed a Black Swan?"

Valerie snorted but Marie nodded.

"Indeed, French girl. She had the makings of the best of us."

"So if you were her sponsor, who was her patron?"

Silence.

"Was it Wales? Wilhelm? Someone else?"

The silence was shattered by a pounding on the door downstairs.

Valerie moved to the window, throwing open the pane to look down on the dark street.

"Gisela."

Led by Gisela von Habsburg, a squad of Silver Hussars burst into the Vetsera Mansion.

***

The room lurched like a cabin on an ocean freighter. The effects of mixing his wines, he knew. He had drunk the last of the red while reading the damned book and now there was not nearly enough for Bastien's last laudanum. He sat perfectly still, waiting for the chair to stop its rocking, waiting for the floor to stop its roll. Something had wakened him but he didn't know what, so he opened his eyes to the first gleam of sun through the window. Morning. It was finally morning. It had been the longest night of his life.

He could hear shouting from the rooms below and he rose to his feet, waiting for the wave of alcohol-induced vertigo to subside. When he looked around the room, he was not surprised to see the bed empty, his brother gone. He turned to the door, still locked with the chair propped under the handle. Impossible. But the impossible was becoming routine and he took a long, deep breath, then another, fixing the mask tight and welcoming the dread calm as it sank deep into his bones.

He crossed the floor, moved the chair and left the room, the remnants of the wine thick as blood in the glass.

***

Ivy's heart leapt into her throat as boots stomped up the stairs.

"She can't find you here," said Valerie and she spun around. "Quickly! The window."

"I'm not going out the window!" cried Ivy. "It's all ice and snow!"

"She will kill you!"

"She's my cousin but she will kill me too," said the Countess and she bolted across the room, throwing open the drapes and then the pane. Like a cat, she sprang up onto the ledge and disappeared into the early morning darkness. Breeches, thought Ivy. Marvelous handy for Girl Criminologists and Black Swans both.

"I will buy you time," said Valerie and she rushed to the door, locking it and leaning against it. "Go with Marie. She'll keep you safe but, on your life, do *not* give her the letters!"

"What about you?"

"I will deal with my sister. Go!"

Hugging the letterbox to her chest, Ivy took a deep breath, hiked her skirt and stepped up onto the ledge.

The cold rain bit her face as she squeezed through the window frame, clutching the shutters and trying not to look down. The wind was strong, the ledge slick and she pressed her back into the wall as she struggled for a hold. The house's outer façade was decorated with wide ledges and ornamental sculpting, giving her a narrow but effective path. Still, she was grateful for her very fine boots. Nothing could have afforded her a better grip.

She looked down at the small yard. It was only three stories down – not a long drop but there was a Hussar leaning against the carriages, *shako* helmet pulled down on his forehead, arms folded tight into his body. She was surprised that he hadn't seen her at the window but the rain was miserable and he looked as though he wished to be anywhere other than where he was. Still, she would have to pass him at the gate if she jumped and that, she reckoned, would be a predicament.

"French girl! Over here!" hissed a voice and she looked to see Marie Larisch on a neighbouring roof. The houses shared walls and it was obvious that she'd made a substantial leap from the window ledge to the concrete balusters that lined the top.

"Quickly! Just think like a cat."

Ivy swallowed and edged along, one hand on the letterbox, the other searching out handholds along the house's façade. She could hear the sisters arguing inside the room, realized Gisela had not seen her sister since Strasbourg and wondered if Valerie would be able to explain her current situation. Gisela was a hard and clever woman. It would not be easy to convince her of something she did not want to believe.

She was as close to the baluster as she could get without a leap. Marie Larisch was pressed onto the roof, flattened as if part of it but she did reach out her hand. Ivy reached back.

"No use," the Countess said. "Throw me the letterbox so you can climb!"

"Not bloody likely," Ivy grumbled. She tucked it under her arm and grabbed the edge of the roof. The rain was bitter and her hands were blue. Her boots scrabbled the limestone but with only one hand, it was impossible.

"I will help you, but you must give me the letterbox! Do it or fail!"

There was noise behind her and she glanced over her shoulder to see Gisela and Valerie struggling at the window. Suddenly, a shot cracked the air and concrete shattered beside Ivy's eyes.

"*Verdammt!*" barked the Countess and disappeared into the shadows of the roof.

Ivy thrashed in the darkness as shots rang out now from the Hussar on the street. Heart in her throat, she tossed the letterbox over the baluster and leapt, pulling herself up as bullets tore through the fabric of her skirt. The force of them jerked her over and into a puddle of wet slush on the other side. She huddled for a moment, eyes shut tight as lead balls struck the concrete, spraying bits of sharp stone across her arms and face. But with a deep breath, she snatched the box and bolted across the rooftops into the first rays of sunrise.

***

As he moved through the *palais,* the servants were eager to send him in the direction of the wine cellar. Vienna was a city where most buildings were as deep as they were high. It was said that cellars connected with vaults, storm sewers and church crypts in a vast underground labyrinth that girded the entire city, including the Hofburg itself. Although he refused to believe such fantastical claims, Christien found his heart sinking into the darkness with each step.

At some point the winding stairway had become stone and on the walls, cogwheels spun inside mirrored sconces, creating sparks that illuminated the narrowing steps. He could hear Franz's voice muffled and echoing off the stone.

Christien followed the voice to a series of wine vaults, housed in brick and hidden behind iron grilles. The ceiling was low and curved, the walls cold and damp. Both Franz and the valet turned at his approach. It was obvious the prince had been recently wakened, for he was wearing a dressing gown over striped Turkish pajamas and his arms were folded across his chest. At the far end of the cellar, Sebastien stood, almost swallowed in blackness.

"I'm sorry," Christien said. "I don't know how he got out of the room."

"He says he is waiting for a horse," said Franz. "We have horses in the stables if he wishes to see one. He will not find one in a wine cellar."

He didn't know what else to say. Nothing in the world could possibly make sense.

He crossed to his brother's side.

"Bastien," he said under his breath. "What in hell are you doing down here?"

"Hell. Yes," echoed Sebastien. "I am in Hell."

He was facing a tumbledown wall, the bricks and crumbling mortar clearly covering the entrance to a tunnel beyond. An icy breeze blew between the gaps, carrying the scent of mold, decay and death, flapping the greatcoat like an airship's sails. It was cold but Christien doubted he felt it.

"Bastien? Why are you here?"

"The black horse."

"There is no black horse. It's only a story from a very old book."

"I called him."

His heart sank.

"Why?"

His brother did not look at him.

"Did you know that Sophie died when she was a child?"

"Sophie? Sophie von Habsburg?"

"She was dead for two days before the doctor got to her. He brought her back to life."

"What has Sophie got to do with the black horse?"

"He was a great doctor, they said. He had done miracles with orphans in Prague. Had given them lungs of iron and hearts of brass. Legs of copper and arms of steel." He gazed at the brick wall as if waiting. "He brought them back to life."

"You can't bring someone back to life."

"He did."

Christien sighed.

"What has any of this got to do with the horse?"

"Upstairs, I looked into an orb."

"I was there, Bastien. There was no orb. It was the laudanum."

"Re obscura. Dark matter. Grey matter. Doesn't matter. It's all in the mind. I looked into an orb and saw this doctor. I saw what he did. I know what he did."

"Bastien…"

"Some of the children could have been saved but he waited. He waited until they died. Then he brought them back to life."

Christien said nothing. It was impossible yet scientifically plausible, the research unethical but exhilarating. Every surgeon's dream. Every physician's nightmare.

"There was no way he could kill a Habsburg but Sophie was already dead so it was perfect."

"What of it?"

"Later, this doctor left Prague and Hungary and Vienna for work in

England, for the royals there."

Suddenly, he understood.

"He was celebrated, rubbed shoulders with the highest of the high, began to take his experiments further, right up to the very gates of death and beyond."

That dread calm, which so often served as armor, began to press in on his chest.

"What if you could kill someone, and then bring them back? It's the question of the age, but he hadn't the nerve. Or the victim. There are still rules against that sort of thing."

"He wouldn't. He couldn't."

"He was invited into the Ghost Club of London and Cambridge, and there he met our father."

"Bastien, he didn't…"

"This man was Arvin Frankow," said Sebastien. He turned now and Christien realized that, at this moment, his eyes were as silver as a mirror.

"The first and last child he killed was me."

***

The building code for Vienna was strict – no residences over six stories and here, along this stretch of fine homes, none over four. Ivy was grateful for this simple fact as she dashed from rooftop to rooftop – some flat, others sloped – all the while the letterbox safely tucked under her arm. Now, as the stretch of adjoining homes ended on a roof with a very steep pitch and a set of black-iron chimneys, she slowed to catch her breath and orient herself to the skyline.

It was dawn and the rain had turned to drizzle, the type that was too heavy for fog but too warm for snow. Down below, throngs of people were trudging through this early morning mist, their steps slow, feet heavy, moving in a common direction like a black tide. To the Hofburg, she knew, to mourn their beloved prince as he lay in state. She wondered if the casket were open and if so, if they had bandaged his head. A self-inflicted head wound was a dead-giveaway. She wondered if any of them wanted to know. They didn't look like they wanted to know. They moved like a dark wave, like tar. Like clay.

Like her heart.

She needed to get to the *palais* of Franz Salvator and to do that, she needed to get down to the streets. She studied the angle of the roof, the chimneys, the worn pipes in the gutter filled with leaves and soot. She looked about for fire escape when suddenly, there was a black blur and someone grabbed her from behind, pressed a blade into her throat.

"The letterbox now, French girl."

Ivy felt the rage well up in her chest. She had come too far for this, lost too much, wasn't about to let an Austrian spy snatch it from her fingers.

She slid the box from under her arm, held it up with both hands.

"You won't hurt me," she pleaded. "Just say you won't hurt me."

"Stupid girl. All I want is the—"

With a roar, Ivy slammed the box over her shoulder into the masked face of Marie Larisch. The Swan staggered backwards, her blade clattering to the roof. Ivy snatched it and bolted but Marie lunged and with one hand, snagged her skirt. The force jerked Ivy off her feet and the letterbox sailed out of her grip. Both women watched in horror as it slid down the steep angled roof and over the edge.

"Bitch!" snarled the Swan and she kicked, sending the young writer after it.

The tiles were slick as Ivy pitched downwards, scrabbling to catch a grip but finding none. Suddenly the roof was gone, leaving only the dark plummeting expanse and the rushing street, when a gutter pipe caught her hem with a jolt. She swung for a heartbeat, head down, legs swinging, suspended three floors above ground. The world spun and twisted in sickening circles and she could see faces staring up at her and the shattered box, its contents scattered all over the street.

Another jolt as the pipe began to pull away from the roof. She doubled up, fighting the ache in her muscles and reaching with the blade to nick the fabric of her skirt. It gave in a perfect line, ripping a wide ribbon and spinning her like a peeled orange toward the ground. The pipe groaned and fell downwards with her, until they both jerked to a stop mere feet above the street. Like that moment in the Chevalier when the trip-masts engaged, Ivy was light-headed, free yet suspended over the ground. But it was only a moment. The pipe cracked and she hit the slushy cobbles with a thud, the pipe landing inches from her head.

She opened her eyes to crowds of people, moving in, pressing in, closing off the morning sky, grey to charcoal to blackness.

***

It made sense, thought Christien. Odd, twisted, sickening sense.

"I'm sorry, Bastien," he said. "I know how much he means to you."

"I trusted him. I trusted him with everything but he's done something to me that I have no control over."

"Perhaps he simply fixed your skull."

"Then why metal? I have always assumed it was aluminium but I doubt it very much now. Father took him to Seventh where they could experiment to their heart's content. They killed me over and over and brought me back. That's why I see what I see. That's why I can control the orbs. That's what Sophie meant by, 'Our Father'. He brought us both back to life."

Christien shuddered. Just thinking of his father made him sick. But the thought of Frankow bringing the dead to life was exhilarating. Every surgeon's dream. Every physician's nightmare.

"You don't know that, Bastien. He loves you."

"He killed me."

"You need to talk to him."

"It doesn't matter. He's coming."

"Who's coming? Frankow?"

"The horse."

"Bastien…"

He threw a look over his shoulder to see Franz and the valet still waiting. Franz had lit up a cigarette but the valet was watching everything as if trying to understand. Good man, he reckoned and for the first time in months, he thought of Pomfrey.

Christien sighed. The cellar was as black as night, save for the glow of the cogwheeled lights along the walls. His brother had not moved. It was almost as if he were a part of the stone. A statue perhaps, like the ones from cemeteries and graveyard and churches. A fitting image, he thought. If only his brother stayed dead.

"Let's go up for some tea, shall we? The black horse will surely wait for that?"

"No tea now. Maybe not ever."

"Bastien," Christien groaned, gripping his brother's arm and leaning in close. "I know what you're thinking. These are just stories in a very old book."

"I belong in Hell, like you said."

"Listen, I was angry—"

"Stand back, please. The horse is moving rather fast."

"Dammit Bastien—"

The silver eyes rolled back into his skull as Sebastien raised his arms, palms up. One hand burst into flame and snowflakes began to circle around the other and Christien staggered back. Both Franz and the valet exclaimed in German, shrunk toward the stair.

"Όταν ο Αμνός έσπασε την τρίτη σφραγίδα, άκουσα το τρίτο ζωντανό ον λένε," Έλα! "Και κοίταξα και είδα ένα μαύρο άλογο και τον αναβάτη του κρατούσε ένα ζυγαριά στο χέρι του. Και μια φωνή μέσα από τα τέσσερα ζωντανά όντα, δήλωσε."

"That's not Latin," growled Christien. "That's Greek."

"Μια φρατζόλα ψωμί ολικής αλέσεως ή τρία ψωμιά κριθάρι για ένα μεροκάματο. και μην σπαταλάτε το ελαιόλαδο και το κρασί."

"When the bloody hell did you learn Greek?"

From the gaps in the brick, shapes were swirling. At first, they seemed like ripples of heat above a chimney but soon, they began to take on the appearance of soot, of fine black powder caught on the breeze. The deadwind picked up then, causing the flames to leap and the snow to swirl in his brother's hands. The coglights flickered and the winds roared as the soot began to congeal into a solid form.

Behind them, Franz began to pray in Italian.

Sebastien closed his eyes and the coglights died, plunging the cellar into darkness.

"Don't, Bastien," said Christien. "Please don't."

Suddenly the wall boomed like a cannon, exploding inwards and Christien was flung back into an iron grille as bricks, soot and mortar sprayed in all directions. He covered his head to avoid flying stone and cursed his luck at the shattering of many bottles of fine Austrian wine behind him.

Slowly, both wind and roar died away and his knees buckled beneath him, leaving him slack against the base of the iron grille. Soon, the cogwheels groaned and flickered to life but there was a black cloud like London's industrial fog hovering over the cellar floor. It was near impossible to see anything.

"Mein herr?" called the valet. Christien felt the man fumble through the rubble towards him. *"Geht es dir gut?"*

"Ya," said Christien and he shook his head, bricks and dust falling from his shoulders as he pushed to his knees. "Bastien?"

And the valet was gone, for at the end of the cellar, there was a new tunnel. Darker than dark, and at the entrance, darker than this –

Sebastien.

"Don't touch me," Sebastien snapped as the valet rushed to his side. "Don't touch me!"

It was too late. At the brush of his fingers, the valet froze in place, mouth gaping in a silent scream. Christien watched with dread as, within a matter of seconds, his flesh withered like a dying tree. Cheeks sunk into hollows, fingers dried to skin-covered bones, lips cracked as they stretched too tightly over yellowed teeth. Without a sound, he sank to his knees, shins splintering as they hit the stony floor.

Christien staggered to his feet and stumbled to the man's side. He was alive, but barely and the young physician looked up at his brother, knowing there could be no rational explanation for this.

Soot drifted from Sebastien's fingers and rained from his hair. In fact, soot floated from his mouth with every breath and his eyes – silver just moments before – were as black as the night. Irises and sclera both, like ink spreading across a parchment, streaking down his cheeks in the form of black tears.

In his hand was a set of scales, weigh scales like those found in markets to measure wheat or fish. After a long moment, they too disintegrated to rise up to the ceiling as flies.

Behind them, the minor prince of Austria, Hungary, Croatia and Bohemia made the sign of the cross, before whirling and bolting up the stairs.

Under his hand the valet moaned, breaths like crackling tinder.

"Bastien?" Christien groaned. "What in hell is going on?"

"Hell," Sebastien said, voice hollow and echoing. "Hell is going on and war is coming on iron feet. Blood and iron rains from the skies."

Christien knew that if Hell did exist, it couldn't be much worse than this.

He gathered the dying valet into his arms and carried him up the stair, leaving the Mad Lord of Lasingstoke to the cellar and the soot.

Chapter 20
Of Strange Angels, a Wall of Bones and the Looming Shadow of the Prince of Wales

The day before the funeral of the Crown Prince of Austria, strange things were happening in Vienna.

Eduard Sacher, owner of the famous *Sacher* hotel and restaurant, was roused from his bed to inspect the foul odours coming from his famous hotel kitchen. He found everything save the vinegar spoiled, including his ingredients for the famous Sacher-tortes. Several chefs and sous-chefs were sacked on the spot, but that did not help his predicament. The food simply had rotted in the cupboards.

Down from the *Sacher* the grocer, Ivan Eisler, went down to his storage cellar to check on his winter store of root vegetables. Upon opening the small door, he gasped at the sight. His produce was gone, having rotted away since checking them the night before. There was nothing save fungus and green slime. He staggered out of the cellar, knowing he and his family had lost everything that might carry them through this long, horrible winter.

Next was the butcher shop run by Pieter Kirchmann and his sons.

His brother owned one of the farms that supplied the Hofburg with beef but Pieter butchered some of the animals and sold them in his own shop. He was awakened to the sharp and recognizable stench of rotting meat. When he went down to check, he was horrified at the state in which he found the carcasses. Mold had turned every cut green and he knew in an instant there was no way to salvage any of it. He prayed his brother had more cattle ready for the saw.

Unfortunately for Pieter, his brother woke to find the same problem with his feed lot. All cattle marked for slaughter were dead, bellies bloated, tongues pushed grotesquely out of their mouths.

And so it went throughout the region. Hector Neuner's barns of wheat, eaten overnight by a legion of rats. Ernst Mayr's sheep, brought down from the high fields to harbor winter in pens, ravaged by wolves. Georg Schatt's seed stock, sacks piled to the ceiling, caught fire and burned to the ground along with the sheds they were stored in. Milk went sour, wine became acid. Cakes became stale, bread grew mold. Overnight, the entire city of Vienna lost its food supply, although they didn't realize the scope of it for days.

As for the historic center of the Holy Roman Empire, the Hofburg had become little more than an airship hangar.

Seven dirigibles hovered over the palace, the latest easing in from the northwest. The *SMAS Eisenklaue,* or 'Iron Claw', dropped her mooring hooks onto the statue of Francis II in the center of the Inner Courtyard, digging up the footings and pulling the bronze figure from the pedestal. Painted across its underbelly, the black eagle of the *Empire of Blood and Iron* as Kaiser Wilhelm II came to lead the summit. It joined the *HMAS Royal Carolina* alongside a strange sleek ironclad vessel, reminiscent of a Viking ship. She was inlaid with steel plates and flying a silver canvas with the insignia of a double-headed eagle in red, clutching a wolf in one set of claws, a bear in the other. The *Twelve Apostles,* flagship of Tsar Nicholas' *Empire of Steel.*

Dwarfing them all naturally, the *Stahl Mädchen.*

Meanwhile, crossing the border at Linz, two Eisnemanner rolled on their track wheels toward the Austrian capital. In any other country *by* any other country, it would have been an act of war but Austria and

Germany were allies, cousins, links in the same immutable chain of history and so it was not yet marked as an act of war.

A grandstand had been erected on the site of the Old Theatre, but it could not contain the crowds. From the Court Chapel to the small Church of the Holy Capuchins, people massed on the streets and laneways along the route, hundreds deep, faces pale, garments black. For days, people had waited in the snow, in the rain, all to get a place to wait for the procession, for a glimpse of the carriage that would carry their Rudolf to his final resting place. The vendors were especially helpful, selling sausages, bread and pies to those lining the streets. That was, of course, before the food went bad.

Unaware of any of this, Ivy Savage huddled in a very old church near the center of town.

She had lost all track of time. She had lost all track of her hands and feet and face as well. The skirt she had been wearing since Melk was now little more than a tattered crinoline over torn breeches and once again she was thankful for them. Marvelous handy for Girl Criminologists fleeing Black Swans. She wondered if she were dead. If she were, then she was being tended by a very strange angel.

After her spectacular fall, the people on the street had brought her, ragged and numb and very much alone, to this old church and left her in the care of the priest. He spoke not a word of English but sat with her in the pew, dabbing her scrapes with a cloth. He had dark eyes, bushy brows and the largest beard Ivy had ever seen. If he were an angel, she reckoned he had to be St. Peter.

He smiled at her, pointed out her torn breeches and bloody knee. She nodded slowly, still numb. At the moment, she fully understood Sebastien – she'd give anything for a cup of tea but hadn't the words to explain.

Sebastien. How she missed him.

A man in an Austrian fedora approached. He was carrying a satchel and leaned in to speak in St. Peter's ear. It wasn't German, Ivy was certain, but rather something that reminded her of Lonsdale and the Russian patient known as Grigori. He had cursed her and called her the Virgin Mary.

Funny. She missed Lonsdale too.

She sighed, let her eyes wander. The little church was beautiful. Not beautiful in the 'Melk Abbey' way, but a simpler, more austere beautiful. Dark wood, white walls, low curved ceilings. Candles instead of gaslight giving off a serene glow. A small choir echoing minor chords to the heavens and soothing souls right here on earth. She had never felt this way in a church, not even at the funeral of her brothers. Masses said over five little black coffins had almost destroyed her mother. She had never thought of a church as safe until today.

She thought of Sebastien, of the morning when he had found her in the snowy gorse. Silently, she thanked him for all the training in the field and out of it and for all the adventures and all the time he'd invested in her and she knew that she loved him and cursed herself for not taking that first terrifying step and kissing him in the gorse.

They might not have ended up as fugitives in Vienna.

Her chin trembled but she lifted it, determined to overcome the rush of emotion. Still, the tears were stinging.

"Maria?" asked St. Peter.

Ivy looked at him, blinked, tried to focus.

"Maria von Vetsera?"

And he held up a stack of letters, wrapped in twine.

"The letters," she gasped as she clutched them to her chest. "Oh thank you, thank you so much…"

Damn her chin now. St. Peter smiled, dabbed it with the cloth and she let the tears win.

He began to speak but she didn't understand. He gestured at the man with the fedora, who nodded. They both nodded. Still, she didn't understand.

"Franz Salvator," she said. "I need to go to the *palais* of Prince Franz Salvator. Can you help?"

"Prinz, yah," said the man in the fedora and he nodded. Ivy rose to her feet.

"Thank you," she said to St. Peter. "Thank you so much."

He smiled, made the sign of the cross. She curtsied and made the sign too, not really knowing what it meant. It seemed like the right the thing to do.

Clutching the letters to her chest, she whirled and followed the fedora back onto the street.

***

It had taken hours for the man to die.

Christien drew the sheet over the body of the valet. It was more of a shell than a body, the man having withered away until he was nothing more than skin stretched across bones, breaths fading like cool air in summer. Christien had called for broth but was told there was none. He had called for bread or fruit puree but apparently there was nothing in the *palais* that could help stave off the advance of the valet's condition.

Truth be told, he hadn't a clue what had killed the man but damn, if it didn't look like starvation.

He shook his head and rose to his feet. The valet's room was tiny and on the fourth floor of the *palais*. Servants' quarters were markedly different from the rest of the building, with low slanted ceilings and tiny windows, limiting the already limited February light. It was morning but there was no sun. It would come out tomorrow, he figured, for the funeral. It would be ironic – such pompous ritual to mark the end of an unorthodox life. Rudolf couldn't have planned it better had he tried.

From these windows, he was barely able to see rooftops let alone the courtyard below. He could see the dome of the Hofburg however, the many airships dotting the sky and casting shadows across the city. Airships with both the black and the dual-headed eagle along with two ironclads – the *Stahl Mädchen* and another, flying the flag of *Steel.* All because of Bastien. He had heard Franz's carriage leave this morning, wondered when the Hussars would come. Ivy would be discovered, Valerie would turn coat. Either way, they were done for. A shame, really. This was not how or where he wanted to die.

He looked back at the airships. He had owned an airship, once.

One of the ships looked familiar. He narrowed his eyes to see it flying the colours of the House Saxe-Cobourg and Gotha.

"By god," he breathed. "Bertie?"

And for the first time in months, he felt his spirit stir with something other than despair until it was suddenly dashed with the sound of hoofbeats.

He sighed, steeling his nerve. At least three carriages and even more horses clattering into the courtyard. Hussars, he knew. He looked back at the body of the valet, wondered how he would explain. Perhaps it was for the best. They could shoot both brothers and purge the world of the hell that came with the name de Lacey.

He left the servant's room, followed the winding stair down to the smoking room. Prodded the fire with a poker, causing it to leap in its bed. Poured himself a large Scotch, swallowed it straight and poured a second as footsteps pounded down the hall.

Six Silver Hussars burst into the smoking room, forming a circle around him, sabre-arms drawn as Gisela strode between, blonde hair pulled back from her severe face. Trailing behind them all was Franz Salvator, with Valerie on his arm.

"Christien de Lacey," said Gisela, raising a pistol to his eyes. "You are under arrest."

***

Conquest. War. Famine. Still, he was incomplete and he knew he needed another horse.

Sebastien blinked slowly. Seeing was difficult now, the edges of his vision blurred by creeping blackness, much like flies crawling across a window. Or, in fact, like the flies now crawling along the ceiling. The dead were too many to count and no matter where he looked, they were there in the thousands, maybe tens of thousands. He could barely see the walls for the empty eyes and gaping mouths of the dead.

Breathing was difficult too. It felt like a weight of bricks on his chest but the bricks were inside and he was drowning in mortar. He wondered what it would be like once he stopped breathing entirely. If his lungs would rebel or accept the change like a new huntcoat or pair of boots.

Truth be told, he wouldn't miss his skin but then a kiss from Miss

Savage would be unlikely. It was a conundrum.

No one had bothered him while he sat in the cellar. Not Christien, not the prince, not a single footman or valet or kitchen boy sent to fetch a bottle of wine. The wine was sour, he knew, just vinegar in fancy bottles. That was only the beginning. By tomorrow, the city would be rotten and filled to brimming with nobility. Germans, Austrians, Russians and English. No French, no Italians. The world of princes was a funny place. And by the day after tomorrow, the entire countryside would be ablaze with cannons and long guns, all because of him. And the lockets.

War was coming on iron feet.

Ghostlight was near but Arclight was nearer. He could hear her voice, sweet like music in his veins and he knew he could summon an orb whenever he wished. Perhaps Arvin Frankow's. A part of him very much wanted to see how the little man died. His throat tightened at the thought and he chased it away, along with thoughts of the infirmary and nights spent by the fire with good Scotch and bedtime stories and Mumford.

He hardened his heart, like the bricks. Like the stone.

It had been Mumford who had taught him to see. Mumford had taught him to speak. Mumford had saved his life, not Frankow. Frankow had conspired with his father and the Ghost Club of London. The Ghost Club had been their life and he their little toy. It wasn't surprising that he had forgotten so much, but then again, there was much he'd never wanted to remember. A shattered skull changed things.

He could feel the sting of tears and he wiped his cheeks, only to study the glistening blackness on his palms. Weeping oil, weeping tar. No wonder he was drowning in mortar. Perhaps he was finally turning to stone. Cold, hard stone.

And Ivy.

He wondered how she was, if she was safe, if she was afraid. She was such a brave woman. She had made him feel like he could live, if even for a brief time. He hoped she could escape the coming destruction but if not, he would watch for her at the doors of the dead. They would be his to rule once the last horse came.

The tunnel ahead was quiet and dark and filled with the dead. They had been here for hundreds of years, a thousand perhaps, most embedded in the earth. He wondered if he could release them from here or if that would cause problems in the foundations of the city. That would be bad, all things considered.

An orb appeared, first black and shiny like obsidian but quickly spinning into the familiar mirrored silver. He cocked his head, wondering who he would see this time and soon, a child came barefoot from the tunnel. She was a very young girl – barely walking, a toddler – with baby blonde curls and sunken eyes. She was wearing a tattered nightgown over desiccated feet, and looked to have been dead for many years. She stopped directly in front of him.

"Sophie," he said. "You found me."

He reached into his pocket for the tiny white bone, held it out to her in his palm. She smiled an infant smile but shook her head, folded his fingers back over it. He marveled at how tiny her hands were before returning the unusual bullet to his pocket. He took that hand and allowed her to pull him to his feet.

The orb hovered a moment before disappearing into the tunnel. Together, they followed and were almost immediately swallowed by darkness.

***

Christien raised the Scotch to his lips, ignoring the pistol marked squarely between his eyes.

"Hello Valerie."

"Remy."

The Archduchess peeled herself from Franz's side, slipped between the Hussars to stand next to her sister. Imperial swans, both dressed in black.

"Where is your brother?" she purred.

"Where is Ivy?"

"I'm not certain."

"Odd. Me neither."

A shot cracked the tension of the smoking room, almost deafening

Christien as the bullet whipped past his ear to shatter a fine landscape framed in gold. Gisela moved the pistol back between his eyes.

"Next time, your head."

"You can't shoot him," growled Valerie. "We need him. Where is your brother?"

Christien sipped the Scotch, grateful he was holding it with the clockwork hand. The right was shaking. He slipped it casually into his pocket.

"Why?"

"Answer the question."

"I don't know."

Gisela cocked the hammer a second time.

"I wasn't lying," he said. "I was tending the valet in an upper room."

"That is true," said Franz from the doorway. "The miracle man was in the cellar."

Gisela nodded sharply and a pair of Hussars spun their torsos to clank down the hall.

"He died, by the way," said Christien. "In case you cared. He seemed a fine servant. I hope you paid him well."

The minor prince swallowed, said nothing.

"You will help us," said Gisela. "And you might be allowed to live."

"I will only help you if I know that Ivy is alive and will continue to be alive after I help."

"Why does that matter to you?" asked Valerie, her eyes cutting him as surely as a blade. "She does not love you."

"Neither do you."

"She is annoying," said Valerie.

"She is that."

"Then why?"

"Scandal and misery come with the name de Lacey." He sipped the Scotch, allowing the heat to burn his throat. "But she's not one of us. She's a silly street girl, all brains and pluck, but she's innocent enough. It would be a sin to let her die."

"What do you know of sin?" asked Gisela.

"You have no idea."

"If we find her, we will not shoot her."

"How comforting. What do you need from me?"

The sisters exchanged glances. Gisela barked orders and the last of the Hussars clanked from the smoking room. She lowered her pistol.

"*Maman* has a plan."

Christien looked at Franz. "I'd like one of those cigars, if you don't mind."

Franz stared at him.

"And another glass of this Scotch." Christien held up the tumbler. "Fetch it for me. Now please."

The minor prince scrambled to obey.

"No more Scotch," said Valerie. "You will need your hands steady."

"Good lord," he said. "Am I to operate?"

"You are."

"I don't operate anymore. I'm a clockwork monster, if you hadn't noticed."

And the gears in his wrist began to whir and click. *Marvelous,* he thought to himself. It was all in the timing.

"It won't matter."

"So what patient is so ill that I am the only surgeon skilled enough to cut him? And remember, I was in line to be a police surgeon. I only ever worked on the dead."

"Then you are perfectly suited for this," said Valerie.

"I don't understand."

"You will operate on a dead man," said Gisela.

"On a dead man," he repeated flatly.

"On our brother Rudolf," said Valerie.

"On Rudolf."

"You will put his head, his heart and his body back together," said Gisela.

Valerie stepped forward, stroked his chin.

"Then *your* brother," she said. "Will bring him back to life."

***

The carriage was not fancy, but she was happy to be rattling her way to the *palais* of Franz Salvator. She desperately needed Christien or Sebastien or even Franz himself –someone who spoke English and read German. The letters were crucial, and currently, scattered all over both seats of the cab.

She chewed her bottom lip as she studied the names and return addresses, looking for connections, praying for a clue. They were all written by one hand, sent by one person and her heart thudded at the sight.

Wales.

There could be no 'Wales' other than Edward, Prince of Wales, certainly not in a secret Austrian letterbox. According to Valerie, they had met at a racetrack. She had asked Marie Larisch if he had been her patron and the silence had been telling. She cursed to herself, wishing now that she had taken those letters from Rudolf's desk, despite the threat of being shot.

Her eyes were strained as they scanned for words she could understand. Baltazzi and Victoria, Rudolf and Wilhelm but there was another word that kept leaping out, a German word that she knew she'd heard before. *Archelicht.* She spoke it aloud and rolled it off her tongue, casting her mind back in an effort to remember when she had heard it and what it had meant.

Archelicht.

Years ago, when she had taught Davis his spelling lists, she remembered the similarity of some English words to German ones, others to Latin ones. Sebastien spoke Latin, had spoken Latin in the gorse when he'd heard the shot and drew eagles in the snow. He had said a word then, first in English then, she realized, in German. He had said Arclight and then, *Archelicht.*

She looked down at the letters, steadied her nerve as a theory began to take shape in her mind. It was an unpleasant theory but there were already two bodies to count for it and there was not much worse than that.

The cab rattled to a halt and she looked out the window, realizing that she was not at the *palais* of Franz Salvator, but what looked like a rather grand hotel.

The door swung open, held by a mustachioed soldier in tartan and tan. He looked like a major in Victoria's Royal Guards.

"Good mornin', Miss Vetsera," he said, his accent undeniably Scots. "His Royal Highness, the Prince of Wales, is expectin' you."

***

"Well," said Penny as she gazed around her room at the Vienna Grand. "I suppose it will have to do."

"What's wrong, dear Penny?" asked Alexandre Gavriel St. Jacques Lord Durand as he directed the baggage-carrying automaton to the bedroom. "Is the room not to your satisfaction? Why, the cream of European aristocracy stay here when in Vienna. I should have thought it right up your proverbial alley."

"There is nothing proverbial about an alley," she snorted. "And the room itself is adequate. Although I do prefer the intimacy of the Sacher, but that is simply a quirk of my nature."

"So, if it's not the room, what is it?"

He slipped the porter a spring. Automatons loved springs. It shewed they were always ready to serve, and nothing made a 'bot happier than service. It bowed and wheeled from the room. He closed the door behind it.

"You presume, sir," said Penny. "Once again, there is only one bed."

"I do presume, Penny," said Lord Durand and he turned, crossing the floor towards her, becoming the rogue Alexander Dunn with every step. "But look, there is this lovely settee..."

"Too short."

"And this charming Chesterfield sofa."

"Too soft."

"And of course, there is that marvelous bear-skin rug."

He was almost upon her now, standing so close that she could feel the heat from his body. She raised her chin and met his eyes, hers filled with defiance, his with mischief.

"I am not a colonial, sir. I could never sleep on a rug that was once a living creature."

"I meant for me, Penny. And besides," he raised a hand to smooth a lock of curls from her forehead. "Who said we will be sleeping a wink tonight?"

Her heart was racing and she suddenly noticed his lips. Damnation, but they were smirking in a most infuriating and fetching way. She arched a brow.

"And what do you propose we do, sir? It is well past ten and all the reputable restaurants will be closed. And I for one will not set foot into one of your seedy burgundy bars or jazz clubs."

"Oh I have plans for you, my dear Penny," he breathed and he leaned in closer. He smelled of brandy and expensive linen. "But you may need to remove some of your finer clothes."

"Oh?" she said, and she swallowed as his fingers ran along her neckline, played with the laces of her corset. "And why ever would I need to do that?"

"To fit into the dumbwaiter, of course. It's rather a tight squeeze."

"Dumb waiter?" For some reason, she found herself rising on tiptoe to almost meet his lips. "Tight squeeze?"

"It's the best way to sneak into the Crown Prince's apartment."
She frowned. He grinned.

"Oh didn't I tell you? That's why we're here. We're breaking into Crown Prince Maximilian's rooms. I have information leading me to believe that he has the Star of Morocco."

"Jolly good," she said. "That will be the only squeeze I'll be allowing tonight."

"Well, there's always tomorrow."

And he turned away to attend the steamtrunks and she sank to her heels, cursing the maddening rush of her heart and wondering why she was just the tiniest bit disappointed.

Chapter 21
Of Dangerous Men, Dangerous Women and the Dangerous Games that Keep Them Playing

It was called simply the 'Grand Vienna Hotel', and Ivy waited in a salon that was larger than her entire house in Stepney. She could hear voices through the walls, all speaking German. Her eyes flicked to the windows but they were sealed and therefore, a repeat of the Vetsera incident was unlikely. Still, while everything inside her wanted to bolt, she would not. She was so close to answers, all of which could be compromised by one impulsive act. And she was a rather impulsive girl.

And so she sat in a chair under a crewel-papered wall, hugging the letters wrapped in twine, waiting for Edward, Prince of Wales or a firing squad. Either one and for the very first time in her life, she wasn't certain if she cared.

"Wo ist das Bier?" came a voice from the door at the far end of the room. *"Hier?"*

She rose to her feet as a man staggered in, wearing a uniform of slate blue with more medals than a military parade. He was fair-haired and fox-like with a very unique moustache. Sharply-shaved, it arched up along his cheeks in the shape of a large W. Because of that moustache, she knew immediately who he was and her heart pounded in her chest. It was his signature, his trademark. The entire world would know him by the moustache alone.

Wilhelm II, Kaiser of the Empire of *Blood and Iron*.

"Wo ist das Bier? Fräulein, gib mir mehr Bier!"

He staggered toward her, stopping as his eyes flicked over her face, her tattered clothes, surprisingly even to the shape beneath them and she hugged the letters a little tighter. A man had never looked at her that way before, not even after so much of her life spent in and around London's East End. She found herself utterly paralyzed at the thought.

"Kein Bier? Kein Problem, Fraulein Vetsera..."

He reached his hand, tugged a lock of hair between finger and thumb. She pushed it away. He grinned.

"Wales," she said. "I wish to speak with the Prince of Wales."

"Ah, you prefer English? You are too good for your own people now?"

"Wales," she repeated.

"He's busy with Bismarck. That makes him Bizzy." And he stepped back, swept his eyes over her once again. Smirked. "How did you lure Rudy into your bed? You look like a streetwalker. Even the whore Kaspar has more class than you."

"Wales."

"Franzi, that old *arschloch,* thinks you are dead. They all think you are dead, even your sponsor. Maybe you are good, after all, to fool your sponsor?"

"Wales."

"Patron *and* sponsor in the next room, and here you are with me. Lucky for me. Luckier for you."

She swallowed, could not stop her chin from rising.

"Wales."

"What are these?" he asked, fingers rifling across the corners of the envelopes. "Love letters from Rudy? Directions from Uncle Bertie? I bet someone would pay handsomely for these, yes? Is that why you're here, *Schätzchen?* Blackmail? If so, then it is a very dangerous game for a little girl like you."

"Wales."

"Do you have it?" He leaned in, foxy eyes shining. "I will pay you double what he is paying. Triple. I don't care. *Blood and Iron* should have it, not *Steam*. *Steam* already has her Ghost. They will be unstoppable if they have two. Is that what you want? Maybe that's what you want since you're an English whore now."

She could smell the beer on his breath and she realized that he was likely more than just a little drunk. That made him dangerous, but the Black Swans were dangerous too and while she wasn't a Swan, she was convinced she was smarter.

Sebastien had called them 'womanly wiles.'

She took a deep breath, turned her face to his.

"Triple?"

His eyes grew wide then but he threw back his head and laughed.

"Mein Gott, you are bold! I can see why even Wales falls at your feet!"

She felt a rush of pride. It was dangerous and giddy but if 'womanly wiles' was the game she was playing, then she'd best play it to win.

"Why do you want it, then?" she asked. "It's just a bauble."

He leaned in again, a conspirator.

"The gold, *Schätzchen.* Rooms of gold! How better to pay for war machines than with a device that turns even wood into gold! You saw it, yes, at Mayerling? The room, the pedestal, the wardrobe? A fortune that keeps replenishing itself. It is like finding the goose that lays the golden egg."

She swallowed, knowing that it had been Ghostlight that had kept the de Lacey family in money for generations.

"And the power! It is not steam, it is not hydraulics, it is not even the filthy Yankee petrol. It is a window to Valhalla and a doorway to Hel. Harness the two and you have a power source capable of running a hundred *Eisenmanner,* a thousand U-boats, a hundred-thousand dreadnoughts. It is said to have destroyed the entire shipping fleet of London with only a small show of its power."

She remembered it well – the steam, the ice, the mushroom cloud over St. Katharine's Docks.

"I thought Gisela would get it for me. She promised but you beat her, you clever thing."

Ivy looked at him.

"Gisela is your Swan?"

"Gisela is my toy. She amuses me."

"With Rudolf dead, she may yet be Empress."

He grinned, his moustache arcing up his cheeks like blades.

"You are far more progressive than your Emperor, *Schätzchen*. There will never be a woman as *Gilded* Monarch. Not while Franz Joseph is alive. Perhaps you could kill him next? Not for me, of course. For Gisela. For your country."

"If Gisela married you, then you could both rule."

His eyes lit up like the wrong end of a firecracker.

"A unified Germany? You know your politics, *Schätzchen*, but maybe not your religion. She is married. So am I. We are both Catholics, and Catholics do not divorce."

"But they can kill." Her blood felt like ice in her veins. "Did she kill Rudolf for you?"

She steeled her nerve, wondering how it would go for her before once again, the game came crashing down on her head.

"Of course not," he growled. "Did *you?*"

"I'm not telling. So, the German hunting party? Why were they there?"

"In case she failed. Which she did." He moved closer still. "You did not."

And then his hand was at her breast, plucking at the laces of her filthy red corset. His lips twitched, along with his moustache.

"Come to my room. Perhaps I will quadruple your fee."

She thought of Sebastien, how she had felt his heart beating back in the gorse, how she had been so tempted to kiss him then but had not. And in an instant, she realized that was not a Black Swan. She was not a Mary Vetsera, seducing princes to get want she wanted. This, these 'womanly wiles', was not a game she wanted to play even if she could. She was made of different stuff.

"I will only speak to Wales."

She tried to slip away but his hand caught her wrist, yanked her back. She gasped as his fingers grew tight and some of the letters dropped to the floor.

"This is an old game, *Schätzchen,* and I have been playing longer than you. Give me the locket or I will break you in half."

Suddenly, the adjoining door swung open. A couple stepped through.

"Willie? Willie, what the deuce?" bellowed the man.

Her heart leapt at the familiar figure standing in the doorway. He looked like a great, noble bear with bright eyes, saggy jowls and silvering beard.

Next to him, a woman in black hunt coat and breeches, currently sporting a black eye.

"Her!" screeched Marie Larisch. "What is that damned Frenchie doing here?"

"Get out, Uncle!" barked the Kaiser. "She's promised it to me!"

"Frenchie? What the deuce are you on about, Marie?" boomed Edward II, Prince of Wales, Crown Prince of the *Empire of Steam.* "You, Willie! Unhand that little *Cymry*! And will someone tell me where the hell is Mary Vetsera?"

***

"What the hell are you talking about?" asked Christien. "Evisceration and embalming? Surely people don't do that anymore."

"We are the Habsburgs of the *Gilded Roman Empire,"* purred Valerie. "Even our bowels are sacred."

He rolled his eyes. They were in a carriage on the way to the city centre, pushing through the throngs of mourners clogging the streets. Gisela was sitting across from him, Valerie at his side. Franz had been conspicuously left behind with a team of Hussars to search the new tunnel in the cellar. Naturally, Bastien had not been found and for the first time in his life, Christien felt a glimmer of pride at his brother's uncanny ability to survive.

"So, let me see if I understand this," he said. "All Habsburgs have their hearts removed, embalmed and interred in a special crypt in one of your churches."

"The *Augustinerkirche,* yes," said Gisela. "It is almost a part of the Hofburg now, it is so old."

"And then the organs? Which ones?"

"I don't know. The bowels, whatever they consist of."

Christien snorted.

"Cut out in one big armful. How very Ripper-like. And these are in another church?"

"In the Ducal Crypt, *Stephansdom.* "

"Stephansdom? "

"St. Stephan's Cathedral."

"And the body is in a third church?"

"Today, in the Court Chapel but tomorrow—"

"Tomorrow," said Valerie. "Is the funeral. His body will be transferred to the Church of the Capuchin Friars for permanent interment. It will be impossible to get to him once he is there."

"So you see," Gisela leaned forward. "It must be done tonight."

Christien stared at her, then Valerie.

"You're both mad."

"Your brother can do it, I know it," said Valerie. "What I saw with the relics—"

"You didn't see him in the cellar!" he snapped. "You didn't see the soot and the black eyes and the dead valet! He can't control himself, not anymore. I don't even think Ivy can control him. No one can."

He stopped his tongue and looked out the window, forcing the mask on tight. The skies were gray and heavy, the snow little more than black slush pushed against the sides of the streets. Black curtains hung from every window, black banners across every door. It was the very picture of despair.

"Besides," he grumbled. "You don't even know where he is."

"We don't," said Gisela. "But Sophie does."

"Sophie knows," said Valerie. "She will find him. He can't escape Sophie."

She reached to take his fleshly hand in hers, gave it a squeeze as if from a lover or old friend. Of which she was both.

"So, you will help us, yes? It is the best gift you could give to our people. You will be allowed to live and my father will be eternally grateful to the house of de Lacey."

He stared into her eyes, remembered the taste of her skin on his tongue.

"Perhaps I'll get an invitation to your wedding," he said before turning his face back to the despair and the streets.

***

This child wasn't Sophie, he knew. This was a ghost, a spirit, an echo brought out by the orb. Yet her hand felt very real in his and he wondered how far the line had blurred since the last horse. Soon, there would be no distinction, and the dead would be more real than the living. It was only right, after all. He couldn't remember a time when life had fit.

They had reached a dead end in the tunnels, a wall he could see as if in daylight. It was because of the black horse. Now with eyes as black as soot, blackness was median and light was the blinding. It was pointless to fight. He had tried his entire life but now, as fate set her course before him, he was free to follow. He knew who he was. He knew what he was. For the first time in his life, he knew.

Little Sophie pulled her hand from his, touched the wall and he understood. It was a wall of bones. Down here, beneath the city, between the churches, likely a repository of ages-old skeletons dug up from all the new construction. The *Ringstrasse* would be filled with them. And someone had done a fine job of piling them neatly and according to bone type – femurs with the femurs, ribs with ribs, skulls with the skulls, like a puzzle. The decaying flesh on the bones had become human mortar, giving the wall stability and strength. He knew this would not be the first wall of bones under the city. No wonder she brought him here.

He reached forward, touched the rounded knub of a femur and a scattering of rubble lit up across the floor. All bits of the same man, remnants of the plague hundreds of years earlier. He knew. He could see it as plain as he would a tree or a church. Catacombs and burial pits rabbiting the city, foundations of bone and skulls and death. Flames leapt in his left hand, snowflakes in his right and the bones began to glow.

"In nomine Patris et Filii et Spiritus Sancti," he said. *"Et nunc absolvo vos."*

With a rush of fire and ash, the bones disappeared, leaving only small pits where they had set.

He closed his eyes, laid both palms flat against the rough surface and prayed. The wall began to radiate like a furnace before disintegrating and the earth roared all around him and dust rained down from above. Earth shake, earthquake. Ash, soot and dust. This was his air now. His lungs would need little else before stopping entirely.

No, life never did quite fit.

Little Sophie smiled at him, folded up on herself and blew away with the ash and dust. But now, the tunnel continued where the wall had been. It was darker than dark and out of the darkness, the orb spun – slowly, sinisterly, hovering just above the stone floor and out of his reach. Archlight was calling.

With a deep breath of ash and dust, he set off to follow.

***

The carriage lurched to a halt, and a Silver Hussar held the door, propped an umbrella as Valerie stepped out onto the cold, wet street. Christien moved to follow but there was a sound like distant thunder and the ground rumbled beneath his shoes. Mourners in the square looked around, faces blank but they did not scream, did not run, did not even move. Panic, it seemed, was not an Austrian thing.

Valerie, however, clutched her umbrella just a little tighter.

"Earthquake?" he asked.

"Vienna never has earthquakes," she mumbled.

"It is a judgment of God," said Gisela. "One of the plagues because He is angry over Rudolf's death."

"The food is going bad," said Valerie. "There was no cheese or cake at Franz's *palais.*"

"Earthquakes and famine," said Gisela. "The plagues are upon us."

"Don't be ridiculous," said Christien. "It's not God. It's Bastien. He'll bring your city to its knees."

"Then we will kill him."

"Doesn't take."

From inside the carriage, Gisela grabbed his clockwork arm and pulled him back with surprising force. She remained dry inside the cab while the drizzle felled on him like a cold lover.

"Then you see why this must work," she hissed. "Rudolf must be revived for balance to be restored. Otherwise, there will be a war and the entire world will burn."

"You are putting your faith in the wrong man."

"We put our faith in God."

"Then ask him to do your dirty work."

"Nein!" barked Valerie, halting the fist that was swinging toward his face. Gisela growled, relaxed her hand, released first a deep breath, then his arm.

"You will meet at the Chapel tonight at midnight," she said. "You will have both the heart and the viscera."

"And if I don't?"

"You will die. If you get the wrong person's organs and Rudolf doesn't rise, you will die. If you only get the heart and not the organs, or the organs and not the heart, you will die."

"I presume these viscera are under guard?"

"Of course. They are Holy Roman relics."

"And how am I to pinch them?"

"Valerie says you are clever. You will think of something."

"And if I do manage to locate and retrieve his Most Royal Viscera, put them all back in and stitch him all proper, what if, at the end of it all, my brother doesn't show?"

"Simple. You will die."

"If the alternative is war and death, then I'm dead anyway. Why not just go have a pint at a local *Heurigen* and wait for it in drunken stupor?"

"Because despite your cynicism and debauchery, Christien de Lacey, you still hope for something better. Hope is a obstinate thing to kill."

She looked at her sister.

"Do not fail. *Maman* is trusting us."

"We will not fail," said Valerie.

Gisela disappeared back into the cab and the coach sped away, leaving them in the middle of throngs of mourners. Black-clad and blank-faced, people pushed their way into the square on their way to the Hofburg, not even noticing the sister of the man they were coming to mourn.

The Archduchess turned to him, the umbrella keeping the rain from her head. He, on the other hand, was soaked to the bone and he rubbed his arms, trying to get the feeling into them. It was pointless. The clockwork arm felt nothing.

"What about surgical instruments? Am I to loot a hospital as well?"

"*Maman* has arranged for those."

"And *Papa?*" he asked. "What part is he playing?"

"You know nothing," she said. "Papa is occupied with funerary protocols. Rudolf's is a state funeral of historic, religious and international importance. Besides, Papa is still Emperor. He first concern is the ongoing stability of the *Gilded Empire.* It is an enormous responsibility."

"And here we are, about to sabotage all that hard work."

She scowled but did not strike. They turned, began walking eastward.

"So where is this church?" he sputtered. The rain had slicked his hair onto his forehead. He didn't care to push it off.

She pointed to a Gothic spire, towering over the square like a fist raised to heaven. It was grey and gruesome, with grinning gargoyles and gravestones embedded in the façade.

"Stephansdom," she said. "The largest, most beautiful cathedral in all the city."

"Do they do ritual executions as well? It smells like an abattoir."

Down the street, a butcher was tossing his wares out onto the walk and the mourning crowd was giving it a wide berth. Sides of beef, slabs of pork, sausage coils and piles of veal, blood running between the cobbles like a spring river.

"That is Kirchmann's," said Valerie, covering her nose with a handkerchief. "Something is wrong with his coolers?"

"It's your curse, remember? Do you have any money?"

"Me? Money?"

"Do you?"

"No. I never carry money. It is vulgar."

"Bloody hell," he groaned. "Well, let the games begin."

And he grabbed her hand and dragged her toward the shop.

***

The floor of the Grand Hotel shuddered as if with thunder, and the gaslights flickered in the room.

"That's the second earthquake this morning!" boomed Edward, Prince of Wales. "I should've known Sebastien de Lacey would be in this thick! Ah ha! Ah ha!"

The Crown Prince of *Steam* stepped toward them, smiling from ear to ear. Wilhelm released her wrist and Ivy curtsied, long and low. Slinking into the room, Countess Marie Larisch scowled at her. Her eye was blackened like a schoolboy and Ivy felt an odd rush of pride that she had caused it.

Pride, she thought. It would be the death of her. Odd. She'd always thought it would have been her tongue.

"Your little spy was telling me everything," said Wilhelm. "She has become almost English. Her accent is quite convincing."

"This is not my little spy, Willie," the Prince said. "But she's bloody well clever enough. Impersonating Mary Vetsera. Brilliant, m'dear. Bloody brilliant."

"What?" bellowed the Kaiser. "This *is* Mary Vetsera! You said so!"

"I was *told* Vetsera was here by the guard at the door, Willie, but I can assure you that this is not Mary Vetsera."

He towered over her now and she dared not look up. Rather, she kept her eyes fixed on the floor, tried to calm her heart. It was racing like wild horses.

"It is *not* Mary Vetsera," hissed the Countess. "She is the French Anarchist's woman! She has letters belonging to me!"

Eyes on the floor. Eyes on the floor.

"Rather, I think," said the Prince. "Letters belonging to me?"

And he lifted her chin so there was nowhere else to look but his face, his big, bushy, bear of a face.

"You look like you've had a time of it, eh wot, little *Cymry?* As wild as I remember. How's the ankle?"

The tears were stinging yet again and her throat had grown tight. She was so very tired.

"Fine, Your Most Royal Highness," she managed. "Healed up right quick, it did."

"How about a cup of tea? You'll have to make due with honey and lemon, mind. Apparently, there's been a spot of trouble with the milk."

She nodded. Her words had fled.

"Right then," and he turned to the Countess. "Marie, be a love and ring for some tea. Better yet, go back to your apartments and fetch some yourself. Clean up a bit while you're at it. You look worse than this child."

He glanced back at Ivy.

"She lives here. Did you know that? That's how we met, over cocktails in the terrace, what, seven years ago?"

"Six," growled Marie and Ivy thought that, right now, she was more black cat than swan.

Wales turned and stared at the woman, intelligent eyes shining, the smile fixed on his wooly face. If he'd had his cane, he'd be thumping it firmly on the floor. Once, twice, three times.

"It's not my fault," Marie moaned. "I'll lose everything."

"Damnable inconvenient, life," he said.

With a snort, the Countess whirled and left the salon. He turned his bearlike gaze on his young nephew.

"Bismark wants you, Willie," he said. "Apparently, Franzi doesn't see your Ironmen as a tribute and has forbidden you from the funeral."

"What? He can't do that!"

"Taaffe is here now. Gisela is on her way."

The Kaiser unleashed a string of German that Ivy knew was not poetry. He stormed from the salon, but paused with one hand on the door.

"*Archelicht* is mine, Uncle. Three lockets, three Empires. That was the deal."

And he slammed the door so that the paintings rattled in their frames.

Wales looked down at her once again.

"Let's sit, shall we? The world is about to go to war over these bloody lockets and I for one, could use some answers."

He slipped a hand into his pocket and what looked like icing sugar fell to the floor. He pulled out a pendant, held it up with two fingers.

"For example, why the bloody hell is m'pocket filled with snow?"

At the end of her serpentine chain, the locket Ghostlight glittered and danced like a star.

Chapter 22
Of Lemon Tea, Moldy Sausages and Black Death at the End of the World

Dunn had been right. It was a tight squeeze.

She had stripped down to corset, breeches and little else to fit into the Grand's dumbwaiter. Antoine Marionette had rewired the cables so that she was sent down the shaft to Maximilian's room, where she was to wait until the Crown Prince answered the door. But it had been several minutes now and she could hear him still reading the lines of a speech to himself. It was hot inside the metal box and her legs were beginning to cramp. She wondered what explanation might best suit her in the event she broke out of confinement and into his room.

Given her attire, that shouldn't prove too difficult.

But there, she heard a knock on the Prince's door, heard him cross the floor to answer. Heard the voice of Alexandre Gavriel St. Jacques in his Lord Durand persona and she had to give him credit. Surely, no one would suspect him if the Prince truly did have the Star of Morocco and if it went missing from his room. He was a smooth one, that rascal Dunn.

"Yes, by George," she heard the Prince say. "I could use a stiff whiskey and a plate of fois gras."

"Le Ciel has agreed to open for an exclusive after-hours tête à

tête," said Dunn. "It is Vienna's premiere hotel for a reason."

"Indeed!" laughed the Crown Prince and together the two gentlemen left the room. Penny waited until she heard the twist of the skeleton key before sliding the dumbwaiter's door up and dropping in an unladylike heap to the floor.

Quickly she bounced to her bare feet, slapped the cobwebs from her knees and drew what looked to be an Oriental fan from her corset. With a twist and a snap, it became a magnifying lens and Penny Dreadful, Girl Criminologist, got down to work.

***

Tea with lemon was not her choice but apparently, there was a problem with the milk in the Grand Hotel. Didn't matter. For Ivy, she was simply grateful that her hands had stopped shaking and that both Wilhelm and Marie had left the room.

"I didn't believe the press. French anarchists, indeed. No bloody anarchist is going to kill a Habsburg. They're too wiley for that! Ah ha! Ah ha!"

She tried to smile. His affable manner put most at ease, but here, with Ghostlight sitting on the coffee table in front of her, it was little more than a well-practiced show.

He noticed and sank back in his wing chair, raising the teacup to his moustache.

"Now, little *Cymry,* don't tell me that was the *Chevalier* that plumb crashed in *Reichsland,* wot? That was one damned fine airship."

"We were shot down, sir," she said. "They thought Sebastien had something to do with Rudolf's death."

"And did he?" Those eyes, so kind, so cunning. "After all, he does have a penchant for shooting folk in the head, wot?"

"Not anymore, sir. He wanted the locket, true enough, but he didn't kill either of them. You remember what Ghostlight did to Christien. It's not much of a stretch to believe Arclight can do the same to someone else, if not more."

"Sticky business, these lockets."

And he sipped his tea, made a face, set the cup back into its saucer.

"Can't abide m'tea without a spot of milk, wot? So where is he then, our Laury boy?"

"I don't know, sir. I left him with Christien in Franz Salvator's *palais.*"

"And when was that?"

"Last night, I think. Yes, last night. He was hiding from horses."

"What's that? Horses? That boy loves his horses! Why, no one loves horses as much as our Laury!"

"Not these horses, sir." She set down her teacup. "They're ghost horses."

"Egad. That boy does get himself into some pretty pickles."

"He does indeed, sir."

She glanced down the locket, her rings flashing merry colours and spinning a pile of fresh snow on the table. She had nothing to lose. Even her heart was weary of beating.

"If you don't mind me asking…"

"What's that, little *Cymry?* "

"How did you get it? The locket, I mean. Last I saw, she was lost in the Thames after the cataclysm at St. Katharine's Docks."

He reached down to gather the Vetsera letters in his hands, straightened them, shuffled them, straightened them again, placed them in a neat stack on the table. Next to the snow.

"Sir?"

"Jack Williams gave her to me," he said finally. "Says he got her sent to him along with an old Frenchie book and a human heart."

"A heart?" She remembered the cold sticky feel in her hands.

"Indeed. So he gave the damned thing over to the Club for safe keeping."

"But it doesn't belong to the Club, sir. It belongs to Sebastien de Lacey."

"And Sebastien de Lacey belongs to the Crown and the Crown funds the Club."

He lifted his clockwork arm, tapped the elbow and a cigarette popped out. She was surprised he'd lasted so long.

"Come now, little *Cymry*, don't act so shocked. The world is governed by politics. Men understand this quite well. That's why there are so blessedly few women in charge, wot?"

"I'd say your mother has done rather well, sir."

"Dear old mummie. She's a horse of a different colour, she is."

She set her cup down next to the locket, heat from the cup causing snow to melt into little puddles on the table. The letters were sitting next to it, each of them stamped in black wax.

"What did Kaiser Wilhelm mean, sir? He said 'Three lockets, three Empires. That was the deal.'"

His intelligent eyes bored into her as he inhaled a deep breath, held it for a long moment before releasing it in a long, white stream.

"Times change, little *Cymry*. Governments change. Allegiances are only as good as the weakest link. The Habsburg locket was, shall we say, a well-known secret among us. Franzi had it but never flaunted it. Flaunting is apparently not the *Gilded* way, wot? But after the docks…"

He lifted the cigarette to his lips, blew the smoke out the side of his mouth.

"After the docks, there was no hiding the fact that there were more."

She held her breath, wondering how much he knew.

"More, sir?"

"Three, to my knowledge," he said. "Although where the third one is, no one knows. If that Czech madman, Frankow knows, by jove he ain't telling."

She sighed, grateful for that small fact.

"So then, if you agreed that *Blood and Iron* should get Arclight, why would you hire Mary Vetsera to steal it?"

"Hold on to your knickers now, little *Cymry*. I never said *Blood and Iron* should get her. That's Willie - all bombast and swagger. Oh no, no, no. I never said that at all."

He flicked ash onto the carpet and leaned forward, eyes dancing.

"I hired Mary Vetsera to steal it, for *me.*"

***

"That smells disgusting," grumbled Valerie. "You should have found a better sack."

"We could use your skirts," he said.

"*You* are disgusting."

Christien grinned to himself. She was completely right. Under the pretense of helping the butcher he'd nicked a potato sack and, while Valerie had distracted him, he'd cut a section of sausage links using the snips he'd had in his prosthetic hand. They had subsequently fled the scene but the trail of evidence was not terribly hard to follow if one still had a nose.

The crowds near St. Stephen's were pressing – some moaning, some praying, some literally genuflecting on the streets. There was a mob around the main doors but she led him around the southeast corner to a set of stone steps that went down below the street. She paused at a small iron door, pressed a code into a keypad and stood back to wait.

"*Zugriff verweigert,*" buzzed the lock.

"Denied?" Valerie frowned, entered the code again.

"*Zugriff verweigert.*"

"That is impossible. It is an Imperial code."

"Your father's been busy," said Christien.

He pushed the sack into her arms and raised his clockwork hand. The skeleton key replaced the snips and he raised a brow at her.

"I think I'm beginning to enjoy this. I wonder what other parts would be better off clockwork?"

And he slipped the key into the lock. The wrist spun several times until there was a clank and the tiny door swung open, the odor of damp stone hitting them like a wall.

"At least it smells better than this," and she shoved the sausages back into his arms.

Valerie went first, ducking low as she went in and he followed, watched as she dipped a finger into a bowl of water on the side and curtsied, making the sign of the cross.

"The Bishops' Crypt," she whispered. "The Ducal Crypt is this way. But there will be security. The Silver Hussars, most likely."

"Are Rudolf's viscera on display yet?"

"As of two days ago, yes."

"Then there will be mourners as well as Hussars. This could be problematic."

They passed rows of simple caskets, some made of wood, others made of copper, and the subterranean walls were whitewashed stone. Cogwheel lights ran along wire tracks and he mapped them with his eyes as an idea began to form.

The hum of voices, low and chanting, and in a corridor ahead of them, a wall of people flowing like a river. Pressed three and four deep, they were shuffling down a tunnel toward a distant, circular antechamber. Beyond that, Christien could see the glint of Silver Hussars.

Valerie ducked back, pulling him to her and the sack dropped to the floor.

"The Hussars," she gasped. "They cannot see me. They have face recognition algorithms. If we are caught, Papa will disown me."

"But he will *kill* me. How equitable."

"We have *Maman*. She understands the spirit world. She believes your brother can do this. She believes with all her heart. Like you, she still has hope."

"Hope," he grunted, "Is not a word in my vocabulary. However…"

Her body was warm in this cold cavern, her eyes – usually so sharp, were wide, trusting. He wasn't certain, but he thought his heart skipped a beat.

"Yes, Remy? However?"

"I think I might have a plan. You'll need these."

And he raised the clockwork arm once again, called the snips and they popped up. With his human hand, he began to work the tiny screws that held them in place and soon, they came free in his grasp. He pressed them into her hand.

"Here," he said.

She took them but did not let go and his heart thudded at the touch of her fingers. She raised the prosthetic to her lips, began to travel along the copper with her mouth, all the while, her steely eyes locked with his.

"Hardly proper behavior from a woman engaged to be married," he said.

"Habsburgs," she murmured as she kissed his cabled palm, "Do not marry for love."

"Come away with me, then. We don't have to do this. We can go and never be found."

"I can't."

"You can. We can."

And he leaned in to kiss her, tasting the salt of her tears, the sweetness of her skin. Brandied peaches forever on his tongue.

He leaned his forehead against hers.

"We can do anything we want, empires be damned."

"And your brother? Your writer girl?"

"They can take care of themselves, believe me. I have nothing back home for me. Nothing at all. That's why I came."

"I'm glad you did."

He wiped her tears with his fleshly fingers, studied her eyes, her blushing complexion, her perfect lips. She was so beautiful, complicated, elusive. Everything he had ever wanted or could ever want. He could lose himself in her forever.

He froze.

"By god."

"Remy?"

"By god, you're playing me."

Straightened. Stepped back.

"You're playing me. You're saying what you think I want to hear so I'll perform, so I'll do what you want and steal those damned urns and patch up your brother. God, what a fool I am."

"No Remy, it's not like this."

"I can't believe I fell for it."

"Remy, please."

"Wait ten minutes then cut the wire to the cogwheel lights. Anywhere along the track, it doesn't matter. I'll have those viscera for you and we can move on to the heart. Perhaps I can give Rudolf mine. It was cut out long ago."

And he pushed away and left her standing, to lose himself in the crush of the crowds flowing toward the Ducal Crypt.

***

He was utterly lost but following the orb and the tunnels alternated low and smooth with narrow and rocky. It seemed that some of the tunnels were old cellars – evident from the petrified barrels lining the walls. Others were storm sewers that ran deep beneath the city, slick with ice now in winter. Others were older, almost Romanesque and then there were the catacombs – mile upon mile of intersecting caverns that connected the churches from underground. Vienna was a city of many, many churches. They buried a lifetime of dead.

He had no idea how far he had come, nor where beneath the city he might be. Bones littered the floors and with each piece, he released the dead attached to it. Here and there, an ossuary pit going deeper, utterly black in the catacombs but with his new eyes, utter blackness was simply a matter of perspective. The release was becoming progressively easier as well, and he found the ash of bones as sweet as water in a desert. He breathed it in and he wondered if he were still alive or something else entirely.

Because I could not stop for Death, he kindly stopped for me.

Arclight was so close now. He could feel her drumming his heart, pulsing his blood. Her voice was music – hypnotic, intoxicating music and he longed to drink her in. High above somewhere, Ghostlight sang with her, and the harmonies were sweet and deadly. Snow and flame, fire and ice. He knew that once he had both, he could amplify their song, releasing the *re obscura* and the city would shatter into a thousand thousand pieces. The *re obscura* would consume everything in its path, city by city, until the world itself was a hole, one large gaping black hole in a universe of stars.

The Carriage held but just Ourselves – and Immortality.

Immortality. Life forever and ever and ever, world without end, except it would end but he wouldn't and he would have everything and nothing and all things would be his to control.

But not Ivy.

The orb was hovering near another dead end stacked with gruesome, grinning bricks. At least twelve feet long and seven feet high, a wall of skulls blocked his path. Most of them were here because of the plagues that had swept the continent over the centuries. The Black Death, it was called. The Black Death had sent them here and now, as he stood with soot raining from his hands and mouth and eyes, it was only fitting that the Black Death would release them.

He laid his palms atop two skulls and suddenly, hundreds of orbs appeared, spinning and flashing, lighting up the cavern like the lights of Carnival. He could see the faces, the twisting of the mouths, the last late flicker of life in the eyes. He closed his own and whispered in Latin. One by one, the skulls disintegrated and the wall disappeared in a rush of ash and soot.

Once again, the earth rumbled and all around him, stones and chunks of earth dropped to the floor, threatening to bring the tunnel down on his head. He didn't mind. Burial was only a temporary solution. It had stopped him before but not now. He wondered if there was anything that could.

As the dust settled, he could make out a figure standing where the wall had been, porcelain mask a beacon in the darkness.

"*Bruder,*" said Sophie.

And around her neck, Arclight flashed like a lighthouse, calling him home.

***

It took seven minutes to shuffle with the mob to the subterranean burial chamber known as the Ducal Crypt. Two minutes to fall into line before waiting his turn at the pedestal and the copper urn containing imperial intestines. Two Silver Hussars standing on either side, sabre-arms held at attention, mirrored faces seeing all. One minute to go and his heart was racing as he counted the seconds. Thirty now as he knelt before the urn. Ten now as he made the sign of the cross like every other mourner before him.

Three as he laid the sack on the ground, clasping his hands as if to pray.

Two as he closed his eyes.

One.

Zero.

Nothing.

Nothing.

Cog-wheeled lights still on, crackling overhead with old wire.

The old woman behind him coughed.

He opened his eyes, certain his heart had now well and truly stopped.

"Move," hissed the old woman. "You've had your turn."

As one, the Hussars turned their silver heads toward him.

"Move," growled the man behind the old woman.

As one, the Hussars lowered their sabres, took a step forward.

He staggered to his feet, released a long-held breath. Swallowed, made the sign of the cross once again. Glanced around for Valerie.

Nothing.

"Move," said the Hussars, with one voice.

There was no word for hope in his vocabulary.

He shoved his hands in his pockets and turned, preparing to take his place in the mob of mourners shuffling out of the Ducal Crypt.

"Your bag," hissed the old woman. "Take it! It smells like dead cats."

Slowly, robotically, he turned back, bent down to pick it up, when suddenly, the earth began to rumble and the Ducal Crypt was plunged into darkness.

***

"Oh look," said the Prince of Wales. "There's another one. Damned quakes. I hear Nippon's a bugger for 'em! Ah ha! Ah ha!"

The crystal clinked in their chandeliers and the cups rattled in their saucers. Soon, the rumble died down and Ivy looked up at the big bearlike man in the chair opposite.

"Not many quakes in Lancashire, I hear," he said, smiling.

"Getting back to our conversation, sir…"

"Dashitall. I was rather hoping you'd forget."

"Never," she said. "I don't understand why would you get Mary Vetsera to steal Arclight for you? Surely Ghostlight is deadly enough."

"Rule Britannia, m'dear," he said. "Anything that can gives you an advantage…"

"Is to be used to your advantage," she finished.

"Bully, girl! I see Laury *has* been teaching you a thing or two." He sat back, dropped the cigarette to the carpet and crushed it under his toe. "He's an asset, that boy. If only he'd do what he's told."

Her green eyes flashed. She was smarter after all.

"He *has* been teaching me, sir," she said. "And one of the things I know is how to get that locket to work."

"What's that?" He sat forward. "What's that you say?"

"There's no power in these lockets in and of themselves. Look at it. It's just lying there like a regular pocketwatch. Oh yes, it can make snow. Oh yes, it can flash like a kaleidoscope. It can even spin rooms into gold. The elements that make it up are wondrous and new but seriously, sir? If you needed more gold, you'd just expand into Africa or India or Arabia. But that's not really what you're after, is it? Not really."

He grunted, raised his arm, proceeded to light another cigarette.

"You would make a bloody good spy, you know that?"

She nodded, knowing it to be quite true.

He sat back again, blew smoke into the air, studied her with eyes that changed like the wind.

"Simple fact is, little *Cymry,* I don't want my nephew to get it. Nothing more than that. He's a willful, dangerous young man, hell bent on proving he's better than all of us, that he knows better. Not at all like his father, God rest his soul. Not like his mother, either. She's a good girl, our Vicky."

Vicky or Victoria, Princess Royal, oldest child of Victoria and Albert. Edward's older sister and wife of Frederick III, the liberal Kaiser who ruled for less than a year.

"Nine months was far too short for Freddie," the Crown Prince said. "I can't believe Willie had his father poisoned. I simply can't. But I don't know, do I? Willie wants what Willie wants, and he's been a spoiled ruffian all his life."

He blew smoke again, watched it as it swirled and changed.

"He's building war machines, you know. And not just airships and iron clads."

She swallowed, remembering them well.

"If he gets his hands on that locket, not only will he fund a war against the Republic, Steel, the damned Turks and us, he'll have his chemists and physicists working on it night and day until they take it apart and discover its secrets. Believe me, the power they will have will reshape the world. And, little *Cymry,* that is something I'm just not ready for. In fact, I am convinced the world is not ready for it."

She looked at Ghostlight. It was a beautiful, deadly piece with her kaleidoscope colours and pretty snowflakes and she hated it with everything inside her.

"Sometimes, little *Cymry, "* he said finally. "Part of being a leader is knowing when to act, and when to prevent an act. Arclight will be much safer in a vault in the Tower of London, along with her sister here."

"That's quite true," she said. "So why did you bring her?"

"What do you mean?"

"Well, if Ghostlight is safer for everyone in the Tower of London, why did you bring her here?"

"I…" He frowned. "Well, that's obvious…"

"Yes?"

He stared at her.

"By God, I don't know. It just seemed like the thing to do."

Ivy reached forward, picked up the locket gingerly as if holding a snake. Ghostlight's rings spun like a top, happily, merrily, innocently. Just as she had when floating through the ice and steam of the Thames.

"Of course it did," she said. "Like Wilhelm, the locket wants what the locket wants. Ghostlight wants Sebastien. And look. She's just crossed an ocean and is currently in Vienna, where he is."

"By jove…"

"The lockets need to be destroyed, sir," she said. "And destroyed completely, or once together, they will destroy the world and use

Sebastien to do it."

***

The rumble of the earthquake died away and the Ducal Crypt of St. Stephen's Church was plunged into utter darkness.

For several seconds, there was absolutely no sound. Not a cough, not a question. Even the Hussars were silent. It was as if the entire world was holding its breath.

"It's the judgment!" Christien shouted in German and his voice echoed through the shadows. "The judgment of God!"

He waited in silence, until the old woman.

"Yes," she whispered. "The holy judgment of God our Father..."

"God has sent the plague of famine!" He grew bolder. "Then the plague of earthquakes! And now the plague of darkness!"

More murmuring from the crowd.

"Cease and desist," said the two Hussars as one.

"Rudolf was firstborn and now he is dead! We must repent and flee this city of wickedness!"

"Vienna is Ninevah!" shouted a voice in the darkness.

"Berlin and London are Sodom and Gomorrah!" came another.

"Repent or we will all be destroyed!"

And as suddenly as they had gone out, the cog-wheeled lights sputtered back on. But it was a dim glow, a pale shadow of the original. Generators, he thought. Should have known.

"*Mein Gott!* A sign," breathed the old woman, and she pointed at the pedestal. "A sign from God!"

On the pedestal, there was no urn. Rather, a pile of intestines that resembled molding sausages.

And from deep within the Ducal Crypt, a woman who sounded suspiciously like Valerie von Habsburg screamed. The crypt erupted in chaos.

Chapter 23
Of International Politics, Imperial Holiness and the Face Behind the Mask

The crowds carried him up and out of the catacombs to the street, scattering a screaming mob in all directions and allowing him to slip unnoticed down an alley between the shops.

The rain had stopped but he could see his breath like white plumes in the grey afternoon. His limbs were a twitching mess as the adrenalin left his body, and he leaned against an old brick wall. He slid down to sit, dropping his arms across his knees and trying to control his breathing. He closed his eyes.

He had done it.

He had stolen the Holy Roman viscera, right out from under their bloody noses.

His heart was still trying to beat its way out of his chest and he looked down at the sack, the shape of the urn rounded and smooth. It was heavier than the sausages. Certainly less smelly.

A black shadow swept past him in the alley.

"Follow me," she said but did not stop, her skirts sweeping the snow from the cobbles like brooms.

He shook his head but pushed to his feet, threw the sack over his shoulders. But for once, did as he was told.

***

"Wo ist sie?" came a familiar voice. Ivy bolted to her feet as Gisela von Habsburg pushed into the salon, Kaiser Wilhelm and two Silver Hussars at her bootheels.

"There!" barked the Archduchess and she pointed. "She is under sentence of death! Guards, take her!"

The automatons clanked forward to stand beside her and Ivy froze, unsure of what to do, what to say, where to run.

For his part, Crown Prince Edward simply released a long stream of smoke.

"What's that, Gigi, dear?"

"Her! The Empress has issued an order. She must come with me!"

"Tut tut. By your own Imperial law, this apartment is British soil and this little *Cymry* is a citizen of *Steam*. She has claimed asylum and I, as ranking official, have granted it."

"You are an Heir Apparent, Uncle," hissed Wilhelm, "Waiting for your crown. *I* am Kaiser of Germany and King of Prussia. *I* am ranking official."

"Not on British soil, Willie."

"This is a *Gilded* hotel, only one step away from a German kingdom. Not one politician will blink if I have her dragged out of here by her breeches! They are far too busy drinking their *Veltliner* and watching their operas."

"That's enough," snapped Gisela. "You are a guest in this city."

"An unwanted one, according to Franzi," grunted Wales.

Gisela turned to Edward.

"I need this girl," she said. "If I promise you that she will come to no harm, will you release her from *Steam's* protection? It is a matter of state importance."

"No sir," begged Ivy. "Please."

"Now now, *Cymry,* you are a bricky thing. Buck up and no

blubbering."

He tossed the second cigarette to the carpet, crushed it as he rose to his feet. He was a tall man, a bear of a man, and even the Kaiser of *Blood and Iron* seemed to pale in his shadow.

"Does this have anything to do with Sebastien de Lacey?"

"French anarchists!" sputtered Wilhelm. "They should all be hung, drawn and quartered, and each piece sent to a different corner of the Republic. They could be used as target practice for my *Eisemanner.*"

"Your *Eisemanner?*" Valerie swung around to face him. "Your *Eisemanner?*"

"You remember them in Strasbourg, surely," he said. "They were part of the birthday parade."

"They are reported crossing the *Gilded* border and closing in on Vienna! Is this a part of your birthday parade, Willie? The *Anschluss* of Austria by *Blood and Iron?*"

The Kaiser's moustache twitched. He straightened his spine.

"Merely a tribute to the life and death of a dear comrade," he said. "Rudy and I were fast friends."

"You hated him," she snapped. "And he despised you. Get your filthy Iron Men out of my country!"

"And what about your bed? Do you want your German iron man gone from there as well?"

She struck him so hard he staggered back, but instead of retribution, he merely lifted his head and laughed.

She snarled but Edward stepped between.

"Enough," he boomed. "Willie has his own apartments here at the hotel and Gigi, you have your own *palais.* If it's a good slap and tickle you want, then off with you but Willie, you're half *Steam.* Behave like one then, will you? And Gigi, there's enough French in you to cool the hot springs at Baden Baden."

"My father asked him personally not to come and here he is!"

"For the summit!" barked the Kaiser. "Against those damned anarchists!"

"This is not about anarchy. This is about *Blood and Iron* trampling Europe under its boots." She leaned in, steely eyes glittering. "I want you to leave."

"I am on English soil," he grinned.

"I *order* you to leave."

"Very well. I will." He turned to march toward the salon door, but paused to bow like a gentleman. *"After* I pay my respects. I will see you at the chapel, Gigi."

And he slammed the door behind him.

There was silence for a moment in his wake.

"Right. That settles it," said Wales and he turned to the Archduchess of Austria. "You want the girl. There's only one reason you might. So I say again, does this secret plan of yours have anything to do with Sebastien de Lacey?"

***

It was a part of the Hofburg itself, white-washed and angular, with tiled roof and a single steeple. Unlike St. Stephen's, however, there were no crowds, there were no mourners. In fact, this second church looked locked up, with two Silver Hussars guarding the main doors, sabres and rifle-arms at the ready.

"Augustinerkirche," she said as they peered out from behind a wall of the Theatre Museum. "St. Augustin's. The *Herzgruft* is not underground, but rather behind the Loreto Chapel. To the right of the main altar."

"A crypt just for hearts," he said. "Sad."

"Holy," and she turned her face to him. "The practice dates back to Emperor Ferdinand IV. He was a great man."

"Will you have your heart cut out and placed in a jar when you die?"

She was close enough to kiss.

"Silver," she breathed. "A silver urn. It is an honour."

"It's a joke."

"Do you see that I am not laughing?"

He dropped the sack to the cobbles and leaned in, pressing her against the wall.

"Tell me everything you know about the inside. Doors, windows, clergy rooms. How do I get in without going through the front doors? Everything. And by the way, give me your gloves."

"Oh, you are dangerous now," she purred. "I'm terrified."

The blade sprang up from his clockwork hand.

"You have no idea."

***

"Gigi?" repeated the Prince of Wales. "I must ask you one last time, does this have anything to do with Sebastien de Lacey?"

"Yes," said Gisela. "But not the way you think."

He sighed, looked down at the golden leaves woven into the carpet. Smiled sadly.

"You know I loved your brother like he was my own," he said softly. "The days we spent shooting in the Vienna Woods or at Sandringham, or all our days at the race tracks, discussing politics and progress and science and ornithology. I think I shall never have such a friend as I had in your brother."

Gisela nodded and Ivy could have sworn there were tears in those hard Habsburg eyes.

"He loved you too, Bertie."

"If there was anything I could do to bring him back…"

"Give me the girl. We may yet have hope."

Ivy's heart thudded in her chest.

"You're going to do it," Ivy whispered. "Don't make him do it."

Wales turned to her now.

"Can he? Can he do this? Mummie's been after him for years but he's elusive, that boy is. Damned elusive like a cat."

"No," she said. "No one can. That is simply grief talking."

"We'll never know unless we try," said Wales. "Mummie would be ever so happy and so would I. Rudolf is the last, best hope for the *Gilded Empire*. For all of Europe, for that matter."

"Yes," said Gisela.

"Well, that settles it. Take her, then."

"But sir! You can't! We're British citizens, Christien and Sebastien too!"

Edward raised his arm. Out popped another cigarette.

"I did tell you, didn't I? Part of being a leader is knowing when to act. So buck up little *Cymry.* You've just been conscripted! Ah ha! Ah ha!"

***

There was something about a church filled to the ceilings with sad music.

St. Augustin's church was very different from St. Stephen's, white walls as opposed to stone, clear windows as opposed to stained glass, terracotta floors as opposed to tile. He found the understated elegance of it appealing. At the far end, Gothic and gold and at the very heart of the altar, a priest was playing a pipe organ. Christien didn't know music – that was one of Bastien's interests, not his – but he thought it sounded beautiful, rich and perfectly sad.

Rather like his life, he thought.

He had slipped in through the Imperial Library of the Hofburg, which was attached to the Augustinian wing which was attached to the Augustinian monastery which was attached to the Augustinian church. The Hofburg was a bloody labyrinth, a maze of tunnels and wings and corridors and passageways. Fortunately for him, Valerie knew them all.

Along with her black gloves, he had nicked a collar and cassock from the monastery residence and slicked his damp hair off his face. He walked now down the long nave toward the altar but veered right, stopping at a black iron door with a tiny window. He could see a priest arranging the urns but a Silver Hussar stepped forward, blocking the view.

"Kein Einlass," said the Hussar.

Christien cocked his head, not for the first time wondering how the Silver Hussars, with their lack of facial features, could talk. At this close range, he could see the slatted box in the throat and he grinned to himself. A clockwork voice box that mimicked speech. Bloody marvelous technology from the gadget set.

"**No Entry,**" repeated the Hussar.

"I'm here to see the Holy Father of St. Augustin."

The mirrored face distorted his reflection and he wondered if the face-recognition algorithms were shared between them, like a collective. That would be an impressive feat of AE programming. Terrifying, but impressive.

"MARCUS?" came a voice from inside. "Is someone there?"

"**Intruder,**" said MARCUS.

Eyes peered through the grilles on the window, eyes and brows the colour of coal.

"Who the hell are you?" the man asked.

Cursing priests. Bloody marvelous.

"I'm Father Dominic from the Diocese of London, *Empire of Steam,*" he said. "I'm here to convey the respects of the Archbishop of Canterbury."

Amazing how well he lied in German. He wondered if he could make a career being the first male Black Swan.

"London? There are no Catholics in London," said the man.

"We are a small number, but very devout."

"I wasn't notified."

"Neither was I."

The eyes narrowed as the man thought it over, and finally disappeared from the window. There was a click and scrape of old locks and the iron door swung open to reveal a man with short-cropped silver hair and the barrel-chested shape of a boxer.

And of course, another Hussar.

"Father Dominic, you say?"

"Indeed."

"Your German is good, my son, but there is an accent."

"Irish," he lied.

"You look like you've been in a fight."

"As I said, Irish," and he held up a flask that he had snatched from Franz's library. "I have been sent with Holy Water blessed by all the bishops and archbishops in London."

"There are no archbishops in London."

"Forgive me. My German is good, but not *that* good."

And he smiled.

The man studied him for a long moment, then stepped back.

"Come in then, Father Dominic from the Diocese of London, *Empire of Steam.* Come see over two hundred years of Imperial Holiness."

And with that, Christien de Lacey stepped into the Holy of Holies, the Hearts Crypt of St. Augustin of Vienna, one Hussar within and one without.

***

Sophie stepped toward him, porcelain mask almost blinding through the blackness of his eyes. Around her neck, Arclight glittered like a star and orbs spun into life like suns in the heavens, creating light out of darkness and death out of life.

Sophie clapped her hands.

"They are so very pretty!" And she giggled, her voice thin and childlike. "I never knew they would be so pretty but they are. Like the tears of a baby."

The cavern was filled with dead, thousands upon thousands in this underground tomb somewhere between heaven and earth. They were frozen, ghostly images in a forgotten photochrome, pressed along the walls, over their heads, under their feet.

"Why are you here, Sophie?"

"For Rudolf." He could hear the wheeze of her throat, the whir of her clockwork crinoline. He still didn't know whether she had legs or wheels. "His was a beautiful death, bleak and alone and sad. A very perfect Austrian death."

Arclight was calling, her rings spinning but instead of snow, sparks. Sparks and shards and *re obscura* and the dead.

"What do you want, Sophie?" he asked.

She moved toward him over the rubble that was the wall, stepping over the remaining skulls and he realized, with an odd detached thought, that she did in fact have legs. She did not stop until she was directly in front of him and he could feel her breath on his face. It was the warmest thing underground.

"What do I want?" she asked. "I want what was taken from me."

"And what is that?"

"Death," she said.

"Death?"

"My death. I want you to kill me. Only you can."

He studied her eyes behind the mask, the tiny pink of her mouth. Her teeth were very small, he reckoned. Like a child's.

"No."

"I have no life. I want no life. I want my death back."

And she reached up with a gloved hand. He stepped away.

"Don't," he said. "Your flesh will wither and die."

"It has already done so. I am a machine. There is nothing left for me but the sweet constant void of beyond."

And she touched his brow. Her hand was cold. Clockwork.

"Your eyes are black," she gasped. It sounded like a dove. "The third horse has found you. It will be easy now."

"I don't understand."

"You know that place, the beyond. You have been there too. Our Father sent you there."

"Frankow," he said quietly. Amazing how his heart still ached.

"You are his last and best. But I was his boldest. Firstborn of the Habsburgs. There was no one more important in the world than I. Of course he could kill you."

"It was my father, the sixth Lord of Lasingstoke. They were a part of the Ghost Club. They wanted to prove life beyond death."

"Did your father tell you this?"

"My father was dead," he said. "Arvin told me."

"He tells you what you want to hear, yes?" And she cocked her head. "And you still believe him?"

He swallowed but had no words.

"Of course you do. You love him. He is your father."

"Arvin Frankow is not my father."

"But he is your creator. You are his creation, utterly and completely. Has he ever told you how you see the dead?"

"That night—"

"No. Not 'that' night. Not any 'night.' Not our Father. Like me, you believe yet you shouldn't." She moved her hand now to his forehead, like a blessing. "The metalwork is almost undetectable. Exquisite."

"Very fine quality aluminium, or so I'm told."

"Not aluminium."

"What else would it be?"

He could see the eyes gleam behind the slits in the mask.

"You must ask him," she breathed. "Ask him before you kill him."

"Kill him?" he stepped away from her. "I won't kill Arvin Frankow."

"You will. The creature must always destroy the creator. It is the cycle of Life and Death."

"No."

"There are many things you must do before you become who you were created to become, before you accept the crown and take the throne. So many people will die, including me. It will be beautiful."

He shook his head, dropped his eyes to where Arclight hung across the iron corset, her rings spinning in opposite directions. She was playing like music now, beating his heart, pulsing his blood. She and Ghostlight owned his body, controlled his will. There was nothing he could do to resist them. And truth be told, he hadn't the inclination.

"You are lucky," cooed Sophie. "She sings to you. Not to me. I am not so perfect."

And she lifted her hand to the clasp of the porcelain mask.

She peeled it away, golden ringlets sticking to her forehead and clinging to the edge of the mask as if pasted. Raised her tiny jaw, face bare and exposed for him to see.

Either the most beautiful woman in the Gilded Empire, the rumours went, *or a machine.*

Neither.

"Give me your hand," she said in her thin, childlike voice. "We will finish this together. I wish to fully live my second death."

With her small blue eyes and tiny teeth, it was neither the face of a beautiful woman, nor that of a machine. Rather, it was the face of an infant who had died at the age of two.

She had never grown. She had lived but had never grown.

He took her clockwork hand and together, they stepped into the new tunnel and the labyrinth of stone and earth collapsed behind them.

***

It was a small room with a low ceiling, curved walls and two wooden shelves spanning them. Urns of different sizes and shapes lined the shelves, all silver and tarnished with age. The Holy Father had given him a history lesson on each one as two hundred years of Imperial Holiness played out like a college tutorial.

One urn was bright as the Queen's tea service and the Holy Father held it up with both hands.

"And this," he said. "Is the heart of our beloved Rudolf, released far too soon from this mortal coil. May God have mercy on his soul."

"Amen," said Christien. "May I see it?"

"You are seeing it, my son."

"Of course. May I hold it?"

"Why?"

The Hussar was standing watch in the centre of the curved room.

"The holy water," he lied. "I was instructed to pour it over the heart to wash it with God's deepest blessings."

"That's not a good idea."

"Why not?"

"It's been mummified."

"Ah…"

Damn.

"Ah, well. That is unfortunate."

He had no words for that.

"Well, you see…" He rocked on the heels of his wet shoes. "You see…"

"Yes, my son?"

"Well, I'm not exactly a priest."

"I knew that." The man's lips quirked as if to a private joke. "It was painfully obvious but I am a patient man and curious. What *are* you then, my son?"

Christien's slid his eyes to the Hussar. It was staring at him with its inhuman face.

He grinned.

"A French Anarchist."

The dagger sprang out like clockwork and he swung a savage arc at the Hussar, severing the cables at its throat. The automaton lurched but Christien grabbed its silver dome, yanking it from the shoulders and swinging it into the side of the Holy Father's head. The man staggered into the wall as two hundred years of Imperial Holiness were sent crashing to the floor.

Even headless, the Hussar came, sabre flashing and the black cassock tore at the waist, spraying a thin spatter of blood across the wall. Christien was quick however and rolled with the machine to duck behind its back. The crypt echoed as the Hussar's torso began twisting one hundred and eighty degrees. The sabre came with it but Christien rammed the head down onto the blade like an impaling pike. Sparks rained over the tarnished silver on the floor.

Swiftly he scooped the brightest urn, locking eyes for one brief moment with the Holy Father as he pushed himself to his knees.

"You will rot in Hell," the priest growled, wiping blood from his lip.

"Where I belong."

And he whirled towards the iron door, only to see MARCUS's mirrored head through the grille and the lock bolt slid home.

There was a moment, a long terrifying moment, and he realized that he had miscalculated, overestimated, undervalued, this situation and that he would likely die for this mistake. After all the atrocities committed by his hand in London, he would die for trying to steal a bloody heart. It was ironic, to say the least.

Suddenly, MARCUS' silver dome struck the grille and disappeared. The lock clicked and door swung open on a woman in black, a bolt of lace over her mouth and nose.

"Come now," snapped Valerie and he rushed out, urn in hand. She peered into the crypt, at the Holy Father struggling to stand.

"Forgive me, Father, for I have sinned."

She closed the door, locking it on him and the two hundred years of Imperial Holiness.

***

Ivy's world had grown very small very quickly, as Edward Prince of Wales reached across to take Ghostlight from her hand. He held it up, rings spinning like a mad top.

"If Laury can do this, little *Cymry,* he will be released from the debt he owes the Crown and will be made an Earl in the House. But I won't make him sit in it, with or without his damned blanket. Ah ha! Ah ha!"

Colours flashed all across the room, across faces, across walls, across empires.

"Remy will be reinstated into the medical program at the Royal with full honours and all his Ripper nonsense will be purged from his record."

"Ripper?" asked Gisela.

"And as for you, little *Cymry,* and your family in Stepney, name it. If you want an island in the Hebrides, if you want a house in Knightsbridge, if you want your mum and dad to spend weekends at Sandringham playing croquet with dear old Mummie, name it. It will be yours."

She stared at him, his intelligent eyes, his silvering chops, his big loveable bear persona. And suddenly she understood. He was just like Christien, just like all of these rabid royals for that matter, shaped by forces outside their control and simply wanting to find their way through the mire of life. Not so different from herself, really. Not if she stopped to think about it.

She took the locket from his fingers, remembered the day Christien had given it to her, a sweet and innocent gift from a loving fiancé. It was a lifetime ago.

"*When* we do this," she said. "We will ask one thing and one thing alone. That you and all the heads of state angling for points and all the broadsheets angling for scandals, that all of you do this one simple thing.”

Ghostlight glittered like a star.

“You leave us alone.”

With that, she slipped it over her own head and it nestled between her breasts, home.

Chapter 24
Of Window Forts at One Hundred Feet, Court Chapels Dressed in Black and a Reluctant Crown Prince Comes Home

He'd always known the Hofburg was a labyrinth. Now he was getting Pan's tour.

Out of the church into the Augustinian Wing, down a hidden stairway and through a narrow courtyard. They had even squeezed through a false wall into an abandoned storeroom with statues covered in cobwebs, and furniture stacked in piles against the walls. Christien wondered if they were awaiting the closing up of an empire rather than the funeral of a Crown Prince.

Before he knew it, they were on the roof. Below, hundreds of people crushed together in the many courtyards, all waiting for a chance to view the body, pay their respects. Above them, at least seven airships including the *Stahl Mädchen* and Bertie's *HMS Royal Carolina* and he wondered how long it would be before they were spied and a cannonball sent down on their heads. Valerie crossed the roof like a cat, leading him to a very large dome with eight round windows. She lifted a latch and they both ducked inside. The casing itself was two feet wide, with a copper railing that had seen better days but even with sack filled with urns, they fit easily. They were also very high up, at least one hundred feet above the floor, and he looked down over a vast sea of shelves and balconies filled with books. No one could see them and better yet, no one could reach them. It was perfect.

Valerie pulled him to sit on that ledge so high above the world, began to unbutton the bloody cassock and peel it from the clothes beneath.

"What is this place?"

"The Imperial Library. We would sneak in here as children, Rudy, Gigi and I. We would read the old texts and spy on the nobles and eat chocolates we had stolen from the kitchen."

He tried to imagine it. Gisela in a playfort.

"Then Gisela was too old and it was just Rudy and I, and then…" Carefully now, she folded the shirt away from wound. "Then, just me. High above everyone else, alone."

"I'm sorry."

"Don't talk."

"Why? It's only a… Oh."

A gash as wide as his thumb and as long as his forearm, sticky and red across his belly.

"Oh damn," he said, fighting a rush of light-headedness. "You can be certain there is no suture needle or cat gut in the prosthetic. Perhaps you could use the fountain pen."

"Hush."

"Valerie, stop it. I'm fine."

"No." She was dabbing at the wound with her black lace, succeeding only in smearing the blood across his skin. "No, this is not acceptable. This should not have happened. It was supposed to be easy, a simple in and out, but—"

Her chin was trembling and he puzzled at the tears gathering behind her lashes.

"But now, you are hurt and Rudolf is dead and *Maman* will leave once again and I'll be left alone in this horrible place for months, maybe for years by myself. All by myself…"

She glanced up, tears spilling.

"I was not playing you, Remy. I am not a Black Swan. I wanted to be but I failed. I failed every task they put before me. I was supposed to seduce you to get the other locket but I even failed at that because I love you and I don't care about the lockets anymore."

"You were supposed to seduce me?"

She nodded.

"Maman encouraged it. She wanted the other locket, your *Geisterlicht*. She knew you had it."

"Geisterlicht," he said, heart sinking like a stone. "Ghostlight."

"She wanted to give it to Rudy so he could be king of the Hungarians as well as emperor of Austria." She dabbed at the wound. It was a sticky mess. "But I don't care about it anymore. I am not a Swan. I am just a silly, foolish girl who loves you."

He studied her clinically, for he was, after all, a clinical man. She looked sincere but then again, her looks were a weapon, much like his. He wanted to believe her because deep down, Gisela had been right. He *did* hope. He hoped that there might be someone who might not find a better prospect, someone who might see something buried so deep inside him that was worth the trouble spent digging it out. He wanted to be more than a pretty face or a prestigious address or a future Baron. And he wanted to know that forgiveness could be offered to the London Ripper, and that perhaps he would not have to die with the blood of so many women on his hands.

But neither life, nor Sebastien, worked that way.

His heart had been cut out long ago so there was nothing left but the scars.

And the mask that had worn most of his life was still a good fit.

"Where is Rudolf's body?" he asked. "I still have work to do."

She wiped her cheeks with her palms.

"In the Court Chapel," she said.

"And where is that?"

"Here. In the very heart of the Hofburg."

"Naturally. Will it be empty?"

"*Maman* is going to pray. It will be empty."

"You have it all orchestrated, don't you? Are the tears on cue as well?"

She said nothing.

"Right," he said and rolled to his feet, began the process of removing the cassock and collar, doing up the buttons on his shirt, waistcoat and jacket. "May I keep the gloves? A souvenir of my wonderful time in Vienna."

She nodded woodenly.

"Shall we go? I have a patient to attend."

She rose to her feet, twisted the latch, pushed open the round window. The cold wind struck them like a fist.

Together, they climbed through and out onto the roof.

***

For some reason, her hand kept going to the locket as it hung around her neck. It was strangely comforting, as if it belonged. Odd, she had never felt that before, not in all the time she had worn it back at Lasingstoke.

It was growing dark, as it did on winter afternoons. Ivy was in another private carriage racing toward the Hofburg. Gisela sat across from her, watching the streets rush by with sharp Habsburg eyes.

"You have this all arranged?" Ivy asked.

"Completely," said Gisela.

"How? I mean, how can this possibly work? You hope Remy can steal the viscera. You hope he can steal the heart. You hope he will be able to put them all back into a man who has already been embalmed and is lying in state in a public chapel."

"Court chapel."

"Court chapel," said Ivy. "Not only that, you hope that Sebastien will in fact do what Sophie asks and show up at that same chapel to work a miracle that he might not be able to work."

"Yes," said Gisela. "I hope all these things. Hope is an obstinate thing to kill."

Echoes of Renaud Jacobe St. John de Lacey that night in Whitechapel. That night. It always came down to *That Night.*

She swallowed.

"Why didn't you just ask then before you shot us out of the sky? Why threaten us at every turn, with Hussars, with sabres, with pistols. Why behave like that, then wonder why we run?"

The Archduchess looked out the window and at that moment, Ivy saw the likeness of Valerie in her – the same profile, the same eyes, the same Imperial mask sliding into place.

"Have you ever loved someone," Gisela began, "So much that you would die for them? That you would not only die but sacrifice everything you are and had just to please them, to ensure their happiness?"

"Wilhelm?"

"Wilhelm is an *Arsch.* I meant Pappa. I love my Pappa. I love him so much. He works so hard for the good of the Empire. People have no idea how hard he works. I would do anything to help him."

Ivy thought of her mother, how she had stopped living after Tobias' death, and as a result in order to tend her, Ivy had stopped living as well.

"Life as a *Gilded* princess changes you," Gisela went on. "It molds you from what you were naturally meant to be, into something that is useful to the Empire. Rudolf was a clever, progressive scholar but he did not become not the military leader Pappa had hoped for, so…"

She turned back to look at Ivy.

"So I did."

"Life is funny that way," Ivy said finally.

"Yes."

"Do you love Wilhelm?"

She smiled sadly.

"I did. Once. He was a wild young man, so different from anyone in the *Gilded* court. He was proud and passionate and funny. And a very impressive soldier. We fit."

"But?"

"But he was told to marry whom he was told to marry, and I was told to marry whom I was told to marry. A Habsburg does not marry for love."

Ivy was beginning to believe it.

"We must get to the Court Chapel before he does. *Maman* will have it emptied so she can pray. There, your Christien de Lacey will put the heart and viscera back into Rudolf's body and stitch him up. Then, we will wait for Sophie and your Sebastien. Your Sebastien will say the words and bring him back to life. All of Europe will be astounded at the miracle that is Rudolf Franz Karl Joseph von Habsburg and we will move from glory to glory."

She looked out the window once again.

"And there will be peace in Europe for a very long time."

Ivy reached up to stroke the locket, wondering if peace was ever in the cards if Ghostlight and Arclight were part of the game.

***

It was impossible for him to breathe, and he paused, reaching a hand to steady himself against a cold damp wall.

"We are here now," said Sophie and she looked at him, her infant-face sickly pale in the darkness. "The Augustinian cellars will lead us to the Chapel."

He closed his eyes, concentrating on the moving of air into and out of his lungs. Not just air anymore. Smaller than air, particles spinning like the rings of the lockets, like tiny solar systems revolving around even tinier suns. The *re obscura* moved around those suns, slipped between them like heavy water. He could see it all with his new eyes.

"Of course, it will not be a good idea to go through the Hofburg. Not like this. I'm quite certain I look more terrifying than you."

She laughed, her voice like a baby bird.

"But you must be strong, *Bruder*. Just for a few moments longer."

"Why?" he panted, not caring for the answer.

"Because you must. Because the world is waiting for you. Can you see Rudolf now, *Bruder?*"

"I can't see Rudolf. I've told you that a thousand times."

"Use the orbs," she said. "You can see him. You will."

"Give me the locket."

"Soon. Soon all will be yours. Just look."

He turned, pressed his back into the wall.

"She's mine. Give her to me."

"Call her."

He reached out his hand and the locket rose from her chest, spinning wildly at the end of its chain. Suddenly, a large orb sprung up between them, spinning like a coin, flashing like running water. In the mirrored surface, he could make out a face, a man's face with thick moustache and large sad eyes.

"Look and see," said Sophie. "Rudolf is waiting for you to see him. Do you see him?"

"I see him."

Sophie squealed.

"What have I done?" His voice was hollow, echoing. "Mary…"

"Yes!"

"Mary, what have I done?"

"Yes, yes!" and Sophie clapped her clockwork hands.

What had he done?

Mary at the bottom of the step, staring up with empty eyes

"Yes, yes, you see him! I know you do!"

Blood seeping from her mat of midnight hair, Arclight rolling through the red, leaving tracks on the lodge's cold floor

"We will use the orb to go directly to Rudolf," said Sophie. "Go deeper, *Bruder*. You must! The Crown is calling."

"No," he gasped. He was underwater and it was heavy. Heavy, heavy water. He didn't know which way was up.

"*Archelicht* will help."

"No, please. I want it to stop. I want to go home."

"You *are* going home, *Bruder*."

The orb was flashing now, hypnotic and wild, and his head spun with the music of it all. The dead pressed in, an audience of thousands, as Sophie stepped forward. She raised the locket and there was a hush as the music fell silent and the world grew strangely still. He was certain his heart had ceased its rhythm minutes ago.

He was going home.

He closed his eyes, held his breath as she slipped the locket over his head.

"Prince of *Hades, Sheol, Nifilheim, Alvilag, and Duzakh*," she said. "You, Sebastien de Lacey, are the Crown Prince of Death."

On her serpentine chain of brilliant gold, Arclight fell to the centre of his chest.

Home.

***

The sight below was both warm and eerie, as the *Gilded* Empress Elizabeth sat vigil over the casket of her dead son.

Christien leaned over a marble balcony, his eyes taking in the scene below. Other than three immense windows and the chandeliers of gold – all else was black. The floor was carpeted black, the pews draped in black, the oratory, the walls, the altar. Even the statues of saints, draped in black. The funeral gown of the Empress was a study in ebony with obsidian pearls twinkling like stars in the train. The only thing not black in the entire room was the military uniform on the dead man himself, whitest of white, with medals of all colours across his chest. It reclined in its coffin on a pedestal of roses, seven feet above the floor.

He looked over at Valerie.

"And now, I must climb that, remove all that military rubbish, open his stitched body, replace the organs, sew them in and correctly I might add and close him back up before I faint of blood loss myself. Speaking of which, have his bodily fluids been removed as well? I would imagine so, if he has been embalmed."

She stared at him, blinking.

"God," he moaned. "I liked you better when you were a Swan."

"This way," she said, turning to lead him down from the balcony to the floor.

***

The Chapel Commons was filled with mourners, waiting for a

chance to view the body, waiting to pay their respects. In fact, it was so filled that the carriage was blocked and both Ivy and Gisela were forced to continue on foot. The sky was dark but the yard well lit, and it wasn't long before mourners recognized her and began to move out of the way, allowing the Most Royal Princess a path to the steps.

Ivy could hear the whispers as they moved, felt her heart pounding within her. Glanced up to see the seven airships floating like bloated dragons overhead, beams of light illuminating the emblems across their gondolas. People bowed, curtsied, made the sign of the cross. Gisela looked straight ahead, acknowledging none as she pushed through them like an icebreaker through a black sea.

Up a short but steep flight of steps, black banners hanging, black flags waving, and soon, they entered what Ivy could only describe as a cave of darkness, the only light being the flickering of tall candles. Her eyes were immediately drawn to the altar, the pedestal and the coffin.

Slowly, with the carriage of a swan, the Empress rose to her feet.

She looked to her right.

"Gisela," she said.

She looked to her left.

"Valerie."

Ivy's heart leapt at the sight of Christien and she immediately she rushed across the floor to wrap her arms around him. He dropped a large bag and to her surprise, hugged her back.

"You're alright, then?" he asked. "Not dead yet?"

"Not yet," she grinned. "Sebastien?"

"No idea." He released her and turned to the Empress. With a daughter on either side, she stood tall and resolute, her beautiful face in a mask of its own. "You have surgical instruments for me?"

She inclined her chin to the base of the pedestal. Almost hidden by the roses, a black medical bag.

He strode over to it, removed his jacket and began rolling up his sleeves.

"Remy," said Ivy. "You're bleeding."

"Hussar sabre," he said. "Devilish quick."

"But are you—"

"Yes," and he pushed the medical bag into Ivy's hands. "I'm quite able to put the innards back into a dead man."

"Show some respect," growled Gisela.

"Now putting the *life* back into him, that will be another story."

He reached high to grip the top of the pedestal. It teetered and his fine shoes scraped but within a heartbeat, he was sitting inside the coffin, straddling the Crown Prince of Austria.

"Please hurry," said Sisi. "The doors will be opened in one half hour."

"One half hour?"

"Yes, there is a late viewing tonight for Taaffe and all the court."

There was silence for a moment, before a sound rarely ever heard echoed through the chapel. Christien de Lacey laughed.

"What?" asked Valerie. "Why do you laugh?"

Still laughing, he shook his head, gestured for Ivy to toss him the bag.

"I don't care what Wales said," growled Gisela. "Once he's done, I will shoot him for that alone."

Ivy swallowed and wrapped her arms around her ribs, glanced around the black cave that was the Court Chapel. *This was madness,* she thought. They would be dead before the night was over. It was impossible to fear anymore, however and she wondered if Sebastien would shoot someone in the head, just for her. Just this once, she thought she might not object.

Suddenly, around her neck, Ghostlight began to hum.

***

Arclight was home.

Because I could not stop for Death...

The tunnel roared and earth rained down as the orb grew with each turn on its mysterious axis, changing from mirror to smoke, becoming black before his black eyes.

The world was turning black.

Re obscura. Dark matter. The darkest in all the universe.

He kindly stopped for me.

He wrapped his hand around the locket, feeling the flesh sear from his palm, feeling his bones leap with frost and fire. Smoke curled from the tips of his fingers, snowflakes from the palms of his hands. He released a breath that rose like ash to the ceiling, another that fell like soot to the floor.

One more, that seemed to stall before it even left his lips.

And that was the last breath to proceed from the mouth of Sebastien de Lacey.

He had stopped all together.

The world was silent, yet amplified. He could hear the drip of a faucet from the kitchens up above. He could hear the footsteps of the people on the streets, the cry of a baby in a top-floor servant's apartment, the rattle of carriage wheels through the ruts in Vienna's streets.

The Carriage held but just Ourselves…

He could hear a man laughing who had never laughed before.

He looked up at Sophie. She was smiling her infant smile, hands clutched beneath her chin. He could see her skull beneath her pasty face, the teeth white, eye sockets black as if viewing the negative of a photochrome.

He looked down at his hands. He could see the multitude of thin white bones within the flesh, the gaps black where the joints and digits met.

And Immortality.

She took his hand.

"Come *Bruder*, the orb is ready."

Pulled him from the wall and led him to the orb, where Rudolf's life and death flashed before his eyes.

Together, they stepped into the orb.

Once again, the tunnel roared as they were swallowed up and the world disappeared around them.

***

"Blast," said Ivy as the colours of the locket flashed across her face.

Suddenly, the candles flickered as the chapel roared and shook with a new, more terrible earthquake. Black candelabras thudded to the carpet, banners dropped from the ceiling, statues toppled to the floor. From his perch, Christien swore and Ivy looked up to see the pedestal tipping precariously forward. There was nothing they could do, there was no way they could stop it and he leapt from the coffin even as she dove to the floor. It came crashing down, crushing the roses with its weight, rolling once and shattering the first row of pews before coming to a halt, upside down.

Outside, the screams of a thousand panicking mourners rose to fill the night sky and the rumble of aftershocks.

"Lock the doors!" snapped the Empress. "Lock them all!"

Her daughters rushed to obey and Ivy knelt at Christien's side. Fresh blood was seeping through his waistcoat and running down his forehead. The clockwork arm was wracked with spasms and sparks sizzled where black glove met sleeve.

"I don't know if can do this, Ivy," he panted. "I've tried. Honestly."

"I know," she said. "I know. We all have. It's too much."

"We don't have time for this!" Sisi cried. "You must help Rudolf!"

"Rudolf is dead!" shouted Ivy.

"Ivy," said Christien.

"He's *dead!*" she repeated and she struggled to her feet. "And you can't bring him back, no matter how many people you threaten! My mum lost five sons! Five! I'm so sorry for your one, really I am, but death is simply a part of life! Grieve your son and get on with it! You'll do no good being stuck. It sticks all those around you too and that's not fair."

Like a slap to the face, the Empress pulled herself straight, stared at her.

"Come on, Ivy," grumbled Christien. "Let's put this coffin aright."

She realized her hands had curled into fists. She growled before whirling to help him to his feet and together they gripped the edge and heaved. The coffin bumped once, twice, before finally rolling over with a thunk. A white-clad arm, complete with military glove, flopped out of the casket but Christien tucked it carefully back in. He looked up at the

Empress.

"Give me some time," the young physician said. "I can do this. I just need time."

"Remy, no," said Ivy.

Slowly, deliberately, the *Gilded* Empress glided over to them and Ivy held her breath. Sisi lifted Christien's chin, kissed his forehead. She took Ivy's hand, squeezed with all her strength.

"Forgive me," she whispered. "Take the time you need."

Christien nodded swiftly, flipped open the lid and crawled back in.

"Five sons?" asked Elizabeth. "How did she survive?"

"She didn't. That's how I know."

"Listen," called Valerie from the stairs.

"I hear screaming," said Sisi. "And the cowardice of Vienna."

"No, *Maman*, listen!"

The sound that had seemed merely an aftershock was now growing and Ivy blanched, so easily recognizable once heard. The rumble and screech of metal track wheels rolling on cobbled streets, carrying soldiers of immeasurable weight.

"Oh god," said Christien from the casket.

"Sentinels," breathed Ivy.

"Eisenmanner," hissed Gisela. "I will kill him myself."

The door to the stair banged as if with a fist.

"Let us in!" shouted the voice of Wilhelm II. "We have come to pay our respects!"

"We told you not to come!" barked Gisela and she leaned against the door as if to stop him.

"You have insulted the *Empire of Blood and Iron* and have caused affront to the *Empires of Steam and Steel!* Let us in our we will blast this door to ashes!"

"Hurry," said Valerie.

"Was ist los? Sisi?" came a voice from the balcony.

They looked up to see His Imperial and Royal Apostolic Majesty, Franz Joseph the *Gilded* Emperor himself, coming down the stair.

Chapter 25
Of Living Dead Men, Broken Living Men and the Man in Between

Penny peered up into the darkness.

"Pull me up, Antoine!" Penny hissed. "Antoine, quickly!"

There was silence from the shaft and even the dumbwaiter was gone, having been sent somewhere other than Crown Prince Maximilian's floor.

"Drat," grumbled Penny and she folded her arms across her chest. Searching the Crown Prince's room had been a bust, turning up nothing in terms of world-renowned lockets or counterfeits of such, and she grudgingly admitted that she was no further along in the case of the Villain of Vienna than when she'd started.

"Of course," she said to herself. "It could be all a ruse of that rogue, Alexander Dunn. For all I know, he could be absconding with the jewel at this very moment."

With a harrumph, she took several steps toward the very fine gold-edged door when there was the sound of a key in the lock, followed by the sound of men's laughter on the other side.

"Blast!" she snapped and whirled, rushing back to the dumbwaiter and ducking her head, slipping one bare foot, then her entire torso

inside. Braced against the sides of the shaft, she slid the door shut and begun to climb the cables, hand over fist, up, up, up into utter darkness.

***

"Was machst du?" barked the Emperor as he marched down the steps. *"Sisi? Gigi? Wer sind diese Leute?"*

It was then that he spied the casket and the young physician kneeling atop his dead son, heart and intestines and exposed cavities and a blade and there was silence for a very long moment as everyone in the chapel held their breath.

Until the *Gilded* Emperor, Ruler and Apostolic King of half the known world, opened his mouth and a terrible sound came forth.

It was the sound of heartbreak. It was the sound of ultimate misery. It was the sound of a strong man pushed too far and for too long and shattering into a hundred different pieces for all to see. His cry reverberated off the walls and the banners and the windows and the floors and threatened to rend the very heavens with his pain.

"Nein, nein, nein, nein!"

He rushed down the steps toward the casket but his daughters caught his arms, held him back even as he flailed against them. He sank to his knees, finally crushed by the weight of his position, sobbing with a lifetime of buried sadness. The girls hugged him now, their own tears joining his, but even still, his gloved hand reached between them, striving for one last touch, one brush of a finger on the polished, final bed of his son.

Watching them all, rigid and unmoved, arms wrapped around her waist was Sisi, her face an emotionless mask.

"Nein, nein, nein," sobbed Franz Joseph. *"Mein Sohn, Mein Rudolf..."*

"Pappa," said Gisela, and she began to speak quietly but quickly, glancing at Christien, nodding and nodding again. Valerie too, whispering and nodding and it took a moment for Ivy to realize that Wilhelm was still pounding on the chapel's door.

She crossed the floor, leaned her cheek against the wood.

"Go away, you horrible man!" she shouted. "People are grieving and they don't want you gloating during their time of sadness."

"You!" came the muffled response. "I will break you in half! I will break you in pieces! I will ravage you on the altar then throw you down to the people where they will tear your arms from your shoulders and your legs from your hips and your head from your neck and they will dance on your bloody torso, you little English whore!"

"I'm Welsh!" she snapped. "And I have the locket so I suggest you shut it, mate, before I turn *you* to gold!"

And there was quiet.

She turned her face.

"Remy, please hurry."

"I am, Ivy," Christien growled. "But if I connect the superior vena cava to the left atrium instead of the right, or the pulmonary artery to the wrong ventricle, I doubt very much that even Bastien is going to get this bugger on his feet. Besides, all the mesenteric tissue has been cut and I have to figure out how to keep his guts from falling down into his boots."

"I don't understand," moaned the Emperor in English as his daughters helped him to his feet. "I don't understand what you are doing."

"That's because you don't believe in the spirit," said Sisi, arms still wrapped around her waist. "You believe in the sword."

"I believe in my son!"

"You never did!"

And now she moved, a panther unleashed from its cage.

"Nothing he did was good enough! None of his ideas were worthy, none of his projects could succeed, not while you and Taaffe and Bismark had the reins. He loved you, Franzi. He loved you and you beat him down like a dog! It is your fault he is dead, Franzi. Yours!"

"No..."

"He killed himself, Franzi. He put that pistol in his mouth and pulled the trigger! It was only yesterday he was just a little boy!"

The Emperor looked as though he was about to sink to the floor once again, but his daughters were bulwarks, holding him up.

"But now we bring him back, Pappa," offered Valerie. "Now we make it right."

She was glancing between both parents and Ivy realized that, of all the children, Valerie was the peace broker, the youngest desperately trying to keep her fractured family together.

No wonder they married whom they were told. Habsburg love, it seemed, was a lethal thing.

"Yes," said Gisela. "And we will use spirit *and* science to do just that."

"This is blasphemy," said Franz Joseph. "He is desecrating my son's body!"

"No sir," said Ivy and she pushed away from the door. "Christien is a man of science. Sebastien is a man of spirit. If there is any chance in this world that can bring your son back, they are the only two in that world who can do it."

Except for the fact that Sebastien isn't here yet, she thought darkly.

There was silence in the chapel, save the rumble and squeal of *Eisenmanner.*

"It is true," said Valerie.

"Yes, Pappa," said Gisela. "Please, trust us."

Sisi said nothing.

The Emperor straightened and released a deep breath, smoothed his hands along his uniform, tapped the ceremonial sword at his hip once, twice, three times. He turned to the chaos that was the Court Chapel, lifted a toppled candelabra, set it straight.

"I must do something," he said. "I cannot be idle. I will busy myself while—"

There was a boom from high above the courtyard, a whistle and crash. An answering boom and sirens began to wail in the Hofburg.

"The *Stahl Mädchen!*" said Gisela. "Those are her cannons!"

She raced to the door, threw it open to find Wilhelm staring out at a battle now being waged over the Chapel Commons. Smoke and sparks rose from a silhouetted Sentinel, while behind it, a red beam swept the clouds from a second iron helm. High above, the airships dropped their moorings, slipping away from each other and jockeying for position and safety. The sky lit up as the *SMAS Eisenklaue* fired now and the *Gilded* dreadnought swung around to face her, the groaning of her hull like thunder in the night. The *HMAS Royal Carolina* and the *Twelve Apostles* gained altitude, obviously hoping to stay clear of the fray and any stray cannonballs that might be sent their way.

Gisela and Wilhelm began shouting on the stair and Franz Joseph moved swiftly to join them, when suddenly, unnatural colours flashed from behind.

"Blast," said Ivy and she looked down.

The locket, Ghostlight, was spinning, sending kaleidoscopic lights across her face, the ceiling, the black-draped walls. Slowly, it began rising from her chest, a magnet pointing home.

"Was ist..." mumbled the Emperor as he stepped back into the room.

High above the altar, a shape began to ripple and blur. An orb, easily the size of a carriage, bloomed into life – large, shadowed and shining like a great black pearl. It hovered over the altar with the hum of a powerful engine. Inside it, Ivy could see stars, suns, clouds, the infinite blackness of space.

Ghostlight leapt, her chain snapping taut against her neck and Ivy grabbed it with both hands. She leaned back but the orb roared and the locket strained and Ivy's very fine boots scraped forward on the floor.

"Remy!"

In the center of the chapel, the orb convulsed, shrinking, expanding and pulsing like a heart and a powerful wind picked up, stirring papers and fabric alike. The skirts of the women whipped around their legs, banners ripped from the walls, candles flew across the room, sheet music and prayer books and roses, all whirling now like a cyclone toward the eye. Even heavier items like pieces of broken plaster were dragged toward the orb, only to disappear into its starry depths.

Where Ghostlight was taking Ivy.

"Remy!" she cried again.

The Emperor's arms were suddenly around her waist, but even together they slid across the floor. Christien joined them, using his body as a shield but the pull was unstoppable and the three of them were dragged closer and closer yet to the massive orb.

"Let it go, Ivy!" Christien shouted over the roar of the winds. "That's what it wants!"

"No!" she shouted back. "Sebastien needs it!"

"He needs you alive, that's what he needs! Let it go!"

Roses whipped past her head, cutting her cheeks with a hundred tiny thorns. Even the Kaiser was being sucked into the room, he and Gisela clutching the doorframes to keep themselves aright. Valerie was behind a pew but its anchor bolts were rattling loose in the vacuum. The casket itself was bumping and sliding and inside it, Sisi held the body of her son to her chest. Even her tears were snatched from her eyes to disappear into the vortex above the altar.

Swiftly, Ivy nodded and the blade sprang up from Christien's clockwork hand, snapping the chain in an instant. Ghostlight flew like a shot into the heart of the orb, disappearing like a coin down a dark well. Immediately, the engine ceased and the wind died and there was silence for a brief moment in the Court Chapel.

With a rumble, the great black orb folded up on itself and disappeared, sucking the entire altar with it.

Leaving two figures where the altar had been. One staggered, losing sparks and springs before collapsing to the floor in a shower of smoke; the other dropping to hands and knees, greatcoat trailing soot like a shadow.

***

Outside, in the Chapel Commons, there were no mourners left. Rather, the Swiss Guard streamed out in double rows, rifles and bayonets at the ready. Hussars – human and silver – joined them until the entire courtyard was filled with soldiers, the Swiss flanking the walls and steps of the chapel, the Hussars surrounding the massive trackwheels of the *Eisenmanner*. High above, the cannons had fallen silent and there was only the creak of hulls and flap of canvas as *Claw* and *Maiden* circled each other, the others drifting just out of reach. Later that day, the papers would call it a monumental display of technology and weaponry and international support, put on for the eve of the Crown Prince's funeral.

Only those inside the chapel would ever know the truth.

Where the altar used to be, a woman struggled, arms flailing, crinoline hissing with steam and hydraulics. As if in a trance, the Empress rose slowly, moved slowly to her side, slowly helped her to sit. It seemed like ages before Ivy realized that the woman with the iron corset and baby-blonde curls was Sophie. Her signature mask was gone and Sisi ran her hands over her daughter's face, kissed her forehead, smoothed her curls.

Either the most beautiful woman in the Empire...

Slowly herself, she turned her eyes to the second figure. She did not recognize what she saw.

"Was zum Teufel?" said the Kaiser.

"Oh god," breathed Christien.

On his knees, Sebastien looked like a crumbling statue, unmoving and weathered. Soot rained like plaster from his fair hair, from his mouth, from his eyes. His greatcoat was tattered and the blanket wrapped his shoulders like a cowl, but they like his face, like his skin, were grey. Around his neck, Arclight, glittering and spinning and wicked.

In his right hand, Ghostlight.

"Ivy, don't," said Christien. "Don't touch him."

But there was only one person in her entire world and she picked her way over the rubble toward him. When her heart should be leaping, she found it was cold and she wondered if she was dead too as she sank down to her knees before him. Slowly, he looked up at her, his eyes black as night, no stars, no suns, only the great, empty void of space.

"Please," said Christien. "Just don't touch him."

She nodded. She had no strength to do anything else.

And the chapel was filled with infant laughter.

"Where is your mask?" asked Sisi.

"Gone," Sophie sang. "Gone, gone, gone, gone..."

"But you must wear your mask. Your face—"

"Is my face, *Maman*. There are no more masks. Not for me. I will enter my death with my face. My own face."

"Ivy," gasped Sebastien. His voice sounded a thousand miles away.

Tears rolled down her cheeks. She didn't know where they came from. Couldn't feel them at all.

"I can't breathe…Ivy."

She nodded.

"And the horse is coming."

It was obvious he was having difficulty speaking. Lack of breathing would do that, she reckoned.

"I know…why I couldn't see…the Crown Prince."

"He wasn't murdered," she said quietly. "He killed himself."

"Yes…with Sophie's help."

"Sophie?"

"Was?" said the Emperor.

"Sophie?" asked the Empress.

Sitting only a few feet away, Sophie von Habsburg clapped her clockwork hands.

"Oh *Maman,* you would have loved it," she said in her sing-song voice. "He was so miserable. He had just killed Mary and he was despondent."

"I saw it…in the orb," said Sebastien. "He carried her…up to the room…laid her on the bed."

"With a rose!" Sophie sighed. "A single, long-stemmed rose. How utterly, beautifully macabre."

Everyone was looking at her as she struggled to her feet. Ivy couldn't tear her eyes away – the infant face, the tiny mouth, the baby curls. All else was wrapped in cable or iron. Fashionably wrapped, so as not to give the impression of full automation, but she could not help but wonder if the little girl's body was contained within all that clockwork or if only the head and neck remained.

Utterly, beautifully macabre.

"I joined him beside the bed and we talked. Oh we talked for hours and hours about death and dying and the joy it brings. We had been talking for months about it. Oh yes, we had been talking for years. But now he was ready," she nodded seriously. "Ready to take that last, best step beyond."

Franz Joseph moved closer, as did Gisela and Valerie. Christien had resumed his work on the body and Wilhelm circled like a crow, watching all with his feral gaze.

"But he was frightened, you see? Even the whore Mitzi Caspar would not help him. Mary said she would but Mary lies. Mary wanted the locket for Wales, like Gigi wanted the locket for Willie."

"The girl was dead when I got there," said Gisela. "And the Germans were waiting in the forest. But I couldn't. I couldn't do that to Rudy, not after all that had happened that night…"

That night, thought Ivy. Somehow, it always came down to 'that night.'

"But *I* helped him," sang Sophie in her little girl voice. "I told him that he didn't have to be the Crown Prince anymore, not when the true Crown Prince was in Vienna. All empires were coming to an end and death for all the world was upon us. We would embrace it together. We sat beside the bed, I gave him my pistol and he gave me his."

She reached into her skirts, pulled out an iron cast in the twin eagles of the House of Habsburg. She waved it wildly and her sisters stepped back. Her parents did not.

"And so he did it. I gave him his morphine and he shot himself in the head. Blood sprayed on my face. It was beautiful, like a painting. Like art. I have never been so proud in all my life."

She laughed. It was the tinkling of bells but no one else joined the music.

"You are a coward," said Wilhelm.

All eyes turned in the direction of the Kaiser of *Blood and Iron.*

"You didn't do it," snapped Wilhelm. "You didn't shoot yourself. Rudolf is dead but you are very much alive, you little machine-girl. You lied to him!"

"Silly man! I wasn't lying. I knew that with *him* in the city, so many more could join us as well!"

And she pointed her finger at the Mad Lord of Lasingstoke.

"The end of the world is here. We are simply waiting for the last horse!"

From his place over the body, Christien looked up.

"Horse?" he asked.

"You are all cowards," said Wilhelm. "And *he* doesn't look like the

Crown Prince of anything. He looks like a dead man!"

And he leaned over Sebastien, eyes flicking from Ghostlight to Arclight. Both were swinging sweetly, happy to be home.

"And what does a dead man need with such pretty things?"

"Go away," growled Ivy.

"What? Or you'll turn me to gold?" He snorted. "You can't control those lockets anymore than he can. They are the future of *Blood and Iron.*"

And he reached his arm across the Mad Lord, fingers stretching to brush the glass, the silent rings.

"Good lord, you people!" snapped Christien. "I said don't touch him!"

Ivy slapped his hand away.

With a snarl, the Kaiser grabbed Sebastien's arm to pull him back, when he froze, eyes bulging, mouth gaping open, wide, wider. The scream wouldn't come.

The man staggered back, sinking to his knees and clutching his left arm. It was nothing but a withered stump, the fingers shriveled, the wrist twisted, the flesh dried like jerky. And still there was no scream, just bulging eyes and ragged breath and a rocking motion, back and forth, back and forth.

And the sound of infant laughter filling the chapel.

And someone else pounding on the chapel door.

***

It was all too loud for him.

"Mein herr! Est dir gut? Öffnen Sie die Tür!"

"Pappa?" asked Gisela. "The Hussars are at the door."

Far too loud and Sebastien rose to his feet, turned to the casket of the *Gilded* Crown Prince. He could see the bones inside his brother's skin.

"Remy?" asked Valerie.

"Finished," said Christien, climbing out of the casket and wiping his hands on his trousers. "Although I don't think the wax they've used for his skull is going to keep. And as I've said before, he has no blood, no lymph, no fluids at all and his brain's bound to be a bloody mess. Well, minus the blood."

Sebastien watched them all. It was like skulls talking. All he could see was the white of their bones.

"If you're hoping Bastien's going to make this body come alive, be prepared for the fact that he will not live very long and if he does, he will not be even remotely the same. I would strongly advise against it."

And with that, he snatched up the medical bag, crossed the floor to kneel beside the still-rocking Kaiser of *Blood and Iron*.

"I don't care," said Sisi. "I want my son back."

"I want my son," Franz Joseph nodded. "If there is anything you can do, please do it."

The Mad Lord looked down at Ivy. She was battered and bruised, but if he concentrated, he could make out her face – her great green eyes, the freckles on her nose, the quirky, grinning mouth. Beneath the skin, the skull white as a cloud, the hollows black as the night. Red washing through tiny rivers, pink coiled like sand castles, sparks racing like firebugs through her brain. But at least, he could see her face.

She tried to smile. It was thin, but still.

"Life," he said, his voice hollow and echoing. "When I look at you…I see life."

He offered her his hand.

"Ivy, no!" hissed Christien.

"I am Death but she…"

She took it and he pulled her to her feet.

"She is life."

He reached up a hand to touch her cheek. His fingers were rough but the touch of her skin was like fairy dust.

"Do you mind?" he asked. "I do marvel…at the fact that…you're real and very soft. Skin is…a remarkable thing, isn't it?"

She nodded, seemed unable to speak.

"I'm not sure…how much longer I will have mine but…yours is like the fall…of fresh snow. You barely feel it at all…and your hair…"

He plucked at a lock, ran it through thumb and forefinger, studying it as if it were a string of pearls. He could see the particles, spinning together far, far beneath.

"It's not like a horse or a dog…or anything else in my world. More like a rabbit or a feather…or a strand of spider silk…"

She made poetry out of ordinary things.

"Rupert… warned me about this," he said. "He said…I was above such things but…I think he was quite wrong. I'm not…above you at all. You are as high above me…as a star above the earth."

"Kiss me please," she said.

He leaned in.

"I…will be the death of you," he said. He could feel her breath on his cheek. "And I won't be able to follow."

"Then I shall live at Seventh and haunt you forever."

She closed her eyes as he kissed her.

Like twin engines, Ghostlight and Arclight began to hum, their rings spinning in opposite directions and colours flashed across the room. Orbs sprang into life along with the colours, turning the chapel into a dizzying carnival of light.

It was beautiful.

She slipped her hand in his but gasped as sparks leapt from twin bands on her thumbs.

"Oh wait."

She slipped two rings from her hands, held them up to gleam in the locket-light.

"Rudolf's wedding ring," she said. "And Mary's. I don't know if you need them but we went to a bucketful of trouble to fetch them, so I'd be pleased if you did."

He so wanted to kiss her again.

Instead, he took the rings in one hand, clutched Ghostlight in the other and the room began to hum once more. Together, they turned to the casket.

Christien had closed up the uniform and the Crown Prince looked as if asleep.

"No," wheezed Sophie. "No, do not do this. Rudy does not want this."

Sebastien closed his eyes. The voices in the chapel began to fade as the dead moved aside for his mind.

"No, *Maman.* Make him stop!"

"Sophie, hush," said Sisi.

The frost whirled and congealed, slowly, reluctantly becoming a man in white uniform.

"No!" wailed Sophie. "This is not the way! I want my death back! Our father took it from me and I want it back!"

"Sophie!" snapped her father. *"Schäm dich!"*

"No! I want it back. He is the Crown Prince of Death! Our father made him for me but he needs to accept the crown. He must accept the crown!"

She raised the holy Habsburg pistol and fired.

Chapter 26
Of the Death of Life, the Death of Death and the Arrival of the Last Horse

"Life," he had said. *"When I look at you, I see life."*

The sound of his voice, echoing through time, deep and ageless and free. At the touch of his hand, sparks and colours, warmth and light, cold and absolute utter blackness. And his kiss. It was perfect, like the kisses in all the stories and fairy-tales and novels she had ever read. The Bronte sisters couldn't have written a better kiss. Not clever Jane Austen either nor lyrical Elizabeth Barrett nor wild Thomas Hardy. She found herself breathing him as easily as a summer evening, ethereal and deep and she wished to write her own prose on his tongue.

He was beautiful – a creature not of this earth and she loved him with more than her heart, with everything that she was. It wasn't enough, not for him, but it was all she had and it was pretty good for a girl from Stepney.

She *was* a good girl from Stepney and she loved a Mad Lord from Lasingstoke and she would love him until the day she died. And for the rest of her life after that, she had promised.

But there was a sound.

Loud and barking like the crack of thunder.

Then there was the force – a shock, an impact and it hit her ribs, lifting her off her feet like a charging bull or a flipping steamcar. Dimly she was aware of flying, then of not flying, of roses and thorns and a face like porcelain, with pale skin and clear blue eyes and dark hair falling into them.

"Christien," she said but there was a sharp taste on her tongue and bitter and she tried to spit it out but more came with the effort.

There was heat, crashing over her like a wave of hot oil.

And then the pain.

***

Damn if it didn't sound like a pistol.

The veil was tearing once again, the veil between death and life, hammering nails into his brain. It was the same as the night behind Dutfield's Yard when Elizabeth Stride had died not fifty feet away, a victim of his father's fury and his brother's blade. Now, Sebastien could hear voices at the periphery of his mind but he was so deep in the deadspace and Rudolf just a heartbeat away. He could see the sadness in the man's eyes, even more poignant than the missing pieces of his skull. Sophie had been right. He didn't want to come back.

"Bastien!"

Ghostlight was flashing, sending snowflakes to the ceiling. Arclight was spinning, raining sparks to the floor. Standing before him, ghostly and pale, the Crown Prince of Austro-Hungary reluctantly offered his white-gloved hand and stepped toward him through the void and the stars. It would be a feat to reunite him with his body, both broken and embalmed. He had never done such a thing. He had never done it, but then again, he had never tried.

"Bastien!"

Christien's voice piercing the deadspace, causing it to ripple like a pebble in a pond.

"Bastien!"

He tore his eyes away. They didn't work well in this world, he knew. Figures were skeletons and tendons, muscle and organ. It took all

323

of his effort to see his brother *as* his brother, and more than that, to see him kneeling over another figure on the black-carpeted floor, bloody hands clutching his sleeve.

There was a woman.

"Bastien! I need your help!"

Her hands, her boots, her blood. The rivers of red now slowing, pooling, the heart coughing red into the cavity, rhythm stopping and starting and stopping and starting. There was a woman and his own heart thudded inside its prison.

Stopping and starting like his world.

He sank to his knees beside them.

"Ivy?"

"Can you touch her, Bastien? Because if you can, I need you to put your hands here. I need you to stop the bleeding."

The words like rainwater, impossible to catch.

"Bastien? Can you? I have to get my medical bag."

"Ivy? How?"

"Here. Do it. Now."

He pressed his hands into her ribs. She arched her back and threw back her head, trying to fill her lungs with anything but blood.

Ivy.

And suddenly, Christien was gone, leaving him with his whole world writhing on the floor.

He wished he had breath to give her but his was gone, like the sunshine. Like hope and reason and daylight and love. Like night and winter and dark and cold. He couldn't believe what was happening. It had the appearance of a dream. A slow, agonizing, distorted dream. A nightmare.

What had he done?

She grabbed his sleeves now, her boots scraping the floor, chest convulsing with spasms. He slipped one hand behind her head, leaned to press his forehead against hers, as if his very closeness could bring relief.

He would be the death of her.

"Ivy," he said. "Ivy, look at me."

"Laury?" she gasped, blood bubbling at the corner of her mouth. "It hurts. Oh, it hurts…"

Then I shall live at Seventh and haunt you forever.

"Breathe," he said. "Please breathe and look at me."

"It hurts…"

"Look at me. Stop fighting and please look at me."

She did. And with it, her struggles quieted as she fell into the black abyss that was his eyes.

"I have something for you, see?"

He reached into his pocket, dug out the slip of paper. It was as thin as an eyelash now, and stained with soot. He could barely make it out.

"*1 Rue Victor Cousin, Paris.* It's for the Sorbonne, the university that accepts women. We were going to stop there before returning home but well, the living had other plans, didn't they? They always do. Almost as bad as the dead, they are."

The paper froze in his fingers, disintegrating like ash and disappearing in a wisp.

She smiled. Her lips were red as roses, stained with blood.

"But I don't want you to go, Ivy. I don't want you to go. I know it's a very good opportunity for you, and you would certainly get top marks and start a new life as a Girl Criminologist but Ivy, I don't want you to go. I never did. I want you for myself but I'm a greedy man and I've been too afraid to ask. I'm was afraid you'd want Paris more than you'd want me so I never said anything but now I am, because I don't want you to go."

She wheezed, her breath ragged and thin. He pulled closer still.

"Ivy, I'm a fool. You've tried for so very long. You've given me chance after chance after chance and I've hidden from them like a coward. You were too alive for me. I've lived with death every minute of every day and the power of your life frightened me. But I'm not afraid anymore, I'm not afraid because if I am Death, then you are Life and the world needs you. I need you."

She was sinking into the floor. No struggles at all now. Her heart was barely beating.

"I need your life. I need your courage and strength and your laughter and ingenuity. You make me think and you make me feel and I can't imagine anything without you at the heart of it. In the Stallburg, I said I didn't know about love but I lied because I know you and I love you and I don't want you to go to Seventh, I want you to live."

She was slipping away, slipping, her eyes turning to glass. He pulled her closer.

"I need you to live." His chest was tight, his eyes stinging and tears gathered behind his lashes but they would not fall. They were like tar. "Please live, Ivy. Please, I need you to live."

She shuddered and he saw it, saw the confusion, the fight, the stubborn determination and a momentary flash of fear. It all stopped in an instant, along with her heart.

I won't be able to follow.

"Move over," said Christien, returning with the medical bag. "I need…"

Even the single tear that had begun to fall stalled in its path along her cheek.

She was standing in the deadspace above her body now, a mere vapour of white, turning in circles as if searching for the light.

"Oh god," said Christien. "Bastien…"

She spied him kneeling beside her body and she opened her mouth, tried to speak. He watched the realization play out on her face and his walls came crashing down.

As if from very far away and very long ago, Sophie began to speak.

"Because I could not stop for Death…"

There was nothing left inside him, save a very dark hole.

"He kindly stopped for me."

A black hole.

He staggered to his feet.

"The Carriage held but just Ourselves…"

The temperature in the Court Chapel plummeted and he turned.

"Bastien, no."

"And Immortality."

He stormed toward the clockwork princess. Her father lunged but the Mad Lord swung an arm, sending the man backwards with a hail of ice pellets.

"No, Bastien!"

He caught her by the cabled throat, pushed her twenty feet backwards into the massive glass panes where the altar had been.

"Nein!" barked Gisela. *"Hör auf!"*

She scrambled after him but ice was racing up the windows, across the floors, forming a wall between them.

"Kill me, *Bruder!"* wheezed Sophie. "Send me to the sweet beyond after your lover!"

She placed her hands over his and closed her eyes, smiled like a child expecting a present on Christmas day.

Ice crackled all around them as he took the temperature down, down, down in the chapel and he gripped her skull, pulling her forehead to his. Her squeal of delight died as her tongue froze to the roof of her mouth and her pasty complexion turned blue in a matter of seconds. Another sound arose from her throat, this time a scream, and it shattered the frost between them, drowned out only by the groaning of clockwork. The temperature dropped lower still until the air sizzled, burning the cables and causing the iron corset to buckle and crack. Wires snapped in her limbs and the room echoed with the squeal of collapsing metal. Suddenly, with the boom of cannons, the three massive windows shattered into a thousand pieces.

Taking what was left of Sophie **Friederike Dorothea Maria Josepha Archduchess von Habsburg** with them.

***

"Sophie!"

The scream would have shattered windows, had there been any left. Empress Elizabeth collapsed to the floor as she lost her second child within a week. Gisela pulled her pistol and fired, but the muzzle was thick with ice and it exploded in her hand, clattering instead to the floor next to the Kaiser of *Blood and Iron*. He merely rocked back and forth, clutching his withered arm.

Silhouetted in the beams of airship light, Bastien stood in the breach with his back to them all, greatcoat waving like a tattered flag on a battlefield. Soot rose and fell on the night wind and snow blew in along with it as the *Stahl Mädchen* lowered herself to chapel height. Cannon ports glinted in the moonlight.

The world was mad, Christien realized. It had simply taken him a few years to catch up.

Through the rubble, Franz Joseph marched to his daughter's side, face streaked with pinpricks of blood. Bastien's spray of ice would have been like buckshot, biting his flesh like tiny needles.

"Gisela, go!" he snapped. "Summon the Hussars! Summon *Steam and Steel!* Tell them to prepare their ships and train their cannons on the Chapel! We will destroy this creature once and for all!"

Gisela whirled and bolted toward the door but the walls were frozen and the door sealed shut. She pounded on it, began shouting instructions to the Hussars on the other side.

The Emperor turned to his youngest.

"Valerie! You know all the secret doors. Find one that is not ice, get out and get Taaffe, tell him to summon parliament and declare a state of emergency."

Valerie was on her feet, eyes glued to the spot where her sister had shattered. There was nothing left, save a blast pattern that exposed the floor beneath the carpet.

I'll be left alone in this horrible place, she had said earlier. *Alone.*

"Valerie! NOW!"

She raced toward the balcony steps, laid her hand on the railing when suddenly the entire staircase became a slick of ice. She glanced around and dashed toward the far end of the chapel, her footfalls echoing as she followed to its end.

The Emperor swung around to face Bastien, slid the ceremonial sword from his hip.

"We will kill you, creature," he barked. "The power of God and might of the Habsburg *Holy Roman Empire* will send you and your brother to Hell!"

"Hell?" came the hollow voice. It rang through the chapel like a bell. *"Hell?"*

"Yes! You belong in Hell!"

Slowly he turned his face, raised the blanket from his shoulders to form a hood. With the greatcoat in tatters and the eye sockets black as night, Christien realized that his brother no longer merely saw Death.

"Hel, Hades, Sheol, Nifilheim, Alvilag, Duzakh," growled Sebastien. "I *am* Hell."

He had become it.

Franz Joseph raised the ceremonial sword and charged but his brother spun, catching it in both hands and ice travelled swiftly up the shining blade. The Emperor gritted his teeth as his hands, then arms, then shoulders began to shake. Finally, he roared with fury and released the hilt, stepping back and tucking his hands under his arms for warmth. Bastien turned and left him, carrying the sword by the blade.

At least he hadn't killed the Emperor, Christien thought. At least he hadn't killed him.

His brother knelt down now beside the woman he had loved. He stroked the wild hair from her face, ran his fingers along her cheek to her chin, bent down to kiss her forehead.

"Skin," he said with a voice that sounded like soot. "Marvelous soft."

Christien looked down at them both and he sighed, his breath frosting in front of his face. Ivy Savage, bringer of chaos, daughter of calamity. She had once been his fiancé, then perhaps his only friend. He felt his throat grow tight. Odd. He'd never wept for anything before. Not his mother, certainly not his father, not his arm or his career or the bird he had found last summer. What a sad, miserable life if nothing mattered enough to weep its loss.

Perhaps he was more machine than Sophie.

He rubbed his arms, watched Gisela approach her father. She had to move carefully not to slip in this holy cavern of ice.

"The airships are ready, Pappa," she said. "But they won't fire if you're in the Chapel."

"They will fire if I order them to fire."

"And what if the creature does not die?"

"Then we will have done our best duty to the Empire." Franz Joseph turned to her. "But you know that. You are bound by honour and duty and holy Habsburg blood. You should have been Emperor, Gigi, not Rudy. You."

He kissed her forehead but she yelped as his lips bit her skin like frost.

The temperature was plummeting once again.

***

He couldn't find her anywhere in the deadspace.

Even her bones were empty, simple lengths of white on a carpet of black. The body was a shell, a vessel for the spirit and once the spirit was gone, it didn't take long to lose heat on the road to dust. He tore the sleeves on the greatcoat, picked up the Emperor's sword.

"No, Bastien! You're not going—"

He waved a hand and a wall of ice rose up between himself and his brother. In fact, he thought, keep it going, and the ice grew up all around them, walls and ceiling surrounding he and Ivy and the casket of the Crown Prince. Just like the Bergl *palais*. A cave of ice within a cavern of ice. The holy of holies.

In its refracting, distorted surface, he could see faces, otherworldly faces frozen in death. For the first time, he realized that the ice wasn't ice, and the frost wasn't frost but spirits from beyond this earth, the manifestations of those who called no place home.

A wall of the dead, creating a barrier between the world of the living and that of the dead. The deadwall.

Christien was shouting and pounding but the sounds were as distorted as his face. Odd. He never thought his brother cared and he felt a pang of guilt. These last days had been hard on his brother, his many wounds not yet healed. Christien was far too young to die like this, following him from frost to fire and back again. He would try to set it right before the end, but had little faith that it would take.

He looked back at Ivy. Her eyes were blank, empty and he reached over to close them. It was like closing the windows on an abandoned house. Seventh was an abandoned house. Frankow and his father had created him there.

Then I shall live at Seventh and haunt you forever.

That was not acceptable. There was only one way to prevent it now.

He lifted the rings, the ones belonging to Rudolf and Mary, placed them on each of her eyes like the coins from long ago. Reached for the ceremonial sword, dragging the point of the blade across his forearms and the bandages fell away like orange peels. The flesh beneath was puckered and raw, but it wouldn't be around for much longer, he knew, and he sliced the skin from wrist to elbow, pleased at the welling of the red. No *ligaturae spiratus* this time. He wasn't binding anything. No, his prayers would be of a different sort entirely.

His blood dripped into a pool on the carpet and he lifted Arclight from around his neck, dipped first her then her sister into the pool. He laid a hand on Ivy's chest, moved his fingers to find the wound and his throat tightened. He had never touched her. In all the months he had known her, he had never touched her. He had wanted to but he never had. Two kisses and that was all and now, his hands on her dead body and he couldn't even weep, for his tears were like tar. He was as dead as she.

But he would change that.

He began to pray, the Latin words turning to frost even as they left his mouth.

He placed Ghostlight – beautiful glittering Ghostlight, his lover, his mistress– over the wound. Clutched Arclight – elusive, wicked Arclight, his siren, his destruction – in his left hand, wrapping the chain around his palm.

He lifted the Emperor's sword, placed the tip under his own heart, and with a prayer in Latin, slid it home.

***

"Bastien!" Christien shouted, knowing what was coming long before he saw it, knowing also that it was too late. Through the distorted ice, he saw the greatcoat bulge as the sword came through, and he closed his eyes, wondering at the madness of the last few days. The things he had seen, the things he had learned. He would not be the same person, if

he lived.

He turned and sagged with his back against the ice cave in the Court Chapel of the Hofburg. His life was absurd. He should have just moved in to Hollbrook, taken a little job maybe as a hospital orderly or a chemist or menswear salesman at Harrod's. Hell, he could even have worked as mad Dr. Jekyll's assistant next door. Didn't matter. He wouldn't be getting out of this alive.

Elizabeth was being ushered to the far end of the chapel by her husband while Gisela was helping a stunned Wilhelm to his feet. Wind whipped in through the shattered windows and beyond them, he could see the *Stahl Mädchen*'s propellers working against each other to keep her hovering and level. He could see the torches lighting up the ports. Death by cannonball. Not a bad way to go, all things considered.

He just wished he had some of that sweet Austrian white or dry red to go along with it.

He could hear bootsteps and as if on cue, Valerie marched back into the chapel, a troop of human and Silver Hussars at her heel. He didn't move. They could bloody well shoot him where he sat if they wanted to.

Valerie spied him. He could see her thinking, weighing her options like the Habsburg she was. She pointed an Imperial finger.

"Bring him," she said. "The Chapel must be empty before the barrage begins."

Two soldiers jogged over, grabbed him by his arms and hauled him to his feet.

***

Wave after wave as his body rebelled. It didn't want to die. Oddly enough, it never did and the pain almost overcame him with its crippling poison and its fear. His hands were slippery now as he dragged the sword out of his body, let it clatter to the floor. Arclight. He needed Arclight. She had fallen from his hand and was sitting in a pool of Ivy's blood. His fingers fumbled as they tried to pick her up. He was tired.

He wanted to close his eyes. He would be lost if he closed his eyes.

And so would she. Not acceptable.

He called the locket and she spun patterns in the blood so he could see. His fingers found her, gathered her into his palm and lifted her up to the wound where his heart still pumped blood like a fountain.

He was tired.

He held both lockets out now in the palms of his hands, both covered in blood. He began to pray, waiting for the flash of colour, the leap of light, telling him that his prayers weren't in vain. Telling him he would not fail because deep down, he knew he had.

He had failed Ivy, he had failed Christien, he had failed his uncle and he had failed himself. He had failed everyone who had ever put their hope or trust in him but truth be told, there weren't all that many. His dogs, at least, but they had Rupert.

He closed his eyes tightly now, forcing his lips to move as he prayed with all of his dying heart in Latin. Snow and ice and frost fell to the floor like flakes on a winter night.

He prayed until his heart stopped beating and even as he fell forward beside her, he prayed. He prayed until there was nothing left in his heart, mind, soul or strength and there was little else to be done after that.

The ice began to melt, just a drip from the deadwall and even in the twilight between life and death, he lingered, his body not quite ready to give up. He had died so many times that it was confused, not knowing how it was done and waiting for the fall of ice that would begin the healing. But not this time, not when the horse was so near.

He was dimly aware of great green eyes, of the smell of rosehips and leather and a flash of colour and the song of elements. It was finished and he smiled, but it was not remotely like the sun.

***

Vienna Extra Daily
Earthquake Reveals Ancient Roman Settlement
On the eve of the funeral of the Crown Prince, witnesses report another earthquake outside the entrance to the Hofburg at St. Michael's Gate. According to witnesses, the circular Michaelerplatz rippled and

heaved before finally belching a great cloud of dust. When the dust cleared, there was a giant sinkhole in the center of the Michaelerplatz, revealing a city here-to-fore hidden underground. Walls, windows, cellars and foundations have been found intact and a local historian claims that they are likely from the times of the Romans. That alone would have been newsworthy but witnesses say that immediately following the earthquake, a large animal was seen emerging from the dust and rubble. Some witnesses claim that the animal was in the shape of a very pale horse.

Police have roped off the sinkhole and are continuing to investigate.

Chapter 27
Of Physics, Metaphysics and the Resurrection of the Crown Prince

She was in the middle of affixing her blouse buttons when Alexander Dunn walked into the room.

"Oh Penny," he whistled. "Don't you look dollymopish?"

She whirled and swung, her palm connecting with his cheek in an instant, and he exhaled, his breath bringing with it the odors of brandy and whiskey and Cuban cigars. He straightened and rubbed his cheek, grinning.

"Well, that was exciting. What was it for?"

"For lying to me! For leaving me hanging in that room without a means of escape! For having me waste my time searching an apartment for a stone that was clearly not there!" She turned her back to him and stepped into her skirt, began the process of affixing the buckles at the hips. "For all I know, this was a ruse to simply see me in my undergarments and had nothing to do at all with the Star of Morocco."

"Oh Penny, that's where you're utterly mistaken."

"I am never mistaken," she snorted. "Except when it comes to trusting international jewel-thieving rogues like you. A mistake I shall never make again."

His hand appeared in her range of vision, dangling the largest diamond locket she had ever seen in her life. Her breath caught in her throat.

"Oh," she gasped.

And she spun back to face him.

"The Star of Morocco! But where was it? It wasn't in his room. I searched high and low!"

"Yes you did, Penny and for that, I owe you my thanks." He stepped back to a silver tray and set about to pour himself a Scotch. "I had my suspicions that he carried it on his person, but I couldn't be sure. Especially when this would likely be our one and only meeting."

He offered her a glass. She took it.

"So what happened to the forgery? Who stole it and how did Maximilian come into possession of the real deal?"

"I suspect he'd stolen it ages ago and replaced it with the counterfeit," he said. "When I saw it that night at the palace, I could tell at once it was a forgery but why? Who would go to so much trouble to steal such a diamond, then replace it with something so perfectly crafted. Clearly, the thief was a man of some means."

"Clearly."

"Also, the Star of Morocco is a symbol of the Empire of the Known World, and who is the heir to that Empire? Who is being stifled politically and socially in that same Empire?"

"Why, Maximilian of course!"

"Precisely! He disappeared moments before the lights went out, leading me to believe that he himself had thrown the switch. He wanted someone to steal the fake locket, if only to become the hero in restoring the original."

"Earning him political and familial points on all counts."

"He was the logical suspect."

He smiled and raised the glass in a toast, drained it in a shot.

She studied him, his devil-may-care attitude, his roguish demeanor, his playboy charm. She swirled the glass, watched the amber liquid splash inside the crystal.

*"And so **you** stole it."*

"They were expecting me too. I couldn't disappoint."

"So tonight?"

He set the glass down and stepped toward her.

"My apologies, Penny. I truly did believe it was in his room."

"So you picked his pocket over drinks, substituted the false locket, and made it back unnoticed."

"I did."

"That's very clever of you."

"Isn't it, though?"

"But I can't let you keep it. Its stolen property of the Viennese government."

"I wouldn't dream of it."

He held it up to the light, colours flashing like a kaleidoscope across her face. But he reached forward, tucking it in her corset between the arch of her breasts.

"Keep it. You have caught me fair and square."

His fingers touched her chin, raising it to meet his.

"I am your prisoner, Miss Dreadful, body and soul."

She swallowed, raised a brow.

"Justice is an uncompromising mistress."

"So I've heard."

She held her breath, her entire body tingling in anticipation when he blinked, then blinked again. He frowned.

"Did you...?"

"Slip opiate into the Scotch?"

"Yes."

"No!"

"Damnably clever for a Girl Criminologist."

Dunn began to buckle to the floor. She caught him.

"No, I didn't. I give you my word!"

"But I did," came a voice from behind.

With the rogue Alexander Dunn in her arms, Penny turned to see Julian standing in the doorway, cigarette holder gleaming in the darkness.

***

They didn't beat him. They didn't need to. He had nothing left to fight with and truth be told, he didn't really care overmuch. They could do what they willed. For the first time in a long time, he was actually an innocent man. It would be poetic justice, all things considered.

The iced door to the chapel shattered inward, courtesy a familiar red beam of *Eisenman* light, and the stairs leading down to the courtyard disintegrated under the blast. Hussars lowered the Empress Elizabeth first out into waiting arms down below, followed immediately by Valerie, Gisela and the Emperor himself. Then it was his turn, and they dragged him by the arms and pushed him out the doorway. There were no Hussars to catch him as he fell.

Guards pulled him to his feet and bound his hands behind his back, taking time to secure the prosthetic so he could not slip free or cut the bonds. They went through his pockets, pulling out the only item he had in his possession – the folded page from Franz Salvatore's old bible with the list of questions on the back. They passed it to Valerie and he looked away from her to study the courtyard. It would likely be the last thing he saw. A firing squad would shoot him at dawn. It was the *Gilded* way.

The Commons were alit with torches and tech, a snowy sea of soldiers and politicians and generals. In the windows of the Swiss Wing and the Treasury, faces were pressed against the glass as staff and servants alike gathered to watch. High above them, airships circled across the night sky, the *Stahl Mädchen* precariously low to the ground and targeting what was left of the Court Chapel. Her cannons were silent and waiting.

There was a fight breaking out behind him as the Kaiser of *Blood and Iron* was lowered onto the snow. A circle of physicians had stepped in to examine him but he batted their hands away, flailed at them with his good arm. Both Gisela and Franz Joseph moved to intervene but he cursed at them in German, Russian, English and all the other languages that found a home on his tongue.

Christien couldn't help it. He laughed.

The man whirled and immediately, the fox-like eyes grew wild.

"You English," he snapped, "are mad, mad, mad as March hares! What have you done to me? *What have you done?"*

And he broke free of the protective ring, staggered over to the young physician, trailing Silver Hussars in his wake.

"There will be no more patience," he growled. "No more good will. The time when *Blood and Iron* lies down like a dog at the feet of *Steam* is over! Do you hear me?"

"Wilhelm, save your strength," said Franz Joseph. "This man will be shot at dawn. You need—"

"You *dare* presume to tell me what I need?" The Kaiser's face was red, the tendons in his neck taut as soldiers at attention. "Wales, the old peacock, has orchestrated this and he will pay! Look at my arm!"

He waved it in front of the Emperor's face.

"This is what his arrogance has done! But *Blood and Iron* will not be crippled. *I* will not be crippled! I will have a new arm, like Wales'! Like *his!"*

He pointed at Christien.

"No, it will be better than his! My *Eisenmanner* are only the beginning! The world will see our new technologies and marvel! The mighty arm of *Blood and Iron* will usher a new day of science and progress and power."

"That 'mighty arm'," muttered Christien. "Looks rather like a desiccated cat."

There was a moment, a brief heartbeat of a moment, when the Kaiser was speechless. But it was only a moment. He bellowed, slamming his good fist into Christien's middle and sending the young physician to his knees. A savage backhand across the cheek and he collapsed into the snow. Valerie was there in seconds, straddling him with her skirts and shielding him with her body. She faced the Kaiser, eyes steely, hands curled into fists.

"Leave him alone," she said.

"Stand aside, girl."

"I said *leave!"*

Wilhelm moved to strike but the Emperor barked and Hussars moved swiftly, grabbing the Kaiser and ushering him ungracefully out of the Chapel Commons and into the safety of the Hofburg. The gaggle of physicians followed, taking the Empress with them.

Gisela appeared and together, the two sisters helped him to his feet. They turned toward their father.

"No firing squad," Gisela said. "This man did what we asked. The shame is ours to bear."

"The plan was ours, Pappa," said Valerie. "Not his. We wanted to bring Rudy back. *We* did."

"Your heart has been broken," added Gisela. "And the Empire compromised. We all wanted to restore it."

Franz Joseph smiled sadly, reached out to stroke Valerie's cheek.

"My daughters," he said. "My beautiful girls. You have the hearts of lionesses. But the law is the law. This man will die now."

He stepped back.

"Assemble a firing squad in the center of the Commons and order the *Stahl Mädchen* to open fire. Destroy the Court Chapel!"

With that, Hussars yanked his arms, dragging him to the center of the yard as the dreadnought opened fire on the Hofburg.

***

Boom boom boom

The cannons of the *Stahl Mädchen* boomed like the ticking of a great clock. In the middle of the courtyard, Christien watched the walls explode and the black draping catch fire as the cannons coughed out their iron balls with flame and fury.

Boom boom boo-

Through gaping holes in the walls, colours flashed and circles spun into life, a display of fireworks from within the chapel itself. The airship's cannons fell silent and all eyes in the Commons looked up.

The dreadnought rippled and pulsed, growing smaller then larger, smaller then larger and suddenly, it disappeared altogether from the sky overhead. There was a moment and Christien realized that like everyone else, he was holding his breath. Without warning, the chapel exploded outwards, limestone and marble and wood raining from where it had been, for 'where it had been' was now occupied by an airship.

Masts sticking out of holes in walls, canvas and sails and iron sheets and twisted metal, balloon hissing with combustible gas, the *Stahl Mädchen* creaked inside the Court Chapel. Airshipsmen could be seen scrambling from the hull and leaping down the short distance to the ground below. Swiss guards and Hussars rushed to the wreckage when a flash of light lifted them all off their feet and a wall of sound sent them soaring as the hydrogen ignited and the dirigible erupted in flames. The roar was louder than anything in the world.

In the sky where the airship had been, however, a crystalline ball hovered, flashing and spinning like the large black orb that had appeared in the Chapel. It hovered only a moment before dropping unceremoniously to the ground, crashing and shattering into a thousand pieces. He threw himself into the snow to avoid being shredded by a thousand icy daggers.

A second boom now as, inside the chapel, the dreadnought's engines exploded, sending out a second wave of heat and light. It was blinding and snow in the courtyard melted immediately, covering the winter grass with water. Sound was distorted as both screams and sirens echoed across the night sky and he lay for a while, waiting for his senses to return. The Hussars had abandoned him in the chaos so he rolled to his knees, waiting for a rifle butt to the head but none came. With a deep breath, he willed his prosthetic to release the metal hand and it did, ejecting it into the puddles and freeing him from the bonds. He snatched it up, affixing it with a twist and scrambled to his feet, ready to bolt. Before he did, however, he threw a quick glance behind him where the orb had crashed.

He realized he was not going anywhere just yet.

For pushing up out of the wet grass in his white uniform was Rudolf Franz Karl Joseph, Crown Prince of Austria.

***

Once, when she'd been younger, it had snowed in London for over a week. Snow never stayed in London but this time it did, and the city had been paralyzed. Not Ivy Savage, however. She had braved the drifts to visit the Library in Whitechapel and that night, she'd read to Davis about houses in Upper Canada made entirely of snow. They had draped blankets between the kitchen chairs, brought in icicles as carrots and slept in their winter coats to pretend.

Odd how she would remember that now.

Her head was spinning so she lay quite still, watching the stars and the moon in the sky above her. Watching the sparks fly high into the night, watching the airships circle like warring dragons over her head. She was still sleeping, still dreaming. It was obvious, especially when the mustachioed face of Crown Prince Rudolf hovered into view.

"Wach auf, junge Dame."

She smiled at him.

"I don't speak German," she said. "But soon. I promise. I'm so sorry you died. I think you would have made a terrific king."

He reached down, plucked two metal rings that had become wedged in the laces of her corset.

"Yes, those are yours. I borrowed them. I'm a borrower. So sorry."

He slipped one on over the white glove, tucked the other into a deep pocket before he disappeared from view. She propped herself up on her elbows to get a better look at the panorama of her dream and her heart thudded once in her chest.

It was no dream.

Flames roared in what had once been the Court Chapel of the Hofburg, airshipsmen dead and dying on the ground all around. Two Sentinels standing guard at the entrance to the Commons and a sea of Hussars staring at her. From every window in the buildings surrounding the square, faces were pressed against the glass, staring at her. In fact, everyone who was not dead was staring and she realized they weren't staring at her, but at the man in white uniform standing in the middle of the field.

Only the crackling of the fires could be heard from the Commons.

It was like a wave sweeping across the ocean of bodies as one by one, people sank to their knees. All the generals, all the politicians, even

Valerie and Gisela and dear, battered Christien, all bowed with reverence and awe before the Crown Prince. Only one other man in the entire crowded courtyard remained on his feet, too overcome to do anything else but stare.

"Mein Sohn," said Franz Joseph, his voice barely a whisper.

The prince raised a hand to touch his head. He frowned.

"Pappa?" he said. *"Was ist das?"*

"Mein Sohn," repeated the Emperor and he took a tentative step forward, then another but ran the rest of the way to throw his arms around the young man. Together, they buckled to the ground as Imperial tears streamed down the proud old face.

"He did it," she heard Christien say. "By god, he did it."

Ivy looked around.

"Where is he? Where's Sebastien?"

She spied a dark mound in the grass and her heart thudded once more. She rolled to her feet and scrambled toward it.

***

"Remy?"

It was Valerie. She had crossed the courtyard and dropped to her knees beside him. In the light cast by the burning dreadnought, he couldn't help but marvel at her beauty. It was his weakness and he cursed himself for it.

"He did it," she breathed. "I knew he could."

He said nothing, began tightening the cables in his wrist.

"He is a miracle man. All of the world will know it now."

He steeled his jaw as he worked, remembering the sight of the sword pushing up through the greatcoat.

"I'm sorry for everything we have put you through, you and your brother and your little girl. You will be rewarded by my father."

He looked up at her.

"All we want is an airship to take us home."

"You will have it. The best in our fleet."

"The best in your fleet is currently inside the Court Chapel."

She looked away now and he felt vindicated.

"Rudolf!"

The crowd parted as Empress Elizabeth rushed through, pausing only a heartbeat before following her husband to the huddle on the ground. It might have been beautiful had it not been so surreal.

Valerie held up a sheet of paper that was illustrated on one side. "What does this mean?"

"I don't know," he said. "Something about horses."

"No, not that. This."

She showed him the list, the last point crossed off.

He stared at her flatly, but truth be told, he was too exhausted to look any other way.

"Do I love Valerie von Habsburg?" she read. "That's what it says."

"I crossed it off."

"Why?"

"It's no longer a question."

"What is the answer?"

"That is none of your concern," he said. "You're engaged to another man."

"But if I weren't?"

His heart had been cut out when he was still a boy.

"Then the answer would still be no," he said. "I am my father's son, my life bought and sold with blood. I don't love you. I don't love anyone or anything. I never have. Just like him."

She looked down at the list. He could have sworn tears fell, smudging the ink.

"Christien!"

Ivy's wail broke the stillness of the courtyard.

And without a second glance, Christien rose to his feet, leaving the Archduchess Marie Valerie von Habsburg with only a slip of paper in the night.

***

"He's not waking up," she moaned. "Why isn't he waking up?"

"Ivy," he said.

"No," she said. "I know what you're thinking but that's not true. He dies all the time and comes back. He does. Honestly, he does. So…"

She looked back down at the Mad Lord. He looked like a broken statue, his face ashen, his eyes empty, cheeks and mouth stained with soot. He was entirely drained of all colour. Like Vienna in winter, a monochrome of grey and black.

"So why doesn't he wake up?"

He sighed.

"It's over, Ivy."

"No, not this way. Not Sebastien."

She reached down to brush the hair from his forehead.

"There's more to him than that. There always is." She smiled sadly. "He's like a cat. That's what Bertie said. Been dead more times than a cat."

"Ivy." He laid a hand on her shoulder. "Ivy, it's over."

She felt rather than saw the shadow of three people standing over her. She would not look up.

"Thank you," said the Emperor. "You have restored my son. It is beyond belief."

Slowly, elegantly, Sisi knelt down beside her. She gathered Ivy's hands in hers.

"Dear Sebastien," she said. "I cannot express how thankful I am."

"Don't, please," said Ivy and she shook her head. "It would sound false."

"I know him," said Rudolf and he bent down beside his mother. "I remember him as if from a dream."

Still, Ivy couldn't look at him.

"He asked me to come home," the Crown Prince continued. "I didn't want to but I could not refuse him. He spoke with authority and kindness, but…he did not use words. I can't explain it."

He shrugged.

"He was a good man, I think."

She looked up now, eyes flashing.

"Then be a good king," she said. "Don't do this. Don't rule like this."

And she swept her arm over the courtyard, across the destruction and the flames, the iron men and the silver.

"*Justo Armas,*" said Rudolf. "Right weapons. Just causes."

He reached over, took her hand and she couldn't stop the tears from welling. She blinked them away.

"Keep the locket. It belongs to the house of de Lacey, not the Holy Roman Empire. Or any empire, for that matter."

"Bury the lockets with him," said Sisi. "Perhaps they will bring him back one day, like they brought back my son."

And the Imperial family left her alone with Christien in the middle of the Chapel Commons. He squeezed her shoulder.

"I'm bleeding, Ivy."

She blinked up at him.

"It's nothing, but I do need to get it looked at. We'll take one of their airships and get the hell out of here as soon as I'm done."

She nodded and he left, Valerie following him like a shadow.

She sighed, reached down to pry open the Mad Lord's hands. The lockets rolled out onto the grass like pebbles. She picked them up, studied them for a long moment.

"These are wicked, wicked devices and I should throw them far, far away. But the world is filled with greedy people and I fear I could never throw them far enough so that someone would not find them."

She gazed out at the faces of soldiers and politicians, the steely glint of the Eisenmanner, of the Hofburg fires quenched by Swiss Guards with water hoses. The sun was beginning to streak the dark sky with pink. She looked back down at the Mad Lord.

"They are wicked and full of dread, but you are not. You, with your life spent on the dead and the dying, you are the master of these accursed things. You redeem them and make them good. You make everything good."

The lockets were quiet in her palms. No flash of colour, no gleam of light. Just intricate metalwork over pieces of cold stone.

"People put pennies on the eyes of the dead. I don't know why. Maybe to pay the ferryman for their trip through the river, maybe to bribe the saint at the gates of heaven. I think it's to deter the crows from taking the eyeballs but that's me. I'm a morbid creature, a real-life Penny Dreadful."

She leaned forward, tenderly kissed each lid before placing the lockets over them.

"So take these because the only pennies I can give you, are dreadfuls."

Beneath her knees, the earth began to move.

Chapter 28
Of Angels in the Turf, Bones in a Wall and the Rider of the Pale Horse

The Cistercian Monastery Graveyard,
Heiligenkreuz, Vienna Woods

The young police constable, Helmut Mansel, looked up from his reading and glanced around the small room. It was a horrible night, the only warmth provided by a few hand-dipped candles. Apparently, the monastery cultivated their own bees, using the wax for candles and the honey for mead. While he was enjoying the fruits of the wax, he knew a little mead would take the chill even better.

"What is that noise?" he asked.

"Probably those macabre journalists," his companion groaned. "Gawkers and gossips, all of them."

Helmut grinned. Brother Georg was not an open-minded man. He had likely never read a broadsheet or newspaper in his long, holy life.

"But listen. It's coming from inside the yard."

Georg frowned, closed his bible.

"It sounds like a woman," said Helmut.

"As I said, gawkers and gossips."

Helmut grinned again.

"Regardless," he said. "I have to investigate. Gorup left specific instructions."

"Vile desecraters. You have your pistol?"

"I do."

"I am a man of peace," said Georg. "Still…"

He rose to his feet and reached for a spade.

"I'm sure I can help them *rest* in peace."

With lantern and spade and pistol in hand, both men left the warmth of the shelter and headed out into the night. The graveyard of *Heiligenkreuz* monastery was a simple one and they made their way through the row of bare trees and headstones to a fresh, unmarked grave. The ground was frozen, the pit hastily dug and it was covered only in a light dusting of snow. There were no looters, no reporters, no gawkers nor gossips. The sounds were coming from the ground, however, from inside a makeshift coffin and they were unmistakable.

"Rudy! I'm sorry, Rudy! Let me out!"

The screams of a woman, muffled and dull. The banging of fists and boots on cheap wood.

"Rudy! It wasn't my fault! It was Wales! Please let me out!"

They exchanged glances before Helmut snatched the spade and leapt into the pit. The impact of his boots caused the voice to scream more loudly and with three good blows of the spade, the cheap wood shattered. A girl with lustrous hair pushed her way out of the snow.

"Rudy!" she cried. "Rudy, where are you, my love?"

"Who are you?" breathed Brother Georg.

Brilliant eyes, wicked and sharp, flashed at him.

"I am Baroness Marie Alexandrine von Vetsera, Black Swan and lover of Crown Prince Rudolf of Austro-Hungary! You will take me to him at once or I will have you both shot!"

Helmut blinked slowly.

"Crown Prince Rudolf is dead, Baroness…"

She stared at him, her eyes the largest things in the entire world.

"Oh no! Oh no. They will come for me next…" She grabbed his sleeves. "Please, my handsome lord, take me far, far away from here!"

And with that, the Turf Angel of Fredenau and Baden Baden

collapsed into Helmut's waiting arms.

***

In graveyards throughout Vienna, the earth tore itself apart, pushing caskets and coffins up from the frozen depths, shattering them open to spill bodies across the snow. In backyards and courtyards and other areas not set aside for burials, the earth still split open, forcing bones from centuries past up to the surface. People screamed and fled into their homes, counting it as yet another symptom of the curse that had befallen all the *Gilded Empire,* a curse which had begun with the worst of all possible beginnings – the death of the Crown Prince.

It would prove to be nothing compared to his resurrection.

***

"Another earthquake!" someone shouted as the ground began to rumble beneath their feet. The sea of politicians and soldiers rippled like a tide and a collective murmur rose as something passed through the crowd under the Swiss Gate.

Christien whirled and tore the page from Valerie's hand. He held the illustration up to see it in the light of the chapel fires.

"What is this?" he shouted over the roar of the earth. "What the hell does this mean?"

"It's a prophecy," she shouted back. "From Revelation, the last book in the Bible."

"But what does it *mean?"*

There was a sound like the booming of cannons and they both turned to the Gate, to the crowd gathered across the courtyard. The mob was moving, rippling aside like a tide as something large pushed its way through.

Christien staggered back.

It was a horse.

"By god," he said.

"The pale horse," breathed Valerie.

"By god," he said again. "He was right."

It was the largest horse Christien had ever seen. The largest and the strangest. Its colour was not white, not yellow, not quite green, and he could see the bones and muscles working beneath its translucent skin. Both mane and tail dragged on the ground, and looked to be ribbons of tendon and cobwebs. The earth thundered and the stone cracked with every hoofbeat. The air grew heavy with the smell of death and as it passed by him, he could see the eye, milky and white.

"I heard the voice of the fourth living creature," said Valerie. *"And it said "Come." I looked, and behold, an ashen horse; and he who sat on it had the name Death; and Hades was following with him. Authority was given to them over a fourth of the earth, to kill with sword and with famine and with pestilence and by the wild beasts of the earth."*

It continued past them and Christien knew where it was going.

"Death," he said. "The rider of the fourth horse is Death."

"Yes," said Valerie. "He is Death."

"I understand. It makes sense. God, I've been an idiot."

"What is it, Remy?"

"That's what Sophie meant. That's what she wanted all along."

"Remy?"

Christien turned. The sun was peaking over the rooftops of the Hofburg, painting everything in strokes of gold. In the middle of the courtyard, Ivy knelt over the body of his brother, unaware and unknowing. The horse was moving like an arrow toward them.

"He won't stay dead," he said. "The horse will bring him back."

And the realization struck him like a dread fist.

"Whatever happens, we can't let Bastien get on that horse!"

***

A great horse was standing above her.

She could feel it more than see it, her skin tingling with its presence, her nose reeling from its stench. It tossed its great head and foam dripped from its tongue, ran down its iron legs. It lowered its head, the forelock spreading across Sebastien's face. It nudged him but he did not move.

"No," she said. "Go away. You can't have him."

It raised a hoof, the rough surface clear so she could see the triangular bone beneath it. The ground thundered when it brought it down.

She bolted to her feet, hands curling into fists at her sides.

"I said *no!*"

It snorted at her, the force almost blowing her off her feet, but she stood firm.

"Go away! He's not yours!"

She pushed against its shoulder with the palms of her hands. It was not moved but rather pawed at the Mad Lord's body with its hoof, rolling him over to lie face down on the stone.

"I said Go!"

And she struck it with both hands. It was like striking a whirlwind.

The horse reared, its squeal shattering the glass in every window and a new quake sent her toppling backwards. The earth erupted beneath her feet, roaring as it split open and she flailed against it, clinging to the stones so as not to be swallowed. Beneath and beside and all around her, she could see bones rising from the depths and she clawed her way up with them, fighting the bite of cold underground and frost above it, the choke of dirt in her lungs, the taste of it on her tongue.

When she managed to pull herself out of the pit, what she saw caused her heart stop dead in her chest.

Sunlight streaming from the dome of the Hofburg and dappling the horse with light, skeletons stood like a fence, like a wall. An army of bones, some white, some yellowed, some stringy with decayed flesh. All across the courtyard, an army of the dead assembled on swaying legs. Skulls watching, bones missing, some with scraps of clothing, others with strands of spidery hair. It was just like in Melk when the relics had crossed the floor, dropping stones as they went. Utterly and completely unnatural.

A human Hussar swung with his sabre, striking one of the corpses and it clattered to the stone, bones shattering as they hit. A Swiss Guard next, pulling his pistol and blowing a hole in a skull as large as a fist. The skeleton did not collapse, however, and lurched toward him with extended arms.

Chaos erupted in the courtyard as soldiers fired and spectators fled and from high above, the remaining *Eisenmann* fired its rockets into the dead, bits of bone raining into the crowds along with pebbles and dust. But with every skeleton that shattered, another rose up from the earth and they swarmed the iron giant with sheer, unstoppable numbers, climbing over the arms, pushing at the torso and finally pulling it to crash in pieces across the courtyard.

It was war, she realized, between the living and the dead, and she had no idea who would win, nor in fact, who should.

Suddenly, both colour and orbs burst into life across the sky, silencing the chaos and causing all living eyes to look up in wonder. It was a terrifying sight, their empty eyes, their dislocated jaws, most missing arms or ribs but taking position around her like an undead army. She didn't know what to think anymore, whether they were protecting her or preparing to tear her limbs from her body.

Christien was trying to push his way through the wall of standing bone, but it was like stone. Like cold, grey stone.

The Chapel courtyard was silent and still.

"Ivy!" he cried. "Ivy, don't let him get on that horse!"

Numb and disoriented, she looked down at Sebastien. He was dead. He would never get on a horse ever again and she felt the last of her heart disintegrate at the thought.

She looked up at the creature, marveled at the unnatural, translucent sheen of its skin and coat, its milky eye almost hidden by stringy forelock. It took a step closer, lowering its head once again and covering the Mad Lord's body with its mane. It breathed out a long, cold, ashen breath.

The earth rumbled one last time.

Suddenly, Sebastien's mouth flew open and his back arched violently as if breaking the wrong way. Soot rained from his hair, from his eyes, from his mouth as he pushed to his hands and knees, the tendons straining in his neck like iron cables. The blanket fell across his face like a hood and Ivy could hear the drum of his lungs filling with ash and smoke.

"Sebastien," she whispered.

He did not look at her. In fact, it seemed he did not even hear.

"No, Sebastien," she moaned. "Don't listen. Don't do this."

She watched his grey fingers wrap around a length of tangled mane, twisting it round his palm and the horse stepped back, its massive haunches engaging to haul him to his feet. He leaned into it, swaying on unsteady legs and pressed his forehead into its translucent neck.

"Don't let him get on!" Christien shouted again.

"Fight, Sebastien!" she gasped as she too staggered to her feet. "Please fight!"

But there was no fight. Rather, his fingers moved in and out of the cobweb mane, along the sticky neck, caressing the creature as though it were a dog. It let out a sound that rumbled in its chest like thunder.

"So beautiful," he said, his voice echoing and hollow. "You are the most magnificent horse I've ever known. I will name you Ash."

He turned slightly toward her now, eyes and forehead hidden in shadow so she couldn't see his face. Somehow, at some time, the blanket had been transformed into a cowl. He looked like all the statues of Death she had ever seen. Death in a grey tattered hood and greatcoat.

"I'm sorry, Miss Savage," he said. "But there is nothing to fight."

"Good," she snapped, chin rising. "Then you come over here and tell me all about it. And we'll go home on an airship and have tea and see all our friends and your dogs at Lasingstoke. That's what we're going to do right now. Do you understand?"

"I do understand, Miss Savage, but that's not going to happen. Not for me."

Her heart was racing in her chest and she wondered if there had been a time when it had stopped. She could almost remember but it was a dream.

"I am still incomplete, you see? I need the last locket but I don't know where she is. Her sisters will help me. They will lead me where I need to go."

"No. You will stop this nonsense and come home with me."

"There is no stopping what has begun," he said. "It is an act of God."

"No," she said. "God is not doing this. The lockets are."

"Yes, the lockets. There is one more."

"The lockets are destroying you."

"No," he said. "They are making me."

He turned his face to look at her and her heart did stop this time.

His eyes, once brown as chocolate, oft blue as the sky or green as an emerald, then white, red, silver and finally black, were the lockets. Ghostlight and Arclight, spinning and flashing behind his lashes. Clockwork eyes of metal and glass and otherworldly elements and angels.

"I will find Lostlight and then I will be who I was created to be."

"And who is that?" Her voice was very small and thin.

"Death."

He twisted his hand into the mane, swung his leg and suddenly, he was up and onto the great ashen back. The horse pranced and the earth died with every hoof fall.

He looked down at her and smiled.

"Sophie was right. I am the Crown Prince of Death. I will find Lostlight, then go north to Lonsdale. I will find Arvin Frankow and I will kill him. God will judge the living and the dead and the world will come to an end."

"You are not Death," she said and she rushed to the horse, laid her hands on his boot. Tears spilt from her own lashes now. "No, you're not. You are Sebastien de Lacey and I love you. Do you hear me? I love you and I don't want you to leave."

He reached down to touch her face, ran his cold fingers along her chin.

"And I love you, Miss Savage, if it is possible for me to love. I suppose then it is only fitting that Death would love Life. We are a set, you and I, matching yet opposite, star-crossed forever."

"Romeo and Juliet," she said. Her throat was tight. She could barely speak. "You said you would be the death of me."

"I already was."

He drew his hand away and the world was colder without him.

"Good bye, Miss Savage. Perhaps I will see you at the gates of the dead."

"I shall live at Seventh," she whispered. "And haunt you forever."

The horse reared on its hind legs, and the bone army shrank back, allowing them to pass through. The human crowd did likewise and with a toss of its head, the pale horse pranced slowly, majestically, like a Lipizzaner towards the Swiss Gate. The bone army moved to follow and the crowd fled before them, some wailing, others mute, all horrified at the things they had witnessed. Together, crowd, army and horse were gone in a heartbeat.

Ivy sank to her knees, finished.

It was the morning of the funeral of the Crown Prince who had lived, and the birth of the Crown Prince who had died. Nothing would ever be the same again.

Christien approached, his shadow blocking the early morning sun.

"What are we going to do?" she whispered.

"Simple," he said and he looked down at her. "We stop him."

He offered her his clockwork hand and she stared at it for a long moment, feeling the breath entering and exiting her body. Breathing, she thought to herself. Bloody marvelous thing. She would never take it for granted again.

She took his hand, allowed him to pull her to her feet and for the first time in days, the sun rose over the city of Vienna.

***

The Orient Express rattled along the track heading east towards Paris, the city of lights. There was a celebration in the dining compartment as unlimited champagne had been ordered, compliments of Emperor of the Known World, his wife the Empress of Avalon and their son, Crown Prince Maximilian. The renowned Star of Morocco had been returned to the imperial vaults and there was only one name on everyone's lips – Penny Dreadful, Girl Criminologist.

"Bully for you, Penny!" guffawed her father, Chief Inspector Charles Dreadful. "It's a regular Coop de Grace, it is. A regular Coop de Grace!"

"Coup de grâce, *Father,*" said Penny with the appropriate pronunciation and she lifted the flute of champagne to her lips. "But I couldn't have done it without help."

"Here's to Julian Terrence Hull!" her father boomed. "We'll make a criminologist out of that boy soon enough!"

"Here! Here!" echoed the boys in blue.

Standing in the corner, Julian smiled at her, his clockwork arm whirring as he lifted his flute. Odd, thought Penny, how often he smiled without his eyes.

She turned back to her father.

"And what about that rogue, Alexander Dunn?"

"What about him, Penny?"

"Well, technically he didn't steal the Star of Morocco. He shouldn't be tried for a crime he didn't commit."

"Balderdash, Penny. He stole what he thought was the Star of Morocco, which is just as bad. If it hadn't been for you, Crown Prince Maximilian would never have been able to return it to his father. As it stands, all of Europe is basking in a fresh glow of world peace."

"World peace," she repeated and stared into her glass.

"Besides, there are so many crimes that rogue has committed, that he'll surely swing for something once we get him back to good ol' Londontown!"

A woman moved through the dining compartment toward them. Penny followed her with her eyes.

"Surely," said Penny. "And you're certain that Prison Compartment 3 in the rear of the train is secure?"

"Oh most secure, Penny. This is the Orient Express, after all. It would take an act of God to break him out of there."

"An act of God," said Penny and she smiled to herself.

The woman was dressed as a French maid, with a white powder wig, striped leggings and tiny spectacles that were as dark as coal. She was gazing absentmindedly out the window and bumped into Penny, causing her to spill her champagne.

"Oh mon Dieu," said the woman, obviously French. "I am so terribly sorry, mademoiselle. I am not good on trains."

"Not to worry," said Penny. "It was entirely my fault."

"I seem to have dropped my room key. Might you help me find it?"

"Oh look," said Penny and she held up her flute. "Your key has somehow miraculously found it's way into my champagne glass!"

"Oh, what a happy accident!"

Both she and the woman laughed merrily.

"Do take it with my apologies," said Penny, pulling the skeleton key from the flute. "And enjoy the rest of the trip. We will be in Paris soon."

"Yes," said the woman. "J'adore Paris. I am expecting to be reunited with my brother soon."

"I expect you will, then," said Penny. "Give him my warmest regards."

"I will, most certainly. Adieu.*"*

And the woman carried on to disappear into the next coach.

"Ah those French dames," said her father. "Such a bloom of innocence and purity about them!"

"Indeed," said Penny. "Il n'est rien de réel que le rêve et l'amour."

"What's that, Penny?"

"Nothing is real but dreams and love."

And she raised her glass as a silent toast to dreams and international jewel thieves and the girl criminologists who loved them.

The End of Penny Dreadful and the Villain of Vienna

Epilogue

It was dark in the town of Over Milling, the crescent moon shedding little light along the cobbled streets. There were no gaslamps save for the four dotting the corners of the town square, and only two of those were burning. Towering over the square, a lone Sentinel stood. It was an old giant, one of the original fleet that had been sent out as a part of Prince Albert's Great Exhibition of 1851. In the summer, he was surrounded by flowers and covered in ivy, a grand hitching post for horses and dogs alike. Come winter, he was home to a resident barn owl and friend to a few snowmen that joined him in the square. He was a fearsome sight nonetheless, standing guard over the town as a symbol of imperial majesty and might.

For thirty-seven years he stood, never having moved from the square. For thirty-seven years, he watched and guarded, and upheld the symbol in a silent, passive but very British manner.

Now, a telegraph signal caused sparks to flicker inside its metal skull and the tarnished eyes to beam and glow. With an indignant hoot, the owl lifted from its perch on the iron shoulder as gears that had not moved in thirty-seven years groaned, remembering their purpose. The bellows roared as mechanisms that had grown rusty sprang to life and gaslight could be seen along all the welded seams. The iron body shuddered as cables sprang taut, pulling gears in the great torso and one leg strained against the hard-packed snow.

From a neighbouring building, a dog barked as the ancient Sentinel broke free of the ice, its iron foot crushing the first of the snowmen beside it. The town square thundered as the second foot completely obliterated all traces of snowmen. Even with the dog barking, the residents of Over Milling would not realize until morning that the Sentinel had moved or that the symbol of majesty and might had left their town square.

It wasn't until noon that it would be found on the road to Lasingstoke Hall.

To be continued in

Cold Stone & Ivy Book 3:
The Seventh House

If you enjoyed this novel, I would be honoured if you left a review.

Other Books by H. Leighton Dickson

Tails of the Upper Kingdom
To Journey in the Year of the Tiger
To Walk in the Way of Lions
Songs in the Year of the Cat
Swallowtail & Sword

Empire of Steam
Cold Stone & Ivy Book 1: The Ghost Club
Cold Stone & Ivy Book 2: The Crown Prince

Dragon of Ash & Stars

Coming Soon:
Snow in the Year of the Dragon
Cold Stone & Ivy Book 3: The Seventh House

ABOUT THE AUTHOR

H. Leighton Dickson grew up in the wilds of the Canadian Shield, where her neighbours were wolves, moose, deer and lynx. She studied Zoology at the University of Guelph and worked in the Edinburgh Zoological Gardens in Scotland, where she was chased by lions, wrestled deaf tigers and fed antibiotics to Polar Bears by baby bottle! She has been writing since she was thirteen and pencilled her way through university with the help of DC Comics. She has three dogs, three cats, three kids, one horse and one husband. She has managed to keep all of them alive so far.

An award-winning indie author, Heather has seven scifi/fantasy novels on Amazon. She also writes for Bayview Magazine and is a photoshop wizard when it comes to book covers.

Come join the conversation at http://www.hleightondickson.com

or on Facebook at http://www.facebook.com/HLeightonDickson

www.ingramcontent.com/pod-product-compliance
Lightning Source LLC
Chambersburg PA
CBHW072011110726
47910CB00005B/1726